N   2008

Fic MACOMBER
MACOMBER, JAMES.
A GRAVE BREACH :
    /
2008/01/04

P9-AGV-139

WITHDRAWN

WITHDRAWN

A GRAVE BREACH

A GRAVE BREACH

A Novel

JAMES MACOMBER

Alameda Free Library
1550 Oak Street
Alameda, CA 94501

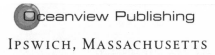

Oceanview Publishing

IPSWICH, MASSACHUSETTS

Copyright © 2007 by James Macomber

FIRST EDITION

All rights reserved. No part of this book may be reproduced in any form
or by any electronic or mechanical means, including information storage
and retrieval systems, without permission in writing from the publisher,
except by a reviewer who may quote brief passages in a review.

This book is a work of fiction. Names, characters, places, and
incidents either are the products of the author's imagination or are
used fictitiously. Any resemblance to actual events or locales or
persons, living or dead, is entirely coincidental.

ISBN-13: 978-1-933515-07-6
ISBN-10: 1-933515-07-4

Published in the United States by Oceanview Publishing,
Ipswich, Massachusetts
www.oceanviewpub.com

2 4 6 8 10 9 7 5 3 1

PRINTED IN THE UNITED STATES OF AMERICA

To the memory of
Larry Gordon

He was a good man, and did good things.

ACKNOWLEDGMENTS

Anyone wishing to learn more about the Balkans and the history of that vital, fascinating, and turbulent region can start with *Bosnia: A Short History* by Noel Malcolm (New York University Press, 1994). It is an immensely readable work that examines the Balkans from the eleventh century to the present and affords the reader, the world observer, the student, or the merely interested a wealth of information on where it is and what has happened there, though not all will agree with Malcolm's "why"?

Acknowledgment also goes to Franklin Lindsay's *Beacons in the Night* (Stanford University Press, 1993), in regard to OSS operations in WWII Yugoslavia and in particular for the manner of insertion of Allied operatives into the area at the time.

I want to particularly thank my friend Alexandar Nis in Belgrade, who calls himself "just a regular guy," but whose encyclopedic knowledge of the history of the region and the relation and effect of that history to events in the recent past and the present was invaluable.

A long overdue and very heartfelt thanks to Joey Petrat at Circle Books in St. Armand's Circle in Sarasota. Way back when, Joey read my first novel and her praise and encouragement —and recommendation—went a long way toward getting this whole thing off and running. And deep, sincere thanks to Deb Stowell, co-owner of Circle

Books, a book lover's bookstore, because Debbie and Eric and all the staff are not merely booksellers but book lovers themselves.

Special thanks to those who read—and, in some cases, reread—the manuscript to help keep the book on track: Geoff Metcalf, journalist, commentator, pundit, and talented writer in his own right, and most importantly, my good friend for more years than either of us care to remember; my sister, Joan Tavernier, librarian extraordinaire, who is usually the first to read a manuscript and never fails to provide valuable advice and insight; my brother Jerry Macomber, who is not only an incisive reader, but who has a grasp and command of detail that borders on the eerie; and to Kris Gordon, Terry and Rosemary Walsh; and, of course, Sandy, for her continued support and without whom none of this would ever have happened.

A GRAVE BREACH

1

Law Office of Loring, Matsen, and Gould
Washington, D.C.

In summer, the humidity in Washington, D.C. can be so thick it appears as fog. This particular evening, it enveloped the upper-level corner office of Arthur Matsen, senior partner of the law office of Loring, Matsen, and Gould like a low-lying formless cloud. Inside the office, senior associate John Cann watched as Matsen leaned forward in his chair, placed his coffee cup on the low table in front of him, then pushed himself out of the chair with a soft grunt. Tall, slender, white haired, still active even in his eighties, Matsen looked like everyone's image of a Supreme Court chief justice.

He crossed to his desk, took a remote control from its surface, then returned to his chair.

"I could have gotten that for you," the three-or-so decades younger Cann kidded.

Matsen looked at him with a distracted smile but said nothing, which was out of character. Normally, Matsen would give Cann a mock retort. But not today.

Cann knew something was preoccupying the man who'd brought him into Loring, Matsen, and Gould many years ago and who was far more than just the senior member of the firm. Matsen was friend, mentor, even father figure to Cann, and the respect and trust between the two was mutual and unconditional.

"Out with it Arthur," Cann prodded. "What's on your mind?"

Matsen didn't answer right away, then, "I may be asking you to clear your plate for a while, John," he said. "There's something I want you to take a look at."

Cann nodded.

Matsen pointed the remote at the television and pressed the power button. The screen lit up, at first snowy then, after another click, going to solid blue before the first image came into view. The videotape began its story.

The image was clear, not at all grainy, and initially showed a static scene, the side of a weathered concrete-block building. The camera panned to the right along the wall and stopped on two individuals who stood facing each other outside a single door at the right side of the building. Both of the figures had weapons slung over their shoulders. One was wearing a baseball cap and the other a high crowned, military-style cap. The man with the baseball cap held what appeared to be a Russian-designed Kalishnikov AK-47 assault rifle while the man in the pseudo-military cap had what looked like a Czech-designed Skorpion submachine gun dangling from a strap over his right shoulder. Except for the one military-style hat, neither man was in uniform. Jeans and jackets. Both men appeared to be in their late thirties, early forties.

The man with the Skorpion went to the door of the building and pulled a railroad spike out of a hasp that kept the door secured. He pushed the door inward with the stubby muzzle of his weapon and stepped back. The other man also took a few steps backward and raised the Kalishnikov to an across-the-chest port arms position.

After a moment, several men filed out of the building, blinking in the sunlight. They were all dressed in civilian clothes, disheveled, unshaven. All were of "fighting age, broadly defined, the youngest perhaps sixteen, the oldest in his seventies. They were all shapes and sizes, but the common denominator was the terror in their eyes.

The captives lined up shoulder-to-shoulder facing the two armed men. The man in the military-style cap separated what appeared to be the four oldest from the rest and moved them over to stand by the wall. Then he repositioned himself off to the side of the main group and pointed the Skorpion at them.

Cann suddenly realized he could hear voices on the tape as one of the captors barked an order. Though Cann was fluent in several languages and conversant in others, he didn't understand what was being said. He recognized the flavor and cadence as Balkan, however. Somewhere in what used to be Yugoslavia, he guessed.

The shouted words were obviously a command, and the prisoners looked at one another with expressions of even greater fear and concern. Some stiffened, others moved nervously. The guard shouted again, and slowly, some of the captives began to take off their clothes.

The four older men stirred, but a few words from the man with the Skorpion stilled them. The others continued to remove their clothing until they all stood naked. Some attempted to cover themselves. Others didn't bother to try. Except for one very large individual who stood silent, unmoving, head bowed. It was as if he were trying against all reason to be somehow invisible.

The command was repeated, more loudly and more angrily. When the large man still didn't respond, the guard stepped forward and whipped the stock of the Kalishnikov into the prisoner's midsection, doubling him over. The initial strike was followed immediately by an upward thrust of the butt of the rifle to the man's forehead. The blow threw the prisoner's head back but he remained standing, bent slightly at the waist, blood dripping down his face. Both guards continued to shout at him, but he didn't respond. The one with the

Kalishnikov struck the prisoner in the head, first with the barrel of the assault rifle, then with the stock. Over and over again until, finally, the large man fell to his knees.

The captor with the Kalishnikov repositioned himself so he could cover all the captives. The other man put the Skorpion on the ground and pulled out a large combat knife. He walked over to the kneeling man, planted his left foot, and unleashed a vicious kick to the side of the man's head. The prisoner fell onto his side and the guard threw himself onto him hacking and slicing at the man's clothing, tearing it off in shreds until the prisoner was, in fact, naked.

But still, the guard kept cutting. When at last he was done, he sat back on his heels, chest heaving. In front of him, a slow, painful wail began in the victim's throat that grew into a tortured howl. Inexplicably, the prisoner attempted to stand but managed only to struggle to his knees. When he faced the camera, even Cann, who had seen just about everything, was tempted to turn away. The man's genitals had been completely cut off. He remained kneeling for a time, his life force ebbing away, then began to sway until he toppled over. Blood dripping between the fingers of his left hand, the attacker watched the man fall, and then casually tossed the man's genitals onto the ground beside him.

The man with the Kalishnikov chose another victim, a slight man who was clearly terrified beyond measure. The armed man put the muzzle of his assault rifle alongside the face of the slight man and fired a burst next to his ear. Terrified, the man lost control of his bowels. The guard with the Kalishnikov moved the muzzle of the weapon so it pointed into the prisoner's face, which was twisted with tears and horror. His lips moved, but he said nothing. Suddenly, the back of his head exploded splattering blood and tissue on several others around him. Without emotion, the man with the Kalishnikov shifted the rifle's direction, selecting his next victim, seemingly at random.

At that moment, heads snapped to the left as a utility vehicle drew up, followed by a large open-rail truck packed with women of all ages, all also naked. As the vehicles braked to a stop, two pairs of arms reached out through the rails of the cargo area in the back of the truck toward the bodies on the ground, and plaintive wails could be heard on the videotape.

The doors of the utility vehicle opened almost simultaneously and several men got out. Only the one who appeared to be the leader was in uniform. He strode over to the man with the AK-47 and spoke briefly but animatedly to him, his hands and arms waving and finally pointing off in the direction from which he had just arrived. The man with the Kalishnikov looked annoyed, even angry, but nodded and gestured for the naked men to pick up their clothing. The men from the utility vehicle fanned out and, not allowing the prisoners to put on any clothing, herded them to the truck, and forced them up and against the naked women and children. The last of the captives had hardly been jammed aboard when the rear gate of the cargo bed was slammed up and secured.

As the vehicles pulled away, a late model Mercedes limousine pulled into the scene. As soon as it stopped, a man let himself out of the back seat without waiting for the driver to come around and open his door. He wore an expensive well-tailored business suit but, judging by its rumpled condition, it looked like he might have been in it for a while. He strode up to the man with the Skorpion, looking closely at the bodies on the ground as he passed, then giving them no further attention. After some conversation, he nodded and pointed at the four older men left standing against the wall. The man with the Skorpion looked at the man in the suit for a moment, then nodded. He crossed to the old men and marched them over to the limousine. With a look and a vigorous nod, the well-dressed man said something to the two armed guards then looked directly at the camera that was still filming and made a beckoning hand gesture. The image tilted and the tape ended abruptly.

*　　*　　*

Cann blew some air through his lips. "What did we just watch, Arthur?"

"*Etnicko ciscenje*," Matsen replied somberly. "Ethnic cleansing. One face of it, anyway."

Cann grunted. "Where?"

"Northwest Bosnia." He looked at Cann. "How much do you know about the Balkans?"

Cann held his right hand out flat and waggled it a bit. He knew Arthur was much more knowledgeable about the area having, as he'd put it, "spent some time there" during World War II.

"I'm familiar with what happened there in the '90s, but I won't claim to understand all the groups or the rivalries and conflicts. I know they go back generations. Centuries, I guess. But beyond that —"

"I'm not sure anyone does. Even the people who live there. I mean, they think they do. They live it. Were raised on it. But the antipathies go deep. Make no mistake, at some point in the conflict, they've all brutalized each other. As one reporter put it, one group's retribution becomes the other's next atrocity."

Matsen dropped the remote on the table in front of him. "Anyway," he flipped his chin toward the screen, "the victims in that scene are Bosnian Muslims and the two men with weapons are reportedly Serb paramilitary irregulars. The one in the baseball cap was killed sometime in 1995. The other one, the man with the knife, is still alive. His name is Dubran Mribic." Matsen shook his head. "What this Mribic is alleged to have done is almost beyond comprehension. And based in part on things like that," he nodded at the video screen, "and on firsthand accounts of eyewitnesses, he was indicted by the International Criminal Tribunal for the Former Yugoslavia."

Cann nodded to indicate his awareness of the ICTY.

"But by then Mribic was in Srpska—the part of Bosnia controlled by Bosnian Serbs—which the Dayton Accords had recognized as an independent entity, the Republika Srpska. So, as long as Mribic stayed inside Srpska, it would be up to the local authorities to arrest him and hand him over. And they weren't going out of their way to do that."

"Right."

"Then, reports came in from an area in southeastern Germany, where refugees had fled to escape the fighting and the slaughter; something like 65 percent of the people in that area are displaced Bosnian Muslims. It appears that Mribic turned up in the middle of a community of the very people he victimized and, in fairly short order, he was recognized and taken into custody by German authorities under an ICTY warrant."

"And Germany surrendered him to the Tribunal, I presume."

"Well, apparently it's not so cut and dried. Germany is not a signatory under the Dayton Accords so technically isn't bound by its provisions."

"But as members of the UN, Germany's obligated to honor the ICTY warrant. Not to mention that they've also signed on to the International Criminal Court, and there's also the Geneva Protocols."

"Right. But as with all such agreements and protocols, national laws and sovereignty can come into play if there's a conflict."

"So what's the conflict?"

"It seems that Serbia and Srpska have an interest in Mr. Mribic and got together to file an extradition request of their own. Few people think they'll send Mribic to The Hague for trial if they get him back. But the petition has to be heard and so, for the moment, Mribic sits in a German federal holding facility while all of this sorts itself out."

Cann tilted his head and looked at Matsen. "I assume you're telling me all of this for a reason."

Matsen nodded. "I'd like you to go over there."

"When?"

"Right away."

Cann hesitated. "I'm flying down to see Janie tomorrow, Arthur. I'd hate to . . ."

Matsen held up his right hand. "No, no. By all means. You go. And give her my love." His gaze drifted briefly then he brought his attention back to Cann. "But immediately after, I'd like you to fly over for the extradition hearing."

"Okay," Cann drew out the single word turning it into a question. "But why? Does the U.S. have an interest in this?" He frowned. "Is the agency somehow involved in the situation?"

The "agency," of course, being the Central Intelligence Agency. Founding partners Gordon Loring and Arthur Matsen (Gould came later) had both been field operatives for General "Wild Bill" Donovan's Office of Strategic Services (OSS) during World War II, and the law firm they founded after the war grew and prospered based in large part on its deep and lasting connection to the intelligence community. Indeed, it was widely assumed, even in the absence of concrete evidence, that Loring, Matsen, and Gould was more than a law firm and many of its associates were more than attorneys.

"No, our involvement will be as private counsel."

"As —?"

"Defense counsel. I want you to represent Dubran Mribic."

2

Whispering Marsh Rehabilitation Center
Outside Savannah, Georgia

"Hi, 'fessa Cann!"

Janie Reston beamed the greeting at John Cann as she came into the visiting area of the Whispering Marsh Rehabilitation Center. In spite of her injuries, Janie lit up the room with her smile and the intelligence in her eyes was evident even from across the room. Her speech was noticeably slurred, though. And, perhaps because she was trying to move a little too quickly, her gait might have been a little less steady than the last visit, even with the cane.

"I thought you were going to call me John. Or do I have to go back to calling you Ms. Reston?"

Janie looked up at Cann's face with her crooked smile and he could see in her eyes that the answer formed instantly in her mind. But he knew it would be an effort to get it out.

"I . . . 'member, John. Jus' f'got . . . 'cause I'm . . . 'xcited."

Cann put his arms out inviting a hug. Janie crossed the room and almost fell against him as she pushed the cane away so she'd have both hands free to throw around his waist. The cane tottered and then fell against the couch.

Cann pulled her in and held her close, conflicting emotions

washing over him. Even as he felt the warmth and the pride he had in Janie, he couldn't help but feel sadness and anger at the contrast between her present condition and the memory of what she had been before her ordeal. And at the role he had played in it.

Two years earlier, Cann had taken a sabbatical from Loring, Matsen, and Gould to sit in the Johnson Chair for Visiting Legal Scholars at Charlestown University Law School. It wasn't a career move he'd have chosen, but he'd been declared persona non grata in Washington by no less a figure than the president of the United States, and Cann and Matsen decided it would be best if he "got out of Dodge for a while."

He'd met Janie after the dean of the Law School at Charlestown asked him to act as her faculty adviser in a disciplinary hearing for which the dean thought she was getting a bad rap. She was. And when the dean explained to Cann that certain campus factions were going after her simply to make their political point of the day, Cann had agreed to do so. Cann faced down the campus politicos and the charges were soon dropped.

But a connection between Cann and Janie was established in some minds — including the members of a terrorist cell within the Middle East Studies Department at Charlestown University. In truth, Cann's presence at Charlestown had no connection with the terrorist cell on campus, but the terrorists didn't know that.

They just knew Cann was the enemy. He'd gone into the military straight out of high school. First infantry, then airborne, then special forces. More than one tour in Vietnam. Then multiple assignments around the world, more often than not in the Middle East. Sent to college and then law school to establish an airtight legend, then more assignments under cover of his lawyer role, often seconded to the Central Intelligence Agency, National Security Agency, or Defense Intelligence Agency. And Cann excelled not only operationally but as a lawyer and thereby came to the attention of Arthur Matsen, who brought him into Loring, Matsen, and Gould. Both before and after joining the firm, Cann had been a fearsome and effective weapon in both the cold war and the war on terror. And he had made a lot of enemies.

The terrorists kidnapped Janie. It ate at Cann's soul that, having been called back to Washington, he didn't even know she was gone for several days. And what was done to Janie in that time was beyond comprehension. He only learned of it after his return, after Janie had been left for dead in the trunk of a car.

Janie survived. Barely.

The terrorists did not. Cann saw to that.

But it still frustrated and angered him that he hadn't been able to prevent the horror in the first place. Janie's injuries had been so extensive that there were many who thought it would have been better if she had not survived. Had she been a broken doll, she would have been thrown away.

Cann was determined that Janie would get the best treatment available. Arthur Matsen concurred without hesitation and visited Janie in the hospital. Cann wasn't surprised by Matsen's compassion, but he was struck by the depth of the emotion in his old friend's face when he looked down at the small vulnerable "broken doll."

When Janie had recovered enough to leave the hospital, Cann and Matsen arranged for her transfer to Whispering Marsh Rehabilitation Center where she'd been for the past two years. Cosmetic surgery had restored her physical appearance, but there had been brain damage as well. It was slow going, but Janie was a fighter. And the staff loved and admired her for it.

Janie swung herself in a half turn and Cann helped her lower herself into a corner of the couch.

"I . . . like . . . it . . . when . . . you . . . visi'." Janie had to take a breath between each word and the labored effort was clearly tiring.

"I like it too, Janie. I wish I could come more often." He sat back down and turned toward Janie bending his right leg and resting it on the seat of the couch.

"Me . . . too." She took several deep breaths before continuing. "But lo's . . . of . . . times . . . when . . . you . . . come," she had to pause and take a breath, "y'ur goin' . . . 'way . . . 'gain. Where . . . you . . . goin' . . . nex'?"

"Actually, I'm headed for Germany as soon as I leave here."

Janie smiled at him again and then leaned back. Her face grew serious and she took several breaths. Cann knew she was in constant pain but resisted taking painkillers when he visited so that she could be sharp for him. Sometimes she overwhelmed him.

"Are you okay?"

"Jes' tired."

"Shall I let you get some rest?"

"No." The word was sharp and lucid and heartfelt. Janie sat up quickly — a move that triggered an obvious jab of pain. She fell back. "No. You . . . jes' . . . got . . . here." She spoke more quietly then.

"I'll stay, Janie. But maybe you can get a little rest. I'll be here when you wake up. That's a promise."

" 'Kay. Maybe . . . I should take a . . . li'l med'cin. Jes' a li'l."

"You bet, sweetheart. I'll get the nurse."

"But don' . . . leave, 'kay?"

"I won't."

He crossed the room and opened the door into the corridor to get the attention of the nurse at the other end of the hall. He mimed taking a pill and then looked back and smiled at Janie who had her eyes closed and her head resting against the back of the couch. When the nurse came in with a tiny plastic cup, Janie held her hand up in a "stop" motion to the nurse. "I don' wan' . . . a full . . . dosag', 'kay? Jes' 'nuf . . . to help me . . ."

"It's a half dose, Janie," the nurse said as she watched Janie take the pill with a small cup of water. "But it will make you a little sleepy.

You go ahead and nap there for a bit and then you can continue your visit."

Janie nodded and looked at Cann. "But you . . . won' . . . leave while . . . I'm . . . 'sleep. Right?"

"Not a chance, Janie. I promise."

Janie nodded and smiled. And then closed her eyes.

Cann watched her for a long while before walking slowly out into the corridor. He'd wait as long as it took.

Cann walked down to the main foyer that looked out through a glass wall into an inner courtyard. Small bonsai-type shrubs were placed around and amid rocks that were threaded by a gently flowing stream.

In the reflection of the glass, Cann saw a middle-aged man of average height, roundish build, and thinning, slicked-back hair come around a corner, stop briefly, and then stride toward him. As the man got closer, he jutted out his hand toward Cann's back and declared in a loud voice, "Mr. Cann."

Cann turned

"I'm Dr. Fredrich. Dr. Nathan Fredrich. Staff psychiatrist. We haven't met before."

Cann knew that. He took the offered hand. "Dr. Fredrich."

"I've been looking for you," Fredrich said. "I saw on the schedule that you'd be visiting Ms. Reston today."

"Yes, I am. She's resting right now."

Fredrich gestured toward an alcove with benches. "Let's talk over here, shall we?"

As soon as they were seated, Fredrich turned to Cann.

"I saw in the records that you're closely involved with Ms. Reston and her parents. Have you been a close family friend for a long time?"

"No. I met Janie at Charlestown University. Shortly before —" He waved his arm in the general direction of the room where Janie was resting. "— all this?"

Fredrich leaned in. "You were there when Ms. Reston was harmed?"

"I was at Charlestown."

"Do you know what happened to her?'

The fact was Cann did know—from a videotape the terrorists had made of Janie's torture. But Cann had shredded and burned it after exacting retribution. He'd told only Matsen about the tape, and only after he'd destroyed it. To his knowledge, only one other still-living person had ever seen even a part of it. But Cann wasn't going to share that information without knowing where this was going. "I've read the medical reports, Doctor," he responded. "I assume you have too."

"Yes, I have. Horrific. I understand they never found the people who did this to her?"

He meant that no one had ever been arrested or tried.

After a long moment, Cann responded. "No, they never found them."

He, of course, meant something entirely different.

Fredrich thought for a moment then said, "I also saw in the records that you're Ms. Reston's lawyer."

"Yes, and a co-guardian but—"

"As is an Arthur Matsen," Fredrich interrupted.

"As I was just about to say, Doctor, I—and Arthur—*are* coguardians, but we see that only as an emergency measure. Janie's parents and Janie are the primary—

"Which is precisely what I wanted to talk to you about."

Cann was getting *very* tired of Fredrich's abruptness. He held up a hand. "Just a minute, Doctor. As you said, we haven't met. How long have you been here?"

"Oh, barely two weeks now. But rest assured, Mr. Cann, our little Ms. Reston is one of the reasons I wanted this position. Her case presents a unique set of issues in my field. That's what I want to talk to you about. I need you to help me straighten out Janie's parents with regard to her treatment and what I want to do with her."

Cann's jaw tightened. In the first place, Janie was not *their/his/our* little anything. In the second place, Cann knew that the Restons adored their daughter and were the last people to need "straightening out." And, in the third place, anything — *anything* — involving Janie's treatment would be based on what Janie *needed,* not what Dr. Fredrich or anyone else *wanted.* Cann momentarily suppressed his fierce protectiveness of Janie and asked, "And what is your field?"

"Memory." Fredrich nodded sharply. "Repressed and recovered memory."

"But Janie was heavily drugged throughout the ordeal. She has no memory of what happened to her."

"I disagree. And that is why I wanted to talk to you. Ms. Reston's parents have declined to accept my recommendation that we begin to treat Janie's potential psychological trauma — particularly what I feel is the virtually inevitable, albeit undetected, dissociative disorder that must of necessity accompany situations of this sort."

Cann frowned with concern. "Has Janie been having problems I'm unaware of. Any symptoms of such a disorder"

"Not yet but having been through what she experienced, how can she not at some point be affected?"

Cann repeated his point. "But if there are no symptoms, you can't know there's a disorder, no? And if she doesn't remember what happened, why would she have symptoms?"

Fredrich's shoulders heaved up and down once in exaggerated exasperation. "As for her having no memory at any level, I simply don't believe that. At some level of her consciousness, she had to be aware of what was happening to her and that awareness is, I believe, stored at some level somewhere inside. What is called 'implicit memory.' "

"That's not good enough, Doctor," Cann said forcefully. " 'Some level, somewhere' doesn't make it. You don't treat someone for a disease if you don't even know they have it. And even you said that there are no apparent symptoms of these memories that may or may not be there."

"Oh, they're there all right, I assure you," Fredrich said haughtily. "And I must tell you that I quite frankly don't understand why you and Janie's parents would be willing to risk her mental health and perhaps even her physical well-being simply because you can't grasp a moderately complicated theory."

The silence was as sudden as it was complete. When Cann did speak, his voice was low and cold. "Perhaps the better question, Doctor, is why you would subject anyone to treatment that might not be warranted."

Fredrich drew himself up in his chair. "I beg your pardon? That statement has some odious undertones, Mr. Cann."

"Undertones? I must have been more subtle than I intended. Let me make it clear. Neither I nor Janie's parents nor Arthur Matsen, for that matter, will consent to any fishing expedition into Janie's psyche. Or memory. Or anywhere else."

Fredrich folded his arms across his chest and sat simmering for a moment. "My work is important, Mr. Cann. Very important."

"Janie is what's important, Doctor Fredrich. If you don't get that —"

"There is an enormous gap in science's comprehension of matters such as implicit memory and —"

"Maybe, but you're not going to fill it by experimenting on Janie."

"Experimenting! How dare you?"

"I dare, Doctor. Count on it. And I'll dare a lot more if you harm that girl in any way."

"Is that a threat?"

"Yes." Cann pointed his finger. "You will act in Janie's best interests. And only in her best interest. Am I understood?"

Fredrich drew himself up straight. "I always keep the well-being of my patients in mind."

Cann stood. "Just remember what I said, Doctor." He walked away without looking back.

Cann pushed his conversation with Frederich aside for the moment and, after Janie awoke rested and feeling better, he visited with her for several more pleasant hours. After the reluctant farewells, he walked out of Whispering Marsh and to his rental car to head for the airport. He started the engine and sat for a moment, thinking. Then he took his cell phone and punched a single button.

"Hello, Arthur. It's John. I'm just heading out to the airport right now — She's well. She sends you her love — I know. She knows that too." Cann paused. "Arthur, listen, there's something I'd like you to look into. There's this new doctor here at Whispering Marsh. His name's Fredrich. Nathan Fredrich. That's F-r-e-d-r-i-c-h."

3

"Come on, Janie, one more. Press."

Janie Reston lay against the backrest of the weight machine and exerted all the strength she could muster to push on the foot pads which, through a series of cables and pulleys, were attached to weights somewhere behind her. *One more, my butt,* she thought to herself. That was the third, maybe the fourth, "one more" in a row and she wondered how many more "one mores" there would be before this session was done. But she also knew that the device of "one more" was the standard way of getting that extra effort and she was grateful even through the pain.

And, let's face it, it hurt a lot less than it used to, so they were doing something right. She gave yet another final push and felt the pad touch bottom.

"Super, Janie. Good work." Sara Furden was genuinely pleased. "Let's call it for now. Okay?"

"I'll shay i's 'kay, Sara. I go' nothin' lef'."

Damn. She hated the way words wouldn't come out the way she intended. Everything in her brain was as clear as it had ever been but somewhere between brain and lips, it got jumbled and slurred. But her speech was better than it had been. A little. Not as significant as the improvement in the rest of her body and she wondered if she'd ever be 100 percent again. In her most truthful moments, she knew it wasn't likely. But that was the goal. The alternative was to aim low. No way.

Janie swung herself off the bench of the weight machine, grasped her cane, and stood. "T'anks, Sara," she said and leaned over to give a brief hug to the physical therapist before heading into the locker area and the showers.

Sara Furden watched Janie falter a couple of times as she made her way to the adjoining shower room and her heart ached. Furden had known Janie all her life. She and Janie's mother had been best friends growing up and had stayed close throughout school and into adulthood. Sara had been Janie's godmother and big sister and surrogate mother all rolled into one. So it was no surprise that when Janie went off to college, it was to Charlestown University where Furden was assistant professor of physical education.

That haunted Furden. She was obsessed with the idea that Janie would never have been hurt if Furden hadn't encouraged her to attend Charlestown. At first, she'd tried to blame John Cann, already resentful that Janie had asked him, not her, for help in the disciplinary hearing. And when Janie disappeared, Furden convinced herself he was responsible. She'd hated him.

At one point, Furden had a gun pointed at Cann and the last terrorist was urging her to shoot him. And she was about to when she glimpsed that few seconds of awful videotape which made her turn and shoot the terrorist point blank in the face instead. She'd never killed anyone before and that, and what she'd seen on the tape, and her conviction that it was all her fault, caused her to have a complete breakdown. In the end it was Janie who brought her back from the brink. Janie's love. Janie's acceptance. Janie's trust. From that moment forward, Janie was the core of Furden's life. She left her position at Charlestown and got certified as a physical therapist. She would never leave Janie's side, she vowed to herself. She would do whatever it took to help Janie and protect her. No one would ever hurt her again.

Furden's thoughts snapped back to the present when a voice asked, "Where's Janie Reston?"

She turned to face Dr. Fredrich. "We just finished a session. She's in the shower."

"Not a problem," Fredrich mumbled as he started to go around Furden toward the shower room. Furden stopped him by placing the palm of her right hand on Fredrich's chest. "I said she's in the shower. I'm sure she'll be done in a few minutes."

Fredrich looked down at the hand restraining him. "I assure you I have no ulterior motives, Ms. Furden. I only need a moment of her time." He went to step around Furden, but she moved her hand to his forearm and gripped it tightly. Furden was tall and her slender build didn't imply great strength. But she was in excellent shape and years of physical training and exercise had given her a grip like a vise. Fredrich flinched.

"It's not a question of time, Dr. Fredrich. It's a question of privacy. As I said, I'm sure she'll only be a few minutes. You can wait or you can leave a message with me. I'll be happy to pass it on."

"Yes, well, there might be another question of privacy if I were to be leaving messages here and there, don't you think?"

Furden kept her hand on his arm. After a moment, Fredrich shook his head. "Oh, very well. Please tell her to stop by the med station before two this afternoon. She needs to take a new med I'm prescribing at least an hour before our three o'clock session." He started to leave then stopped. "And oh, yes. I noticed in her medication record that you're recommending Reflexeril for her. Be sure to clear any and all meds with me. I'll be adjusting her other medications from time to time and we wouldn't want any drug interactions, would we?" He walked away without waiting for a response.

Like just about everyone else at the center, Furden was put off by this new staff psychiatrist, but traditional medical protocols argued against the less than cordial answer that initially formed in her mind. So she settled for mumbling, "Asshole," to his back as he left.

Janie stood in the shower feeling just a bit sorry for herself. She missed being home. Or at school. She missed her parents. She missed her friends. To be sure, Whispering Marsh was luxurious and top of the line; Cann and Matsen would settle for nothing less. And she got away now and then for visits and trips. But no matter how you looked at it, it was still an institution. And therefore virtually impossible to be alone. Except maybe in sleep, and even that required the artificial palliative of drugs. So Janie luxuriated in the warm cascade and in the escape that allowed her to be alone and to recapture the sense of what she was before her injuries.

The warm tingle of the stream of water lowered the chronic pain to a dull ache. The enveloping sensations and sounds created a refuge in which she could briefly be whole. In her mind, at least. For just a few moments, reality could be suspended and she could revel in the clarity of her thoughts without the futility of trying to articulate them.

And there was the sense, the burden she sometimes felt, that everyone was depending on her. Expecting that she would be strong. She knew that they cared for her, loved her deeply. But sometimes she just got so frustrated. Frustrated with their encouragement. They didn't know. Frustrated with their praise of her strength. How amazing she was. Sometimes she didn't feel strong. She felt small. And hurt. And scared.

She shook her head. Okay, enough of that. She'd be strong. As strong as they say she is. Maybe even stronger. To herself, she sang, 'that's what friends are for. In good times —' It came out clear and correct in her mind. She didn't want to think what it would sound like if she tried to sing it out loud.

Arthur Matsen's Office
Loring, Matsen, and Gould
Washington, D.C.

" 'Well, dear, I am afraid zat I cannot permit zat.' "

"Uh-oh," Matsen raised his eyebrows. "He called you 'dear'?"

"That's what he said," Katherine Price repeated the statement in a mock French accent and with a chuckle of her own. "I mean, it's not the word, Arthur. Dear, shmear. Who cares? But in this case it was clearly intended as a put down." She shook her head. "Uh-uh.

Price was a full partner at Loring Matsen, and about as far removed from the stereotyped image of the proverbial fat cats or old boys who hibernated in their posh offices as one could get. Brilliant, superbly capable, at once aggressive or persuasive as conditions warranted, she was adept at incisive legal analysis as well as both scathing wit or warm humor depending on the circumstances and goals. She was also what Arthur Matsen thought of as a handsome woman. Other partners and associates, male and female, described her as stunningly attractive and, among the younger associates, the word "hot" was not uncommon even though she had ten or fifteen years on most of them. But for everyone in the firm, including Arthur, it was the whole person that generated the admiration and respect. Arthur was in one way or another close to all the employees, associates, and partners, but Katherine was one of his favorites. And the feeling, grounded in both respect and affection, was mutual.

"And you said?"

"I kind of pouted and said, 'And why would zat be, dear?' "

Matsen chuckled. "With the fake accent?"

"No, in French, but he got the idea."

"And?"

"Well, he harrumphed a bit. Then he said, 'I have discussed it wis my government and zey utterly refuse to go along with ze provision zat equalizes ze licensing rights for all parties. *Corseaux* must retain superior rights as well as a right of first refusal on all content proposed for ze merged companies.'

" 'Or?' I asked him." She smiled and continued. "He gave me his best Gallic sneer and leaned back in his chair, shrugged, turned his palms up, and said, 'Or zere will be no merger.' "

Price uncrossed her legs and immediately recrossed them with the opposite leg on top. "So I let that sit out there for a while and then said, 'It's not negotiable?' He pursed his lips in that oh-so-Gallic fashion once again and said, with a smirk, 'No, dear.' "

Matsen shook his head back and forth.

"So I just looked at him. And finally I said, 'Zat's too bad,' and started to pick up my papers. At first he didn't flinch. But by the time I zipped my portfolio and started to get up, he wasn't smiling anymore. 'Where are you going?' he says. It was my turn to shrug. 'Obviously zat point is critical to you so I don't see where we have any place to go.' I shrugged again.

" 'But zere are so many other aspects to zis transaction,' he says. 'I cannot believe your clients would allow it to fail on zis basis.'

"So I said, 'And yours would?' "

Matsen nodded approvingly.

"There was a very long pause after that. Then finally he says, 'Perhaps zere is some room for discussion after all.' "

"Would you have walked if he didn't come around?" Matsen asked.

"I was going to. But I really didn't have the authority to do that on a licensing issue. It was a bluff. But, all's well that ends well, right?"

"Often but not always, my dear." He put his hands up in front of him. "Oops. Sorry."

Price's smile was broad and warm. "As I said, Arthur, dear,

schmear. It's not the word, it's the intent. I've told you many times, coming from you, it's a compliment." She stood and came around his desk and kissed him on the top of his head. "Now that's unprofessional," she said and stepped back to watch him flush. Not blush. Arthur Matsen wasn't one to blush, but he did feel the warmth come across his face at this delightful breach of protocol. He knew and accepted it as a form of teasing, but he also knew it came from a heartfelt affection and respect.

"Yes, well, please don't do that at a partner's meeting, Katherine," he said with a feigned severity that was belied by the smile on his face. "People will talk."

They laughed together.

"Anyway," he said after a moment, "I wanted to discuss something else with you. Not firm business, technically, but I'd like your help on it. You know Janie Reston."

She did. She'd met Janie when she'd come on a visit with her parents some time ago. Price very clearly remembered the lovely young lady in a wheelchair with the brightest eyes imaginable and slightly crooked smile that communicated so much more than mere amusement. She also remembered the pain in those eyes and in her own heart when Janie needed to move or wanted to speak She nodded to Matsen.

"She's still at Whispering Marsh and it seems that John has some concerns about a new psychiatrist on staff there and some proposed treatments he wants to try. I remembered that you're admitted in that jurisdiction and wanted to ask if you could make some inquiries — Board of Licensure or whatever equivalent they have down there. Get some background on the guy. Dr. Nathan Fredrich. Also, and I realize this is out of the legal realm, but could you also make some inquiries of others down there with expertise in dissociative disorders and repressed and recovered memory? Also, something called 'implicit memory.'" Price noted that Matsen rattled off the terms without consulting any notes.

Price narrowed her brows. "I was under the impression that Janie didn't have any memory at all of what happened to her."

"That's the point. On his last visit, John met this Dr. Fredrich who wants to try to elicit whatever may be buried inside — if anything. But John had some fundamental disagreements, questions anyway, with what the doctor said as opposed to what he described the condition to be. Of course, John may be being somewhat overprotective but —"

Indeed. Price remembered how both Cann and Matsen had hovered over Janie during that visit to the firm. Like a couple of mother hens. Or father hens.

Price was aware of the extent of Janie's injuries — Arthur had spoken about it on several occasions — but she didn't know all the details. She also had a vague sense of the events that had followed Janie's ordeal and knew that John Cann had done something. Taken some action. But she didn't know the details of that either.

What she did know was that seeing that wonderful young lady struggle and knowing that there were animals capable of committing such atrocities, she'd liked to have been there when Cann had done whatever he'd done. Legal constructs and abstract theories were all well and good in their place. Direct action had its place too. She knew from experience.

Like Cann, Katherine Price and Loring, Matsen, and Gould were a good fit. Also, like Cann, she'd been recruited by Arthur Matsen for more than her legal skills.

Actually, in the case of Katherine Price, much of the recruiting of Loring, Matsen had been done for them by the Department of State. An honors graduate of a small, private law school, Price went directly into the Department of Justice upon graduation. Then there was an interesting lateral into DEA out of Miami that lasted about a year before she went off to a stint at the Glynco Federal Law Enforcement Training Center — referred to as "fletsy" — before returning to other assignments at Justice, often in the role of "legal attache," the euphemism used for FBI agents on foreign soil. Then another stint, this time at Quantico. Very specialized training.

After that, the assignments got even more interesting. And often coincided with events in varied parts of the world: crises, coups, assassinations, and accidental deaths. Some made the headlines. Most did not. But even the latter were known to one degree or another within the intelligence community. No names, of course, but those in the know knew.

Then Price had gone over to State. It was her intent and she had been led to believe that she would be attached to the Bureau of Diplomatic Security — the Intelligence and Threat Analysis Office specifically. Counterterror. A perfect fit.

But in her intake interview with Secretary of State Marilyn Sutton, the secretary interpreted Price's confidence and strength as a lack of proper deference and, for no other reason than to prove that she could, switched Price's assignment to staff attorney. An utter waste of talent and experience but par for the bureaucratic diplomatic course under Sutton.

Price also didn't score any points by rejecting the cult of personality under Sutton; like the way virtually every female employee adopted Sutton's fashion signature of a loud, garishly patterned scarf tied around the neck and draped over a shoulder. Refreshingly different, Katherine Price dressed like a professional. Normal businesslike clothing. She was and would be her own person, a clear sign of the inner strength so prized at Loring, Matsen.

It was Cann who'd brought her to Arthur Matsen's attention. He'd seen Price for the first time at a meeting of the legal staffs of several agencies and had been mightily impressed. More than just appearance, he'd noted the way she made her presentation at the meeting in the most professional manner of anyone there — including himself, he admitted — and did so without notes, without posturing, and without missing a beat. And there was a sense of inner strength. He didn't know about her other activities.

But there was little Matsen didn't know. Or couldn't find out. So he did some checking, as only he could do, and he liked what he found — that Katherine Price was very, *very* good at what she did.

A phone call. A return call. A meeting. It was done.

State, or Sutton at least, had already recruited Price for something else. She just didn't know what.

Until Arthur Matsen called.

4

"How are you feeling, Janie?"

"Fi'."

"Good. Did you stop by the med station? Did the physical therapist give you my message?"

Janie nodded. "Wha' was the new med'cin'. It doesn' feel much dif'ren' than my pain pills."

"It's not, really. Same class of drugs actually. I just wanted to relax you a bit more for this session. Remember that when we met for the first time last week, I went through that long list of questions with you?"

"Did I pass?" Janie's crooked smile made it look just that much more mischievous.

"What? Pass what. I don't understand."

"You as'ed me all those questions. Like a tes'. I always did well on tes'."

Janie's attempt at humor was lost on Dr. Fredrich. "Oh, yes. Well, it wasn't that kind of test, of course."

"Nev'r min'." Janie waved her hand loosely in dismissal of the subject.

"But now I'd like to see if we can take a look at more internal matters — see what's inside and what we need to do about it. Are you relaxed?"

"I s'pose so. I'm not sleepy or an'thin'."

"That's good." Fredrich got up and went around behind the upholstered recliner where Janie sat. He pushed down on the back-rest until Janie was tilted back in a semireclined position and went back behind his desk. "I'm going to talk to you very softly, Janie, and I'd like you to focus in on the sound of my voice and what I'm saying and let your mind go where I direct it. Okay?"

" 'Kay."

"You remember when we spoke before, I asked you about your favorite places, don't you?"

Janie nodded.

"And you remember your most favorite place of all, that grove of Spanish oaks you told me about with all the moss hanging from them, the soft grass on the ground all around them, the tiny pond with the frogs."

"An' the salama'ders. They were ev'r'wher'."

"Right. Let's go there."

" 'Kay."

"Okay. To get there, I want you to walk down a hill, not too steep, Janie. But you have to go downward to get to your favorite place. And I want you always to know that your favorite place is your safe place. No one or nothing can hurt you in your safe place. And that means it's okay to remember things in your safe place, Janie. You can remember anything and everything and it won't hurt you. Do you understand that?"

"Yes."

"Okay. Start going down the hill. Picture that there are steps you can use to go down so it's easier. As you go farther and farther down the hill, I want you to let yourself get more and more relaxed. You're going to your favorite place and that means you're safe and you can just relax and concentrate on what I'm saying."

"Mmm."

"Okay. Now you're in your favorite place, Janie. Is it nice?"

"Mmm. Yes."

"Why don't you sit down with your back against one of the oaks and lean your head back and let your mind wander. Can you do that?"

"Mmm."

"Okay. Now, let your mind take you somewhere else. You're not going to be somewhere else for real, though, Janie. You're going to be in your favorite place—your safe place—at all times. But in your mind, I want you to go back to the university when you were attending there. Can you do that?"

"Mmm."

"Where are you then?"

"Doin' 'robics."

"Doing what? I didn't understand."

" 'Robic's. Esercise. Dancin'."

Fredrich though for a moment, then, "Oh, aerobics. You're doing aerobics?"

"A class. Mmm."

Fredrich didn't know the details of the events that left Janie so badly hurt but, if she was up and doing aerobics, then it was clear that that would have to have been before the injuries occurred. "Let's move ahead in time, Janie. Can you do that? Just fast-forward for me and tell me where you are now."

"Lunsh. With John and Sara."

"Would that be John Cann?"

"Mmm-hmm."

"Who's Sara?"

"My mom's frien'."

"But you're at the university. Why would your mom's friend be there?"

"She's a 'fessa there. Phys ed."

Fredrich made a note. "What's her last name?"

"Fur'then."

"Can you spell it for me, Janie?"

"F-u-r-d-e-n."

Frederich snapped his head up. "The therapist?" The surprise in his voice was apparent.

"Mmm-hmm."

"Why —?" Fredrich stopped himself. He made a note to follow up on that later.

"Okay. Can you fast-forward for me again?"

After a moment, Janie's voice quavered and she emitted the single sound, "ohh."

Fredrich's attention level jumped.

"What, Janie? What is it?"

Janie's body stiffened in the chair and her face grimaced in pain. Fredrich scribbled without taking his eyes off her. Then, the tension in Janie's body began to lessen.

"Janie, what is it? What's happening?"

Janie didn't answer.

"Janie! What's happening now?"

"Nothin'."

"Nothing?" Fredrich snapped the word out then regained control. "Don't let go, Janie. Stay there. What do you see?"

"Nothin'. There's nothin'."

Fredrich's mind was racing. There had been a hint of memory. A beginning. He needed to get it back. He composed himself and spoke calmly. "Okay, Janie. I want you to remember that your favorite place has different levels. I want you to go down the hill, the steps, some more into a deeper, safer place where you can see even more. And as you go down, I want you to fast-forward until you come to something else you can remember. And don't forget, you'll be safe there, so you can remember anything you want. Can you go down the steps some more?"

"Mmm."

After a moment, "Where are you now?"

"Don' know. Can't see anythin'. Nothin' here."

Fredrich's tension grew but still he spoke gently. "Janie, there can't be nothing. Your mind has everything in it. Go down some more steps."

" 'Kay."

Fredrich watched and waited.

"Where are you now, Janie?"

"Nowher'. Can' see anythin'. Open space."

"But you can't see anything?"

"No. 'T's dark."

Frederich felt his breakthrough slipping away.

"Sa' light."

Fredrich's heart skipped.

"What, Janie?"

"A light. An' . . . oh . . . oww! . . . oh . . ." Again, Janie stiffened. No words came out but she twisted in the chair, writhing in apparent agony. Fredrich was making notes as fast as he could write. Janie's respiration was rapid and very shallow, her body rigid in the recliner, her knuckles white as she gripped the arms of the chair, her face contorted. A single tear ran down her cheek.

Fredrich was exultant.

I knew it. His left fist was clenched and pumping as he wrote with his right. *I knew it!*

5

Bayerischen Staatsgericht
Detention Facility
Outside Garmisch–Partenkirchen
Germany

Cann waited outside his hotel in Garmisch-Partenkirchen in south-eastern Germany until a green and white sedan with the word "Polizei" on its sides drew up to the curb. One of the uniformed men in the front twisted and reached back to open the rear door for Cann, who muttered *"Morgen"* as he got in. They drove in silence for about twenty minutes until they came to a complex of single-story, wooden structures surrounded by ten-foot barbed-wire-topped fences. It was a former U.S. Army stockade long since turned over to the German government and was now the facility where Dubran Mribic was being held.

Cann was checked in, first at the outer gatehouse and then again in the administrative building. From there, he was taken across an open area of grass bisected by a paved path and into another building where he was finally deposited in a comfortably furnished interview room to await his first meeting with his client.

He wasn't happy about it. He wasn't a criminal defense attorney and never wanted to be. In fact, he didn't have a very high opinion of criminal defense attorneys at all. He remembered back to law school where, unless his memory was failing him — and it wasn't — he was quite clear on what the legal Code of Ethics had to say about defending people accused of a crime.

You didn't.

If you knew they were guilty, you didn't take the case. If you found out they were guilty in the course of representation, either by evidence or the defendant telling you he'd done it, you dropped the case. Recused yourself. And the judge was duty bound to allow it.

No more. Now it seemed too many lawyers would take any case as long as the retainer check didn't bounce. And the judges added to the problem, often denying a recusal request usually on the specious assertion that *every* defendant was *entitled* to a defense. Bullshit. Cann's view was that you're only *entitled* to a defense if you actually have one.

Not that the prosecutors were any better. Equally as offensive to Cann as the defense lawyer knowingly defending a guilty person was the prosecutor with a winnable case knowingly pursuing an inno- cent accused. He knew one assistant D.A. who liked to brag — thought it was a sign of professional toughness — that he "didn't care if they're guilty or not. It's the wins and losses that matter." The system was broken. And the only people who could fix it were profiting from it.

And here *he* was about to undertake the defense of a man whom he'd seen on videtape committing the crimes he was accused of. And who'd probably committed a lot of others that were just as bad or worse. Yet, he'd taken on the duty of affording this man as good a defense as he, Cann, was capable of giving him.

It bothered him a lot. More than a lot. So why was he doing it?

Arthur had asked him to.

The click of the door handle brought Cann back to the present. The door swung in and a uniformed guard leaned in and nodded to Cann.

A second later, Mribic walked in. He looked essentially the same as he had on the videotape. Older, maybe fifty or so. A couple of inches shorter than Cann. Squarish face with pronounced cheekbones. Light brown hair combed straight back from his forehead. He appeared fit, apparently none the worse for wear from the rest of the Bosnian war, the years since, or his present incarceration.

"Mr. Cann." Mribic nodded as he spoke but didn't offer his hand.

"Mr. Mribic." Cann answered with a similar nod and sat down. Mribic followed suit on the other side of the rectangular table.

They looked at each other for a brief moment before Cann spoke. "Deutsch? Englisch?"

A sardonic smile appeared on Mribic's face. "Yes, I rather suspected you wouldn't know any Serbian." He shrugged. "English would be best, I think." He spoke with very little accent, more American than British.

"Okay. Hearing you speak it, that makes sense. Where did you learn English?"

"How disappointing, Mr. Cann. A good attorney should take the time to learn about his clients. If you'd done your homework, you'd know that I have spent some time in the United States."

"And you would know what a good attorney would do?"

"Yes, actually, since I am one. Another thing you would know if you'd done your homework." Mribic's attitude was more one of smugness than contempt.

Actually, Cann did know that. And a lot more than this arrogant man realized. Which was how Cann wanted it. Not only would his apparent ignorance work toward eliciting basic information from Mribic; it also gave Cann an excellent way of confirming how forthright Mribic intended to be.

Cann shrugged. "Where did you get your law degree?"

"University of Belgrade, of course," Mribic said with a cluck of his tongue.

"Of course," Cann repeated back at him.

"With course work toward a Master of Laws in International Relations at the University of Chicago. Interrupted by," he waved his hands around the room, "all of what led me to this."

"So how did you get from there to here? Briefly."

Mribic's eyebrows arched at the last word. "Briefly, Mr. Cann? Can't be done. It's taken me more than a thousand years to get here."

Cann shook his head. "Spare me the profundities. You've been indicted by the International Criminal Tribunal for the Former Yugoslavia for grave breaches of the Geneva Protocols and crimes against humanity. Let's address the matter of why we're sitting here across from each other."

"In good time, Mr. Cann. First you must —"

"No. Not in good time, Mr. Mribic. Now. I've seen the tape. And that's only part of what —"

"What tape is that, Mr. Cann? May I call you John, by the way?"

"No."

Mribic shrugged. "Yes, well, the tape. I assume you mean the one that was sent to Mr. Matsen. Let me tell you, that's nothing."

"Assuming we're talking about the same tape, I wouldn't call it nothing."

"Compared to what was done to Serbs in World War II? Seven hundred fifty thousand dead. Executed. Murdered. Because they were Serbs. Nothing more. And not just shot, John. Skulls were crushed by hammers, eyes gouged out, heads sawn off while the victim was alive and conscious, whole villages thrown alive into mass graves, rapes, drownings. And if you choose not to believe me, it's preserved in photos. Look at them some time, John. You would not forget."

"I have seen them. But what happened in World War II doesn't justify what you did on that tape."

Mribic clicked his tongue. "How very judgmental. Perhaps you might take into account what those men on the tape did earlier themselves. Maybe they deserved what happened to them."

"And the women. The children. What did they do to deserve it?"

"Deserve what? Being transported in trucks?"

"Naked?"

"Very little chance of hidden weapons that way. A tactical alternative to harsher methods. Look at it positively. Give me credit. And it's nothing you probably haven't done yourself."

"Bullshit."

"No. Not bullshit. I think perhaps you've seen war. Vietnam, perhaps?"

Cann nodded.

"And when you were shot at — or worse — by women. Or children. You didn't respond? You know you did."

"But we didn't respond by rounding up every one of them and trucking them off to God knows where. Or what."

"You just shot them on the spot."

"No. That's not how it worked. If we got attacked, they were by definition combatants. And we reacted as such. What's on that tape is you brutalizing prisoners."

"Ahh. Yes. Prisoners. Helpless, blameless individuals entirely at our mercy. And to whom we owe extraordinary consideration. Is that what you're saying? Tell me, John, how does what I did on that tape differ so greatly from throwing a man out of a helicopter from several thousand feet for no other reason than to persuade one of his colleagues to talk." Cann said nothing and Mribic issued an amused huff. "The only difference I see is that you don't get his blood all over you. A moment ago you asked me to spare you the profundities. I ask you to spare me the self-righteousness."

Neither man spoke for a moment, then Mribic continued. "You speak of your acts in the context of cause and effect. I agree. Let me tell you something. Those men in the tape were from a village that supported and in many cases were members of a Bosnian Muslim militia that themselves had run the Serbian population out of a village called Doblici some months earlier. In the process, they killed thirty-seven people, then they systematically raped every single female in the village. Regardless of age, John. The oldest was in her seventies. The youngest was eight. Eight! They were paraded out in front of the men of the village, stripped naked, and raped over and over again while the men of the village were made to watch. Those women who resisted in any way were staked out on the ground spread-eagled while the militia men lined up for their turns." He leaned in toward Cann. "The large man you saw on the tape? He was especially fond of the eight-year-old I mentioned."

Cann was silent for a long moment. Finally, he said, "So it's all about vengeance. Okay. But what about the people on the tape? Or their relatives or friends. Wouldn't they have the same excuse?"

"Sure. That's how it works. So long as the victim is Bosnian Muslim or Croat, it's assumed the villain is a Serb. But then, in fairness, if the victim is Serb, the assumption would be that a Muslim or Croat is to blame. And it isn't always Croat versus Serb versus Muslim. Sometimes it's Eastern Orthodox versus Catholic. Sometimes it's a neighborhood feud that has nothing to do with any of those other factors, but the usual categories come in handy as an excuse or pretense. It goes on and on. Why? Simple answer, really. Habit. That's the way it has always been."

"Arthur Matsen quoted something to me about one man's revenge being the next man's atrocity."

"Absolutely," Mribic agreed. "But do you think we are unaware of that? We're brutal, John. Not stupid. Ultimately, it comes down to why should I be the one to forgive or forget? Let the next guy turn the other cheek."

Cann, in his way, understood. He had long since reconciled actions of his own to necessity or survival or his personal sense of justice. To be sure, there were differences of degree but ultimately he knew Mribic was right about one thing. For good or ill, it was all about context.

When Cann didn't speak, Mribic concluded, "All of which has brought me here, no?"

"No," Cann answered. "What's brought you here is what you did on a date certain. Not what someone else did in the past."

Mribic tilted his head and shrugged. "Correction, John. What I *allegedly* did. And it is your job to give me a defense. But I can help."

Cann put out an upturned palm inviting Mribic to go on.

"Consider this. The indictment, as you accurately said, charges me with 'grave breaches of the Geneva Protocols' and I submit that what I am accused of does not constitute a grave breach as defined under international law. The indictment itself describes me as an 'irregular.' A thug. A loose cannon. Very well. For the purposes of this proceeding, I won't disagree. Because it is clear that, for an act to be a grave breach it requires action by a state. Some degree of government involvement. Or at least government sanction. Whether my activities did or did not have such sanction is actually quite irrelevant at this point. The charges as written don't describe any grave breach. So the indictment is flawed on that ground alone. And we shall argue that, under the ICTY's own rules, the charges have to be dismissed."

"Sounds like the defense argument in the Kalic case, which the court didn't buy."

"Not really," Mribic countered. "Kalic argued that a grave breach had to involve an *international* conflict. And that the relevant events in his situation were an *internal* conflict. My point is that, whether the conflict was international or internal, a grave breach requires action by a state and cannot refer to acts by a nongovernmental individual. An 'irregular.' Their term for me."

It was a sound legal argument, one that Cann had already considered and would, in fact, make. But, as in all legal matters and processes, it would not be that cut-and-dried. "Well, before you get too confident, the German courts may not even listen to the argument. They may well say that's a substantive point that should be heard by the ICTY."

Mribic went on. "But they will at least hear the jurisdictional arguments, which is a very large distinction in my favor. Kalic had to make his case to the ICTY tribunal itself. He was already in custody in The Hague when he filed his motion to dismiss the indictment. We, on the other hand, will be arguing before the German court in an extradition proceeding. I don't expect the German court to find me innocent. But I do want them to say the ICTY can't have me."

"You can't always get what you want."

Mribic raised his brows and pointed a finger. "The Stones. 1969. Remember the album?"

Cann just looked at the other man.

"*Let it Bleed*," Mribic said with a smirk. "Ironic, no?"

Cann closed his eyes and shook his head slowly. He did not get this guy.

"Anyway," Mribic said, "your job is to get me what I want."

"And if I can't?"

"Then we'll just have to think of something else."

6

Retracing their morning route, another green and white Polizei vehicle dropped Cann back at his hotel. After a quick shower and change of clothes, Cann set out at a leisurely pace with no specific route in mind in search of a place to eat.

It was the randomness of his actions that tipped him off that he was being followed. He'd turned off one quaint postcard-like street onto another and gone only halfway down that one when, for no good reason, he changed his mind and turned to head back the way he'd just come. The sudden move caused a car containing four men to brake sharply and then continue past, its occupant's eyes riveted forward. Cann gave no indication he'd noticed them but followed the car with his peripheral vision as he walked. When he reached the corner he continued around it at the same pace but immediately sped up as soon as the sight line between him and the vehicle was broken. Two doors down was a bookstore, and he quickly went in and positioned himself behind a chest-high shelf away from the window where the shadows permitted him to see out much better than someone could see in.

Even though Cann didn't know for sure exactly what was

happening, he was distinctly uncomfortable about being unarmed. Through connections and Arthur's considerable influence, he'd been able to bring both his Sig Sauer P228 and the smaller Colt Mustang Pocketlite into the country legally, but he still had to be conscious of the strict European Union restrictions on firearms in the hands of private citizens. Being aware of no specific threat, he'd left his handguns back in the hotel.

For several moments, no car came by. Then Cann recognized one of the men as he came walking around the corner on the opposite side of the street. Cann worked his way to the back of the bookstore, looking for a rear exit. At the front of the bookstore, another man peered through the window into the relative darkness, then came in, the traditional bell tinkling as he did so. Cann moved behind another set of shelves but not before the man's eyes adjusted sufficiently to see the movement. Through an opening between the books, Cann saw him speak into his collar.

Cann found a door in the rear but couldn't be sure it was an exit. And having seen the man speak into his collar mike, he had to assume that, even if it was a way out, it wouldn't be for long. Making his choice, he charged back around the shelves and ran straight at the man who stood between him and the door, slamming hard into him and sending him sprawling into a table of books. As the man fell, he pulled out a gun. Cann moved quickly around the overturned table and put his left foot on the wrist of the hand now holding the small semiautomatic pistol and dropped his right knee heavily into the man's diaphragm. The man emitted a whooshing grunt as the air was forced out of his lungs. Cann reached down to take possession of the weapon but stopped when he felt a vague sense of enclosure that told him he was surrounded even before he saw the men around him.

"Be still, Mr. Cann," a voice from above him said. "And leave the gun."

Cann spread his fingers in compliance but moved nothing else.

"Now stand, please."

Cann shifted his weight onto his left leg releasing the pressure on the other man's midsection as he stood. The man on the floor gasped as his lungs regained full capacity, then he started to raise his gun.

"*Ne!*" the apparent leader shouted at the man on the floor. To Cann, he said in English, "I just want to have a word with you. We intend no harm." He held up his left hand, indicating a desire for restraint. His right hand held a gun, which was pointed at Cann's chest. Cann looked down at the man's gun and then past him to where another man held a gun to the head of a very frightened clerk who stared wildly at Cann, her eyes and mouth wide open, clearly on the verge of hyperventilating. Then he looked at the group of armed men surrounding him. "Yes, I can see that," he said sarcastically.

The other man shrugged. "I understand, Mr. Cann. But the fact remains we are not the enemy."

"Then who are you?"

"I am called Rade."

"That's you. Who's the 'we'?"

"I'm afraid I cannot tell you that."

"What do you want?"

"Information"

"Such as?"

"Why you are representing Dubran Mribic."

"Well, I'm afraid I cannot tell you that either."

"Why not?"

"Because I don't know."

The man called Rade frowned. "Mr. Cann, we have a legitimate interest in Dubran Mribic. And we were very surprised to learn he is represented by a leading Washington law firm. We did not think that Mribic operated in such circles. We would like to know how this comes to be."

"Mr. Rade, you seem to know about Washington law firms.

Perhaps you know about issues like privilege and confidentiality. But the fact is I don't know what went into the decision to represent Mribic."

Rade gave Cann a look of unconcealed disbelief. "You are a beginner just doing what he is told," he said, his voice dripping with cynicism.

"No. Not a beginner, but the fact remains —"

"Yes, yes. You don't know why you are representing Mribic." He sneered the words out.

Cann shrugged.

A very long moment passed without either man saying a word. Finally, Rade expelled a breath and broke the silence. "What I said about not being the enemy was true, Mr. Cann. That could change."

Cann said nothing except, "Are we done?"

Rade nodded. "But we will talk again. And we will be watching." He lowered the weapon. The man on the floor got to his feet and moved around Cann to join the others. The man holding the clerk took his gun away from her head and joined his companions as they backed out the door.

"Are you all right?" Cann asked the clerk who responded by slowly sliding down the wall to the floor.

Loring, Matsen, and Gould
Washington, D.C.

"I don't have enough information yet to say whether I have good news or bad news, Arthur. As always, just penetrating the bureaucracy is an initial major hurdle in its own right." Katherine Price had barely begun her briefing of Arthur Matsen when the phone buzzed.

Matsen had a questioning frown on his face as he reached out and pressed the flashing intercom button. He'd asked for his calls to be held.

"John Cann on three, Arthur," his secretary announced.

"Thank you." He looked an "excuse me" at Price as he pressed the button putting them on the speaker phone. "John, hello. I have Katherine Price here with me." It was standard procedure at Loring, Matsen to make such an announcement.

"Am I interrupting something? Should I call back?"

"No," Matsen answered. "I've asked her to make some inquiries into your concerns about this Dr. Fredrich. She's admitted in that jurisdiction."

"Great. Hi, Katherine. Thanks for your help. Found anything?"

"Hi, John. No. But I've just started the wheels in motion. I've made an inquiry to the Board of Licensure for background information on Dr. Fredrich — bio, CV, disciplinary history, if any, et cetera. I'm also trying to get the records from where he's practiced before. But a lot of states keep those confidential."

"Anything on the Web?"

"Done. Nothing of note there. Some published material. Almost all on what appears to be his specialty — implicit memory. Apparently the theory that everything that happens to us is stored somewhere, even if we aren't aware of it. Even if we weren't aware of it as it happened. That last part I find a little odd but don't worry, I'll stay on it and I'll take good care of her."

"I know you will. She couldn't be in better hands. Great move, Arthur." He was genuinely delighted that Arthur had involved Katherine, particularly since he was on the other side of the world. He'd always been both pleased and proud that he'd been instrumental in getting Price into the firm and, over time, his respect and admiration for her had only grown. And not just for her legal abilities. Being Matsen's closest confidante in the firm, he now knew quite a bit more about her background. And he meant it when he said that Janie couldn't be in better hands.

Price had an equally high opinion of Cann. Ironically though, in the several years that Price had been at Loring, Matsen, their paths had rarely crossed professionally or personally. This was because they were both international lawyers and spent a great deal of their time away from Washington. One day they could be at an office function or the Christmas party or the like where they'd talk and often sit together and get along famously — and it was universally agreed that the six foot tall, salt-and-pepper-haired Cann and the five foot nine auburn haired Price made a handsome couple indeed. And then the next day, Cann would be off to Tel Aviv, and Price would be off to Paris. Or Cann to Geneva, and Price to Moscow. It drove the office matchmakers nuts.

"We'll keep you posted on it, John," Matsen said. "But unless you're even more prescient than usual, you called for a reason. Developments?"

Price pointed to the door in an offer to leave.

Matsen shook his head and motioned for her to stay in her seat. As Cann reported on his meeting with Mribic, Matsen glanced self-consciously at Price. She was aware of the nature of Cann's assignment and Matsen knew she was as troubled by it as Cann was.

Then Cann told Matsen about the other "meeting" — the one with Rade. When he was done, Matsen was quiet for a moment, clearly conflicted. "John," Matsen began, "I don't know what to say about that. I don't know who those people were. Perhaps I should come over —"

"I don't think it's come to that yet, Arthur," Cann countered quickly. "I'm fine." Whatever the encounter with Rade had been about, it had been tense and had ended with an implied threat. Cann was determined that, no matter what, Arthur would *not* be placed in harm's way. "Hold off. Let me play this out a bit longer and see where it goes. Maybe it's nothing and today was the beginning and the end of it."

Matsen took a breath before he spoke into the phone. "I appreciate what you're doing. Especially that you're doing it on trust. I wish I could tell you what it's about but —"

"I know that, Arthur." Cann was fully prepared to go on just as things were.

Matsen expelled a burst of air through his lips. "I —" he began then stopped. "John — it's on the tape. One of the — I'm sorry. I can't say more but —"

"Then leave it at that," Cann cut in. "Let's take it a step at a time. There's an initial hearing scheduled. I'll keep my eyes and ears open and I'll touch base with you as needed. Okay?"

"Thank you, John. I . . . thanks."

"Take good care of him, Katherine."

"I will, John."

"And of yourself too."

"You too."

The call ended.

Price looked at Matsen, who sat shaking his head. "I'm shamed, Katherine. I should not be asking John to do this. Without giving a good reason. Such loyalty. I'm shamed."

"He trusts you, Arthur. And loves you." She leaned forward in her chair and reached across the desk to take Matsen's hands in hers. "He's not the only one, you know." She squeezed his hands. "Shall I stay with you for a while?"

Matsen smiled weakly. "No, no. I'm fine. You go ahead."

She gave his hands one last squeeze and got up to leave. As she went out the door, she glanced back at Matsen and saw that his eyes were no longer focused on anything in the room but seemed to be looking at something far, far away.

7

3,500 feet above Cazin, Bosnia
(Independent State of Croatia)
March 1944

Nothing.

He could see absolutely nothing beneath him.

Twenty-five-year-old Captain Arthur Matsen, U.S. Army, presently seconded to Office of Strategic Services out of Brindisi, Italy, looked down through the round opening in the floor of the long-range British Halifax bomber through which he was about to plunge.

"One minute," the sergeant announced over the sound of the air rushing beneath the vertical tube into which Matsen's legs dangled. Matsen looked up at the man who would oversee his jump, the dispatcher, who was checking the static line that was attached at one end to the inner fuselage of the airplane and at the other end to the parachute on Matsen's back.

"Yes, by all means, please make sure that thing's connected, would you?" His wary smile was matched by a wry one from the sergeant.

"Don't worry, Captain, I haven't missed one yet."

"Has anyone?" Matsen asked. As soon as the words were out of his mouth, he realized he didn't really want to know.

"One of ours, recently, I'm afraid," the British noncom said. "Too caught up in the excitement, neither he nor his dispatcher remembered to make sure the static line was hooked to his parachute."

And, Matsen knew, the Brits didn't use reserve chutes. "I get the message, Sergeant. Thanks — I think."

The dispatcher pushed against his earpiece and listened briefly.

"Twenty seconds."

Matsen had been gripping the rounded edge of the opening and now raised his weight up from the surface and slid his rump forward a matter of inches, his weight now distributed precariously out over the hole at his feet.

"Ten seconds."

Matsen leaned forward a little more and held. The idea was not to fall forward but to drop straight down and into the blackness.

"Go."

A 120-mile-per-hour wind slammed Matsen as his body exited the bottom of the tube. A few seconds later, he felt the saving yank of the static line pulling on the chute and heard the rustle of the silk as it spread itself properly above him. Then it became surreal. In total silence and total blackness, he cast his gaze downward. He could see only the tiniest pinpoints of light at very great distances.

Several moments later, he began to feel the inexplicable sensation that the earth was rising to meet him, even though he still couldn't see it. He peered down, looking for the prearranged signal, and then, finally, spotted the rapid double flash of light. Unbelievably, it was almost directly below him. He understood navigation, but how did they get him this close in the dark without lights and with the winds and all the other variables? Unless of course, this wasn't the right spot and the light below was a coincidence. Or a trap.

It wasn't a perfect landing but it was close enough. He didn't land in a tree. Or a river. He did strain his right ankle. Not a sprain. Just a strain that would work itself out quickly.

He quickly gathered his chute into a bundle against his chest and hurried into the surrounding trees in the direction where he'd seen the lights. As soon as he broke the tree line, one of the lights flashed for just an instant and he adjusted his direction. When he was close enough to make out shapes he spoke just loud enough to be heard.

"*Nauciti pameti.*"

"*Dvaput nedjeljno,*" came the reply, a non sequitur intended to assure Matsen that he was now in the right hands.

Matsen was in Yugoslavia to establish contact with Huska Miljkovic, a Bosnian Muslim and native of the Cazin region who had established a resistance force of several thousand in northwest Bosnia. The tide of the war had turned against the Nazis, and the allies were looking to establish a foothold in what was referred to as the soft underbelly of Europe. Indeed, Trieste on the Yugoslav–Italy border was considered a possible invasion point.

The allies would have preferred one of the two major resistance groups — the royalist Chetniks under former Royal Yugoslav Army Colonel Drago Mihailovic or the partisans under Tito. But logistical reasons argued against the Chetniks — Mihailovic's forces were concentrated far to the east — and political reasons argued against Tito — he was a Communist. In addition, the two groups often expended more resources fighting against each other than they did against the Nazis.

Then there was Huska Miljkovic.

Miljkovic's force — the Huska Legion as it was called — was comprised of a few soldiers and deserters from other forces, ex-partisans, and Bosnian Muslim resisters. At one time a Communist and ally of Tito, Miljkovic had been stripped of all authority and rank in a power struggle. Undaunted, he immediately transferred his loyalties to the fascist pro-Nazi Croatian regime and was rewarded with the rank of colonel in the Croatian Domobranstvo forces. In that capacity, he fought in concert with the German Army as well as with the Ustachi, the quasi-military force noted for outdoing even the Nazis in the atrocity business.

But Miljkovic's commitments remained ever flexible and, in early 1944, he agreed to join with Mihailovic and his Chetniks to mount a joint campaign against Tito. The more optimistic in the Allied intelligence world wanted to see this as a sign that Miljkovic might be trying to distance himself from the Independent State of Croatia and the Nazis. Most didn't. But it did signal that Miljkovic's loyalties might be up for grabs, and thus for sale.

And so it was that Captain Arthur Matsen, U.S. Army Intelligence, seconded to OSS for an indefinite term, found himself dispatched from Brindisi, Italy, to Cazin Province to seek to bring Huska Miljkovic and his Legion into the fray on the side of the Allies.

Having read up on the man, Matsen didn't think much of the idea.

Matsen buried his chute in the trees and met up with the three-man party waiting for him. The apparent leader, the oldest of the three, nodded to Matsen as he approached, but did not accept Matsen's outstretched hand. Instead he pointed at Matsen's sidearm and turned his own hand palm up indicating he wanted Matsen to surrender his weapon. To a field man, this was akin to asking him to surrender his testicles. It wasn't going to happen. The leader looked hard at Matsen and saw the determination. After a moment, he shrugged and, with an outstretched arm, invited Matsen to head out.

Matsen hesitated. It made no sense for him to be in the lead. He extended his own arm in an "after you" gesture. The leader stared for a moment then stepped past him. Matsen looked back warily at the two men falling in behind him, then followed.

Call it training, experience, logic, fear, or whatever it is that makes the hair stand up on the back of the neck, but Matsen sensed what was coming before he consciously heard or saw anything. As one of the men behind him swung his rifle butt toward him, Matsen leaned to his left and tilted just enough so that the blow caught his right shoulder instead of his head. He managed to grab the stock of the weapon with his right hand as he turned and then got his left hand on the barrel. In little more than a second, Matsen had control of the weapon and was bringing it to bear on the man who'd tried to crack his skull. Unfortunately, the other man who'd been behind him had his own weapon pointed at Matsen. As did the leader of the greeting party.

Matsen slowly lowered the gun he had seized and the man he'd taken it from angrily grabbed it back just as the leader smashed his own rifle butt into the back of Matsen's head.

It was morning before they reached Cazin. Matsen, minus his weapon and with a splitting headache, noted the normalcy of the scene: shops and homes and streets filled with people who appeared to be going about their daily business at the beginning of a normal day. It seemed like any other village on any other early morning.

Except for the shots. The first time Matsen thought he'd heard gunfire was about an hour before they got to Cazin. A single shot. When it was not followed immediately by others, Matsen thought it might be a hunter. He'd heard two more single shots about twenty minutes apart by the time they reached the village square. It was filled with people. At the center, about two dozen men stood with their hands stretched high above their heads. Roughly half were in German Army uniforms and the rest wore civilian clothes. Encircling them was a larger group of men numbering about forty, all armed but, strangely enough, not particularly attentive to the captives in the middle.

Another shot rang out. Very nearby. Matsen's peripheral vision caught movement on the roof of the dominant building in the square, and he looked up just in time to see a body fall off the edge and plummet down the left side of the building, disappearing behind a wall.

A moment later, an armed man emerged from the front door of what was apparently the town hall and, ignoring the uniformed German soldiers, walked briskly to one of the groups of captives in civilian garb. He pointed at one man who gave a negative shake of his head and for his trouble received a vicious jab in the kidney from another armed man behind him. The man who'd pointed grabbed the front of the captive's jacket and threw him forward then pushed him repeatedly until they got into the building. The armed men in the square went back to their smoking and chatting.

The leader of Matsen's group gestured for them to proceed down the west side of the square. "*Mi ici zatim,*" the man uttered in a conversational tone which Matsen knew meant, "We go now."

They'd just reached the opposite side of the square when Matsen heard yet another shot. He turned in time to see another man fall from the roof. From the clothing, it appeared to be the man who had just been summoned from the square. He too disappeared behind the wall.

"*Zasto?*" Matsen inquired jutting his chin in that direction.

"*Izdajica,*" the man replied. Even though Matsen knew how to ask "why," he realized he didn't understand the answer.

But obviously, whatever *izdajica* meant, it wasn't good.

The man leading Matsen's group pointed down a side street and they walked past a few buildings before the man said "*Ovdje.*" Stop. They were at what appeared to be an ordinary storefront but Matsen saw a handwritten sign in the window that said "*klinika.*" "*Dojilja,*" the man said pointing at the door. That was a word Matsen knew— "nurse." The leader prodded Matsen in the kidney with the muzzle of his weapon, and they all went inside.

8

Matsen noted his escorts didn't feel the need to stay with him while the young nurse tended the wound on the back of his head. It was nothing serious, but did require a few stitches. He was seated on a small, metal table while, opposite him, sitting on a small footstool and saying not a word, a girl about six years old with a roundish face, prominent cheekbones, blond hair, and two of the bluest eyes he'd ever seen stared at him with unconcealed curiosity.

Matsen smiled. At first the child didn't react. Then, slowly, a slight tentative smile appeared on her face. Matsen winked. After a moment, both of the girl's eyes blinked in response. That made Matsen chuckle causing his shoulders to bounce. The nurse placed a restraining hand on him to steady her work. The little girl kept on smiling, and Matsen continued the moment by crossing his eyes. This time the girl's attempt to mimic Matsen consisted of her pouting her lips and tilting her head forward as she darted her wide-open eyes from side to side but never quite got them to face each other. This got Matsen laughing even harder and the little girl joined him with a growing giggle.

"Be still." The nurse spoke first to the little girl in their native language. Then she said, "Still, please," to Matsen in clear but heavily accented English. But she was smiling also. And while her hair was somewhat darker — still blond but with a more almond hue — the face was similar to the child's in shape and contour and the smile was identical. And there were the blue, blue eyes. Matsen put her age at early twenties, which meant she'd given birth to the little girl in her midteens.

"He is pretty, Mama, no?" the little girl said.

"Handsome, Milica. Men are not pretty. He is handsome."

"I think so too, Mama," the child said with a shy grin.

Her mother smiled again and nodded. Then, with a remnant of the smile remaining, she turned to Matsen who hadn't understood much of the exchange. He'd been given the basics of the predominant language of the Balkans in his premission training, but his vocabulary was still minimal. He knew he would get it quickly, but for now he had deduced only that they were talking about him.

"You are finish," the nurse said in accented English.

"Thank you," Matsen replied, still smiling at the little girl. Then, turning his gaze to the nurse, he asked, "How do you say that in Serbo-Croatian?" he asked.

"It is Serbian we speak, not Serbo-Croatian," the nurse said a little sharply. "There is difference."

That was news to Matsen. He knew the Serbs used the Cyrillic alphabet and the Croats used the Roman alphabet, but it was his understanding that the spoken language was essentially the same.

"What is the difference?"

"We Serbs speak Serbian. It is our language. What Croats and Bosnians speak isn't their language. It is ours. That is difference."

"I see," said Matsen, quickly grasping that the differences were more political than linguistic. He decided not to pursue the subject.

"Well, how do you say, 'You are finished' in Serbian, then. I want to learn."

"*Ti si zavrsiti.*" She said slowly. Then, "*Zasto?*"

"Because every time I learn a new word or a new phrase, I also learn something about how your language works. Oh, another one. What does *izdajica* mean?"

The nurse turned her head sharply and looked hard at him for a long moment. "Why do you ask me that? Where did you hear that?"

"The authorities — I guess that's who they were — were shooting some men when I came into town and I asked my escorts why. The man told me one word — *izdajica*. I assume it's not good. What does it mean?"

After a pause, the nurse responded, "The word means . . . how you say . . . betrayer. Traitor. That is word. It does not mean those men were truly *izdajica*."

"Do you know them?"

She shrugged. "Sometimes. Often they are from other villages or regions and come for many reasons. Some are, how is said, scouts or even Germans sometimes. Some are . . . what is word? . . . run away? . . ."

"Deserters?"

"Is that what is called?" She absorbed the word. "Yes. Some from Tito. Some from German army. Some are pretending to join Huska but are really spies, informers. *Izdajica*." Another shrug. "Some. Not all. Some only get neighbor angry." Once again the shoulders rose and fell resignedly.

"What about today? Do you know who those men were?"

"I think no. I hear shots, but I was here with, ahh . . ." She made a move with her hands as if breaking a stick.

"Wounded. Hurt," Matsen offered.

"Ah. Hurt. What was other word?"

"Wounded? It means the same thing. Mostly."

"Wun-did? That is how you say?"

"Yes. So you are busy here?"

She frowned. Matsen could see her mind working behind her eyes and he searched for another word. "Ah . . . much work?"

The nurse turned and reached for a small book that she handed to Matsen. Dog-eared, dirty, and worn, it was a small English-Serbian dictionary. When he opened it, Matsen saw the English words were in recognizable western script but the Serbian equivalents were in the Cyrillic alphabet. He quickly found the word "busy" and then slowly transliterated the alien characters to pronounce its Serbian equivalent.

"*Pos . . . lo . . . va . . . ti?*"

"*Poslovati.*" She frowned again, then muttered. "*Ah, dati kome posae.*" She looked up at Matsen and nodded. "Yes, I am very bee-ze."

All through the conversation, the little girl had sat with a bemused expression looking back and forth from Matsen to her mother. Matsen looked down at her and couldn't help but smile. "Her name is Milica, no?" he said to the nurse, who nodded while casting a smile of her own over the child. "May I ask yours?"

"I am called Savka."

Matsen smiled and nodded. "I am Arthur." He extended his hand and Savka took it in a firm grip and gave it a single sharp pump then quickly released it. "Artur," she repeated.

The sound of footfalls outside the door to the room caused Savka to quickly grab the dictionary out of Matsen's hands and put it back. Then she moved quickly aside and busied herself cleaning the instruments she'd used to tend to Matsen.

The door opened suddenly and forcefully and the man who'd led Matsen's escort from the landing zone stood in the doorway. Ignoring both the woman and child, he spoke directly to Matsen.

"*Zavrsiti?*"

"*Je.*"

"Come." The man spoke the word in English though the way he pronounced it, it sounded like "comb."

The rest of the "escort" was waiting just outside and they fell in behind Matsen and the leader. Instead of heading back toward the village square, however, they turned into a narrow alley that led off in the opposite direction. Matsen held back. "Wait," he protested. "I want to see Miljkovic." He jabbed his finger back toward the town square. "Uh ... *ja* ... uh ... *movriti* ... Miljkovic." The head of the group gave a negative shake of his head and continued down the alley. The other men behind Matsen moved toward him, convincing him he'd not win this battle of wills either. He stepped off after the leader with the others following.

Fifty yards down, the group exited the alley and continued past a series of almost identical small houses whose front doorsteps lay practically on the roadway itself. The leader stopped at one of the homes, stepped to the side, extended his arm with palm upturned, and told Matsen, "Go." Matsen gave a quick look around, then stood on the single raised step, and opened the door. Inside he saw a central living/cooking area with two smaller rooms off to either side. Light came from two large windows at the front and two more at the rear of the house. Through one of the rear windows, Matsen could see a solitary man in the backyard area sitting stiffly erect in a straight-backed wooden chair. The man's hands were down by his sides gripping the seat of the chair and he was holding his chin very high, face tilted upward in what seemed a pose of defiance. Matsen got the sense he was about to witness an execution. Followed by his own, he wondered?

The head of the escort came in behind Matsen and suddenly let out a guffaw followed by a laughing challenge to the seated man outside. "Bloody hell, Talbot," he chortled, "it's four flippin' degrees out there and you're takin' the bloody sun?" He roared with laughter. "If ya get any color it's as like to be rosy cheeks from the chill as a burn from the sun, ya know."

The man outside released his grip on the seat of the chair and turned his face toward the inside of the house. "P'raps, old chum. But that'd be no different from any good day at Brighton then, wouldn't it?"

Matsen suddenly realized that the leader of the escort had

spoken English. Very good, very colloquial English. Without a hint of a Slavic accent. He snapped his head around sharply with a questioning look. The leader saw the look, shrugged one shoulder, and twisted his mouth into a wry expression. "Sorry, mate. Spent my youth in Birmingham. One of those things ya hold in reserve in case it proves useful, right?" He turned back to the man outside. "Brought ya a playmate, Talbot. Just in time, I'd say the way yer startin' to behave. Sittin' there lookin' up like a bleedin' plant or somethin'."

"Exactly like a plant, Predrag, joining with nature, revitalizing, and all that." The man rose from the the chair and came inside. "Tony Talbot," he nodded to Matsen. "Nice to meet you." Then he turned back to the man he called Predrag. "Does this mean you feel my current housemate isn't company enough for me?"

"Well, I figured this one speaks yer mother tongue, anyway. Sorta. In any case, yer stuck with 'im for now. Explain the rules to 'im. Keep 'im happy. Content, anyway."

"To obey," Talbot responded as he went up on his toes and clicked his heels together. The man named Predrag looked coldly at him for a moment, then left.

Matsen extended his hand to Talbot and they shook. "I'm Arthur Matsen."

"As I said, nice to meet you. Shall I call you Art? Or Artie, perhaps?"

"I prefer Arthur, actually."

"Ah. I see. Fine. I prefer Tony, if you don't mind."

"Of course."

The two men stood nodding silently at each other for a moment before Talbot spoke. "So, welcome to this humble abode, Arthur. What brings you here?" He immediately held up a palm in a "stop" gesture. "Not that I'm prying, you understand."

Matsen smiled, but hesitated to answer, and the two men continued to nod and wonder who the other was — or wasn't.

A Brit and a Yank. Natural allies, right?

Maybe.

The problem was people in the field got so used to being something they weren't that it was difficult to accept that anyone else was what they said they were. And it was a given that the degree to which truth was accepted was proportional to the difficulty involved in eliciting it. It was a world that fit Churchill's description of Russia — "a riddle wrapped in a mystery inside an enigma" and one that famed CIA spycatcher James Jesus Angleton would describe years later as "a wilderness of mirrors."

So Matsen told Talbot that he was in Bosnia to liaise with the indigenous population and observe the damage done by the war to the countryside and the populace and to gauge the degree of support that would be required after the war. The story had elements of truth, as all good covers do, and it allowed for the implication that he would learn things of value to — well — to all sorts of things.

Of course, Miljkovic knew why Matsen was there and that information had likely found its way to other interested parties. That, too, was acceptable. So long as the enemy couldn't know for sure where or when an invasion was coming, it would need to expend resources covering all the possibilities. Matsen was aware his role could be nothing more than a ploy, a feint to keep the enemy off balance. That was the way the game was played, and Matsen knew he might well be nothing more than one small, expendable component in an often unduly contrived diversion. "Wilderness of mirrors" indeed.

Talbot gave no sign that he didn't accept Matsen's story, drew himself to exaggerated attention, and announced as though he were reporting to a superior officer, "Flight Lieutenant (pronounced 'left-enant,' of course) Anthony Talbot, Royal Air Force. I won't identify a unit, of course, you understand." He relaxed and positioned his rear on the windowsill and gave Matsen his story of being part of a mission to resupply British agents in Slovenia, being shot down, picked up by the partisans, and then routed from their operational area by a huge antipartisan sweep by the Nazis. While evading the Nazis,

Talbot explained, they met with a force of Chetniks on their way to join Miljkovic, "and that," Talbot said, "brought me here."

Matsen didn't necessarily believe Talbot's story either. But he had no inclination to try to separate fact from fiction. And, again, as with any good legend, there were elements of truth to Talbot's tale. He was indeed a flight "leftenant" but he was also an expert with demolitions. And he had been working with the partisans, not merely supplying them. And the huge Nazi sweep that routed them from their area was the direct result of Talbot's handiwork when he blew up a railroad bridge in an attempt to destroy a train carrying the Grand Mustafa of Jerusalem, Haj Amin el-Husseini, one of Hitler's greatest admirers, one of the strongest proponents of the ultimate solution to the "Jewish Question," and also, by the way, an *Obergruppenfuhrer*— Lieutenant General—in the Nazi SS. Unfortunately, the timing of Talbot's blast was off and while the bridge collapsed into the deep ravine, the train had plenty of time to stop. Hitler was not, as Talbot put it, best pleased. It was not so much that the Nazi leader recipro-cated the Grand Mustafa's admiration. He didn't. But it was an embarrassment to the Führer and he ordered the area cleansed of resistance.

The two men's exchange of fables was interrupted when a figure stepped through the door and stood for a brief moment backlit against the opening. His posture was exaggeratedly erect and he was tall enough—something over six feet—to be able to look down his nose by titling his head back only slightly. He looked at Talbot and Matsen and, without saying a word, veered off toward one of the side rooms.

Talbot called out. "I say, Ger." Talbot pronounced the name with a hard "g" as in "get." "Come greet our guest? Unspeakably rude of you not to, what?"

The tall man turned sharply back and glared icily at Talbot but said nothing.

"There, that's better," Talbot said in a patronizing tone. He extended an arm toward Matsen and formally announced, "Allow me to introduce Captain Arthur Matsen." He then extended his other arm toward the man he called Ger. "Arthur, allow me to present my dear, dear friend of, oh, not so very long actually, and our housemate for what would appear to be the immediate future at least. One of Herr Hitler's finest—at least he clearly thinks so—Captain Gerhardt Weil. Hauptmann Gerhardt Weil, I mean." Talbot finished with a flourish and a mocking bow.

Weil glared venomously and then pointedly corrected him. "My rank is Haupt-sturm-führer." He overarticulated each syllable. "As you well know."

"Ah, yes. Haupt-sturm-führer." Talbot mocked the precise pronunciation. "Wouldn't want to confuse you with the common folk, would we?" After only a second's pause, Talbot added a further jibe. "And where's your funny little hat, anyway?"

For a long moment, Weil continued to stare at Talbot then he turned and fixed his gaze on Matsen. "*Amerikaner*," he said his voice dripping with contempt. Not waiting for a reply, Weil turned his back and left the room muttering something about "*verdamt untermenschen.*"

9

"See how tall I am, Mamice?"

Milica stood on the child-sized footstool at the outdoor basin and ran water over the breakfast bowls, all the while moving her hands in ineffective circular motions imitative of her *mamica's* dish-washing efforts. Savka knew that she'd have to do them over, but it could wait until Milica was occupied with her lessons.

Milica put down the last dish and stepped carefully backward off the stool, using the front edge of the basin to support her descent. Then she turned, wiped her hands on her little apron just as she'd seen her mamica do so many times, and announced that she had completed her morning chores.

"Yes, Milica, I see. Thank you. You are the best helper in the world." Milica beamed. "I don't know what I would do without you," Savka continued. That last part was most undeniably true. She took the few steps over to her daughter and bent down and lifted her up into a snug embrace which Milica reciprocated by squeezing with all of her might, emitting a childlike grunting sound in the process. They held the embrace for a long moment.

"Uhh," Savka let out a grunt of her own as they finished and she put Milica down. As soon as her feet hit the ground, the little girl started to run to the door that led into the kitchen then suddenly stopped and turned.

"Will we have patients today, Mama?"

Savka's smile at the collaborative "we" faded almost as soon as it appeared. "I don't know, *ceri*. We don't know when they will come."

Milica's eyes opened a tiny bit wider as she asked, "Will Artur come again today?"

Savka shook her head. "I don't think so, Milica. He was not so badly hurt. He doesn't need to come again so soon, I think."

Milica screwed her face up in thought for a moment then announced, "I think he will, Mama. He liked me. Don't you think?"

"Yes he did, Milica. I like you too, remember."

"But you are my *mamica*. You must like me."

"But I would like you even if I weren't your *mamica*, you know. You are a wonderful girl, my Milica."

This elicited another beaming smile from Milica.

"You make me smile, Mama." Another thoughtful pause. "Artur made me smile too. He made me laugh. It is fun to laugh, Mama."

"Yes, *dusho moja*. It is fun to laugh, isn't it." There was a distant touch of sadness to Savka's voice as she made the last statement. But it disappeared as Milica began to stride purposefully into the house. "Should we clean the surgery, Mama?"

Savka saw through the ploy. "The surgery is fine, Milica. And it is time for your lessons. You know that. Come. We'll start with your numbers today. You like to do your numbers." Savka took Milica's hand in hers and started for the tiny room at the end of the house that they had set aside for Milica's studies.

"No." Milica dug in her heels and pulled from her mother's grasp. She folded her arms in front of her and pouted. "I don't want to," she cried.

Savka hated these moments. "But you like your lessons. And your numbers. Especially your numbers, no?"

"No!" Milica repeated, lips pursed. "I mean, yes. But I hate that little room. I want to go to school. Why can't I go to school with the other children?"

More than that she hated these moments, Savka hated that she had no answer. No answer that could help this little girl understand anyway. Not yet. Not for many years, Savka hoped. Perhaps not ever.

So she lied. "It is because you are so smart, Milica. Too smart. The other children would feel badly if they knew how smart you are." There was a lot of truth to it, but still Savka felt shamed for the telling of it.

And in fact Milica was too smart to be persuaded by it. "Then I will pretend to be not so smart, Mama. I will forget my numbers. Please, Mama, may I go to school with the other children?"

Savka heard sounds from the front of the house and stiffened. She bent over her child and looking at her through eyes that were now wet, she gently took her face in her hands. "Please, Milica. Maybe some day. I don't know. But for now —"

Milica looked up and the sight of her mother's tears stemmed her own. She reached one of her own small hands up and touched her mother's face in the same way. "Yes, Mama. Some day. But don't cry, Mama. Please don't cry." It was at moments like these that Savka wasn't sure who was protecting whom.

"Come, *ceri*, then. Your lessons are on your table." They went into the tiny room and Savka got Milica settled at the small desk with her books and pencils and tablets. "Do your lessons and I will be back to sit with you when you are done. And," she tilted Milica's chin up to her and smiled down at her, "be smart, *dusho moja*. Be as smart as you are. Always." They exchanged small, sad smiles and Savka turned and left the room pulling the heavy wooden door closed behind her. As it closed, she placed her forehead against its cool surface and allowed another tear to fall. "I am so sorry, my little Milica."

The sounds from the front of the house grew louder and more frequent and several deep voices could be heard saying her name in questioning tones.

Savka reached down and quietly turned the key in the lock on the door and then slid over the bolt that was oddly and uncharacteristically on the outside of the door rather than the inside. It made a subdued click-thud as it slid into the hole in the frame. There weren't many things she could protect Milica from. But at least she could protect her from this. She turned and made her way to the other tiny room at the far and complete opposite end of the house.

"So where's Captain Sunshine?" The last word in the sentence was drawn out considerably by Matsen's early morning yawn.

After Weil's abrupt exit of the previous day, Talbot had the remnants of a smirk on his face when he turned to Matsen. "Don't care much for that chap, I must say."

"Well, he is the enemy, Tony," Matsen offered with a grin. "It's allowed. Encouraged in some circles even."

Talbot smiled absently. "Quite. Yes. I suppose. But —" He shrugged. "Aside from the obvious — between his obsession with rank and that funny little hat of his, I just find him — insufferable, I suppose."

Matsen understood the reference to rank. As soon as Weil had entered the room, Matsen saw from his uniform that Weil was a captain, a Hauptsturmführer, in the Schutzstaffel — the SS. Talbot had addressed him as Hauptmann, the word for a captain in the regular German army — the Wehrmacht. To the SS Hauptsturmführer, to be called a hauptmann was to be addressed as a common soldier. Talbot, of course, knew that, which was precisely why he did it.

But Matsen needed some explanation about the reference to the "funny little hat." In Matsen's experience, SS officers wore visor hats with the *totenkopf* — death's head insignia. And there was nothing funny about that. So he asked.

"The bloke wears a bloody fez," Talbot explained. "A fez! Like a bleedin' wog." He looked more sharply at Matsen. "Apparently he's a something or other with that Muslim SS division.

Matsen knew about the Muslim Handschar Division. About 30,000 Bosnian Muslims formed the 13th Waffen SS Gebirgs Division, known as the Handschar Division. Handschar was the German word for the scimitar, the curved sword of the Mohammedans and the Saracens and the Ottomans and it was the symbol of the division — along with the swastika.

But the last he'd heard of the Handschar Division was that it had recently been assigned to antipartisan activity operating out of the Srem region of northeast Bosnia. So what was SS Handschar Hauptsturmführer Weil doing over here in northwest Bosnia?

At the moment, Hauptsturmführer Weil was sitting on a hard wooden bench against the front outer wall of the building in the village square where Huska Miljkovic conducted business. All around the square, individuals and pairs and groups of people, most armed, milled about. The scene resembled the gathering of supplicants at a medieval court.

Predrag Djilic stood at a window in Miljkovic's office looking out over the square and then down at the impatient Hauptsturmführer Weil who sat erect, almost at attention, with a thick file folder on his lap and his green officer's fez neatly placed atop the folder. Djilic smiled knowing Weil resented being kept waiting and particularly resented Djilic's ready access to Miljkovic.

Miljkovic got up from behind his desk and walked over to the window and looked out over Djilic's shoulder. He scanned the people in the square below all of whom, he knew, wanted something from him, often at cross purposes to one another. "Do you know the proverb, *Gde mnogo babica kilava deca*, Predrag? Where there are midwives, there will be children? I look at all these 'midwives' out there and wonder if we are giving birth to too many children."

Djilic nodded. "Perhaps that means you are involved in too many courtships. Perhaps it is time to take a 'wife,' so to speak."

Huska Miljkovic nodded. He trusted Predrag Djilic as much as anyone and relied on his counsel. "The problem is, my friend, that too often the choice made doesn't seem such a good idea in time."

"And by the time we learn that, it is too late."

Both men smiled at the continuing metaphor but both also knew the problem was very real. Djilic turned to Miljkovic. "Seriously, Huska, this endeavor is getting out of hand. And out of our control. It was supposed to be us and enough Chetniks to help, but not enough to be dangerous to us. We would hit the partisans often, and always at different places and times. Always letting the Chetniks take the lead. A campaign of attrition for both the Chetniks and the partisans. Now, somehow it's become a major military campaign and we are in danger of losing our identity. It's bad enough we have so many filthy Serbs sleeping practically in our beds. We will be lucky if Weil does not try to absorb us into the Handschar Division itself. Look at how he names our men as deserters from his division, and we allow him to shoot them on the roof."

"We have been with the Germans for a long time now, Predrag."

"Yes, but as equals."

Miljkovic snorted a sharp laugh. "Please." He looked over his nose at his lieutenant. "In theory we are equals. Perhaps. But in forces. In power. Let's be realistic."

"You're saying we have no choice in this matter?"

"We have choices. But they have costs. And the cost of our separating at this stage would be high. Very high."

10

Matsen and Talbot were making twice-daily trips to the village square to join the milling crowd outside Miljkovic's headquarters. Matsen hadn't yet gained an audience, but he was duty bound to keep trying. Talbot accompanied Matsen, he said, to keep Arthur company and himself occupied, but it was not lost on Matsen that Talbot was being used as a conduit to the Chetniks. Although the Chetniks were, at the moment, allies in the antipartisan force now being assembled, they had been billeted well outside the village and were rarely seen in the village itself, let alone Miljkovic's headquarters.

Both Matsen and Talbot had mixed feelings about being in the midst of a force gathering for a coordinated attack on Tito's partisans. Neither man had any particular liking for Tito, but both knew there were Americans and Englishmen among his ranks.

For the moment, there was no fighting in the area and, except for the occasional shot coming from the village square, it was quiet. The sky was constantly overcast and the dull gray of the buildings of the village and the clothing of the inhabitants dominated a landscape devoid of variety. Indeed, the only color in the entire picture for Matsen was the blond hair and blue eyes of Milica who waited

every afternoon for him on the corner of her street when Matsen
returned to the house he shared with Talbot and Weil.

"Artur, how is your head?" she would ask in a serious tone.

Matsen, who was picking up the language quickly, would
respond, "Good, I think. But perhaps you should have a look." And
he would turn around and squat down so that the back of his head
was at the same height as Milica's face. She would then step forward
and push his hair aside with her tiny fingers and give a long and
serious look at his stitches and then pronounce, "All seems well."
Matsen had taken to searching out what sweets or candies he could
find in the village so that he could reward little Milica for her
"medical services" each time he saw her. He was pretty sure she, too,
saw it as a bit of a game, but it was a moment of brightness for both.

Toward the end of his first week in Cazin, Matsen saw an example of
the depth of the ethnic divisions and enmities in the region. Earlier
that day, he'd found some sugared nuts in a little store, and he was
looking forward to giving Milica the sweets. When they met, Milica
gave Matsen a message from her mother. "Mama says I am a very
good nurse, of course," the little girl related with pride, "but perhaps
it is time for Artur to come by and have his stitches taken out."
Matsen smiled and thanked Milica for the very good care she had
given him and said he'd come by in the morning. He gave her the
sugared nuts and he and Talbot started to leave.

They'd just turned the corner when they heard a high-pitched
squeal, more like a squeak, cut short. Matsen ran back expecting to
see another child perhaps trying to take Milica's candy. Instead, he
was astonished to see a grown man — a large one — with a handful
of Milica's blond hair pulled up so tight that only the little girl's toes
were touching the ground. The man was using his other hand to
bend Milica's fingers away from her palm to get at the sugared nuts
she clutched protectively, in spite of her fear.

For a moment, Matsen was unable to absorb what he was seeing. When he spoke, it was in a sputter, a series of disconnected words that he couldn't put together into anything approaching a coherent sentence. "What the...? You can't... Get your..." Then his brain finally said, "Fuck it." He crashed his fist into the middle of the man's face, bloodying his nose and knocking him into a sitting position. The man reached his left hand under his coat and pulled out a huge two-edged knife. As he placed his hands on the ground to raise himself, Talbot pinned the knife with his boot and Matsen executed a front kick that caught the man full in the face, snapping his head back, and crushing his nose.

Matsen reached out and pulled Milica to him. The man on the ground propped himself on his elbows and looked up at Matsen with a face contorted by hate.

Matsen shouted down at him. "Are you crazy? How can you do that to a little girl?".

"She is Serb!"

"She's a little girl, you fucking moron." Matsen realized he was shouting in English. He repeated himself in Serbo-Croatian, except that he changed "moron" to "pig" because he didn't know the word for "moron."

The man on the ground slobbered through his own blood. "She is little Serb who will grow into big Serb. They are the pigs. All of them. From the day they are born."

Matsen bent over the man and spat the words. "If you touch this little girl again, I will kill you." He stood erect and, still holding Milica's hand, walked her down the street to the clinic. She stared straight ahead as they walked, knowing even at her young age that it would not be wise to gloat.

Behind them, Matsen heard the words, "Serb lover!" It was intended to be the ultimate insult.

* * *

Savka greeted Matsen and Milica at the door with a smile that faded as she saw the grim look on Matsen's face and the fear on her daughter's.

"What?" She bent and picked Milica up in her arms and looked questioningly at Matsen. He shrugged and put his hands out to his side, palms up.

"There was this guy — He wanted to take her candy — and —"

"Her candy?"

"Sweets. Sugared nuts."

"You gave her?"

"Yes. I'm sorry."

"No. No. Is fine. Is good. She likes sweets." A wry smile and a shrug of her own. "She is child. Like all children. That is perhaps why another child wanted to take her sweets, yes?"

"But it wasn't another child. It was a grown man."

"What is 'grown'?"

Matsen struggled for the word in Serbian. "A man. Not a boy." He held his hand up in the air palm down. "Big man. Not child."

Savka squinted as she processed the information and slowly the puzzled expression remolded itself into one of sadness then despair. "Oh. I — I see."

"See what? I don't understand. How can a grown man —?" All Matsen could do was shake his head side to side.

"We are Serb."

"Yes, I know. But Milica is just a child."

"Does not matter. To these people Serb is Serb."

Matsen recalled the man on the corner saying something to that effect. It still made no sense to him. It was so alien to his own frames of reference that he was struggling to absorb it. Milica had her arms around her mother's neck but was looking at Matsen with an expression that combined fear with a smile. Matsen felt a surge of affection begin to dissipate the lump of bile that remained in his throat.

Savka suddenly realized that they were still standing in the open door. "Perhaps you should come in." She shook her head at her own discourtesy. "And I must thank you for looking out for my little Milica."

"That's not necessary. I couldn't do otherwise."

They stood looking at one another for a moment before Savka said, "Will you have some tea?"

"Thank you. That would be nice."

Savka turned her face to her daughter's. "Shall we make Artur some tea, *ceri*?"

Milica nodded vigorously and squirmed her way down through her mother's arms. She ran to the stove and went up on tiptoes to grab a small kettle that she took outside to fill. She carried the filled kettle back and, with some difficulty, slid it onto the surface of the stove. Then she stood back and waited for her mother to light it. "Mama says I must not touch the fire, Artur," she said gravely. Matsen nodded. "That's very good. Your mama is right." Matsen spoke to Savka. "She's a wonderful girl, Savka. You should be proud."

"I am. Thank you." Again, there was a bit of an awkward silence until Savka suggested she look at Matsen's stitches while they waited for the water to boil. She led him to the surgery and sat him on the table as Milica assumed her position on the stool opposite and, throughout the process, watched Matsen's face intently.

Savka completed the brief examination and pronounced that everything did indeed look fine, but it would be best to wait another day or so to take the stitches out. Upon hearing the prognosis, Milica's expression brightened with animation.

"So you must come again, Artur, yes?"

Matsen and Savka both smiled and nodded at the same time.

"It will be my pleasure to come again, Milica."

"Can you come everyday?"

"That may not be possible, *ceri*. Artur has other things to do."

"But I will try. With your mama's permission, of course."

"Oh, Mama likes you too. She will say yes, won't you, Mama?"

Savka pursed her lips and clicked her tongue at Milica in silent admonishment, but she was smiling as she nodded her assent. Milica clapped her hands quietly and then announced that the water must be ready by now. As the three of them left the surgery to return to the kitchen, Milica managed to insert herself between the two adults taking Matsen's right hand with her left and her mama's left hand with her right.

11

The next morning, Matsen and Talbot again made their way to the village square in what Matsen now thought of as his daily exercise in futility. Around 9:00 A.M., he told Talbot that he needed to have his stitches taken out and, since he had no more reason to think he'd see Miljkovic this day than any other day so far, would Talbot cover for him and send someone to Savka's should Miljkovic call.

Talbot agreed.

As Matsen turned the corner onto the street where Savka and Milica lived, he saw several men hanging around the entrance to the clinic. He nodded to the men as he neared the front doorway and strode without slowing through their midst. One of the men reached out as he passed and grabbed him by the arm.

"No, no, American. You must wait your turn like the rest of us." The man laughed and looked around at his companions who reacted with smiles, nods, and guffaws. Matsen pulled his arm from the other man's grasp. "Don't worry, I won't be long."

This elicited another, louder round of laughter accompanied by finger pointing and lewd comments. The man who had first grabbed Matsen did so again. Matsen again pulled himself free, but this time, he grabbed back. The other man, expecting Matsen to pull him in, resisted and leaned away so Matsen used the man's own movement against him and shoved instead. The man stumbled and fell backward onto a low bench which tipped over, and the man ended up on his back with his legs sticking straight up in the air.

It was a comic scene, but none of the men saw the humor in it. Almost as one, they stepped toward Matsen, most reaching for weapons. Most were in the street and only two stood between him and the doorway. Matsen was confident in his ability to defend himself, but he wasn't stupid. He knew his best chance would be to get inside, but that would bring the danger closer to Savka and Milica. Instead, he lowered his head and charged between the two men who stood between him and the wall. Then he turned and positioned himself with his back to the wall so that his attackers were in front of him. Unfortunately, they were all armed and every one of them was pointing a weapon at Matsen. Matsen noted the absence of the clicking, snapping sounds of weapons being charged. These men always had a round in the chamber. Ready to go.

At this point, so was Matsen.

"Boys, boys," Predrag Djilic's voice came from the doorway. "This is not how we treat our guests."

The men slowly, reluctantly lowered their weapons.

Djilic looked down at the man who had originally grabbed Matsen. Then he looked back at Matsen. "But this ain't the way a guest treats his hosts either, Matsen," Djilic said in his out-of-place Birmingham accent. "From what I understand, this is the second time ya put hands on one of my men. It's to be the last, mate. Understand?"

"I didn't start this, Djilic, and yesterday your man was hurting a little girl."

"The last time, mate."

"Tell it to them," Matsen said tossing his head at the men in the street.

Djilic stepped to within inches of Matsen so that their faces were almost touching. "All I need to do, Matsen, is snap my fuckin' fingers and yer dead. Got that? Yer bleedin' safe conduct has its limits."

Discretion might be the better part of valor, but something in this circumstance wouldn't allow Matsen to unconditionally surrender. "Okay, then, convey my apologies to your men, but tell them not to harm Savka or Milica."

Djilic widened his eyes and leaned his head forward an inch or two. "Ya think yer in a position to bargain, Matsen?" He turned to his men and translated what Matsen had said. The response was jeers and contemptuous laughter. Djilic turned back to Matsen. "Just don't worry about them, Matsen. We'll take care of them properly. Rest assured of that." He again translated his own words to his men and again got cheers and jeers in reply, which abruptly turned to groans of protest when Djilic gestured for the men to follow him back toward the village square.

Once again, Djilic turned back to Matsen. "Yer gettin' a pass this time, mate. Don't push your luck." He nodded rapidly for emphasis, then turned and led his grumbling entourage up the street and around the corner.

Matsen inhaled deeply to let the adrenaline rush subside, then took another breath and proceeded into the clinic. "Savka?" he called out. No answer. He went down the hall. The door to the examining room was open and inside he saw Savka with her back to him. She was standing at one of the glass-doored cabinets aimlessly moving jars and bottles and bandages around inside it. There was no apparent pattern to the rearrangement; just putting a jar where a bottle had been and then a roll of bandages from where she'd just taken the jar.

Matsen stood uncertainly for a moment then repeated her name, more softly this time. Savka stopped what she was doing but didn't turn around. Matsen crossed to her and stopped a couple of feet away. Yet again he spoke her name.

Nothing.

He stepped to his right and could see her face in profile. So pretty. So young. But she had a strange look on her face. A look of apprehension. Fear. He knew what it meant. She didn't want him to know. But now he did.

The lewd remarks by the men outside. The double meanings. Most of all the blunt sexual content of the men's protests when Djilic made them leave.

Matsen wanted to comfort her. He started to reach his hand out but stopped. She was alone and vulnerable in an incredibly hostile environment. She might misinterpret his touch. So he settled for words. "Savka, it's all right." God, what a stupid thing to say, he thought to himself. Of course, it's not all right. He searched for words that would make it better but knew there were none. That he understood? So what? He had neither the authority nor ability to "understand." Nor was it his place. She was ashamed. Could he absolve her of her shame? He would if he could. Or her blame? What blame? She had none to be absolved of. The bottom line was that *it* was whatever Savka thought *it* was. And felt *it* was. And his role, if he even had one, the best he could hope to do, was not make *it* any worse.

He decided to take the chance. He reached out and put his hand gently on her shoulder. He felt her stiffen.

"You know what they do to me? What I must do?" Savka said softly still staring into the air in front of her.

Matsen nodded, unsure if she even saw the movement.

But then Savka nodded back.

"I am not bad person."

"Savka. I know that. Please know that I know that. I understand. As much as I am able to, I understand. This world is so — I have seen so much —" Suddenly Matsen thought the unthinkable. Could these animals be abusing Milica as well?

"Where's Milica, Savka?"

Savka turned and looked at him, focused for the first time since he'd come into the room.

"Oh, no, Artur. Not Milica. Never Milica, I'll die first."

Matsen and Savka sat at the kitchen table. Milica was in the back, engrossed in a game involving sticks that Matsen didn't know. He had accompanied Savka to the little room to get Milica and had noted how the locks were set up to keep Milica in and others out. That it was Savka's only means to protect her from what her mother was forced to do made Matsen sad and angry.

"Why do you stay?"

Savka looked at him as though she didn't understand the question. "I have always lived here. I know nothing else." She looked at Milica. "We have nowhere else to go."

"But if you've always lived here, these people are your friends, neighbors, no?"

"Neighbors? Perhaps. In way. Friends?" The laugh was short, subdued, and anything but humorous. "I do not even know most of them." She took another deep breath. "As far as I know, I have lived here all my life. And I do not know them."

"As far as you know?"

She nodded. "I don't remember my parents. The people at the orphanage told me they were killed when I was very small." She glanced lovingly at her daughter. "Smaller than my Milica even," she said with a smile.

"Do you know how? Why?"

Savka gave Matsen a long look before she answered. "What does it matter, Artur?" The smile had faded. "But no. I don't know why or how. The orphanage never told me. I don't know if they knew."

"So you were raised in an orphanage?"

She nodded. "Not far," she added, pointing absently to the east.

"Good people?"

Pursed lips and a shrug. "I think they meant well. But it was cold. Not just in winter." A small distant smile. "But mostly I think they meant well."

"Is the orphanage still there? Could they help? Could you go there?"

Savka shook her head slowly. "No. Is not there. No one is there. Even building is gone."

Silence hung between them, Matsen not wanting to press, knowing that the present was painful enough. Not wanting to cause her to relive a painful past.

Still, wondering.

"Can . . ." He hesitated. "I don't mean to pry. But, where is Milica's father?"

Savka looked at Matsen for a long time then lowered her eyes before she spoke. "I do not know where." She was silent again for an even longer time. Then she spoke even more quietly. "I do not know who."

Matsen said nothing.

Savka didn't look up. "I am not whore, Artur," she said.

"I know." Matsen regretted asking, and his mind raced counter-productively in an effort to find something else — anything more benign — to talk about. But Savka continued in an almost lifeless voice.

"The orphanage was run by Orthodox Serbs who were against a separate Bosnia. So one day the Bosnians came. All the men were killed immediately. All the women, the nuns too, were raped. Many times. Regardless of age." She glanced over at Milica. "I was not the youngest." Then she looked down. "There were so many men. I grew tired. I lost count." Savka breathed a deep sigh. "Then there was young boy. Perhaps my age, I think. I remember he didn't want to — I think he felt pity." She glanced up again. "I cried whole time, you see," she explained matter-of-factly, unnecessarily. "But the other men. They forced him to — I remember he looked at me while he — none of others did." She then smiled perhaps the saddest smile Matsen had ever seen. "I tell myself he is father. It doesn't make differ-ence. Not really." She shrugged.

12

"The American will be trouble, Huska. Is trouble now." Predrag Djilic sat slumped in a chair opposite Miljkovic's desk. "He has fought with two of our men and today he attempted to defy me in front of some of the others. It was only your safe conduct that kept me from dealing with him severely."

"The safe conduct has its limits, Predrag. You do not need to be subjected to disrespect because of it. And we have always known what the American intended to propose. I have already decided we would not accept."

"But the Americans could give us much arms and supplies."

"Only if they are serious, which I doubt. And even then, they do not have sufficient presence here to prevent the consequences we would suffer if we allied with them."

"Then there is no reason to tolerate Matsen's arrogance. It will not be difficult to provoke him again. He has apparently developed great concerns for the nurse Savka and her child."

Miljkovic frowned, genuinely perplexed. "The Serb girl? Why?"

"Who knows? Americans have no depth. They see only the surface." Both men shook their heads in wonderment. "Or perhaps he just wants to be like one of their cowboys. Ride in and save the girl from the wild red Indians." He chuckled derisively.

Miljkovic puffed air through his lips. "Except he is . . ." he struggled to find a word. "What is it they call the detention areas where the red Indians are placed, Predrag?"

"Reservations is the word they use, I think."

"Yes. This American is on our reservation is he not? Perhaps he will find we do not give up our . . ." He searched his mind again. ". . . squaws, yes?" He looked inquiringly at Djilic and nodded back at the nod he received. "We do not give up our squaws so easily."

Miljkovic was interrupted when SS Hauptsturmführer Weil walked into the office unannounced. The German officer came to a halt and clicked his heels as he snapped to attention. "I regret that I must protest my treatment —" Weil began in flawless Serbo-Croatian.

"You forget our respective ranks, Hauptsturmführer," Miljkovic answered in equally flawless German.

"*Aber nein*, Herr Oberst." Weil, reverting to his native language, used the Wehrmact term for a full colonel. "But with all due respect, my business — our business — is most pressing and becomes more pressing by the minute. I wish to report that the 13th SS Gebirgs Handschar Division is approximately one day away from the rendezvous point and the local forces here have not yet been sent out to link with them."

"Thank you, Hauptsturmführer, but I assure you I am well aware of the precise location of the Handschar Division and my men" — Miljkovic took pains to place special emphasis on the words "my men" — are prepared to go where they are directed at a moment's notice. I appreciate your concern but —"

"May I ask the Herr Oberst then what the plans are in this regard? I have regrettably been kept sitting in the courtyard when we should be closely coordinating matters. As the High Command has directed, I would remind the Herr Oberst. With all due respect."

Miljkovic tolerated the SS officer's arrogance, but found it tedious. "Thank you, Hauptsturmführer, rest assured my plans are to carry out my role in this operation, and I fail to see why I need to clear such plans with you. You need only know that my forces will meet with the Handschars precisely on schedule. My schedule."

"*Aber naturlich*, Herr Oberst. But perhaps it would be better if we moved the rendezvous point closer to this location. As I have suggested to the High Command," he added pointedly.

This was going beyond tedious. "Perhaps you need to be reminded that this is my command, Hauptsturmführer, and such suggestions should come to me."

"As it would have, Herr Oberst, if I were not kept waiting interminably in the courtyard."

Djilic wasn't as fluent in German as the others, but understood enough. In Serbo-Croatian, he said to Miljkovic, "Perhaps if he spent less time on the roof killing our men, he would have been more available for meetings."

Weil stiffened and spoke directly to Miljkovic, also in Serbo-Croatian. "I am duty bound to accept the Oberst's authority but," he turned and looked squarely at Djilic, "I am not required to tolerate the drivel of a common bandit."

Djilic smiled coldly and rose slowly from his chair. "This common bandit will —"

Miljkovic held his palm out to Djilic. "This common bandit is my lieutenant and operates with my authority throughout my command. In all respects, Haupsturmführer Weil. Remember that."

Weil returned Djilic's glare, then turned to Miljkovic. "Again, Herr Oberst, with all due respect, I must disagree that my oath and my duty requires that I submit to such authority."

"Then perhaps you should return to your troops. You will no doubt be more comfortable in a more traditional environment."

Weil drew himself to further attention and nodded sharply. "I would like nothing better, Herr Oberst. I will advise the High Command of your suggestion, and this conversation. Rest assured I will indicate my complete agreement." He raised his chin. "With permission?"

Miljkovic nodded. Weil clicked his heels, turned, and left without looking at Djilic.

Matsen stayed with Savka and Milica the rest of the day and into the evening. Milica was delighted. She played outside occasionally but only for brief periods and then was back at his side. When she wasn't chattering at him, she was sitting off to the side and staring at him. Just like that first day. She seemed to take particular delight in the interaction between Matsen and Savka. Just a simple conversation, in some ways the more inconsequential the better, made her happy and content. Her little world was good. For now.

After a very simple supper, Matsen went over to Savka as she washed the evening's plates and utensils. Milica followed with her eyes.

"Are there ever problems at night. In the evening?" he asked Savka.

She shrugged. "Is possible. Not often. But sometimes."

"It's just that I need to go talk to Tony Talbot." Savka looked inquiringly at him. "The British soldier."

"Oh." She looked at him with a sad smile. "Of course, I understand."

Matsen didn't. "You understand what?"

Before she could answer, Milica was at their sides, looking up at Matsen. "You don't go, Artur?" she asked. "Please stay."

"Artur has duties, *ceri*," Savka replied. "He cannot always stay."

Milica grasped Arthur's hand and looked up at his face. "Please, Artur?"

Matsen looked down at Milica and then up at Savka who had been washing the same dish for some time now.

And suddenly he understood.

Savka couldn't ask him to come back or to stay as she wanted to because it might look like she was too open to him or worse, just trying to secure his protection. Matsen knew he would never take advantage of her. But Savka couldn't know that. And Matsen didn't feel he should ask to stay or offer to stay, as if he were doing her a favor, because Savka might see it as him assuming she would sleep with him since —

"Artur, Mama?" Milica looked back and forth between the two adults, her lower lip jutting out and quivering.

"Savka," Matsen looked uncomfortably down at Milica, "I'd like very much to come back. Tonight. After I've talked to Tony. There's the table here in the surgery. I don't want you to think —"

Savka put her fingers on Matsen's lips. "Please come back. You can see how Milica wants you to," she said smiling down at her daughter. She looked back up into his eyes. "And I too."

"You're out of your dashed mind, Matsen. You do realize that," Talbot said shaking his head. "Making an enemy of Predrag Djilic is a singularly bad idea. He's one of Miljkovic's closest lieutenants. Been with him for years. And even if he weren't, he's a dangerous man in his own right."

Matsen nodded. "I know that. And I know things like this happen a thousand times a day all over the world. As an abstract concept, it's one thing. But I can't see Savka and Milica as abstractions."

"Quite," Talbot said quietly. He went silent, clearly deep in thought, then, "All right, then listen. And don't start prying for sources, old boy. But I can tell you that all sorts of undesirable material is about to hit the proverbial fan from all sorts of different directions at once."

"How so?"

"I have learned," the Brit canted his head and shook a cautionary finger, "that your presence is no longer required. Miljkovic has no intention of allying himself with our side." Talbot ignored Matsen's raised eyebrows at the revelation that Talbot knew why he was here.

"And Djilic plans to provoke you into a confrontation using Savka and Milica. Not that he needs a provocation. Perhaps he and Miljkovic want to keep some tenuous avenue open to the allies just in case. But I assure you you're not to be in that picture in any event."

"Great."

Talbot grinned slightly. "On a more global scale, quite literally, it seems the whole bloody alliance is falling apart all at once. Our favorite Hun, the noble Hauptsturmführer, came storming in here earlier today muttering about the *verdamt untermenschen* and how the high command had designated him to coordinate, and he would not tolerate the insolence of a bandit. Djilic, I assume." He shrugged. "Very shortly thereafter, he was on the radio — in the clear — reporting that the fighters here were unprepared and worse, would not join the Handschar as directed. Frankly, I doubt that Miljkovic would be that blatantly contentious toward the Germans, but it appears the command accepted Weil's version and ordered the Handschar Division to advance and enter Cazin. I don't foresee pitched battles, but neither do I see Miljkovic being very happy about that. Not to mention the Chetniks. Now that they know the Handschar are on the way —"

"And how might they have learned that, Tony?" Matsen asked with a wry smirk.

Talbot mimicked the smirk but ignored the question.

"They've never been happy about Mihailovic's decision to send them here and are under no illusion they would be anything but cannon fodder when the time comes. But now that the Hanschar are on the way, they've been sending messages and runners constantly to try to finally convince Mihailovic that if this was ever a good idea, it isn't any longer."

"So what happens next?"

"Nothing till the local Chetniks hear from Mihailovic. They're fiercely obedient. Perhaps fatally so in this case. But they're urgently advising that they be ordered out."

"When?"

"As soon as they hear. If they hear. They'd like to go immediately, I know."

"Would they take Savka and Milica with them?" Talbot and he looked at each other until Talbot raised his eyebrows in a "who knows" sort of look.

"I mean the Chetniks are all Serbs, aren't they?"

This time Talbot nodded. "Mostly. Yes, almost all. But —"

"What?"

"You should understand that to some of them, at least as contemptible as a Bosnian woman is a Serb woman who's been with Bosnian men. I don't know if she'd be any better off with them. And, aside from that, it may be a running battle."

"And, if Savka and Milica stay here, what happens to them when the Handschar arrive?"

"Yes. Point taken. Their atrocities have rivaled the Ustachi, haven't they?"

"So —?"

Talbot thought for a moment. "I'll talk to Captain Popovic."

"Who is?"

"Chetnik second in command. Toughest soldier they've got. Nobody challenges Popovic."

13

They made love. Both of them wanted to. Neither of them planned to.

Arthur had been determined that they would *not* make love. Not because he didn't want to. But because it more important to show Savka she was more than what the other men had used her for.

Savka did know that. And for her, the very idea that she *wanted to* was an epiphany. She had never wanted to before. But she was concerned that Arthur must know this would be something she would hold dear. Beyond the physical act, for the first time there would be a sharing, a mutual giving. That would be different. So very different.

Milica had greeted Arthur's return with a squeal of delight and a running leap into his arms. He carried her into the kitchen where Savka was readying the evening meal. She turned to them with a smile and was warmed by a sensation that this was the closest she had ever been to knowing what a family felt like. They ate. They talked. They all cleaned up afterward and, when that was done, Arthur let Milica teach him the game with the sticks while Savka watched. Milica won every time.

When it was time for bed, Savka took Milica into the room they shared for sleeping. Milica insisted that Arthur help tuck her in and so he did, with a kiss on the cheek that Milica immediately returned. She fell asleep secure that the world was now a good place.

Arthur and Savka tiptoed out and went to the clinic waiting room, which also served as a sitting room of sorts. Arthur sat on one of the couches and was warmed when Savka sat down next to him. It wasn't a particularly large couch, somewhere between a love seat and a sofa, and when Arthur turned to Savka, their knees were almost touching. Savka asked Matsen to tell her about his life and listened raptly as he described his own privileged upbringing in northeast America. Savka was fascinated and yet mystified by a world she couldn't imagine.

At one point, Arthur stopped speaking for a moment and Savka placed her hand on his cheek. "Artur, I thank you so much for what you are doing." Arthur started to offer a peremptory disclaimer, but Savka moved her fingers from his cheek to his lips. "But this is not thanks. This is what I want to do." And she leaned forward and kissed him. Arthur's planned resolve evaporated, and he returned the kiss with gentle fervor. Their lips separated and Savka turned herself so that she could nestle under Arthur's arm with her head against his shoulder. Without looking up, speaking out into the room, she said, "You know about what I must do here. This, now, with you, would not be same. You know this?"

Arthur turned her head and tilted her chin up to him with his hand and looked into her eyes. "I do, Savka. I do know that."

She raised her mouth up and he brought his down to meet it.

They made love.

And it was special.

It was the first time Savka had ever made love.

At the sound of the first bang on the door, Matsen leaped from the couch and fell forward onto the floor. He looked around for Savka before he remembered she had gone to the bedroom sometime ago to be there when Milica awoke.

More pounding rattled the front door. Outside, a man shouted, "Open!" There was raucous laughter as other voices repeated, "Yes. Open! Open your legs, whore!"

Matsen grabbed a metal poker from the fireplace, crossed the room, and flattened himself against the wall by the door that finally gave way under the forceful pounding. Three men charged in. Matsen crushed the skull of the third and last man with a baseball swing to the back of his head. As he cocked his arms to do the same to the second man in, a hand grabbed the poker from behind and stopped its forward momentum, then pulled back on it. The hand belonged to Predrag Djilic.

Matsen immediately reversed direction and threw his weight into Djilic. The sudden and unexpected push caught Djilic off balance and slammed him back into yet another man who was entering the house behind him. This man, Matsen saw, was the one who had tried to take the candy from Milica. All three men fell into the street. As Djilic fumbled for his pistol, Matsen jumped to his feet and threw a front kick into Djilic's face. It missed high but caught enough of Djilic's forehead to momentarily stun him.

Matsen turned and charged back into the clinic but was halted by the barrel of a rifle pointed directly into his face. Behind the man with the rifle, another man stood with a pistol pointed at Savka's left temple and his left hand curled around Milica's neck. The little girl's blue eyes, wide open and staring at Masten, showed fear but also complete and utter trust.

Djilic appeared in the doorway, his face and neck red with rage. With Matsen neutralized, he stopped and took a series of deep breaths. Then, he closed the distance and placed his face only inches from Matsen's. He raised the pistol in his right hand and rested it at an angle along the left side of Matsen's head.

"Yer a fuckin' dead man, Matsen." Djilic looked around the room then brought his gaze back to Matsen. "But first, since ya like these Serb girls so much, I'll let ya have a bit of a show. Let ya see what they can do. There's something about Serb women, Matsen. They seem to know their purpose in life — for Bosnian men, that is." He exchanged leers with the other men. "Even at an early age. Here, we'll show ya." He pointed his left hand at Milica, and an evil grin appeared on the face of the man holding her. "In fact, Matsen, we'll let you have the first taste. See if you're half the man we are."

"Fuck you, Djilic," Matsen said. "Never."

"Yeah?" Djilic grinned. "Well, if you don't, we'll torture the little Serb bitch in ways ya can't imagine." Djilic grabbed the front of Matsen's waistband. "So show us what ya've got." He laughed a filthy laugh. "Show the little Serb bitch what ya've got." Savka emitted a visceral growl and the man holding the gun on her rapped it into her face.

Even in his rage, Matsen felt an eerie sort of calm come over him. The almost detached equanimity that accompanies the absence of alternatives. Matsen knew he would be dead in the next few minutes. And saving Savka and Milica was more than he could hope for. But he would exact a terrible price and he would die trying. It was all he could do. And he would do it.

He breathed in, his body marshaling its energy into its core, readying the explosion. He crooked the fingers of his right hand into a claw that would rake Djilic's face, gouging his eyes, and, if Matsen was lucky, penetrate beyond the optic nerves and muscles and into the brain. With luck, such a thrust could even be fatal.

At that precise instant, a strange guttural sound, half hiss and half gurgle, caused all heads to snap in its direction. In the doorway, the man who had tried to take Milica's sweets stood tottering, an enormous knife, almost a short sword, running through his neck parallel to his shoulders. From haft to tip, the knife was three feet long and the blade was as deep as the man's neck, its back edge brushing the spinal column as the razor-sharp front edge severed everything from the inside out. For a long suspended moment, the man stood there, staring at nothing. Then his eyes began to roll back and his head flopped rearward like the hinged lid of a jewelry box. The weight of the head had been all that was holding the sword in place and now it clanged to the ground. The body remained erect for another moment, appearing headless, blood erupting upward in diminishing spurts until the center of gravity shifted and the man fell backward into the street. The force of the landing caused the head to separate from the torso and it rolled onto its side, its eyes toward the doorway, its pupils moving from side to side as if taking one final survey of the scene.

An arm reached out from the side and reclaimed the sword just as someone stepped into the doorway and shot the man holding the rifle on Matsen. Matsen immediately shoved his clawed right hand into Djilc's face and whipped his left arm up and out just as Djilic started to squeeze the trigger of his pistol. The shot flew into the ceiling. The middle finger of Matsen's clawed right hand penetrated into Djilic's left eye and Matsen hooked the finger onto the lower socket bone and yanked sharply down. Djilic grabbed at Matsen's wrist as he dropped to his knees, losing his pistol in the process.

It was over in an instant. The hand that had retrieved the sword came in through the front entrance attached to a tall woman, about five foot eleven, in her forties, with unkempt dirty blond hair tucked into the collar of her jacket and tied with a strip of leather. She took two quick steps and leaned forward to place the tip of the sword against Djilic's neck. Matsen looked at Savka and Milica and was pleasantly surprised to see Talbot standing there with his own weapon pressed harder than it needed to be into the temple of the man who'd been holding mother and daughter.

"Popovic." Djilic spat the name at the woman holding the blade to his neck. His left hand covered his wounded eye.

"Captain Popovic to you, pig," the woman replied. "I heard your plans for the little girl, Djilic. Maybe you'd like to feel something like it yourself, eh?" She spat directly into his face, then sneered, "Yes. You probably would like it."

"You are dead, Popovic. And all your men. You are all dead. If you think you can do this to me. Huska will have your heads on poles for this. And I will cut the rest of you into little pieces and feed you to the dogs, you bitch."

Popovic pressed the tip of her sword harder into Djilic's neck and told him to stand. When he didn't immediately comply, she kicked him hard in the shoulder and sent him sprawling across the floor. Two men came from behind her and roughly lifted Djilic to his feet pinning his arms to his side. Matsen watched with satisfaction as Djilic alternately squinted and squeezed shut his severely damaged eye in a futile effort to alleviate the thudding pain.

"Strip!" Popovic commanded.

Djilic didn't move.

Popovic laughed coldly. "Do it or I'll do it for you with my friend here," she said brandishing the sword in Djilic's face. "And I won't be gentle about it." She looked back at the man Talbot was holding at gunpoint. "You too. Do it!" Talbot jabbed the man with the barrel of his pistol and he slowly began to comply. Savka pulled Milica to her and turned to leave the room. Popovic switched her gaze to Matsen and waggled her sword in the direction of Savka and Milica. "Go with," she said tersely. "Men behind house. We come later."

Matsen nodded and crossed the room to Savka and Milica. He stopped and looked back at Djilic, who stood unmoving and still fully clothed. The fatalistic calm of a few moments earlier had dissipated and now, as Matsen looked at Djilic, he felt the rage rebuilding inside of him.

Popovic saw the look and waved her sword again. "Go now. Quickly." She nodded her head toward Savka and Milica again. Matsen hesitated, then nodded. As he left the room, he heard a grunt from Djilic and the tearing of cloth.

14

Matsen was impressed at how quietly so many people could move through the woods. Operational discipline was in full effect and each individual knew their life depended on getting as far from Cazin as rapidly as possible. They were moving so quickly, however, Matsen wondered how Popovic and Talbot would catch up.

So he was startled when Captain Lidija Popovic appeared from behind without a sound. Matsen quietly thanked her and they exchanged a firm handshake. Savka too mouthed a silent, "thank you." Popovic nodded briskly. "We must make Bosanski Novi before dawn. Another twenty kilometers," the Chetnik leader said quietly, looking first at Savka, who nodded, and then at Matsen, who indicated he understood. Popovic gave him a tight smile and a powerful squeeze to the shoulder. Her expression softened as she looked at Milica's arms curled around Matsen's neck and her little face pressed against his chest. She reached out and patted Savka and started to trot off toward the front of the column as quietly as she had come up from behind.

Matsen stopped her with a touch to her arm. Then he asked her softly, "Is Djilic dead?"

Popovic just looked at him for a moment then said, "No. He lives." She looked to the rear. "He will come."

They reached Bosanski Novi before dawn, changed direction, and went south a couple of kilometers before stopping at the base of foothills in the Kozara range. According to Chetnik intelligence, the Handschar Division was moving west toward Cazin just to the north of the route the Chetniks were taking. Swinging south and east into the Kozaras placed that much more distance between the Chetniks and the Muslim SS division.

Matsen and Savka were sitting side by side against a large tree, with Milica now asleep in Savka's arms, when Talbot came over to them. Even the normally cynical Brit couldn't help but smile at the sleeping child. Settling himself next to Matsen, Talbot shook his head in feigned exasperation and whispered, "So I suppose we both need our heads examined."

Matsen reached down and pulled the large piece of canvas they were using as a blanket up and over their heads so they could speak more freely and still maintain operational silence.

"Thank you isn't enough, you know."

Talbot shrugged. "Miljkovic is dead, you know."

That was one thing Matsen hadn't been expecting to hear. "How? Who?"

"Don't know, actually. We were rather pressed back there. Some were saying that Weil had shot him. I've no doubt the Hauptsturm-führer would have liked to. Others were saying that some of Tito's partisans had infiltrated into Cazin, which is true, by the way." He looked at Matsen. "Miljkovic was talking to Tito's people. Planning on switching over to the partisans at the last minute — full circle. So I doubt the partisans would have killed him now. Most likely scenario to me was that his own lieutenants got wind of the impending switch and —"

"Djilic?"

"Djilic was too busy trying to get his pants back on," Talbot laughed without humor. "And he was genuinely loyal to Miljkovic. Not that he would have taken to joining Tito, mind you. But, no, I don't think Djilic would have done it. Not personally, anyway."

"What happened back there? Popovic said Djilic is still alive. And coming."

"Yes, to the first point. Probably, to the second."

"What happened?" Matsen repeated.

"Interesting chemistry between Djilic and Popovic. Djilic never could stand the idea of a woman officer. And a Serb woman at that. So the whole time the Chetnik's were in Cazin, he was insufferably rude and offensive to her. But Popovic is almost always all business. She let it roll off her back. But back there earlier, she couldn't resist imparting a little humiliation of her own. The problem being that the brief time it took for her to slice Djilic's clothes off gave a number of his men time to come charging down to the clinic. We barely got out." He paused in thought for a while, then, "Our friend Predrag is not a forgiving person. He'll be along, I suspect. Sooner rather than later."

They were soon on the move again, marching at a forced-march pace that grew increasingly difficult to maintain as the elevation of the trail increased. Well below them was a less arduous but more exposed route through a pass in the mountains. The route they were following was thickly wooded and high on the mountainside, making them harder to track and less visible to any stray unit or Handschar scout from above or below.

They'd been climbing for a couple of hours and all but the hardiest were in that automaton state—bodies forging on, minds elsewhere. That changed abruptly when shooting erupted in the distance. They were still below the tree line of the mountain with the terrain sloping up and away to the north and the east. To the south, on their right, was a sharp drop-off to the floor of the pass. Behind them, to the west, who knew? There was nothing to do but keep on and so they did, no longer automatons but focused on the relative distance between them and the sounds of the firefight.

The shooting stopped as abruptly as it had started, but the troops deployed along the north of the column remained in place and on alert. More contact came within the hour and when it did, it was in fusillade. Virtually the entire picket of sentries fell as one. Matsen spun away from the direction of the fire and wrapped the arm that was not holding Milica around Savka, steering and pushing her in the only viable direction — south. By now the fire from the attackers came from the east and west as well as the north. The Chetniks fell back toward the south firing as they went, desperately trying to form a cohesive defensive formation, fully aware that their retreat was blocked a short distance away by the sheer drop-off into the valley.

A Chetnik fighter fell mortally wounded a few feet from Matsen and without hesitation Matsen picked up the man's weapon and began searching for targets. They were not hard to identify. SS uniforms. The Handschar Division.

Fortunately, it was not the entire division but a unit left behind to clean up the aftermath of an earlier engagement with some bandits. After the initial skirmish, which ended quickly with the deaths of the Chetnik scouts, the Handschar officer in charge had sent out scouts of his own who quickly found the larger force. Seeing he was out-numbered, the Handschar officer decided against a pitched battle and opted instead for a quick hit-and-run. As soon as the outer ele-ments of the Chetnik line re-formed and began to push back against the flanks of the attackers, the Handschar troops disengaged. In moments, the shooting diminished in frequency and grew more distant until all was quiet again.

Matsen and Savka sat next to each other in silence, Savka holding Milica close to her. There was no sound at all. No matter how quiet it might be before a battle, somehow the aftermath is immeasurably quieter. It was the contrast, not the absence of sound, that made for the almost ponderous silence.

Which was suddenly broken by a voice saying, "Now. Where was we, mate?"

Matsen was up and moving toward Djilic in an instant. He'd barely taken two steps when he was struck at the base of his spine by the butt of a rifle swung fully and violently by one of Djilic's men. Matsen felt an electric jolt and crumbled to the ground immediately aware that there was no sensation anywhere in his body. He lay on the ground unable to move, fearing he was paralyzed and knowing he was helpless. Several pairs of hands grabbed him and dragged him over to a tree where they sat him up and then stepped back, weapons trained on him from several directions.

"Oh, yeah. I remember where we was," Djilic said sourly. Matsen looked up and saw the strip of cloth covering Djilic's eye. Noting Matsen's stare, Djilic lifted the makeshift bandage to reveal a very blackened eye socket and an eyelid that was now more concave than convex. "Ya done a good job on it, Matsen. It's no good anymore. What's left of it." He pulled the cloth down again. "But I've still got another one and that'll be enough to watch ya suffer. And have a good bit of fun in doin' it."

He pointed at Savka who stood off against another tree with Milica half hidden behind her. "Strip 'em. Both of 'em."

Matsen's brain ordered his body to react — to move, attack, protect. But there was no part of him that would move. The barest hint of a tingle in his furthest extremities perhaps. Knowing what was to come, he found himself wishing he'd been blinded as well as paralyzed.

One of Djilic's men reached out to grab Savka, but she took a quick step forward and slammed her knee into his groin. As the man reacted to the painful blow, Savka ripped a stick grenade from his belt and stepped back between Milica and the evil before them. She held the grenade out by its wooden handle, the metal explosive container pointing directly at Djilic.

Matsen felt pride in Savka's defiance. But Djilic just scoffed.

German grenades were not the simplest devices to operate and it was unlikely that this girl — this Serb girl — would know anything about such weaponry.

"What are you going to do with that?" Djilic sneered. "Throw it at me? Go ahead." He took several steps toward Savka, but stopped when she reached down and unscrewed the cap on the end of the stick handle allowing a white lanyard to tumble out, ready to be pulled. Djilic realized he'd underestimated her. Actually what he'd underestimated was his own men's desire to show off to a female, even a Serb. Still he goaded her, "Go ahead. Throw it."

Savka yanked the white cord of the grenade and threw it well and accurately at Djilic who reached up and caught it neatly in his right hand, no mean feat for a man with only one functioning eye. He flipped the device over in his hand and held it by the wooden handle. He read the writing on the side of the metal explosive canister.

"'Vor Gebrauch, Sprengkapsel Einsetzen.'" Savka didn't understand German but Matsen knew what it meant. "Before using, insert detonator." The grenade hadn't been armed.

Djilic flipped the grenade in his hand again and now held it by the canister with the wooden handle projecting upward. "Well, look at this, bitch. What does that remind you of?" He wiggled it from side to side then pumped it up and down in an obscene pantomime. Then he pointed at Milica. "Bring me the child."

To their credit, Djilic's men hesitated. In the moment it gave her, Savka swept Milica up into her arms and stepped backward until she was standing on the edge of the precipice.

"No!" The sound croaked from Matsen's throat barely loud enough for Savka to hear. But she did. She looked at him with warmth. "Thank you, Artur. You tried," she said softly. "But I said it. Not Milica. Never Milica." Then she whispered something in her little girl's ear. Milica's face contorted with tears as she turned to Matsen and opened and closed her little fingers in a wave. Both she and Savka held Matsen's paralyzed gaze as the young mother took two more steps back and then a third that took them over the edge and into the abyss, their blue eyes never leaving Matsen's face.

Half a world away and more than half a century later, Arthur Matsen put his face in his hands and did what he had done so many times over the last six decades.

He cried.

15

"Thank you for holding. All of our staff are busy assisting other citizens, but your call is very important to us. Please stay on the line and the next available staff assistant will be with you as soon as possible."

"Oh for—" This was the fourth time Katherine Price had gotten that message since the staff assistant had put her on hold some ten minutes before.

Finally, a person came on the line. "Records."

"Hello, my name is Katherine Price. I'm with the law office of Loring, Matsen, and Gould. I'm calling about an inquiry my office made regarding the professional history of a Dr. Nathan Fredrick who is —"

"There's a form that has to be filed for that. I can give you the fax request line where —"

"No, no. We filed that form already. The Form 9386?"

"Well, it normally takes three to five working days."

"We sent it at least that long ago."

"Well, things can get lost in the mail."

"We faxed it."

Silence.

ALAMEDA FREE LIBRARY

"Do you have a copy of the request in front of you?"

"Yes."

"There should be a filing number in the upper left-hand corner as a reference."

"There's no number in the upper left-hand corner."

"If it was filed, it would have been given a number, ma'am."

"I'm sure it would. But since the copy I have is a copy of what we faxed, it wouldn't have it, would it?"

"No need to be abrupt, ma'am." A long exhalation of air. Then, "What was the name?"

"Fredrich. It's a somewhat unusual spelling. F-r-e-d-r-i-c-h."

Click.

Several minutes passed.

Click.

"Those records aren't available, ma'am."

"But that information is public record."

"Yes, ma'am, that *kind* of information is public record," the voice droned, "but it has to be *recorded* before it can be public, right?"

Price considered that response. Then, "You're telling me there's no historical information contained in Fredrich's file?"

"That's right. Have a good day, ma'am."

Click.

Sara Furden debated whether to do another circuit of the training regimen she had devised for herself before she finally went and checked Janie's room. The session was supposed to have started almost a half hour earlier and Sara, rather than sit and stew, had opted to work off her growing tensions through exercise. She did one ten-minute circuit, and when Janie hadn't turned up, did another. But Janie still hadn't shown up.

And that wasn't like her.

At least it didn't used to be like her.

Lately, Sara had noticed a change in Janie's personality. Her positive attitude and commitment declined and then disappeared. She grew sullen and resentful of Sara's efforts. Then came the verbal snapping, the resistance, the refusal to try. Finally there was outright hostility. It broke Sara's heart. And to be on the receiving end of Janie's venom revived the feelings of responsibility and guilt.

Sara looked at the large, round clock on the wall yet again and exhaled. This wasn't about her, she told herself. It was about Janie. And if it was less pleasant, less satisfying than it had been, it was still all about making Janie better. It had to be.

Sara knocked softly on the door to Janie's room and got no response. She knocked a little harder, and then harder again. Nothing.

Okay, now what? Assuming Janie was in there, just bursting in won't help the situation. Still, what if something was wrong?

Sara took a deep breath before trying the knob. It was unlocked. She turned it quietly and pushed the door open just a crack.

"Janie?" Sara put her face to the opening and called softly. Still there was no response. Sara opened the door a bit more and again called Janie's name. Silence. Now she was worried. She pushed the door until she could see most of the room.

No Janie.

Her eyes moved to and rested on the almost-closed door to the bathroom. Just as she started across the room, the door flew back and Janie emerged. For an instant, Janie had a startled, almost angry look. Then suddenly, without transition, she became excited, elated. Too much so.

"Sara!" Janie almost shouted as she lurched across the room to throw her arms around Sara's shoulders. "I was jus' comin' to look for you. I'm takin' us to lunsh, 'kay? How d'wi look" Janie held out her arms, which threw her off balance. Sara reached out to steady her, but Janie caught herself and made a cautious fashion-type turn. She wore slacks and a print blouse and looked nice. Before Sara could say so, Janie pressed on. "I knew you would'n' min' if I skipped today's sessi'n. I know I havn' been as nice as I could be so I wan' to do somethin' for you. And I fig'red a nice lunsh would be nice." She laughed a little more loudly than the comment warranted. "I guess a nice lunsh would be nice, huh? I mean what else would it be, huh?" She laughed again. "A nice anythin' would be nice, I mean. Or it wouldn' be nice, would it?" Yet another laugh.

Then Janie focused in on Sara and her sweatpants and T-shirt. "But I didn't tell you befor' so you're not dressed for lunsh, are you?" Janie struck a pose of mock sternness with her hands on her hips, a move that caused her to wobble just a bit. "Well, you jus' get y'rsef to your room, young lady," she laughed again, "and put on somethin' more 'propriate." She waggled a finger at Sara and again lost her balance. Fortunately, the bed was right behind her so she just fell into a seated position on it. In an instant, a look of immense sadness appeared on Janie's face and she looked as though she was about to burst into tears. In the next instant, the expression changed again and Janie went back to laughing. "Oops. Le's work on that in the next sessi'n, 'kay?" She laughed again.

Sara felt a growing knot in her stomach. She hadn't known what to expect, but it certainly wasn't this. For a moment when Janie had first come out of the bathroom, Sara had felt relief that Janie was in a good mood. But it was clear that this something other than a good mood. Something was terribly wrong.

"Let me go get changed, Janie. I'll only be a minute. Have you decided where we're going?" Sara watched as Janie's grin faded and her expression turned quizzical, then contorted into a childlike grimace of pain and sorrow. "I didn' think of that, Sara," Janie wailed. "I f'got to pick a place to go and —" She began to sob. "I'm so stupi' 'cuz I said I'd take you to lunsh and I f'got to even pick a place to go." She looked up at Sara, who was reaching out to her, and waved her off.

"No, I — Jus' go, Sara." She wasn't crying now. Now she was angry. "You prob'ly think this is funny. The stupi' cripple can't even do this." She glared. "Tha's wha' you think, Sara. I know i' is. Jus' go."

"Janie, I don't think that at all. You know —"

"Go, Sara!" Janie shouted. "Ge' out of my room. Righ' now! Ge' out." Janie tried to throw the small clutch purse in her hand but it slipped out of her fingers and fell harmlessly at her own feet.

16

"Furden. F-u-r-d-e-n. First name Sara." Dr. Nathan Fredrich leaned his elbows on the counter of the Whispering Marsh personnel office and tapped his fingers as he waited.

"The physical therapist?" The human resources assistant stood before a bank of file cabinets and looked over her shoulder at Fredrich, who nodded. The assistant then angled to a cabinet on the left and opened the second drawer from the top. She riffled through the folders until she came to the one she wanted and pulled it from the pack. "Of course, you realize this is confidential information?" she cautioned as she handed it to Fredrich.

"Of course," Fredrich said absently as he reached for the folder. He started to leave but the assistant stopped him. "That can't leave this room, Doctor. Sorry."

"Fine," Frederich grumbled. He found a chair, sat down, and opened the folder.

"Sara M. Furden. B.A. in Physical Education. Master's in Educa-tion. Doctorate in Exercise Physiology." He raised his eyebrows at that and flipped through the other pages. Assistant professor of physical education at Charlestown University up until about two years ago. Then suddenly she resigned. Next entry: licensure as a physical therapist. Fredrich looked up and considered what he'd just read.

Furden. A Ph.D. Almost surely on a tenure track at the university with a career capped by a full professorship suddenly left all of that behind and converted to physical therapy. It had to be related to Janie Reston. He knew from Janie's history that her injuries had occurred about two years ago, which would be right around the time that Furden resigned from the university.

Janie had said that Furden was her mom's friend. Okay. But would that been enough to motivate Furden to give up a stellar academic career? There had to be more to it.

Fredrich caught up with Furden as she was crossing the grounds.

"Ah, Ms. Furden, I was hoping to find you. Do you have a few moments? I'd like to speak with you in my office about Ms. Reston."

Furden's gut instinct was to blow him off. She didn't like Fredrich. But he *was* on Janie's treatment team. She remembered her unreasonable hostility toward John Cann when he'd arrived on the scene at Charlestown and her jealousy at how Janie had looked to him for support and help. Perhaps if she'd worked with Cann instead of distancing herself from him and his efforts, Janie might have been spared her ordeal. Bottom line, Sara, she thought to herself, this isn't about you. It's about Janie. Whatever it takes.

Fredrich got right to the point. He leaned forward, resting his forearms on his desk. "In the course of my most recent session with Ms. Reston, I was a bit surprised when she spoke of you on a personal level."

"What did she say?"

"That you were a friend of her mom's." Furden nodded. "She talked about you being a friend of the family and, well, frankly, I wanted to learn a little more about that."

Furden hesitated. Fredrich put on his best deskside manner. "This is about Janie, Sara. Helping Janie is everything. Anything you might be able to tell me could be a great help." He waited a moment, then stood and crossed to a credenza where he poured some water from a carafe and carried the glass over to Furden. She took it, paused briefly before taking a small sip, and then took a second larger draught. Fredrich nodded and went back to his chair. He sat, leaned forward again, and resumed, "So, you knew Janie before she came to Whispering Marsh?"

"Yes. I grew up with her mother. And I've known Janie all her life. I was there when she was born."

"And you were close to her?"

"Very. She called me her second mom and I guess I felt that way myself. A big sister at least."

"Is that why she chose to attend Charlestown University? Because you were there?"

Furden nodded. "Partly. I mean, it's an excellent school so that would be reason enough. But I did press the issue. I wanted her to come to Charlestown. I figured I could help her make the adjustment. Keep an eye on her." Her voice trailed off briefly then she spoke again. "So, yes, I had some influence on the decision."

"Does that make you feel responsible for what happened?"

Furden didn't answer for a long time, then nodded.

Fredrich's attention was riveted on Furden. "I don't know what happened to Janie," he said. "I know the medical results. The physical effects. But of course, I don't know what happened."

Furden said nothing.

"Do you, Sara?"

Fredrich held his breath as he waited for an answer.

"No."

Fredrich's shoulders slumped and he bowed his head.

"Not really," Furden went on. "Not all of it."

Fredrich's head came back up.

"Janie disappeared. Nobody knew where she was for several days. Some men —" She started to be more specific but stopped herself. "Some men had taken her and abused her." She looked at Fredrich. "You know what the results were. But you can't know how —" Her gaze grew distant. Then she said, almost to herself, "If you'd seen what they were doing to her —"

It took a moment for it to register, then Fredrich blinked. "Seen? Do you mean you were there?"

Furden shook her head slowly in the negative. "No. God, no. I wasn't there."

"But you saw Janie being — hurt?"

She nodded.

"How?"

"On the tape."

Fredrich gasped.

"Tape? You mean a videotape?"

Furden nodded.

Fredrich's brain just couldn't seem to get a hold on this.

"There's a tape of — what happened?"

Furden's eyes were unfocused, still fixed on an unseen image. "There was."

Fredrich felt like he might burst.

"Where is it now?"

Furden shrugged. "I don't know. I assume he took it."

"Who? Who took it. Who is 'he'?"

"John Cann."

17

Conference Room
Landesgerichte
Garmisch–Patenkirchen

Cann saw through the glass wall of the conference room that he was the last to arrive. As he entered, the man seated at the head of the round, polished walnut table flashed a peremptory smile and extended his left hand toward the seat he wished Cann to occupy.

This was Karl-Heinz Stihlmann, a slightly overweight man with a round face and thinning hair who looked more like your friendly neighborhood butcher than the chief judge of the Bayern Oberlandesgerichte, the regional court for the state of Bavaria, and a specialist in *strafgerichtsbarkeit* — criminal jurisdiction.

"*Guten morgen, Herr Cann,*" he said in German. Cann replied in kind.

Stihlmann nodded around the table at the three other men and began. "Thank you for coming, gentlemen," he smiled.

"The first order of business is to decide on a language for this meeting. While German is my native language, I can conduct this conference in French or English, if need be. Is there one language among us that we are all sufficiently comfortable with?" He looked first to the man on his right.

"I know French, Flemish, and German, Herr Richter. I would be less comfortable with English, I confess," the man said. He nodded toward Cann with an expression that might or might not have been slightly apologetic. Cann accepted the look at face value and turned to the two men to his left. One of the men said he was fluent in German as well as English and Serbian but not French and, speaking for the man seated next to him, said that Herr Cesic knew only Serbian and German. The judge lastly turned to Cann who told him he didn't know Serbian and Flemish but any of the others were fine with him.

"So, we shall speak German, yes?" Stihlmann asked, polling with his eyes. He was answered with nods and murmurs of assent all around.

"Good. Let us begin. I believe we all know who is who, but for the record," he tossed his head back at the stenographer seated against the wall in the corner, "let me identify the parties present. Seated to my immediate right is Herr or Monsieur, if you will, Emiel Loens, of the prosecutor's office of the International Criminal Tribunal for the Former Yugoslavia." The two men exchanged nods. "Henceforth, gentlemen," Stihlmann said wryly, "for efficiency, we shall refer to it as the Tribunal." All the men indicated agreement.

Judge Stihlmann next extended his right hand toward the two men opposite and announced, "Herr Anton Divjak, deputy consul of the Serbian delegation. Or rather the Former Federal Republic of Yugoslavia. May I simply say Serbia?" Divjak nodded agreement. "And," Stihlmann went on indicating the man next to Divjak, "Herr Obrad Cesic," he looked down at a sheet of paper in front of him, "legal representative with the diplomatic legation to the Federal Republic of Germany for the Republic of Srpska." He turned to Cann. "And Herr John Cann of the United States of America and the Washington law firm of Loring, Matsen, and Gould, representing the defendant, Dubran Mribic." Cann bowed his head slightly and looked around the table, then turned back to the judge.

Stihlmann reached out and patted a thick folder with his left hand. "I have the pleadings and briefs before me, gentlemen, and I have read them carefully." He looked around the table. "May I assume we have all read them carefully?" Nods all around. "Good. I will not dwell on the details then. Herr Mribic has been indicted by the Tribunal for grave breaches of the Geneva Protocols and crimes against humanity based on events alleged to have taken place in Bosnia in the 1990s." He tapped his fingers on the folder again. "As I have said, the details are in here, but since we are here to discuss purely legal issues there is no need in this context to dwell upon them."

Stihlmann was silent for a moment as he gathered his thoughts. "Yes, then. As we all know, notwithstanding his indictment, Herr Mribic remained at large for a period of time." The judge glanced at Divjak and Cesic for just a second and then went on. "Recently, however, he was found and arrested here in Germany and the Tribunal has requested he be surrendered to its custody for trial pursuant to the arrest warrant issued subsequent to the indictment.

"As you all know, the International Criminal Tribunal for the Former Republic of Yugoslavia was formed by the United Nations Security Council by Resolution 827 pursuant to Chapter VII of the UN Charter and, as a member of the United Nations, Germany is bound to cooperate and aid the Tribunal in its work. Moreover, Germany has, like many other countries, actually incorporated the provisions of the Tribunal into its own federal laws. The point being," he glanced meaningfully at Cann, "that the Federal Republic of Germany considers itself both duty bound and honor bound to comply with a valid Tribunal request for the surrender of a suspect in its custody."

Out of the corner of his eye, Cann could see Loens bouncing his head in agreement. Stihlman noted it too, and glanced at the Belgian for a second before continuing. "Herr Mribic, through Mr. Cann, has filed objections to the Tribunal's request on the grounds that the indictments are invalid and flawed on their face, in that they do not constitute offenses under the Tribunal's procedures and provisions or the governing statutes. We also have before us a competing custodial matter in the form of an extradition request initiated by —" he nodded at Divjak, "Serbia, in concert with —" he nodded at Cesic, "the Republic of Srpska."

Loens began to speak, but Stihlmann held him off with an upraised palm.

"The Tribunal, through Herr Loens, has filed its objections to Herr Mribic's filings and seeks dismissal of his objections on the grounds that the matter of the sufficiency of the indictment and the subsequent arrest warrant is properly and exclusively a question for the Tribunal itself to determine and is not a bar to, and indeed should not be, a consideration with regard to the surrender of the accused. The Tribunal also seeks the denial of the competing extradition request on the grounds that its arrest warrant and surrender request supersedes the extradition request by Serbia and Srpska."

Stihlmann folded his hands in front of him and looked at each of the men seated around the table. "Are we in agreement, gentlemen, that I have characterized the issues we are dealing with accurately?"

Loens jumped in first. "Indeed, Herr Richter Stihlmann, you have stated the respective positions quite clearly and succinctly, and I would only like to emphasize the threshold matter of the authority of the Tribunal with respect to both of the defendant's objections."

Stihlmann motioned for Loens to continue.

"Clearly, Herr Richter, the substantive elements regarding the sufficiency of the indictment are questions for the Tribunal itself. The offenses for which the defendant stands indicted constitute criminal acts under the Tribunal charter. To be sure, the components of the offenses — murder, kidnapping, rape, torture — are also criminal acts under the penal code of Germany. But the context of the specific charges, or perhaps it is more accurate to say the universe in which the charges exist, is broader, more global, if you will, to the extent that they encompass and are part of the offenses of genocide and crimes against humanity.

"Now had the offenses had taken place on German territory, and clearly they did not, Germany would have a competing claim to adjudicating jurisdiction over the offenses as well as over the person. But, the offenses took place outside Germany's territory and, with respect, for that reason also, are outside the authority of the German courts to decide."

Stihlmann looked over the top of his glasses at Loens, then turned to Cann. "Herr Cann? A response?"

"Thank you, Herr Richter Stihlmann." He pointed at the folder still under the judge's left hand. "Our position is that the defense does not dispute that the Tribunal has jurisdiction over such charges as are alleged in the indictment. We do differ on the issue of Germany's concurrent jurisdiction over the elements of the offenses, however. As the court knows, there is an ongoing conflict that pits individual states' sovereignty against the reach of international law and the authority of tribunals and forums and organizations established to implement such law. The acceptance of such laws and tribunals and forums by individual states is entirely voluntary. The sovereign state *agrees* to accept the authority of the international tribunal or forum or organization. It is not, and cannot be, imposed on them. In this instance, Germany has, in fact, implemented the Tribunal's charter but in doing so has expressly reserved to itself the authority to make a determination under the provisions of its own laws whether or not a person in its custody will be surrendered to another state or, as in this case, to the Tribunal."

Loens jumped in uninvited. "Herr Richter, with all due respect, Herr Cann is making an argument that is directed at the court's jurisdiction over the person, not its jurisdiction over the offenses —"

Stihlmann raised his hand in a "halt" motion. "Herr Loens. I do not allow interruptions of a party by another in my court. I will give you every opportunity to respond as I find appropriate, but please do not interrupt or speak over anyone." He looked back at Cann. "Herr Cann?"

"Herr Richter, the two questions are sufficiently intertwined that it is impossible to discuss one without the other. However, the essential point is whether the offenses with which Herr Mribic is charged are cognizable offenses under the Geneva Protocols themselves. As we have stated in the briefs, Herr Mribic's position is that he was not acting for any state force or agency, but on his own."

"Which —" The voice belonged to Cesic, the legal representative for the Republic of Srpska who stopped himself after the single word, remembering Stihlmann's caution. He immediately put his hands up in front of him in a display of apology.

"Briefly, Herr Cesic," Stihlmann directed.

"I beg your pardon, Herr Richter Stihlmann. I wished only to say such a characterization of the acts alleged make them criminal matters that should be handled at the state level, not in an international tribunal. And I respectfully call the court's attention to the established principle of *ne bis in idem*."

"*Ne bis in idem*." Stihlmann looked at Cesic over his glasses.

Roughly translated from the Latin, *ne bis in idem* means not twice for the same thing and is essentially the international law equivalent of "double jeopardy." What it means in practice is that, between states that have an agreement on the matter, a person won't be tried by one state for something he's already been tried for in the other country. Significantly, the ICTY had adopted the principle of *ne bis in idem* in its proceedings.

"But Srpska hasn't tried Herr Mribic, have they?" Stihlmann noted pointedly. "And I will tell you that I would look very negatively on such a ploy at this point. Even if a trial in absentia were conducted, and I repeat none has been, or if one were to be convened now, my position would be that neither the Tribunal nor Germany would be under an obligation to honor it. Article 20 of the Rome Statute specifically makes it clear that *ne bis in idem* doesn't need to be applied when an alleged prosecution is done for the purpose of shielding the accused from prosecution by the Tribunal or when it's inconsistent with an intent to bring the person concerned to justice. I'd say both apply here."

Cesic protested. "Herr Richter, I assure you that no such motivation would —"

"Then don't bring it up, Herr Cesic." Stihlmann closed the discussion with an upraised hand.

"If I may, Herr Richter —" Loens jumped in.

Stihlmann nodded.

"The validity of Herr Cann's assertion is, again, a question to be determined by the Tribunal. Consideration of such an essential element of the crime is clearly premature at this stage."

Stihlmann pursed his lips in contemplation. "Frankly, Herr Cann, to my mind, the weight of the argument on this issue, custodial matters aside for the moment, is on the side of the Tribunal. While I would agree that there is some legal merit to the argument you have made, it seems clear to me that the proper forum to determine the sufficiency of the charges is the Tribunal itself, assuming it is entitled to custody of the accused in the first place. And while I am convinced that I and the German legal system are intellectually and morally competent to determine the question, on a purely legal basis, I am less convinced that we are jurisdictionally competent to do so."

"And the competing request for extradition, Herr Richter?" That was Divjak.

"That is a different matter entirely." He looked at Loens. "And one that clearly falls within the competency of this court to decide, don't you agree, Herr Loens?"

"Respectfully, Herr Richter, I do not," Loens regrouped quickly. "It is the position of the Tribunal that its request for surrender of the defendant clearly supersedes not only the extradition request of an individual state, but the authority of the custodial state to do anything other than comply with the request."

Stihlmann raised a single eyebrow at Loens. "So you are saying that the judicial system of Germany, the nation of Germany, is subordinate to the authority of the Tribunal?"

Loens knew he was in a minefield. "In this context, yes, Herr Richter, again with all respect. The extradition request — indeed any extradition request from one state to another — involves what is essentially a peer relationship. An interaction between equals. The relationship between an individual state and the Tribunal is more hierarchical — a relationship of . . ." Loens hesitated, knowing any word he used that said what he wanted to say could offend.

He was right. "Subservience? Superiority? Master-servant?" Divjak helpfully offered Loens a series of unpleasant options.

Stihlmann continued to look at Loens with the upraised brow, offering no comfort or aid to the prosecutor.

"Herr Richter Stihlmann, under no circumstance is my argument intended to question the judicial integrity or the sovereignty of Germany. But, again, with respect, in this context I would point out that Germany has voluntarily and enthusiastically signed on to the Tribunal's charter. Indeed, as Herr Cann has noted, Germany has implemented the Tribunal's charter as the law of Germany. And Article 29 of the Tribunal statute requires member states to co-operate with the Tribunal in many ways including the surrender or transfer of an accused. I would much prefer a different word than 'subservient' but if I must use it, I would say that Germany is not 'subservient' to the Tribunal except in so far as it has chosen to be."

"Not so," Cesic responded.

Stihlmann nodded for Cesic to continue.

"First of all," the Srpskan ticked off his points on his fingers, "the very fact that the individual state must agree to be bound by the Tribunal's protocols is persuasive evidence in itself that the sovereignty of the state cannot be set aside or subordinated unilaterally by the Tribunal. Secondly, to elaborate on Herr Cann's point, Germany, in its implementing legislation specifically applied German extradition procedures to surrender or transfer proceedings to the Tribunal. That alone, in the context of this court and this hearing, should be conclusive as to the court's authority in this matter. And lastly, while the Tribunal protocols themselves do not expressly provide for an individual state to make this kind of determination, the drafts of the protocols for the impending International Criminal Court, into which this Tribunal may ultimately be subsumed, do in fact recognize that it is the right of the individual sovereign states to determine the disposition of the custody of an accused in the presence of competing requests. I —"

"Yes, yes, yes, Herr Cesic. Your point is well taken. I have already considered that."

"But to adopt it is to undermine the whole premise of the Tribunal." Loens sounded almost panicked. "The entire —"

"In which case," Cesic interrupted, "the ICC has already undermined the very principle you are —"

Stihlmann rapped a knuckle on the table, and both men stopped. "Enough, gentlemen. I have read the briefs and I have heard your arguments. I am prepared to issue a ruling.

"The initial question before me is the matter of whether Germany has no choice but to surrender the defendant to the Tribunal." The judge looked at Loens. "With regard to that issue, Herr Loens, it is clear to me that if I am to accept your arguments, I must find that Germany is, as you have argued, subservient to the Tribunal, at least in this context, and has no say over the disposition of a person in its custody. I cannot. I simply do not find your argument to have sufficient weight in either an historical or a present legal sense." Loens looked pained but resigned.

"That leads to the question of whether Germany will surrender the defendant. And to whom?" He looked at Cann. "Your client would like to be released outright, no doubt, Mr. Cann. That will not happen. While you have argued the defense position well, I am convinced that the question of whether the acts alleged fall within the definition of what is prohibited by the Geneva Conventions and other cited laws is clearly a matter to be determined by the Tribunal itself." Stihlmann turned to Cesic. "And with regard to your position Herr Cesic, that the acts alleged constitute criminal acts that should be dealt with by local, state courts, I find that may be so, but at best that would afford an additional forum to address the charges against the defendant. It in no way gives Srpska a claim superior to that of the Tribunal."

Stihlmann turned back to Loens. "What carries the day, Herr Loens, is, as you forcefully presented earlier, both the fact of and the depth of Germany's commitment to the Tribunal and its goals and purposes. A moment ago, I ruled that Germany was not *required* to surrender the defendant to the Tribunal. That in no way means that Germany is unable or unwilling to do so." The judge looked around the table and rapped a knuckle once again. "And it is so ordered."

18

UN Conmmision for Refugees and Human Rights (UNCRHR)
Garmisch–Patenkirchen
Germany

The taxi dropped Loens off in front of the office building where the United Nations Commission for Refugees and Human Rights kept a suite of offices. In recent years, the UN workforce there had been primarily concerned with the vast number of refugees who had fled the war in the Balkans, some estimates running as high as 2.7 million people, most of them Bosnians. Now, with many of them returning to their homes, the workload had diminished. It was, however, unaccompanied by a comparable reduction in the size of the staff or the facility.

Still, there was always room for a "guest" and, given his affiliation with the ICTY, a creation of the UN Security Council, it was both logical and practical that Loens work out of the existing facility while he was in Garmisch for the Mribic hearings.

The office he'd been assigned was on the first floor and to the rear, but he still had a view of the courtyard and even a glimpse of the top of the Zugspitz to the southwest. Loens placed his attaché case on top of the desk and draped his jacket over the couch then walked over and seated himself behind the desk. He picked up the phone and gave the operator a number at The Hague. He waited while the call was transferred several times before reaching the desk of the assistant deputy prosecutor for the ICTY, Jan VerFaar, who was overseeing the matter of Dubran Mribic from his office in The Hague.

"Emiel," the Dutch prosecutor came on the line, his tone jovial. "Good to hear from you." He and the Belgian were friends, having grown up within miles of each other on either side of the Dutch–Belgian border.

"And you, Jan." Although the official languages of the ICTY were English and French, the men spoke Flemish whenever they conversed.

"So," VerFaar said, "I understand you were quite successful today, yes?" As prosecutor in charge, he had direct access to the court clerks and knew what had transpired. What he wanted now from Loens were the details, the nuances, the intangibles that fleshed out the bare bones of the ruling.

"Yes, Jan. Mribic isn't in our custody yet but —"

The conversation was one-sided — all Loens's for some time with VerFaar's role limited to an occasional grunt of assent. When Loens finished, VerFaar was pleased, but cautious. "Very well, Emiel. I will dispatch our security people immediately so they can be on the scene as soon as possible. Let's take nothing for granted. Until we have him, one never knows."

At the reception desk at the front of the building, the operator who'd put Loens's call through to VerFaar was frantically preoccupied with trying to sop up the coffee she had spilled all over the desk, keyboard, and papers she'd had in front of her when the panic had hit.

While Loens' call was being routed, the operator, a trained stenographer, waited ready to transcribe the conversation. She'd been placed in this high position of trust for her specific skills as well as the fact that she was fully fluent in seven languages.

Unfortunately, Flemish wasn't one of them.

When the conversation began, at first the woman thought the men were speaking Dutch, which *was* one of her languages and one to which Flemish is closely related. But within a few sentences, the woman realized she was hesitating at unfamiliar words and inflections and what made it worse was that the men's long acquaintance meant that they were using unfamiliar regional idioms and even childhood slang that she couldn't hope to interpret, let alone transcribe. For a long moment she froze—and, as a result, missed still more of the conversation. It was then that she decided to tape the call for later translation. As she hurriedly reached down to open the desk drawer where she kept the small recorder, however, she turned in her seat and bumped the surface in front of her, spilling the coffee.

Trying to ignore the spill, she fumbled to get the recorder going. The cord was twisted, the jack wouldn't go in, and when she hit the eject button instead of "record," the cassette popped halfway out. She pressed it back in with her thumb, pushed the correct button this time, and saw the red "record" light finally come on.

Shortly thereafter, in an office two floors above Loens's, Helmut Frank, project manager for Rettungsboot, the UNCRHR's non-governmental organization partner in the Bosnian refugee rescue and reintegration project, pushed the stop button on the recorder and gingerly lifted the soggy paper on which the operator's notes had been scribbled and smudged. He looked over at the woman who sat opposite him, her hands clasped formally in her lap and her eyes fixed on a spot somewhere just over the top of Frank's head.

"Not a lot here, Frau Leider, is there?" he said softly. He raised his eyebrows and pursed his lips as he took a breath before saying, "In the future, may I suggest you have the recorder ready at all times? Perhaps even record everything in the first instance? Just in case."

Frau Leider nodded without speaking and, at Frank's dismissive hand gesture, stood and left the room.

Frank sat and pondered for a few moments before lifting the phone and punching a single button that speed dialed its way across several borders directly to its intended recipient's desk.

"Bakken."

"Frank here."

"What is it?" the other man asked brusquely.

"It would appear things are coming to a head," Frank said. "The judge has ordered Mribic turned over to the ICTY."

"As I said he would," Bakken stated smugly. "Well, that's it then. This has gone on long enough. They must be told to stop this foolishness."

"I cannot make that call, Gustav. You know —"

"Yes. I do indeed. Very well, I will make the call."

Detention Facility
Outside Garmisch-Patenkirchen

"So what do you suggest?" Mribic asked after Cann related the day's events.

"Learn to speak Dutch?"

Mribic ignored the remark.

"When will the actual order be issued?"

"Some paperwork is involved. But no more than a day or so, I would imagine."

Mribic looked at Cann for a moment. "Perhaps Matsen would have done a better job."

Cann answered evenly. "Perhaps. There's nobody better. But even Arthur can't make an argument that doesn't exist."

"He should have come himself."

"Why?"

"You don't know? He didn't say?"

Cann shook his head. "He just asked me to do this. On trust."

"And you did. How noble."

Cann was beginning to savor the idea of wiping the smirk off Mribic's face.

"Perhaps he would have come if he knew more than just what he saw on the videotape he received. Perhaps you should tell him that the man he saw on the tape isn't the only one who survived."

Cann didn't understand the reference but said nothing. After a moment, Mribic said pointedly, "Tell Matsen that Savka survived too. The fall didn't kill her."

"Savka?"

Mribic ignored him.

"Tell him she survived the fall and was found by people from a nearby village who cared for her. She recovered from her injuries. And in the course of treating her, they learned something else."

"Which was —?"

"That she was pregnant."

19

Janie was gone. Her room was empty. Not just unoccupied. Vacant. Cleaned out. No clothes. No toiletries. No personal effects. Nothing. No Janie.

Please God, not again.

But this was different. Furden knew that. This was Fredrich. It had to be. This was how he would "address your concerns"? *God, Furden, you're such a jerk!*

She recalled the conversation of the day before when she'd caught up with Fredrich outside his office.

"I want to talk to you about Janie."

"Ms. Furden, I appreciate the information you shared with me recently. It's been a great help. But I can't discuss a patient's therapy with someone not involved in her psychiatric treatment plan. Even if they are staff. I'm sure you understand."

"I shared that information with you, Doctor, because I hoped it would help her."

"As I said, it has."

"It has not. She's gone downhill. She getting worse in every way —"

"We're in a particularly intense stage of her therapy. It can be stressful, I'm afraid. But it's for the best."

"The best? She looks terrible. Her weight's plummeting. Her eyes are hollow. She won't work. Or talk. No, Doctor, it's not for the best. And you can bet Janie's parents won't think it's for the best when they see her this weekend."

"This weekend? I wasn't —" Fredrich's tone changed from patronizing to reasoning. "Ms. Furden — Sara, the therapy really is working. I think we're close to a breakthrough and to interrupt now — You should prevail on the Restons to postpone their visit."

Her eyes widened. "Postpone? It kills them that they can't visit more often. And if I *prevail* upon them for anything, it'll be for them to make you stop what you're doing. *I* may not have the authority but they do and —"

"To disrupt the treatment protocol could be disastrous. If you — and they — truly care about —"

"Don't even go there," Furden spat, jabbing her finger into Fredrich's chest.

The doctor backed away, his hands up in front of him, palms turned out. "All right, Ms. Furden, all right." He considered for a long moment. "Let me think on this. Just please don't do anything rash. I assure you I'll address your concerns."

Sara pressed her hands against the doorjamb and took several deep breaths. Outwardly, she appeared to calm down but inside her emotions raged. After a moment, she blew a burst of air through pursed lips and pushed herself off the door frame. She stepped into the hallway and almost collided with a nurse's aide carrying a tray of meds.

"How long have you been on the floor?" she demanded of the young man who was maneuvering and juggling the tray in an effort to keep the small paper cups from falling off.

"Since seven. This morning."

"Do you know where Janie Reston is? What happened to her? This is her room." She pointed a thumb back over her shoulder.

"The girl in there? She was moved this morning."

"Moved where?"

"She was already gone when they came and told us to pack up her stuff."

"So where'd you take her stuff then?"

"Storage."

Furden felt a sudden wave of dread as the worst, which she had not previously considered, occurred to her. She hesitated. Then, "Storage where?"

"The Alger Wing. The basement. Those closets they have down there."

The Alger Wing. The closed unit. For the patients with more serious psychiatric problems. She should have been furious. But her first feeling was one of relief.

Then she got furious.

Whispering Marsh Rehabilitation Center is among the world's foremost institutions with facilities spread over six hundred wooded acres. The buildings are roughly equidistant from each other in a geometric pattern, except for the Alger Wing. Given it's function, it was isolated from the remainder of the campus both by distance and by landscape.

Sara Furden covered the distance in minutes, burst through an opening in the hedges surrounding the Alger Wing, and ran straight to the first of three buildings laid out as points of an equilateral triangle. Unlike the main campus buildings, these doors were locked. Furden climbed to the top of the steps, not even out of breath, and pressed the button at the right of the frame. The muffled buzz could be heard through the glass, and Furden saw the attendant inside look up. She lifted the ID that hung around her neck and saw the attendant reach down. The movement was accompanied by another buzz, and Furden yanked the door open.

She crossed to the reception desk and held out her ID for the attendant to take a closer look. He gave it a cursory glance, then looked up without expression.

"I'm Janie Reston's physical therapist," Furden said. "She's just been moved here, but her regimen stays the same."

Still without speaking, the attendant slid open the top drawer on his right and lifted out a clipboard. He flipped up a couple of pages. Without looking up, he said, "She's in building two." He flipped his head back and to the right. "But Dr. Fredrich's notes specifically say no visitors." He finally looked up.

"Yeah, but visitors means others. Nonemployees. You know." Furden forced herself to seem almost disinterested.

"And the therapy room's in this building, so she'll have to be brought here if you want to work on her." The attendant reached for the phone, a slightly quizzical look on his face. "That I *will* have to check on. It's pretty unusual to have physical therapy or much of anything on the first day. Give me —"

"That's right. But I'm not doing any therapy at all today. Just a check on her condition. And her attitude to tell you the truth. See how she's settling in. It's been rough at times, so we need to tread carefully. I just have to observe her for a while. *Maybe*," she emphasized the word, "talk to her, if she even seems receptive to that. I'll have to play it by ear. But I won't be doing any work with her today no matter what, that's for sure."

The attendant's hand stayed poised above the phone for a second or two, then he nodded. "Okay." He reached into the second drawer and pulled out a credit card-sized electronic door key, scribbled its serial number on a sheet on the desk, and then turned the sheet around for Furden to initial. "The key will get you in the front door and the observation corridor. But not into any of the rooms. If you need that, come back here. But I will have to call if you want to do anything like that."

"Fine," Furden nodded.

She crossed to the second building at a fast walk. This time the attendant was inside a small room behind a sliding window. Furden quickly flashed her ID. The attendant nodded and went back to her work.

Furden had been in the Alger Wing a few times and was familiar with the layout. One main corridor ran down the center lengthwise with eight rooms on either side. The rooms were fairly large and comfortable, not at all cell-like. But the thick locked steel doors left no doubt that the Alger Wing was a very different place from the rest of Whispering Marsh. As did the foot square, hinged panels on every door that opened only from the outside.

Furden went down the left side of the corridor quietly opening each viewing panel to look for Janie. Several of the rooms were empty. In the sixth room on the left, Furden saw Janie sitting on the single bed with her back to the wall, her eyes closed. Furden had to admit she almost looked at peace.

Immediately, though, Furden's eye caught a movement to the left and she moved to widen her angle of view. Fredrich sat in a chair opposite Janie with a pen in his hand and a pad on his knee. He was speaking, but the sound was blocked by the plexiglass panel in the opening.

Fredrich looked up from the pad, and Furden quickly but quietly closed the panel and stepped back from the door. Then she remembered the observation corridor that ran the length of the building behind the walls of the treatment rooms. She forced herself to walk at a normal pace and nodded to the attendant as she passed. She turned right and walked almost to the end of that hallway where there was a small door on the right. Furden inserted the pass key and opened it.

The observation corridor was about three feet wide and was unlit, the only illumination coming from farther down, about where the one-way acrylic window into Janie's room would be. Furden pressed against the wall until she was opposite the lighted panel and could see inside. Janie was still immobile on the bed and Fredrich still appeared to be doing all the talking. Furden reached down and gingerly turned a knob on the face of a perforated metal speaker set into the wall. Fredrich's voice came through.

"Remember, Janie, no matter what you see from before, from the past, you're in your safe place now. No one can hurt you here." Fredrich spoke softly without looking at Janie, head down, scribbling on his notepad.

Janie kept her head back and said nothing.

"Do you understand that, Janie?" He looked up. "It's okay to remember. It's good to remember." He leaned forward a bit. "He can't hurt you. But you have to remember."

" 'Member," Janie mumbled. Outside in the corridor, Furden caught her breath as she began to realize how Fredrich had used the information she'd given him.

"You told me, Janie," Fredrich lied. "You told me about the man hitting you. Over and over."

Janie flinched and her face tightened.

"No, Janie. You're in your safe place. You can't feel it now. You can know it, but you can't feel it. Okay?"

Janie's face relaxed a bit. " 'Kay." But she made another face.

"Now it's important that you see who's hitting you, Janie. You can see his face if you open your eyes. Not here. Not now. Open your eyes in your mind and look up at the man who's hitting you."

"Don' wan' to."

"I know, Janie. I know. You don't want to because you don't want to remember, do you? You don't want to know. But you do know, don't you?"

Janie's face contorted even more.

"Think, Janie. Remember what you know. Remember the tape." Fredrich looked down at his notes and rapidly scribbled. "You watched the tape with me, remember?" he lied again. "You've seen the tape and you know the man. He doesn't want you to remember. He wants you to think he's your friend. But he's not. I am. And I want to help you." Janie began to rock her head back and forth. "He hurt you, Janie, and doesn't want to help you. I do. You know who it was. I told you. Now *you* need to tell *me*."

Janie's head rocked more and more until she started hitting the back of it on the wall behind her. And still she continued. Harder and harder. A red smear appeared on the wall and still Fredrich sat taking notes, doing nothing about it.

Furden couldn't stand by. She lashed out a fist and pounded on the high impact acrylic. "Stop, you bastard!"

Fredrich couldn't hear the shout, but the first thump on the glass caused him to jump up and look around wildly. He took a step toward the sound and peered into the window. "How dare you!" he shouted. "This is privileged. Who is that?" He quickly spun around and darted out of the room, turned right, and charged down the hall. As he reached the end of the central corridor he shouted over at the attendant to follow him as he turned right to the door to the observation corridor. The attendant caught up just as he got the door open and charged in.

Furden ran back down the observation corridor to confront Fredrich. She was just at the door when it opened. Fredrich saw her and lunged forward, punching his index finger at her chest. "How dare you?"

Furden screamed at him. "How dare you, you little prick?" She grabbed Fredrich's extended finger and twisted his hand around so that now his palm faced up but his finger pointed down. She followed with a short front kick to the doctor's groin that wasn't precisely on target but caused Fredrich to step back. That gave Furden the range she needed to plant the sole of her right foot into the doctor's chest and send him slamming back into the wall opposite. As he fell, he took the stunned attendant down with him. She bent over Fredrich.

"That's not therapy," she spat at him with her thumb jerked back over her shoulder. "That's not treatment, you asshole! What the hell do you think you're doing?"

Fredrich flinched at the volume of her voice and the spittle that accompanied it, but still shot back, "I don't answer to you, Furden. I'm in charge now. She's mine. I'm her attending psychiatrist and I Baileyed her." He snorted loudly. "You want to interfere? Well, no more. You're finished. Your unprofessional behavior. This — this assault on me and another employee. Interference in a treatment program to the extreme detriment of the patient. You're gone. And so is your license."

Furden knew he was right. He was the *doctor* and in the hierarchy she was the serf. He had the power and she had — she had — *fuck it!* She had had enough was what she had. She reached down and grabbed the flinching Fredrich by his tie and twisted it around its knot until his face started to turn red. She spun him and pushed him back into the observation corridor where he stumbled backward and fell into a sitting position. The attendant put her hands up in surrender. Furden mumbled a semisincere *"sorry,"* relieved her of her pass cards and master key, and ordered her into the corridor with a flip of her head. But not before using the hall fire extinguisher to disable the inside locking mechanism to prevent their escape.

"I'll call and tell someone you're in here." She started to slam the door but quickly yanked it open again. "Do you have wheelchairs here?" she asked. The attendant nodded and pointed toward a door near her station. Furden slammed the door to the observation corridor and gave it a tug to make sure it was locked. Then she dashed over to where the attendant had pointed, which turned out to be an equipment storage room with several wheelchairs in it. Furden grabbed one and ran with it to the sixth door on the left, which she opened with the master key.

Janie was still slumped on the bed with her eyes closed but at least she'd stopped beating her head against the wall. Furden crossed quickly and wrapped her arms around Janie, cradling her head in her hands. She checked Janie's wound and saw it didn't require immediate treatment, then gently lifted her almost deadweight into the wheelchair. She grabbed a blanket off the bed and threw it over Janie's lap and wheeled her out into the corridor. She stopped at the emergency door when she saw the red circle on the push handle. "Alarm will sound if door is opened." She reversed direction and wheeled Janie to the front of the building, watching carefully for activity.

She darted into the attendant's station and grabbed a spare white coat. Then, taking a deep breath, she pushed open the front door, turned to her right, and wheeled Janie along the landing and down the ramp onto the sidewalk. She still saw no one and tried to appear calm and leisurely — an attendant taking a patient for some air. At the bottom of the ramp, Furden continued down along the side of the building and along the paved path that led to benches and tables in a wooded grove. Here, shielded from Building One by Building Two, Furden looked around one more time and then wheeled Janie off the path and into the surrounding woods.

Now came the hard part — leaving Janie alone.

She knelt down in front of Janie, smoothed the blanket on her, and looked at her face. Then she checked Janie's breathing and pulse. It was steady. Knowing that was as comforted as she was going to get, she took off through the woods behind her and emerged into one of the rear parking lots. There, she broke into a steady run and took an indirect route back to her own building and entered it from the rear. In and out with her purse and keys in less than a minute, Furden got her car and drove back to the rear lot nearest to where she'd left Janie. This was as remote as Whispering Marsh property got and Furden's car was the only one in the lot. She jumped out and retraced her steps through the woods to where Janie sat just as she'd left her.

Since the ground was too soft to push the wheelchair through, Furden lifted Janie up into her arms. She was so light it amazed and concerned her at the same time. Still, it was a difficult trek back to the car, but she made it and propped Janie up in the reclined front-passenger seat. She left the Whispering Marsh grounds by the rear entrance and turned north toward her apartment. As soon as she did, she realized she couldn't go there. In fact, it suddenly occurred to her that she hadn't thought this through at all. And now, she had no idea what to do next.

20

Loring, Matsen, and Gould
Washington, D.C.

"*Schade. Es muss behoben werden. Gleich.*" Katherine Price spoke into the mouthpiece that curled around the front of her face. She listened for a further moment then said, "*Ja. Bestimmt.*" She nodded. "*Tschuss.*"

She put the phone down and closed the file folder in front of her and plopped it on the upper-right corner of her desk. She pulled the headset off with one hand and turned to take a different folder off the credenza behind her just as the phone buzzed. Foregoing the headset, Price punched the intercom button.

"Katherine, there's a woman on the phone who's calling for the second time in just a few minutes. She asked for Mr. Cann the first time and when I told her he was out of the country, she asked for Arthur. But he's still in that meeting with the Secretary, and I didn't know if I should interrupt. She sounds upset, almost panicky. I asked her if anyone else could help her. She said she didn't know. Her name's Sara Furden and it's about Janie Reston, and I knew you'd been doing something for Arthur related to that. Do you want to take the call? I hope it's okay."

"It's fine, Phyllis. I'll take it. What line?"

"Three."

"Okay." Price punched it up. "Katherine Price."

It was quiet at the other end of the line, then, "Um . . . my name is Sara Furden and —"

Price waited a moment then said gently, "I know who you are, Ms. Furden. We've never met, but I know your name. And I do know you had — you're a friend of Janie Reston. Her family."

"What else do you know?" Despite the urgency of the situation, Furden was cautious.

So was Price. "Well, I know you were at Charlestown when Janie was — hurt. I know a good deal of what happened there. Not all. And I know that you gave up a lot to be with her. I'm a partner here at the firm. And good friends with Arthur. And John. Because of that, and because I'm licensed down there, Arthur asked me to make some inquiries."

"What kind of inquiries?"

Price hesitated but something about Furden's tone, the strain in her voice, made her answer. "John had some concerns about certain aspects of Janie's treatment and —"

"Dr. Fredrich?"

Price's leaned forward. "Yes, it does have to do with Dr. Fredrich. Why?"

The dam burst on Furden's control. "He was killing her! I had to get her out! But now I don't know what to do."

Price immediately became a tightly coiled spring. "Okay, take a breath. Tell me what happened," she said briskly.

"He had her so heavily medicated. He was —"

"Medicated with what?"

"God, I don't know," Furden answered impatiently. "But she was practically in a trance. And he kept asking her — pressuring her — to remember things. And she couldn't. And then she started to hurt herself. She was banging her head against the wall, and he wasn't even trying to stop her. So I got her out."

"Got her out. You mean out of Whispering Marsh?"

"Yes, I —"

"How? What exactly did you do?"

As Furden related the series of events to her, Price's eyebrows raised, but she said nothing. Instead, she absorbed the information and drew some conclusions.

"Okay. For what's it's worth, Sara, I think you did the right thing. There'll be some legal issues but there are also defenses. We'll stand with you all the way. And I can guarantee you that Arthur will back you on removing Janie. As a co-guardian he can approve that. Janie's parents would too."

"Except Fredrich said he'd Baileyed her. That's got to change things, doesn't it?"

Price was caught off guard for a moment, the term "Baileyed" not immediately registering with her. "He what?"

"He Bailey Acted her."

Then it registered. The Bailey Act. Involuntary commitment. Price was familiar with it in general. And, yes, it changed things.

"Okay, Sara. You're right. That does make a difference. But, let us work on it. We're still with you — and Janie. So, right now, you're in the car with Janie, heading where?"

"South. Just south. That's just it. I don't know! I should have thought this through, I know. But I didn't. I just acted."

"Sometimes you have to," Price reassured her. "South, you said. Is that where you live?"

"No, I live north. But I figure they know that so I decided to go in the opposite direction. Maybe go back later."

"Good thinking. But don't go back. Not till we stabilize the situation. Now, first things first. Is Janie unconscious?"

"Well, out of it anyway. She seems okay, but how can I know for sure?" Furden was close to snapping.

"Stay calm." Price had put on the headset to free her hands and was already tapping on her computer keyboard as she spoke. "Okay, Sara, listen." She ran her finger down the the list that had popped up on her computer monitor. "Do you know where Blanding is?"

"The town? Yeah."

"Okay. Drive to Blanding. Somewhere along the way — give me ten minutes — then call this number." She rattled off twelve digits. "Got it?"

"No, I don't," Furden protested. "I don't have a pen or —"

"Punch the number into your cell, but don't hit send. Just save it. Okay?"

"Okay."

"I'll tell you more when you call me back."

"Okay. I guess I have to trust you."

"I guess you do," Price said abruptly, then softened. "Look, you can trust me. Think about it. You called the firm. Asked for John or Arthur. They gave you to me. I didn't seek you out. You found me. I'm going to track Arthur down right now. He'll be with me when you call back. You can trust me." She paused then said, "And anyway. What choice do you have?"

Furden nodded.

"Ten minutes, Sara. We'll be waiting."

Arthur Matsen was on the phone when Katherine Price came in and he watched with interest as she placed an Iridium satellite phone down on his desk. Still listening to whomever was on the other end, he slid two yellow message slips toward her. One said, "Whispering Marsh. Urgent." The other said "Sara Furden. T-frd to K. Price."

Price held out the one that referred to her and nodded. Then she held out the other and pointed at the phone with an inquiring look. This time Matsen nodded and put his hand over the mouthpiece. In a strained whisper, he said, "Janie's gone missing."

Price shook her head sharply in the negative while holding her index finger to her lips.

Matsen focused an intense stare on Price's face, but kept listening to the party at the other end. Finally, he spoke into the phone, "Well, keep me posted. Anything you learn I want to know at once." He listened a couple of seconds longer. "No. We'll find her parents and let them know." He hung up and immediately said, "Tell me."

"Sara Furden called me a few minutes ago," Price explained. "She's taken Janie out of Whispering Marsh." Matsen's questioning frown grew and he raised his eyebrows. "Here's why."

Matsen listened without interrupting and when Price had finished, he said quietly, "Fredrich." He thought for a moment longer. "Never doubt John's instincts." Price nodded. Matsen thought a bit more and continued slowly. "And I do agree with your analysis of the legal issues, by the way. We'll get staff on those right away. Particularly this Bailey Act business. If it's anything like the statutes I'm familiar with, if they find Janie they'll give her right back to Fredrich."

Price grimaced and nodded.

Matsen flicked his eyes at his phone and said, "As you surmised, that was Whispering Marsh. The medical director. He said only that Fredrich and an attendant had just been pulled out of a locked room. And that Fredrich was claiming that Janie had been taken off grounds by a staff member. That's how he phrased it. He didn't name Sara." He tightened his lips. "Said he didn't know a lot of the details yet. He did say they'd notified the authorities."

"Janie's parents don't know?"

Matsen shook his head. "Apparently they're en route for a visit. No cell phone or anything. We'll track them down. Maybe we can get the situation a little better in hand in the meantime."

Price hesitated then asked. "Arthur, I don't get this impression, but I have to ask. Is there any chance Janie might be in danger from Sara?"

Matsen shook his head firmly. "Only from smothering, maybe. Sara went through a very bad time after Janie's ordeal. She blamed herself for it. Unreasonably. It's true she'd been instrumental in bringing Janie to Charlestown, but she wasn't the cause of what happened. Only the bad guys are to blame for that. But Sara couldn't separate her role in bringing Janie to Charlestown from the sheer horror of what was done to her, and she snapped." He looked at Price over his glasses. "My term, not theirs. But Sara withdrew. Isolated herself. Wouldn't leave the house or see anyone. Then, as I understand it, one day Janie's mother went over and physically dragged Sara out. Brought her to the hospital to visit Janie. And Janie responded. Squeezed her hand and tried to speak. Sara collapsed. But afterward, from that point on, she's been utterly devoted to Janie. Maybe even to an unhealthy degree. But if it is, it's unhealthy only to Sara. Or others perhaps. Not to Janie, I'm convinced. Sara would die for her. I have no doubt."

Price looked at the Iridium phone. "She's going to call me in," she looked at her watch, "about five minutes. I told her to head toward a town called Blanding and call me from there."

"Why this Blanding?"

"Mostly to keep her moving in a direction away from the scene. Though I did try checking the secure database for any safe facilities we might have in the area that have medical capability."

Matsen reached out and pressed a single digit on his phone, waited a moment, then spoke. "Ted. Arthur. Who — yes, fine. No. Listen. What have we got in the area of the Georgia–South Carolina border? Secure. With medical resources." He listened, then, "East coast. Do a radius from Savannah." Matsen scribbled numbers on a pad in front of him and pushed it over to Price. Price shook her head no, gesturing to remind him that Furden was about to call on her phone. Matsen, nodded, ended the call to Ted, and dialed the numbers himself. At that moment, Price's Iridium phone warbled.

Simultaneous conversations ensued.

"Hi, Sara. Listen. I'm here with Arthur. We're going to give you a location. Get the both of you out of sight until we get a better handle on this. And get Janie looked after too." In her other ear, Price could hear Matsen asking about distances and times and then he put up his index finger to get her attention. "Hold on, Sara," Price said as Matsen handed his phone over to her. Now Price was sitting with a phone against each ear. She listened briefly to the man on the other end of Matsen's phone.

"Sara," Price relayed. "Change of plans. Someone's coming to you. It'll be a lot quicker. Where are you?" Price listened and repeated the location into the other phone. Then back to Sara, "The driver says he's almost there."

Furden hung up the phone and walked back to the car. She leaned inside the open passenger-side window as if she were carrying on a conversation. Parked off in the corner of the convenience store parking lot, it was not a difficult charade to pull off. Within minutes, an ambulance pulled into the lot—no lights, no siren—and the driver caught her eye. Furden got back into the driver's seat of her car and followed the ambulance out onto the road.

After a short distance, they turned onto a dirt road that led into a wooded area. The ambulance stopped and two men got out. One stood by the driver's side door watching the surrounding area while the other one walked around to open the rear doors. Furden crossed around the front of her car and opened the passenger side door. Janie was still lying back in the reclined front seat with her eyes closed. When Furden reached in for her, Janie responded ever so slightly. Furden and the ambulance attendant lifted Janie up into the rear of the ambulance where they strapped her in.

Furden touched Janie's neck and got what seemed to be a good regular pulse. She also observed that Janie's breathing appeared smooth and regular. Furden hardly noticed when the man who had helped with Janie touched her arm and told her that he would take care of the car and that she should stay with Janie.

As if.

21

Club Interpole
Schwabing District
Munich

It was late afternoon and the Club Interpole was already picking up steam. The name was a take-off on the ubiquitous Metropole clubs throughout Germany and Europe — the world for that matter. It was also a tweak at the authorities in that the owners were fully aware that the mockery would bring them to the attention of the real Interpol and other police forces. But they didn't care. Such was the power wielded by organized crime, particularly Erwin Jost, in this part of Germany.

A few customers sat at small round tables in the dimly lit room, but the bar stools around the perimeter of the raised dance floor were all occupied by men with upcast eyes. The object of their attention was a naked young woman moving with a robotic languidity. The men looked up at her. She looked down on them.

In the background, a tinny saxophone blared a slow, throbbing whine of accompaniment, which didn't stop or pause when one dancer replaced another. It was up to them to pick up the beat, such as it was.

As a new girl climbed the steps to the platform, the one finishing her stint crawled around the floor picking up bills and coins. One man, seated near the stage exit, toyed with her by holding out a bill then quickly withdrawing it when she reached for it. After several such games, the girl turned away in disgust and frustration. As she did, she caught the eye of a man standing at the door to the back rooms who glared the message that she should not leave without the money. Forcing a smile, the girl knelt down on the stage and wrapped her arms around the man's head, pulling his face into her breasts, distracting him long enough for her to grab the bill and leap gracefully back. As the girl went backstage, she handed all the money to the glowering man at the door who looked down into his palm and shook his head. Then he looked through a glassed opening in the wall at the opposite end of the stage into an office where a dark-haired, middle-aged man watched from his desk. The man at the door shook his head in the negative again and Branko Jost, the manager of Club Interpole, nodded and pushed an intercom button. A scratchy voice responsed.

"Have Oma bring Doina to me."

After a few minutes, the office door opened and Doina, the girl who had been on the stage, entered accompanied by a silver-haired woman who looked to be in her sixties and who walked with an odd side-to-side rocking gait. Branko ignored the older woman and initially said nothing to Doina. He just stared at the young woman before giving his head a slow negative shake. "How much did you make in your last set, Doina?"

Doina said nothing until Oma translated the question into Romanian. "Oma" means "granny" or "granma" and the old woman was sort of a housemother to the girls. She also had a facility with languages and acted as interpreter. The pretty, dark-haired Doina listened and then answered, "How can I know since I must give all to you." She spoke with her head held high and she stared unwaveringly into Branko's eyes.

Oma translated the Romanian into German for Branko. "Yes, well, that was the agreement wasn't it, Doina?" he replied. "We provide you with transportation and a job and you must repay us our costs plus our fee. Is that not so?"

After a moment's pause for the translation, Doina's eyes flared. "Transportation and job, and I repay and pay fee, yes, that was agreement. But this," she waved her arm around her head, "was not job I was told. The man said I could be au pair to good family. I am good girl. I am not naked dancer. That was not agreement."

Branko nodded some more. "But this job, if you try, pays more than au pair ever does. If you apply yourself, you can pay your debt much more quickly by doing this." He raised his eyebrows in a gesture of inquiry.

"But I don't want to do *this*." Doina spat the word. "I want to —" her composure began to break and she stopped to catch her breath. "I want to go home," she said softly.

"Home," Branko repeated after the translation. "Fine," he said. "We can do that." Doina looked up, hopeful but wary. "Of course, you will need to pay for your return transportation. In advance. In addition to what you already owe. How do you propose to get the money?"

Doina seemed to shrink as she stood there. After a long time she said, "Let me work as waitress. Maid. Anything. I will pay. I promise."

"But you promised to pay us to bring you here. And now you don't want to keep that promise. Why should I believe you now?"

"No," Doina said earnestly, "I keep that promise. And this one too. I work hard to pay."

"But how will you get a job? You have no papers here. No passport, no identification card, nothing."

Tears began to form in Doina's eyes. "But you have my papers." In spite of herself, she was starting to cry. "You took my papers. You give them to me and I get job and pay." She swallowed a sob. "I promise!" she cried.

A small smile had formed on Branko's lips as he watched Doina's growing sense of defeat. "Oh, Doina, if we give you your papers, you will run away. We both know that."

"No, I promise. I will work hard and pay. Just —" Again she waved her arm around. "Just not this."

Branko pretended to consider it, then shook his head. "No, it would take far too long for you to pay us that way. We need our money more quickly. Please," he adopted a gentle tone that almost sounded sincere, "you must dance."

Doina drew on her reserves and straightened. "I would rather die."

Branko stared at Doina for a long time. *Schade,* he thought. *Such a pity.* Doina was stunningly pretty and, still just seventeen, had that childlike innocence that sold so well. If only she could see that the dancing is so much easier. The other will use her up so much more quickly. *Schade,* he thought again. Finally he spoke. "Very well, Doina, you won't dance."

Oma translated the words for Doina giving them the same inflection of finality that Branko had used. And though the words might have given comfort, his tone instilled a sense of dread. He flicked his hand in the air. "Go back to the room and wait." He looked at the woman called Oma. "Stay with her."

When they were gone, Branko looked through the open panel in the wall until he caught the attention of the bouncer. He called the man in with a gesture and told him, "Doina is going to the 'Park.' She will need to be — broken in." The man smirked. "Call our off-duty people and have them meet you there. You can go first if you like, but stay there when the others are with her. Don't leave her alone. Understood? We don't need damaged goods. It's not good business." As the man started to leave, Branko added, "And have Oma nearby. Doina will need her when you are done."

United Nations Commission for Refugees and Human Rights
Tuzla, Bosnia-Hercegovina

Assistant deputy high commissioner for the Tuzla field office of the United Nations Commission for Refugees and Human Rights, Gustav

Bakken was a tall man who carried himself in such a way that he appeared to be puffing out his chest all the time. With his slender frame, spiky crewcut black hair gone gray except for the streaks at the temples, angular face, deep set dark, piercing eyes, and hawkish nose, he closely resembled a six foot four osprey.

The image was particularly apt at the moment because he stood at his office window peering intently down from his third-floor aerie at two young girls who were walking briskly down the street. He followed them visually, like the predator he resembled, head bent to the left, telephone crooked between his shoulder and his left ear, until they turned the corner and went out of sight. Only then did he refocus on the beeping tone at the other end of the connection. Finally, the phone was answered by a velvety female voice saying, "*Club Interpole. Fur Deutsch, bitte Drucken sie eins, for English, press two, pour le Francais, appuyez le numero trois.*" Bakken knew the extension he wanted and impatiently punched the numbers into his handset. The message stopped immediately and an instant later a voice answered, "Branko."

"Bakken here." As always, no chitchat. "I want this Mribic business concluded. At once. Do you understand?"

After a suitably insolent pause, Branko replied. "What I understand is that it is not your decision to make."

The Norwegian's eyes narrowed and his mouth pursed at this effrontery. "This should never have been allowed to proceed. Now it has reached a point — do you even know what has developed? Do you not have any intelligence?" Bakken congratulated himself on the double meaning.

"We know of the hearing, if that's what you're referring to," Branko retorted. "Unlike you, it does not make us pull the covers over our head or hide under the bed."

"Mistaking caution for fear is a very dangerous thing to do, young man. Don't make that error."

"I am not making an error. And I am not acting out of fear, as are you. I repeat that this decision is not yours. And I certainly do not take orders from you."

With a great effort, Bakken forced himself to answer evenly. "It is not a matter of taking orders, you fool. It is a matter of doing what is best for the overall picture. Even you should be able to grasp that."

Branko snapped back. "Take care who you call 'fool,' Bakken. I'm not one of your lackeys. Stick to bullying the ones who can't fight back. That's all you're good at." He laughed derisively. "Things are under control and will be handled. If you cannot at least pretend that you have testicles, you should not be playing in this man's game."

Bakken decided he would not argue with this hooligan. "Your interest in my testicles is noted, Branko. But I repeat. This has gone far enough. I want it fixed."

Branko smoldered at Bakken's insult. "And once again. It is not your decision. It will be dealt with."

"Yes, it will." He broke the connection.

At both ends of the conversation the two men looked at their respective phones.

"Cretin," thought Gustav Bakken.

"Arse," thought Branko Jost.

Hanging up the phone, Bakken allowed himself to seethe with indignation because he was the kind of man who enjoyed it. Other's deficiencies ratified his own superiority. After a moment, validated, he would move on. Let others sort these things out.

He glanced at his watch. He had time for a quick drink before the evening's scheduled delivery. He would not miss it. The product — his smile grew at the thought of them as such — were so fresh, excited, always a bit unsure. Vulnerable. That's what he liked the best.

He tugged his cuffs down over his wrists and looked around to see that all was in order. Then he locked up and headed for Arizona. The Arizona Market in Brcko to be precise.

• • •

As the Bosnian war wound down, NATO forces were charged with keeping the warring factions apart. One of the zones of separation enforced by NATO was in northeast Bosnia, near the town of Brcko, which is about an hour's drive northeast from Tuzla at a point where Bosnia, Srpska, and Serbia all come together. The demarcation line between the Serbs and Bosnians in that area was an existing road that ran along and between the lands controlled by the opposing forces. Because of the sandy nature of the road and the surrounding areas, US forces nicknamed it the Arizona road.

In 1996, the U.S. Army graded and prepared a large area adjacent to the Arizona road to create a marketplace for individuals and merchants so the displaced and disadvantaged could begin to put their shattered lives into a semblance of order. The idea was a sound one and what came to be known as the Arizona Market sprang up and grew larger and faster than envisioned, so large and so fast that the authorities could not keep up with it. And when the Dayton Accords set up boundaries and spheres of authority after the conflicts ended, somehow Brcko was left out, so that when all was said and done, Brcko was officially part of none of them. Lacking any form of authority and requiring allegiance only to one's self, it became a magnet and a haven for those who exist best in a vacuum of decency.

Bakken's first trip to the Arizona Market came within weeks of his posting as assistant deputy high commissioner in the Tuzla office of the United Nations Commission for Refugees and Human Rights. It was a good posting. The salary of a P-4 United Nations official was good, the perks satisfactory, and the prestige suitable for a man with Bakken's high self-image. But there were three additional off-the-books perks that Bakken especially liked about being a UN official: visibility, opportunity, and impunity. And ever since he'd attained Professional Grade, he'd never had an assignment that didn't offer all three.

But the Tuzla posting was to add an entirely new dimension for him.

In Tuzla he and the power he possessed by virtue of his office were known throughout the region. That was the visibility. From the visibility, came the opportunity. Within weeks of his posting, a voice on the phone invited him to come to the Arizona Market to discuss a "mutually beneficial arrangement." Bakken had been briefed on the lawless, no-man's-land that was Brcko, and knew from reports that the Arizona Market was the baddest part of this badlands. But he was UN. And with that came the impunity.

That first time he'd been picked up in Tuzla by an armored Land Rover and driven to Brcko accompanied by two bodyguards in addition to the driver. Upon their arrival, the Land Rover was driven very slowly down the Arizona Road so Bakken could see the incredible black market in action. Wherever he looked, something illicit was taking place. On one corner, there was an open-backed, half-ton truck stacked with what appeared to be bales of marijuana. Bales of it! In the middle of the next block, a man stood with a Soviet-era RPG launcher casually resting on his shoulder as he accepted a light for his cigarette from another man who was wearing a very large sidearm in a holster on his belt.

They drove on, passing shop after shop, booth after booth, open area after open area, some with apparently legal goods for sale but, the driver had explained, even those products had been obtained illegally.

The Land Rover continued farther down the Arizona Road and then slowed even more as it approached yet another intersection. Bakken couldn't believe his eyes. There, on a corner, stood about fifteen girls, all, to his eye, exquisitely young and exquisitely beautiful.

And they were naked.

Bakken sat up and twisted in the rear seat of the Land Rover, his face pressed against the window. In his travels and postings he'd seen many of the public sex emporia throughout the world: Canal Street in Amsterdam, the Reeperbahn in Hamburg, Luz in Sao Paolo, Kabukicho in Tokyo. But those were different. Older, mostly. Jaded. Resigned. Innocent once but no more.

Here, these were girls. Children. Not posing or strutting. Some trying to cover themselves, others just looking stunned. All were afraid. Shy, vulnerable, innocent. Bakken was unconsciously rubbing his groin as he craned his neck to view the scene as the Land Rover moved on.

The negotiation, such as it was, took mere moments.

Bakken had seen the girls on the corner, he was asked.

Yes, he had.

Well, the people who matter in Brcko were having some difficulty in transporting the girls to their ultimate destinations. Paperwork difficulties. Do you see?

He did, indeed.

So if they could just travel under United Nations documentation. As refugees. Well, the people who matter in Brcko would be most grateful. And would be happy to reward Bakken. Most generously.

And would that generosity extend to the lovely young things he had just seen?

His pick. Any time. Any group. Anything he wanted.

It was the proverbial offer he couldn't refuse.

And neither could the girls.

Bakken's earlier conversation with Branko Jost was the furthest thing from his mind as he sat in a straight-back chair, legs crossed, body turned slightly, left arm draped along the back. His chin was raised, his lips pursed as he watched the seven new girls walk through the door.

They were all pretty. And they all exhibited a combination of apprehension and youthful excitement about the expected overnight stop on their way to their final destinations. Several of the girls were quiet. Two of them, a raven-haired Moldavian and a blond Ukranian, who looked even younger than the rest, whispered to each other as they gathered. When all seven were inside, the driver of the van closed and bolted the door. Across the room, another man who had been waiting with Bakken for their arrival shouted a command.

"*Skinuti se!*"

The girls grew silent, but didn't move. None understood Serbo-Croatian. The men smiled at one another.

"*Разденьтесь!*" The man repeated the word in Russian. The look on one girl's face told him she understood but, whether from shock, disbelief, or defiance, she still didn't move.

"*Desbracati!*" the man finally shouted in Romanian. Now, they understood. Still, none moved to comply. Mostly because they didn't think they'd heard what they did.

Bakken, who'd watched the game played out many times, shifted in his chair and recrossed his legs. The man next to Bakken nodded to the driver who immediately grabbed the blond Ukranian by the arm and led her to the center of the room. Placing his hands on her shoulders, he positioned her in the center where all coud see. Without a word, he slapped her across the face, then grabbed the front of her dress at the top and yanked downward, ripping it violently off her body. The two actions took no more than five seconds.

The blond girl stood in shock with her hand to her cheek. Still without saying a word, the man went over and grabbed another girl, one of the tall ones, and pulled and pushed her into the center where, without warning, he punched her. She dropped like a stone and the man bent down and ripped her clothes off as she lay unconscious. The message received, the rest of the girls started to undress, most with tears in their eyes.

Bakken watched raptly as the girls disrobed. Every one of them halted when they got down to their underwear, but it took only one "example" to make them realize they were to leave nothing on. The blond Ukranian girl hadn't been wearing a bra but still had her white cotton panties on and hadn't moved to remove them. As the driver turned toward her, Bakken held up his hand to him. He uncrossed his legs slowly, then stood and walked over to the girl. He curled his forefinger under her chin and lifted her head. She looked up at him blankly. No tears. No nothing.

"I know this is difficult," he said softly. "Shall I take you out of here?"

The girl just stared at first, then began to focus on his words. Then she nodded, hope beginning to rise.

"But you will be nice to me, yes?"

It took a moment, but then she understood, the spark of hope left her eyes.

She nodded again, this time looking down at the floor.

God, he loved this!

The Park
Schwabing District
Munich

The last of the Interpole staff had finished with Doina and the head bouncer ordered her to clean herself up. Utterly broken, she got out of the bed and crossed to the single sink and robotically obeyed. When she was done, she sat back down on the bed and began to cry. After a moment, the bouncer left the room and sent Oma in. The old woman went and sat next to Doina and took her head in her arms and rocked gently, tch'ing and shh'ing and doing what she could to calm the convulsive sobs that wracked the young girl's body.

"I was wait for Stefan," Doina said. "I was always wait. I was good girl, Oma. I was good girl."

"Shh, shh, Doina," Oma had said. "You are still good girl. Nothing can change this. You are still good girl. Shh, shh."

Doina's sobs grew quieter but they never stopped.

22

Loring, Matsen, and Gould
Washington, D.C.

Matsen enumerated the priorities on his thumb and index finger. "One, keep Janie safe. Immediately and for the long term. She's not in danger for the moment. Only I know where she is and that's how we're going to keep it." Everyone around the conference table — Matsen, Price, two junior associates, and one very experienced paralegal — nodded. "Two, we need to mount a defense for Sara." Matsen gestured to Price to take the lead.

"There's a BOLO — 'be on the lookout' — for Sara and Janie," she began. "And I guarantee you there's a warrant in the works for Sara. Assault, false imprisonment, kidnapping. Although, given the guardianship situation" — she nodded toward Matsen — "we should be able to defeat the kidnapping issue. Approve Sara's taking Janie out retroactively." Price pointed at their top paralegal. "Helena, get us a quick memo on local law and procedure. That includes profiles on the local prosecutors and judges. I'm admitted down there, but it's been a while." She switched her gaze to one of the associates. "Check out their self-defense law, too, Richard. Protection of others issues. Imminence of harm, and so forth." The young man nodded. "And

153

look at lesser charges — interference with a custodial order versus kidnapping. Anything like that.

"Also, people," she pointed a pencil across the table, "let's hit back. See what we can throw at Fredrich. Hit him hard and put him on the defensive."

They nodded.

"Beth," Price turned to one of the associates, "you've reviewed the Bailey Act. Give us what you've got."

"Okay. The Bailey Act allows for the involuntary commitment of a person under three scenarios. By court order, by a law enforcement officer, or certification by a mental health professional that the person is a danger to himself or others." She looked up. "In this case, it sounds like the third scenario; that this Dr. Fredrich just signed the papers and took her."

"No corroboration. No second opinion?" Richard asked incredulously.

Beth shook her head. "Not at this stage. Initially, all that's required is the certification."

"Surely, there's a review of some kind," Matsen said.

"The statute requires the 'receiving facility' to confirm the initial certification 'without unnecessary delay.' "

"So what's the receiving facility?" Helena Valdez interjected.

"Sara said she took Janie from a secure wing at Whispering Marsh," Price replied.

"Can they do that?" Richard jumped in. "Commit someone to their own facility?"

All eyes turned to Beth. "I'm sorry. I'm not sure," the associate answered. "Probably they can." She reached for the statute volume she'd brought into the conference room.

A single rap on the door was followed immediately by one of Helena's assistants carrying a sheaf of papers.

"Excuse me. I know you didn't want to be interrupted, but this is directly related to what you're discussing. And it is important, so —"

The young man started to hand the papers to Valdez who directed him with a lift of her chin to give them to Price.

Price scanned the top sheet, then held it up where all could see the familiar format of a legal caption.

"Whispering Marsh, LLC, PC," she read, "Alger Wing Ltd., PC, and Nathan Fredrich, M.D., PC versus Jane Doe, by her guardians and next friends, Ivan and Bella Reston, Arthur Matsen, and John Cann, and as individuals. Petition for Involuntary Placement and Injunctive Relief." She looked around the table. "Okay folks, let's see what we're up against."

A moment later Price read aloud. "Petitioner Whispering Marsh maintains limited administrative and other contractual contacts with the Alger Wing, PC, which is an adjunct but independent secure facility under the management and control of Nathan Fredrich, M.D., PC."

"Sounds like they might be reluctant participants," Matsen commented. "A wedge, perhaps?" Price nodded as she read.

"Here," Price said a moment later. "Petitioners submit that respondent has been examined by a competent physician and has been found to be a danger to herself and/or others and requests the honorable court to order that she be placed in a secure facility as designated by Petitioner for the statutorily prescribed period."

Price saw Matsen shaking his head.

"Further, Petitioners respectfully request the court to sever —"

Price stopped and reread the paragraph to herself, then again out aloud. "Petitioners respectfully request the court to sever and nullify the guardian-ward relationship that exists between the Respondent and those named as next friends herein on the grounds that the said relationship(s) is/are an ongoing threat to the safety and well-being of the Respondent and continuation of the status quo in that regard constitutes a risk of severe and irreparable harm to the Respondent.

"Petitioners respectfully aver to the court that the Respondent suffers from severe psychological and physical trauma that was not adequately treated or addressed for a prolonged period of time and that said lack of treatment was the direct result of the failure and refusal of said guardians to initiate, effect, and cooperate with an effective treatment regimen and protocols."

Price looked over at Matsen who stared grimly ahead.

"Petitioners state further that once an effective and beneficial treatment regimen and protocol was initiated under the guidance of Petitioner Fredrich, the guardians and next friends named herein embarked upon a concerted and purposeful effort to interfere with and thwart the successful implementation of the aforesaid treatment regimen and protocols culminating in the unlawful removal of the Respondent from the secure facility to which she had been admitted under the provisions of the Bailey Act, and that they did so specifically for the purpose of intentionally thwarting the effective continuation of the aforementioned treatment regimen and proto-cols. Petitioners strongly advise the court that the failure to order the immediate reinstitution of said regimen and protocols will cause immediate and irreparable harm to the Respondent.

"Wherefore, Petitioners request that the honorable court enter its order that the aforesaid guardian-ward relationship is and has been null and void *ab initio* based on the fact that the aforementioned injuries and trauma to respondent were caused by the tortious and criminal—" Price audibly gasped and the others looked at each other. Matsen was rigid.

"— acts of co-respondent Cann and at all times relevant hereto the motive and purpose of all co-respondent guardians and next friends has not been the well-being of Respondent but rather a con-certed and coordinated effort to conceal both the source and cause of Respondent's injuries and to prevent her recovery therefrom."

A short time later, Price and Matsen adjourned to his office. "Just when you think nothing —" Price began as they sat down but she was interrupted by the intercom. "John Cann on line three, Mr. Matsen."

Matsen looked at Price who opened her eyes as wide as they'd go and shook her head back and forth, reinforcing their decision not to tell Cann what was happening. Not now. Not yet.

"Hello, John," Matsen said into the speaker. "It's good to hear from you."

"Maybe not." Cann got right to the point. "I couldn't pull it off. The judge is going to surrender Mribic to the Tribunal. Sorry."

Matsen shook his head. "No, no, John. It was a long shot. If you couldn't do it, it couldn't be done."

"Thanks, Arthur. But Mribic doesn't agree with you. He says you should have come. And there was something else he —"

"I have to tell you, John," Matsen interrupted. "The way I've dealt with this situation has been a mistake." As he spoke, he looked at Price so that she knew his words were for her too. "I've been unfair to those I care about. And the firm. I owe you an apology, John, for asking you to do something without giving you all the details."

"Well, that's not exactly a first, Arthur," Cann said jokingly.

Price smiled and Matsen emitted a short mirthless chuckle. "Yes. But, this was different. Particularly in that it involved my using you and the firm for what is essentially a private matter. I will tell you that I've given thought to resigning over it —"

Cann and Price both spoke at once. "Oh, come on, Arthur." "Don't be absurd."

"At the very least, I owe you an explanation."

"You don't *owe* me anything, Arthur."

"I disagree, John. I insist you let me tell you what this is — was — about." He took a breath. "On that tape I showed you —" Matsen interrupted himself and looked at Price. "You haven't seen it, Katherine. I'll make it available to you. I'm a little old-fashioned and there are things I don't think you should see. But I'll leave it up to you." Price nodded and Matsen went back to his narrative.

"On that tape, you recall, John, there were four older men separated from the rest. One of those was a man named Predrag

Djilic. The tape arrived with a note pointing out Djilic. Without that, I don't know that I would have realized that it was Djilic on the tape, but once it was pointed out I was quite certain it was him. The tape showed that Djilic was alive, at the time the tape was made anyway. Early to mid-nineties. And the note said he was alive still. And, it said if I represented Mribic, I would be given information on Djilic's present whereabouts." He shook his head. "Sounds awfully foolish now. An old man's fantasy. What was I going to do if I got hold of him? Beat him with my cane?"

"Oh, Arthur," Price said softly. Matsen gave her a wry smile.

"And the note said not to say anything about Djilic to anyone. I wanted to tell you, John. I knew I could trust you with it. But — I'm sorry. That's all I can say. I'm sorry."

"Arthur —"

Once again, Matsen interrupted. "But I'll tell you now what this is about." He framed his thoughts for a moment. "I had dealings with this Djilic fellow in the forties. During the war." His mouth tightened. "They were not pleasant dealings. I don't want to be melodramatic here but —" He cleared his throat. "What happened has haunted me all these years."

By the time Matsen finished his story, his voice was gravelly. "I passed out. Maybe I was knocked out. I don't know. It was a couple of days before I regained consciousness. When I did, the first person I saw was Popovic, the Chetnik captain. I learned that she and her men had chased Djilic off and carried me back to the main force. Even before I could ask Popovic about Savka and Milica, she asked me where they were. When I told her, she sent men to look for the spot. But they came back saying they either couldn't find the ravine. Or the animals had —

"My paralysis was temporary. Less than a week. But by the time I was mobile again, we were many miles away. I wanted to go back." He looked directly at Price and she could see his eyes were moist. "I did go back. After the fighting stopped and before I came back to the States. I think I found the spot. I've never been completely sure."

Price dabbed at her eyes with a tissue. On the other end of the phone, Cann was absolutely quiet.

So that's who Savka was!

No one spoke for a long time. Then Matsen cleared his throat and asked, "John, you said there was something else?"

Cann hesitated, his mind racing. *Should he tell Arthur what Mribic said about Savka surviving the fall. And being pregnant? What if it wasn't even true? And, either way, what would it do to Arthur to learn — after all these years? He hated keeping it from him but — No, not without more.*

"Ah, no ... nothing specific, Arthur," Cann stammered. "I was just considering whether there might be alternative theories of — Or maybe if this Djilic is still around — I — maybe I can make some inquiries."

"I don't know how much could come of that," Matsen said, "but if you want to take a few more days ..."

"And I'll play out the string with Mribic and see what happens."

"But if it comes to it, feel free to walk away. I mean that."

"Okay," Cann agreed. "Everything okay with Janie?"

Matsen and Price exchanged a look. "We're watching out for her, John."

Price had the videotape brought to her office. Notwithstanding Arthur's sensibilities, it was, sadly, nothing she hadn't seen before.

She was focusing on the four older men on the tape wondering which one was Djilic when her direct line rang. She picked it up and heard Cann's voice at the other end. Her first thought was that they hadn't fooled him about Janie and somehow he had sensed that something was wrong.

"Hi, Katherine. It's John. Are you on speaker?"

"No," she said with curiosity.

"Are you by yourself?" Cann asked. "Is Arthur with you?"

"No, I'm alone. Why?"

"How's he doing?"

What was he getting at?

"He's well, John. Is there something specific you're concerned about?"

"No. Well, yes. It's about what he told us today."

"Yes, it's an amazing story. Had you known any of that?"

"No. I knew he'd been in the Balkans during World War II. Involved with the partisans. Just generally. That's why I'm calling you."

Price waited.

"There's more to it. The 'something else' I was going to tell Arthur when I called? It was something else Mribic said. About this Savka Arthur spoke of. I didn't even know who Savka was when Mribic brought it up."

"Mribic spoke of Savka? Djilic too?"

"No. Nothing about Djilic. Check that. He did make a reference to 'the man Arthur saw on the tape.' No name, though."

"I'm watching the tape now."

"Nice, huh?'

Price emitted a harsh humorless grunt. "Not the word I'd use. Do you know which one is Djilic?"

"No. I was going to ask you. Can you find out from Arthur and let me know? Also send me a copy of the tape?"

"I'll have IT make a digital file and e-mail it to you."

"Okay, good. Thanks."

"But what was it Mribic told you?"

"He said that the man Arthur saw on the tape wasn't the only one who survived."

"Survived?" Price thought for a moment then it hit her. "Savka? Milica?"

"Savka. He said that Savka survived the fall. At the time I didn't know what he was talking about. Like I said, I was going to tell

Arthur about it. See if it meant anything to him. But after hearing that story —"

Price was nodding on her end of the phone, her thoughts and her heart going out to Arthur as she considered the implications. "Right. I agree. Even if it's true, it could cause more pain than anything else. Did Mribic say anything about Milica?"

"Nothing. But there's more about Savka."

"What?"

"What Mribic said was, 'Tell Artur that Savka survived too. The fall didn't kill her. That she was found and cared for. And it turned out she was pregnant.'"

"Pregnant?" It took barely a second for the implication to hit Price. "Oh, my God, John!" she said. "Do we even have a right to keep this from Arthur?"

"No, I don't think we do, Katherine. But what if it's not true?"

"Then why would Mribic say it?"

"To get Arthur over here? It was fairly clear when I showed up that it was Arthur they expected. And if Mribic wants Arthur here, that alone is reason enough for me to want him to stay away."

Price accepted the logic. "Okay. What can I do?"

"For now, the tape. Which one's Djilic? And keep an eye on Arthur."

"You know I will. And, John, you be careful too."

23

Riessersee Hotel
Garmisch–Partenkirchen

Cann got a good night's sleep even though he dreamed about pirates
with eye patches. He'd viewed the digital file when it came in, but still
hadn't heard from Price about which one was Djilic. So he'd examined the four older men as closely as he could for some sign of the eye
injury Arthur had inflicted. It was really the only clue he had so far.
But he found nothing and all his search got him was a night filled with
images of Blackbeard and Long John Silver types running around
brandishing cutlasses and yelling "me hearties" all over the place.

Cann decided to forego the hotel breakfast and headed for a
pastry shop. He walked several blocks to the narrow street where
he'd seen the *Feinbackerei*, turned right, and had only gone about fifty
yards when he sensed a car slowing as it approached him from
behind. He angled closer to the walls and storefronts and used the
reflections in the windows to see what was going on in the street.

An older Mercedes sedan had slowed down to match Cann's
walking pace. Once again, to his chagrin, he wasn't armed. He was
meeting with Mribic after breakfast and weapons weren't allowed in
the detention center.

The Mercedes pulled to the curb just ahead of Cann, and both passenger-side doors began to open. On the alert, Cann shifted his briefcase from his right hand to his left just as a man who'd been sauntering up from behind suddenly lunged at him. But Cann had seen that man too in the reflection and met the charge with a back fist to the man's forehead, stunning him. Cann shifted his attention back to the Mercedes as three men jumped out of the car, one from the front and two from the rear. Two of the attackers went low, going for Cann's legs while the third held himself a step behind, waiting to take Cann down once his balance had been upset. Cann braced his left leg and shot out a vicious front kick with his right that caught one of the charging men full in the face. That man went down but managed to wrap an arm around Cann's straight left leg even as Cann dropped a powerful hammer fist onto the head of the other charging man. Seeing that, the third man went to Plan B and pointed a 10mm semi-automatic pistol at Cann's face. In almost the same instant, a man in a black turtleneck and waist-length leather coat appeared to Cann's right, pointing a weapon of his own straight at the the man who had his gun on Cann.

Everybody froze.

Stalemate.

Then, to his left, Cann saw the man he knew only as Rade — who'd led the team that "approached" him in the bookstore — standing in the street by the driver's side window of the Mercedes glancing down frequently even as he kept his eyes moving about the scene. Inside the vehicle, the driver of the car slowly placed his hands on top of the steering wheel.

"Such a public scene, gentlemen. Perhaps we should call it a draw?" Rade proposed.

The man holding the gun on Cann darted his eyes about, assessing the situation. Finally, he nodded. Rade nodded back.

The two men on the ground in front of Cann got up and helped the man whom Cann had backfisted get back on his feet. Only when those three had squeezed into the rear seat of the Mercedes did the last man move toward the car, never taking the pistol off Cann. He, in turn, remained covered by the man in the leather coat as he folded himself backward into the front-passenger seat. No one made any sudden moves and no guns were lowered until the Mercedes was well down the street.

Cann and Rade looked at each other across the space where the Mercedes had been. Rade put the pistol into his waistband in the small of his back and crossed over to Cann, hand extended. Cann took it and said, simply. "Thanks."

Rade nodded. "I told you we'd be watching."

"I'm glad you were."

"Any idea who those men were?"

"I was going to ask you."

Rade shrugged. "One of my men was assigned to get photos. We'll see what we have." He looked hard at Cann. "But we do need to talk. More productively this time."

"It's the least I can do," Cann agreed. He gestured to the *Feinbackerei*. "Over coffee?" Rade glanced at the small shop and then gestured to another man across the street to be on the alert as he and Cann went inside.

The two men carried their Bavarian crèmes and a steaming cup of hot strong German coffee to a small table in a corner at the back of the room. Without discussion, both men rearranged the chairs so that each had his back to the wall. As soon as they settled in, Rade dropped the bombshell.

"You know, of course, that Mribic is gone."

Cann looked at him blankly. "Gone?"

"As in no longer at the detention facility."

"But —"

Rade stared for a moment then said, "I consider myself a decent judge of people, John. May I call you John?"

Cann nodded.

"— and I believe you are as surprised as you seem. You knew nothing of this?"

Cann pointed at his briefcase as if it somehow stood for Mribic and said, "My next stop was the center to meet with him. I had no idea. What happened?"

"Very early this morning. Some federal polizei, or people dressed as federal polizei, arrived at the detention facility in an official transport van and presented what appeared to be a perfectly valid custody warrant. The guards, quite properly, called their supervisor who had seen such documents before and, well, everyone knew of the pending order from the judge so —" He shrugged his shoulders.

Cann was shaking his head. "But no order's even been issued yet."

"Yes, you know that. And I know that. Unfortunately, the supervisor didn't know that. I did learn that the ICTY had acted quickly and their security people were already on the way here. Perhaps whoever took Mribic somehow learned of that and that . . . how do you say it . . . spooked them?"

"So I assume he's not on his way to The Hague then?"

Rade expelled a sharp burst of air through his lips. "The van was found abandoned outside Munich, I'm told. No one knows *where* he is at this time."

Cann continued to shake his head. "I really don't know anything about this." He looked more keenly at Rade. "What about you? Who told you? Hell, who *are* you?"

Rade considered Cann for a moment. "We will be open with each other?"

"Yes."

"Good. You first."

Cann had to laugh at the way Rade had slammed the trap shut. "Okay, John Cann, senior associate, law firm of Loring, Matsen, and Gould —"

"Yes, yes," Rade interrupted. "Here representing Dubran Mribic. I know. What are you going to tell me next? That you are just a simple American lawyer? Don't insult me, John. I know who you are."

Cann turned his head slightly and squinted. "So, who am I?"

"This is what you call open?" Rade snapped.

Cann knew he was cornered but old habits die hard. "Tell me what you know and I won't deny the truth. How's that?"

"Less than open to my way of thinking," Rade said dourly, "but it will do."

Cann listened as the man opposite rattled off a reasonably accurate overview of Cann's professional history. When Rade was done, he looked at Cann and raised his eyebrows.

Cann had promised not to deny the truth so all he said was, "How do you know all that?"

"It is a small world, isn't it, John," Rade said pointedly. "And the intelligence community, tight-knit."

Cann considered that for a moment. "Have we crossed paths?" He didn't think they had.

"Not that I know of. But in the course of my inquiries, I learned that we do have a mutual friend. Rudi Sperre? You remember him?"

Cann did indeed remember the diminutive Dutchman who'd gotten him out of one of the tightest spots of his life. "Of course I remember him. I can't speak highly enough of him. If he's a friend of yours, that tells me a lot."

Rade tilted his head slightly to the side and lifted a shoulder. "I would like to think he considers me a friend."

"You've worked with him?"

"He was in Sarajevo for a time as a NATO liaison during the conflicts." Rade brought the subject back to the matter at hand. "What about you? Have you ever operated in this area?"

"Never."

"So we must assume this morning's incident is related to your representation of Mribic?"

"I don't know of anything else. Do you?" Cann gestured toward

Rade. "I went first. Isn't it your turn?"

Rade thought about it, then, "I am Radovan Nikolic, captain in the Specijalna Antiteroristicka Jedinica. You know it?"

"I know of it. SAJ." The Serbian Special Anti-Terrorist Unit.

Prior to the breakup of the Yugoslav federation, Tito had a number of police and paramilitary and secret police and intelligence services units all keeping an eye on each other as much as on the populace. After Tito's death, some of the units evolved — devolved — into the perpetrators of the atrocities for which the period of the nineties is infamous. One unit, the Organizational Group (OG) was reputed to have worked closely with Arkan, the Tiger, an organized crime figure who turned his gang of criminals into a paramilitary force. Later, the OG was rumored to be responsible when Arkan was very publicly gunned down in a hotel lobby after he'd "returned" to civilian life and was about to embark on a political career.

Ultimately, the OG was a victim of its own excess. After the Dayton Accords, an adjunct antiterrorist unit — the SAJ — was formed and placed under the nominal control of the OG. That didn't last long. The goal of recruiting and filling the ranks of the SAJ with men of the highest skill as well as the highest integrity virtually guaranteed that it would not remain with the OG. The SAJ did not simply break away from the OG. It subsumed it, absorbed much of what was good and jettisoned the rest.

But the SAJ was no boy scout troop. Their tasking included not just hostage rescue and hijack prevention but also the occasional, less public removal of undesirable or embarrassing elements. Internationally, it was often a welcome and effective participant in actions aimed at the drug trade, the sex trade, and international terrorism.

"So what was SAJ's interest in Mribic?"

Rade Nikolic shook his head. "Not yet, John. You haven't told me why you were representing Mribic? I need to know that."

"Me first again?" Cann said with a sardonic smile.

"Indulge me." Nikolic returned the smile, but it was clear he wasn't about to budge.

Cann did owe the man. And he really had nothing to hide at this point. "When you asked me that in the bookstore, I really didn't know. I know more now. It has to do with the senior partner in my firm, Arthur Matsen."

Cann related the story of Matsen and Djilic. Before he got to Savka and Milica, Nikolic interrupted with unconcealed irritation.

"You're telling me your involvement is because of a World War II . . . what is the word . . . grudge?"

"It's significant to Arthur —"

"It's ancient history is what it is," Rade countered. "Look, I know who Predrag Djilic is. All Serbs do. But he has been been dead for over fifty years."

"Arthur received a tape. From the nineties. He recognized Djilic on it."

"This, Arthur, no disrespect, John, but he is very old by now, no?"

"Yes. But don't make any assumptions. He's still sharp. Believe me."

Nikolic nodded. "As I said, no disrespect. This tape. Where is it?"

Cann reached for his briefcase. "I downloaded a digital file of it last night. Would you recognize Djilic?"

Nikolic shrugged. "I've seen some grainy pictures from half a century ago." He watched as Cann pulled a laptop out of his brief-case. "He would look very different now. That's why I must question your partner's identification. You understand."

"I do." Cann opened the file Price had sent and spun the laptop around so the screen was facing Nikoloic. "Click there to play it."

Cann said nothing as he watched the expressions on Nikolic's face. Anger, revulsion, sorrow. After a while, Cann noticed an expression of recognition. Nikolic looked up at him.

"I don't know if Predrag Djilic is one of those men," he said as he turned the laptop so they could both see the screen. "But I will tell you," he said pointing to a freeze-frame of the four older, "this one," he placed his finger on the second man from the left, "is Erwin Jost."

24

Chatham County
Georgia

"The second man on the left," Price said into the phone. The D.C. office had relayed the message to her that Cann had called just as she and the rest of the Loring, Matsen team were setting up the temporary offices they would use during Janie's commitment hearings. She used her cell phone to return the call knowing if she used a landline, Cann's caller ID would tip him off that she was in the same area code as Whispering Marsh. "Arthur said Predrag Djilic is the second man on the left."

"The plot thickens," Cann observed.

"How's that?"

"You remember that Rade guy I asked Arthur about. Well, I ran into him again this morning." Cann didn't tell Price about the incident that had preceded his "running into" Nikolic. Instead, he made the encounter sound incidental and the ensuing discussion more like a working breakfast than anything else. "It turns out that Rade is Radovan Nikolic, a captain in the SAJ."

Price whistled softly. She, too, knew of the SAJ.

"And," Cann continued, "when I ran the tape by him, he very

definitely indentified the second man on the left on the tape as one Erwin Jost."

"Who is?"

"The local godfather apparently. A major player in European organized crime."

"Is it possible that Jost and Djilic are one and the same?" Price asked after a moment.

"Nikolic said that Jost would be in the same age group, but he also stressed that all the evidence suggests Djilic died right after the war. Likely executed when a lot of former fighters were turned back over to Tito."

"So how did you leave it?"

"Nikolic and his team are taking a new look at their files on Djilic. See if they can find any parallels."

"And if they do, what does it mean about Mribic and Arthur? And Savka?"

"I have no idea," Cann admitted. "I'm at that stage where all I can do is put one foot in front of the other."

"Well, I'll put our research team on this too. See if they come up with anything. In the meantime," Price's voice changed slightly, "about this breakfast meeting you had this morning? What aren't you telling me?"

"What do you mean?"

"I mean," she said mock-wearily, "isn't it just a teensy bit odd that this guy who had you jumped in a bookstore is suddenly your breakfast buddy? And he is now so taken with this new found friendship that he just offers up to you that he's with a secret antiterrorist organization in the Balkans? Am I supposed to believe he was just feeling chatty?"

Cann smiled to himself. Price never failed to impress.

His response was, "Don't ask."

"Oh, but I will ask. For Heaven's sake, I understand as well as you do the need for holding back sometimes. Playing it close. But I also understand there are times when you need to trust the people who care about you."

"It's not a matter of trust," he protested sincerely. "It's a matter of not getting other people involved. Or hurt. Especially those you care about."

Price was briefly quieted then she said, "All right. For now. But think about this. What would you do if it was the other way around? If Arthur or I shut you out when you thought you could help?"

"I'd find a way."

"Yes, John, you would, " Price said pointedly, "and so would I."

"I know," Cann said. "And I appreciate it."

"Just don't forget it. Keep us posted and don't do anything reckless. Okay?"

"Okay. Take care."

"I will if you will."

Matsen rarely drove himself anymore, but the fewer people who knew Janie's whereabouts the better. Someone inside the safe house was watching for him and as soon as he entered the driveway, the garage door started to open. He drove straight in and the door closed behind him. Even before he was out of the car, a man opened the door from the kitchen and scanned the garage, then waved Matsen in.

Furden was in the kitchen when Matsen entered. She approached him and extended her hand. Matsen took it in both of his and patted it repeatedly.

"Thank you so much," Furden said sincerely.

"No, thank *you*, Sara," Matsen responded. "It took great courage for you to do what you did." He jutted his chin toward the interior of the house. "How's she doing?"

"Her head's okay," Furden explained. "Several stitches. The doctor found no other physical injuries." Then her face twisted into a grimace. "It's the withdrawal that's the worst. That bastard."

"Withdrawal?"

Furden nodded. "The therapy Fredrich was doing —" She stopped herself. "Therapy. How can I even use the word? The program ..." She threw her hands up and waved them around in confused dismissal ... "Whatever you want to call it. The toxicology analysis indicates he used a variant amylobarbitone, but the analysis also shows the presence of an opiate, maybe even heroin, the theory being that the combination would enhance the effects." Her lips twisted in hate. "Amobarbiturates are addictive after prolonged use, but with an opiate it happens quickly. And opiates increase the tolerance for pain. That's why she was hitting her head and didn't even notice. Damn it, he could have killed her." Her voice cracked under the strain. "We're getting her off it," she said finally. "But it isn't easy for her."

"I want to see her."

They went down the hall to the rearmost bedroom. The door was slightly ajar. Matsen pushed it open and saw an attendant seated by the side of the bed. She had a book in her lap but she wasn't reading.

Matsen crossed over and looked down at Janie. He studied her sweet young face with its roundish shape and prominent cheekbones. Underneath the closed eyelids, he pictured the blue, blue eyes. She looked pretty and peaceful.

The moment ended abruptly when Janie's eyes flew wide open with such suddenness that Matsen actually took half a step back. The rest of Janie's face twisted so grotesquely that Matsen's eyes squinted and his teeth ground into each other as he unconsciously mirrored what he was seeing. Janie's eyes, however, saw nothing and she emitted no sound.

The attendant jumped up and held Janie's left arm and leg down as Furden crossed quickly and did the same with the right. "There's always the possibility she could hurt herself," Furden said through gritted teeth. "But I won't have her in restraints. That's why we've got the twenty-four-hour attendants. If I have to sit by her bed myself all the time, I won't have her tied down."

"She won't be," Matsen promised. "I swear that to you."

Slowly the rigidity lessened in Janie's body and her eyes began to focus. When she saw Matsen, a small smile formed on her face and she croaked almost inaudibly, "Hi, Mis'er Ma'sen."

"Hello, Janie. How do you feel?" He winced at his own question.

" 'Kay," she whispered. Then she grimaced and her eyes grew moist. "No' so 'kay, I guess," she struggled to get the words out.

Matsen squeezed her hand and felt a tiny squeeze back. Again, as he had so many times before, he was humbled by the strength of this young lady. His eyes clouded as he watched Janie slowly, blessedly, slip back into unconsciousness.

25

When Cann stepped off the elevator into the hotel lobby on his way to dinner, he was surprised to see Rade Nikolic waiting for him. "You have something against letting people know in advance that you're coming?" he asked with a smile.

"Generally, yes," Nikolic replied. They both chuckled. Then Nikolic got more serious. "But in this case, I have some information I want to share with you. And ask you about."

Cann nodded.

"First of all, we have identified the men who attacked you this morning. Three of them, anyway. They are KLA. You know what this is, of course."

The world is full of acronyms, but Cann was certain the KLA Nikolic was referring to was the Kosovo Liberation Army. Painted by the Western media, the UN, and NATO as freedom fighters struggling for Kosovo's independence in the face of first Yugoslav and then Serbian oppression, the KLA was a terrorist organization seeking to align the province of Kosovo with the former Stalinist and now Islamist-leaning regime of Albania. Nonetheless, after the Serbs were expelled from the province of Kosovo, the UN peacekeeping force gave the KLA its imprimatur as the official governing entity and allowed it to maintain the only remaining armed force in the region. As a result, the only "peacekeeping" that needed to be done by the UN thereafter consisted of turning a blind eye whenever the KLA did to the Serbs what the Serbs had been vilified for doing to the Kosovars.

"Right," Nikolic said in a tone that conveyed his contempt for the group. "The question is why they are involved. Have you had dealings with them in the past?"

Cann shook his head slowly. "Not that I'm aware of. Not directly as an organization. That's not to say I couldn't have crossed paths with a freelancer."

Most, if not all, terror groups are ready, willing, and able to work with, for, or in place of others in a loose network of exchange. Syrians, Chechens, Afghanis, and a host of others in Iraq. Britains, Australians, and Americans fighting alongside the Taliban and Al Queda in Afghanistan. Middle Easterners with the Irish Republican Army. Palestinians working with Libya to bring down Pan Am 103 over Lockerbie. As far back as 1972, the Japanese Red Army acted for the Popular Front for the Liberation of Palestine when they perpetrated the Lod airport massacre in Tel Aviv. The common bond was a commitment to indiscriminate slaughter.

"Possibly so. Like the others, pretensions to ideology aside, the KLA are always willing to hire themselves out for money. They are deeply involved in purely criminal activity. Assassinations, trafficking in drugs, smuggling — including humans. Prostitution. Slavery."

"But would Mribic be involved with the KLA?" Cann asked. "Serbs and Kosovars, the KLA anyway, are committed enemies, aren't they?"

"You're looking for honor or consistency where there is none," Nikolic responded. "In this case, Mribic is connected to Jost, and Jost is connected to all of the things I just mentioned. It may be that the KLA role in this business is nothing more than hired muscle, I believe is the American term, no?"

Cann nodded. "Okay, so Mribic is connected to Jost. You still haven't told me what your interest in Mribic is. Shall I assume it has to do with Jost as well?"

Nikolic shrugged. "Yes and no."

Cann shook his head in exasperation. "Look, Rade, earlier you said—*you* said, not me—that we'd be open with each other. I went first. Hell, I went second too. Your turn."

Nikolic looked at him for a moment, then led Cann over to an alcove off the lobby with chairs and a small couch surrounding a low table. The SAJ captain sat in one of the armchairs and Cann took the end of the couch closest to him.

"You said earlier that you knew of my group, the SAJ," Nikolic began.

"Know *of*, yes."

"Then you may know that we are multitasked, yes?"

"Aren't we all," Cann observed. Nikolic nodded.

"As such," Nikolic went on, "we have intelligence functions as well as law enforcement functions and some paramilitary functions. All in one. Sometimes they are separate. Other times, they overlap."

Cann said nothing and waited for Nikolic to continue.

"Mribic came to our attention in two separate ways. What you saw on that tape? Those kind of things did happen." He raised his index finger. "On both sides. But I don't say that as an excuse for any of what was done. One difference, though, is that we have tried to deal with our own . . . what is the phrase in English . . . dirty laundry. Unlike others." His expression became stern. "Unlike the way we have been portrayed in the Western press." He looked directly at Cann. "And let me assure you, to us Mribic is 'dirty laundry.'"

"There is a list," Nikolic continued, "of people who have done such things as we are discussing. Like on the tape. And we, the SAJ, are sometimes charged with dealing with these people. Removing them."

"Why not just turn them over to the ICTY?"

"Because when these people are placed on trial, it is Serbia that loses," Nikolic said bitterly. "We cooperate, we seek them, we find them, we arrest them, we turn them over, and they are tried. And what does the world say when the facts come out in these trials? The world doesn't say, 'See what this man has done.' Or 'See what these men have done.' No. The world says, 'See what the Serbs have done.' It says, 'See what animals are the Serbs.' So, no, we take care of it ourselves. You understand?"

Put that way, Cann did.

"Anyway, Mribic was on that list. He was one of many targets, but we did not have an active search going for him in particular. He was on a watch list. Then, not so long ago, we received information he was in Brcko." He looked at Cann. "You know about Brcko?"

Cann shook his head.

Nikolic explained how Brcko came to be and what it is. "Essentially lawless, Brcko is," he concluded. "But such lawlessness would only make our job easier."

Cann understood.

"Now this is where the multitasking comes in," Nikolic went on. "The information on Mribic came from our people working with a combined task force aimed at halting the international trafficking of children for sex." Nikolic saw Cann's jaw clench. "It's a terrible business, John. Heartbreaking. And Mribic was deeply involved.

"Let me tell you, with many of these removals, we don't really give it much thought. The target has to go. It goes. But Mribic's involvement in this horrible business — that made it different. We had more volunteers than we could use. And we were prepared to move quickly to take him out.

"But our people on the task force asked us to hold back. They had

Mribic under close surveillance hoping to learn how the victims were being transported to and from Brcko. No one could figure out how they were crossing international borders, even where they were coming from. They would just appear in Brcko." He described the scenes of naked children in the streets, "— as if out of nowhere. Some never went any farther. Some died there. Some were sold to local brothels. Most go to Western Europe through Bosnia, Croatia, Slovenia, up through Austria, and into Germany and beyond. But no one could figure out how it was done.

"We were finally able to learn that they are transported in groups by van. One night we were tipped off that one was leaving Brcko. We followed it to the Croatian border and stopped it southeast of Vidovice. As soon as we did, the two men in the cab jumped out and ran for the woods. We didn't shoot them because we wanted information. We did catch them. But not before they blew up the van with all the children inside."

Once again, both men were silent. There was nothing to say.

"Did you get anything from the men who ran?" Cann finally asked.

"Very little. The operation is very compartmentalized. These two didn't know much. All we got out of them was that they were given different routes every trip and papers that enabled them to get across all the borders without any difficulty. They claimed they didn't know what the papers were. And the papers were in the van. So —"

"Dead end."

Nikolic nodded. "Now, as for Mribic, while he was still under surveillance, he made a trip to Bavaria. South of Munich. Schloss Grunberg, to be precise." Nikolic's eyes bored into Cann. "This is the primary residence of Erwin Jost." Cann's eyebrows went up.

"This was a surprise," Nikolic continued. "Not that Jost was involved. He controls organized crime in southwest Germany and is very powerful in the rest of Europe. What was surprising was that Mribic would visit him at home. Few people have such access. So we

intensified and redirected our efforts in Brcko and learned that
Mribic was reputed to be a..." Nikolic, like Cann, was fluent in
several languages but struggled with the particular word he wanted
to use. "It is called *savetodavac* in Serbian. Like a... in the Godfather
films — a consigliere."

"Okay. Consigliere. I understand," Cann responded. "Is he?"

"It may be so. Mribic is not a stupid man. And he is a lawyer. Did
he tell you that? Yes," he acknowledged Cann's nod.

"So how did he end up in custody in Garmisch?"

Nikolic shrugged. "From Munich, he came to Garmisch. And
was promptly arrested by the German authorities. He did not
even attempt to conceal his presence. It makes no sense. Arrogance,
perhaps."

When Cann spoke, his voice was cold. "I knew nothing of this sex
trade business, Rade. I would never have represented Mribic —
wouldn't have been in the same room with him — and Arthur never
would have asked me to if he'd known." Nikolic nodded acknowledgment. "But none of this tells me what the tie in is to Arthur, or me."

"I agree. Perhaps Mribic just wanted a good lawyer."

"Then why not just hire us? Why bring up this Djilic business?"

"Would you or Artur have taken the case without it?"

Nikolic had a point.

"What about Jost and Djilic being the same person? Did you find
anything?"

"We reviewed what we have, and I still cannot tell you that they
are one and the same. But, in truth, I can't say they are not. Djilic disappeared after the war, and Jost first appeared on the radar a couple
of years later. He was arrested by the American forces for black mar-
keteering. Cigarettes, liquor, that sort of thing. A couple of U.S. NCOs
were court-martialed and punished severely. Jost was treated less
harshly. Turned over to the German authorities, which was unusual
under the Status of Forces agreement in effect at the time. But there is

no record of his having served any time in jail for that offense. Or any other." He clicked his tongue. "A career of crime that spans a half century and he has never been in confinement."

"So he's due, hey?"

"Due, indeed." Nikolic's looked away and didn't speak for a moment. Then, "Let me tell you, to get Jost would be a significant achievement in my professional life. But that would be nothing compared to getting Djilic. In my heart. In my soul. As a Serb." He looked back at Cann. "What do you know of Djilic?"

"Just what Arthur said. Enough to know he was a bastard."

"That and more. After Miljkovic was killed, Djilic, as brutal as he was, couldn't hold the Legion together. It ceased to function as a unified force. Djilic did put together a good-sized band of marauders for a time; not particularly political in their motivations, more bandits than guerrillas. But his obsessive, abiding hatred of Serbs took precedence over anything and everything else. He passed up plunder, rape, loot, everything if there was even a slight opportunity to inflict horror on just one Serb — the more horrific the better.

"Eventually that cost him many of his followers," Nikolic went on, "who preferred material gain to the satisfaction of Djilic's blood lust. Little by little, they broke away to engage in their own pursuits. So Djilic took a page from Miljkovic's book and allied himself loosely with the Handschar Division. By the time he was done, he was responsible for the deaths of thousands of Serbs. He was — is — for us our Adolf Eichmann. Or Klaus Barbie. You know who Barbie was?"

"Butcher of Lyon."

"Yes. Butcher. That is what Djilic was to us Serbs." Nikolic went silent. After a moment, he continued.

"At the end of the war, thousands of ex-fighters made their way up through Slovenia and into Austria, seeking the protection of the British occupation force. The last reports of Djilic say he was one of them. But Tito demanded that all forces fleeing into British controlled territory be turned back over to him and to a man, and woman, they were executed — on the spot. The general consensus is that Djilic was caught up in that."

"Why?"

"Mostly, I suppose, because he was never heard of since; that and the fact that the expulsions were absolute and complete. Virtually no one was allowed in by the British. Why would Djilic be the exception?"

Cann stared hard at Nikolic before speaking. "What if he pretended to be British?"

Nikolic laughed. "I hardly think so. It was not like today where every schoolchild studies English." He shook his head. "No. In those days, people spoke only their local dialect and sometimes a little of whatever was spoken nearby.

Cann shook his head. "Arthur says Djilic spoke perfect English. Midlands accent and all. Apparently spent the greater part of his youth in England."

Nikolic looked long and hard at Cann before he spoke. "This is true?"

Cann nodded and threw another question at Nikolic.

"Does Jost have any physical impairments that you know of?"

Nikolic nodded very slowly. "But *you* tell *me*, John," he finally said.

"One bad eye."

"How do you know this?"

Cann described how Matsen had destroyed Djilic's left eye.

"I think," Nikolic said quietly, "I would like to talk to Artur Matsen."

26

The six people seated around the oval table stood as Judge Paul Belker walked into the conference room adjoining his chambers. Belker looked like a *New Yorker* magazine caricature of a judge; fifties, portly underneath the flowing robes, round jowly face, pencil mustache, wire-rim glasses. The Loring, Matsen team had learned Judge Belker was generally considered to be intelligent and knowledgeable of the law. They'd also learned he was opinionated, dogmatic, and arrogant. The jurist looked at no one as he went straight to the head of the table at far end of the room and sat down. "Be seated, please."

He slapped a folder down, flipped it open, and scanned it briefly. Then he looked up, first at the two lawyers on his right. One was a thirty-something slender, brunette woman and the other was a slightly overweight, fiftyish man with graying hair. He then turned his gaze to the five people on his left: Matsen, Price, associates Beth Quinlan and Richard Marks, and paralegal Helena Valdez.

"I'm more impressed by quality than quantity," Belker said with a humorless smile. Without waiting for any response, he pointed at the lawyers on his right. "Identify yourself for the record."

"Martha Kewen, representing Dr. Nathan Fredrich and Alger Wing, PC, Your Honor." She spoke in a clipped monotone without greeting or acknowledging anyone else at the table. "Jonathan Priestly for Whispering Marsh Rehabilitation Center, LLC," the second attorney said. In a chair by the wall, the court reporter repeated the words into what looked like an oxygen mask over his mouth.

Belker shifted his gaze to his left.

"Arthur Matsen, Loring, Matsen, and Gould for respondent." Matsen turned to introduce Price, but was interrupted by the judge.

"Are you authorized to practice in my court, Mr. Matsen?"

Price jumped in. "I'm admitted in this jurisdiction, Your Honor, and would —"

"Yes, I know you are, Ms. Price, but I don't believe Mr. Matsen is and I'm not aware of any request that he be allowed to do so. Have you taken it upon yourself to admit him *pro hac vice* for this?" *Pro hac vice* basically translates as "to speak for this" and refers to an attorney not otherwise admitted to a jurisdiction being allowed to appear before a specific court for a specific matter.

"I apologize, Your Honor," Price said. "We intended to do so at this time, if I may —"

"You may not," Belker stated shortly. "It's too late. I would have considered a motion before but —" he looked at Matsen "— please move to the end of the table, Mr. Matsen. Ms. Price can handle this, I assume."

"She can indeed, Your Honor." Matsen accepted the judge's action with grace. Price felt it was unnecessarily demeaning, but knew there was nothing to be done.

"Proceed," the judge said, and Price, Quinlan, Marks, and Valdez identified themselves for the reporter.

"All right, then," Belker said, looking down at the file. "Initially, we have the Petitioner's request for an involuntary placement of Ms. Reston under the Bailey Act. That petition has been objected to." He looked at Price. "Are there any procedural objections or assertions that the technical requirements of the act have not been complied with?"

"Yes, Your Honor," Price began. "Regarding technical compliance with the Bailey Act, the fact is that we only received the papers yesterday and that was by fax so we can't even know if we've seen the entire —"

"Are you making an objection to the sufficiency of service of the papers on you?"

"No, Your Honor. Although we are not waiving our right to do so at —"

"Hold on, Ms. Price. I'm not leaving issues, especially procedural ones, to come up later. Either object to it now or you will be deemed by this court to have waived that objection."

"And if we do object to the sufficiency of service of process, Your Honor?"

"I'll rule against you and we'll proceed anyway." He flashed a mock smile at Price. "So, do you waive it?"

"No, Your Honor, I don't." If she waived it, it was dead as an issue. "And I will note my exception for the record." That way, it was appealable at a later time.

"Both process and service of process are found to be sufficient," Belker said crisply.

"Exception."

"Noted. And I repeat my question, Ms. Price. Are you contesting any part of the procedural steps?"

"Indeed we are, Your Honor. Our position is that the entire basis of the initial —" again she looked at Kewen "— commitment was based on false and fabricated data —"

"What you are raising there, counselor," the judge asserted, "goes to the question of the substance of the examination, even the motivation of the petitioner. Those are issues to be addressed in the evidentiary hearing with the parties present. Now," he said patronizingly, "what I am asking you is if you are making any *technical* objection based on a *procedural* error in how the initial commitment came about. Get the distinction? Did he not file a paper? Is something procedural lacking in the filings themselves?"

"I understand the distinction, Your Honor," Price replied. "The point is you can't excuse or ignore flaws, or worse, in the process just because they're contained in a technically correct document. I would note that we've seen only the pleadings and have not yet received all supporting documentation, including the records of the actual examination."

"Yes, well, in the absence of a specific objection, then, I find that the technical requirements of the Bailey Act were met by the petitioner with regard to the initial certification and involuntary examination."

"And I will take exception to *that*, Your Honor."

"Fine."

"Does your finding include admitting Janie into his own facility and then conducting the subsequent examination himself?" Price kept her tone even.

"Yes to the first question since I'm aware of nothing in the statute that prevents it. As to the second, I'll hear evidence on that at the hearing which, as you know, is required within five days of the filing of the petition." He looked at his watch, "That was yesterday."

The judge looked over at Kewen. "Ms. Price is correct, however, that they have every right to see the records pertaining to the examinations of Ms. Reston and any other materials the doctor is basing his petition on. When can you provide them?"

Kewen spoke as she lifted her briefcase onto the table. "I have copies of the relevant materials with me and can provide them right now." She gestured at the team across the table from her. "Although, I only have two sets."

"One set for them is fine. They can make their own copies." He bent his head forward and looked over his glasses at Price and the others before turning back to Kewen. "Dr —" he looked at the file in front of him, "—Fredrich will testify, of course." It was not a question. "Will there be any other testimony at that time. Any other witnesses?"

"We will be calling Whispering Marsh staff members to testify to Ms. Reston's behavior and condition in the period leading up to the initial certification by Dr. Fredrich, Your Honor."

"Opinion testimony?" Price interjected. "Are they experts?"

"Not opinion, Your Honor," Kewen retorted. "They will testify to objective observations of Ms. Reston's actions and appearance and behavior. It will relate to and corroborate Dr. Fredrich's findings and recommendations."

"Well, ultimately, I'll be the judge of that."

"Of course, Your Honor. We also have audiotape evidence of interaction between Dr. Fredrich and Ms. Reston, but that is relevant to the guardianship issue, not the placement issue."

"Do we have that?" Price asked looking through what Kewen had provided. "There's no audiotape in the materials we were just given."

Kewen directed her response to Judge Belker. "As I was about to say, Your Honor, it's my impression that the first order of business is the placement issue. Not guardianship."

Belker nodded. "I'm not formally severing the issues, but the statute clearly puts the urgency on the placement issue. We can address that first and, depending on my ruling, assess the urgency of dealing with the guardianship issue at that time."

"Regardless, Your Honor," Price contested, "Ms. Kewen's determination of what the taped evidence is relevant to is not controlling. The fact that she wants to introduce it as evidence of one thing doesn't mean it isn't evidence of more — like Dr. Fredrich's methods — which we intend to challenge. If the court prefers, we can make a formal discovery request but —"

Belker put up a hand to stop her. "Give them the tape, Ms. Kewen."

"I'll have it couriered this afternoon," Kewen said tersely.

"That it, then?" Belker inquired of Kewen who nodded.

Belker turned to Price. "Which brings us to the respondent side." He read from the folder in silence for several moments. "Your responsive pleading is somewhat sparse. What will you be presenting at hearing?"

"Clearly, Your Honor, we need to review the petitioner's materials but we would anticipate having expert testimony to address the issues of Dr. Fredrich's theory of treatment as well as his actions in treating Janie."

"Expert testimony as to what?"

"We have reason to believe that Dr. Fredrich's so-called treatment regimen lacks sound medical foundation and is both coercive and abusive."

"And your reason to believe that is based on what?"

Price hesitated. Her source was Sara Furden.

"Your Honor, I respectfully claim privilege and attorney work product on that." She raised her palm as soon as she saw the frown begin to grow on Belker's face. "Judge Belker, I want nothing more than to have everything laid out fully before the court, but I need to know what we're looking at before I can formulate precisely what we're going to do. Please allow us until tomorrow to provide the court with our theory of the case."

Belker, still frowning, flipped through the file in front of him until he found what he wanted. Then he asked, "When was the last time you visited Ms. Reston, Ms. Price. You personally."

"At Whispering Marsh? Never. I've met her elsewhere. But what —?"

"What about you, Mr. Matsen? When's the last time you visited Ms. Reston?"

"It would have been about two months ago, Your Honor."

"So," the judge continued directing his question back to Price, "who, to your knowledge, has visited Ms. Reston at Whispering Marsh since Dr. Fredrich's arrival? According to this," he tapped the file, "he's only been there a matter of weeks."

"Her parents visit as often as they can," Price responded.

"Are they the source of your information, then, Ms. Price?"

"Your Honor, again with respect, I've claimed privilege and work product. It's inappropriate to try to penetrate it."

Belker's mouth pursed with evident irritation. "Very well, disregard that question. Anyone else visit Ms. Reston recently?"

"To my knowledge, only John Cann," Price offered.

"Who is accused of inflicting the very harm for which Ms. Reston is being treated, is that correct?"

"It is *not* correct," Matsen interjected earning a glare from the judge. "Accused of it? Yes. By Dr. Fredrich. As a smokescreen for his own —"

"You have personal, firsthand knowledge of this, Mr. Matsen?" The judge shot the question at him.

"No, Your Honor, I do not."

"Then you will not be testifying to it in my court. I don't know how you folks do it in D-C," he overarticulated the letters, "but down here we actually enforce the hearsay rules." He looked at Price. "Will the Restons and Mr. Cann be testifying at the hearing, Ms. Price?"

"The Restons will be here, Your Honor. Mr. Cann is out of the country at the moment and —"

"I see," Belker said somewhat cryptically. "What about this Sara Furden?" He glanced down at the folder. "It says here that she was Ms. Reston's physical therapist. I assume she would have relevant information but — oh yes, she's a fugitive, isn't she. Have you heard from this Furden person, Ms. Price?"

"I respectfully claim privilege on that, Your Honor," Price said, aware the evasion told the judge what he wanted to know.

"Privilege goes to the content of a conversation not whether or not there was one, Ms. Price. But I'll let that go for now." Belker shook his head slowly. "I will tell you, Ms. Price, that I have more than a fleeting suspicion that you have had contact with Ms. Furden. Whether it was after she took Ms. Reston out of Whispering Marsh, I don't know. If I learn it was before, I will recommend you be charged as an accessory. And I will also tell you that if Ms. Furden shows up to testify, I will have her taken into custody. Lastly, I suggest you get Mr. Cann here. If he cares about this young lady, it seems to me he'd be here already. Unless, of course, his reasons for staying away have something to do with the assertions in the petition."

"This is completely out of order," Matsen started to protest.

"Shut your mouth, Mr. Matsen. You're not recognized in my court."

Belker leaned toward Price. "Now pay attention. There are two primary sources of information in a hearing under the Bailey Act. The medical information and the respondent him- or herself. I will hear Dr. Fredrich's testimony — and be advised that I do not discount such testimony lightly. The only opposing testimony that will be given equal weight is from another medical professional based on his or her examination of the patient, period. Has that occurred?" He looked harshly at Price, let his eyes graze slowly down the two associates and the paralegal, held his gaze for a moment on Matsen, then returned to Price. "Will it occur, Ms. Price? Because in order for that to happen — am I stating the obvious yet? — they have to go where Ms. Reston is. So someone would have to *know* where she is." He raised his eyebrows. "Will such testimony be presented. Ms. Price? Hmmm?"

"I don't know, Your Honor."

"So it might? Meaning you know where she is? I would say that does make you an accessory, a coconspirator perhaps in an —"

"It most certainly does not," Price said sharply. "It hasn't even been established that a crime has been committed, Judge. And I can tell you that Ms. Furden's actions have been ratified by the guardians and thus there's no basis for her fugitive status anyway."

"Ratification or not, what she did was in violation of a statutory procedure that I have already ruled was in technical compliance with the law. Once Dr. Fredrich *properly* admitted Ms. Reston to the facility, even the guardians themselves would not have the authority to contravene that admission. What do you say to that?"

"I say that the very question of whether the admission was or was *not* proper is the ultimate issue you're *supposed* to be holding a hearing to determine." Price was now leaning forward jabbing her forefinger onto the table as she spoke. "And it is highly inappropriate and prejudicial for you to be predetermining what might happen at the hearing or what you will do about it if it does."

Matsen could see that the tension between Price and Belker was reaching a boiling point and jumped in. "And I can tell you, Your Honor, that my ratification of Ms. Furden's actions in this matter are based on information received from Ms. Furden herself. Subsequent to her actions."

Belker gave Matsen a long look of disbelief. "Are you acknowledging you have had contact with Ms. Furden?"

"I am."

"And you are sitting in my court telling me you know the location of a kidnap victim and the fugitive who perpetrated it?"

"I am telling you that I am aware of the whereabouts of Ms. Reston and Ms. Furden, neither of whom is a kidnap victim nor a kidnapper."

"You know where they are."

"I do." Matsen was as calm as ever. "And I have not shared that information with anyone, including Ms. Price. And will not."

"I order you to disclose their whereabouts."

"I will not."

"Then I will hold you in contempt."

"Then we're even."

Belker exploded. He pointed to the court reporter and screamed at him to get his bailiff from the office. Then he looked back at Matsen. "You're going to jail, Matsen. Until you tell me what I want to know."

"Judge Belker —" Price tried to intervene.

"No." Belker shook his head at Price. "And let me tell you some-thing, Missy —"

"Missy! What kind of —"

"It's my kind, in my court!" Belker yelled. At that moment, the court reporter came back in with the bailiff who went and stood behind Matsen. As soon as the reporter sat down, Price quickly said, "Let the record reflect that in the absence of the reporter, the court has referred to counsel in clearly inappropriate, if not sexually harassing terms, threatened counsel for the respondent with unwar-ranted sanctions, and indicated that the judgment of the court has been predetermined before the presentation of evidence."

"Strike that," the judge ordered the reporter.

"Do not strike that," Price commanded with equal force. She turned back to the judge. "You have no right to —"

"Wrong, Counselor, I have all the rights in my court," Belker countered. He pointed at the bailiff, "Put cuffs on that man, Everett, and put him in a cell. He will be released only on my say-so. And no visitors."

Price rose out of her chair when the bailiff grabbed Matsen roughly by the elbow and lifted him up. Matsen made a quick face to dissuade her and left with the bailiff, hands cuffed behind him. Price whirled back on the judge.

"What is wrong with you?" she asked with her voice cracking in anger. "That most decent man — and you —" Quinlan put a restraining hand on Price's forearm and gave her a "we need you out here, Katherine" look. Price forced herself to calm down.

Judge Belker watched smugly as Price sat. Then he looked at the reporter and spoke for the record.

"Ordered. Hearing on the petitioner's request for involuntary placement of the respondent is set for two P.M. the day after tomor-row in this room. This pretrial hearing is continued until two P.M. tomorrow at which time counsel for *both sides*," he said looking directly at Price, "will formally declare and will provide for examination and preliminary review all evidence they intend to present at hearing. Counsel are also ordered to have present at the continued pretrial all witnesses they intend to call. Any evidence or witnesses not specifically listed will be excluded. Failure to comply will be grounds for default and judgment will be entered forthwith." He stood and left the room.

Price spun in her chair as soon as the door closed behind him. Jabbing a finger at the court reporter, she asked, "How long before I can get a copy of the transcript?"

"Overnight if you want to pay a premium."

"Double the premium, and get it to me today."

27

Price stormed out of the courthouse, the rest of the team hurrying to keep up with her. As she reached the sidewalk, her cell phone beeped. She slid it out of the pocket on the side of her briefcase, hit connect, and put it to her ear.

"Katherine, it's John."

Christ. Not now, was her first thought. But she gathered herself. "Hi, John. What's up?" she said with a forced pleasantry.

"Arthur. I need to talk to him and he's not answering his cell. The office said he was at a hearing with you. What's that about?"

The office in D.C. had strict instructions not to tell Cann about the hearings involving Janie or where Price and Matsen were. *This is getting too complicated,* Price thought.

"No, he's not with me. But I'll track him down and have him get back to you."

"Okay. Listen. Nikolic now considers it at least possible that Erwin Jost and Predrag Djilic are one and the same. He wants to talk to Arthur about Djilic. I haven't told Rade about Savka so I think it's safe to —"

"And this Nikolic is who?" Price interrupted impatiently.

"Rade. The SAJ guy," Cann said slowly. "Katherine, are you okay?"

"I am. Yes. I'll tell Arthur to call you."

"Okay. How's Janie doing?"

Price didn't expect the question and it threw her. "Why do you keep asking me that?" she snapped.

Cann pulled the phone away from his ear and looked at it before he answered. "I guess because I always do," he said coldly. "What's up with you?"

Price scrambled to cover her gaffe. "Sorry, John. There's just — everything is going wrong with this merger I'm dealing with and — Janie's fine. She's fine." Price assuaged her conscience with the thought that was true at least. For now, anyway.

Cann, not entirely convinced, accepted the explanation. "All right. I'll wait for Arthur's call."

Price's phone clicked off even before Cann had a chance to say "Good-bye."

Janie was sitting in a wheelchair on the screened-in back porch of the safe house. Every angle had been checked to ensure she couldn't be seen and one of the security team patrolled the tree line that backed up on the small open space at the rear of the structure.

The fresh air was invigorating and added to the thrill of just being awake, reasonably alert, and free of the agonizing pain and pressure that had been twisting her insides. She still felt a sporadic jab or involuntary shudder but, for the most part, she felt normal. Such as it was. Never far away, Sara Furden sat just behind Janie on a bench that ran along the rear wall of the house. She, too, was relaxing a bit now that the worst of Janie's withdrawal seemed to be over.

" 'S pretty out here, Sara," Janie said with a crooked smile Furden couldn't see. She reached her right hand back and Sara took it in one of hers. "So wha' happ'ns now?" Janie asked over her shoulder,

Furden gave Janie's hand a tug. "Don't even think about it, Janie. You're safe. And we're going to keep it that way."

•   •   •

Price marched into the conference room of the rented office space followed by Quinlan, Marks, and Valdez. She threw the file Kewen had provided onto the long, rectangular table and had to lunge after it to keep it from sliding off the other side. Then she sat down, flipping the file open, and scanned the contents. After a moment, she culled some papers and handed them to Valdez.

"Helena, this is the medical documentation — diagnosis, examination notes, and so forth. Get them scanned and out by e-mail to Dr. Nieves ASAP, will you? Let him know they're on the way. And that I need his input immediately. Thanks."

Valdez grabbed the sheaf of papers and was out the door. Price then assigned one of the office staff to make three copies of the remaining contents of the file. As that was being done, she spoke to Quinlan and Marks.

"Beth, I need you to touch base with one of the clerks for the appellate court. See if I can get an appointment with one of the justices. I can at least try to get an order releasing Arthur." She shook her head. "It kills me that he's sitting in a cell right now because I couldn't control my own temper. You'd think I'd know better, wouldn't you?" Quinlan and Marks both declined to respond to what they fervently hoped was a rhetorical question from a senior partner.

The clerical assistant came in and distributed the three sets of copies. They read without speaking until Price slapped her set of papers down onto the table in frustration. "This seems like so much crap, but what do I know?" She looked at her watch. "Where the hell's our expert?" It had been all of twenty minutes since Valdez had sent the papers to Dr. Nieves.

Price looked at her watch again for the second time in a minute. "Okay, look, you two get some lunch. As pressed as we are for time, we need to step back and get a fresh perspective. That, and some evidence we can work with."

*   *   *

To Price's amazement, the transcript was delivered only a little more than two hours after the hearing concluded. Paying double the premium had the desired effect. Not that it would do any good. She checked the last few pages and, as she expected, the exchange with the judge about his actions and the "missy" comments were nowhere to be found. When a judge says "Strike that" and a lawyer says "Don't strike that," no prizes, as they say, for guessing who wins.

Quinlan and Marks stood behind Price, looking over her shoulder. "Okay, let's make the best of this," Price said. "We'll try to show this transcript doesn't match what happened — throw doubt on it. Richard," Price directed, "I want a memo I can give the appellate judge on this. Affidavits from you and Beth and Helena — wait a second." She turned in her chair and called for the paralegal. Valdez stuck her head in the door a moment later.

"Helena, how's that eidetic memory of yours?"

"Not eidetic," Valdez smiled. "I keep telling you. I just pay attention."

"Well, I pay attention too," Price said, "but I don't have the recall you do."

Valdez shrugged the compliment off.

"So, may I assume you were paying attention in the hearing then?" Price asked.

"Of course. That's my job."

Price was serious. "I need you to put down what you recall of the exchange between me and the judge at the end. Word for word. Like a transcript."

"Already done." Valdez stepped away from the door and came back in an instant with some sheets of paper. She handed them to Price. "I did this right after. It should qualify as a contemporaneous recollection. Hearsay exception. All that."

"When do we send you to law school, Helena?" Price said with genuine admiration.

"No, thanks. I value my reputation," Valdez joked. Price and the others smiled.

"Can our stuff overcome the transcript?" Marks asked.

Price shrugged. "Your statements, Helena's notes? They're a start. Add the fact of Belker jailing Arthur for contempt. And what he said earlier is in the transcript. Taken together, we can try to establish bias." Another, bigger shrug.

The receptionist stuck her head in the door again. "There's a Dr. Nieves on the line. Shall I put it through?'

"Finally!" Price looked at the two associates. "Let's hear what the good doctor has to say."

Price had been looking for an expert in the memory field ever since Arthur had asked her to check into things, but after Sara called Price had turned up the pressure on the research department to find someone. She was pleased when they located a Dr. Richard Nieves, who was not only a leading expert in the memory field, but who also had apparently indicated to the researchers who found him that he was familiar with — and not particularly well disposed toward — Dr. Fredrich. But this would be Price's first conversation with him.

She took the phone from the credenza behind her, put it on the table, and set it up for speaker. "Dr. Nieves. Good to talk to you. Thanks for calling so promptly."

"Not at all. How can I help?"

"You've read the materials we sent?"

"I have."

"And?"

"Typical Nathan Fredrich, I would say."

Price felt a tinge of optimism and looked at Quinlan and Marks. "How so, doctor?"

"I've given some thought as to how to best explain this to people outside the field of memory. That's not meant to be patronizing," he interjected. "It's just that this is a pretty esoteric field." He cleared his throat. "The materials you sent me reflect Dr. Fredrich's experimentation with recovering what he calls 'implicit memory.' "

Price lasered in. "Experimentation? Is that how you'd characterize what he was doing with this patient?"

"Oh, clearly. No reputable physician or therapist would — I mean, what he was doing would not be justified even if his premise were valid. Based on his notes, I would say that the frequency of the sessions was abusive in itself. The medication was rather standard, but the dosages were excessive in my opinion."

"What about more than one medication being used at the same time. Was there any indication of any particularly addictive drug being used?"

"Dr. Fredrich's notes indicate the use of an amobarbiturate. Sodium pentathol is the most well known. Quite standard in memory recovery as I said. It can be addictive with prolonged use, but shouldn't have been in this case. And there's nothing in the notes about any other medication or drug. Why?"

"Because there's a toxicology report that indicates that a combination of drugs was being used; the amobarbiturate and another that was highly addictive." Price asked another question. "Would using a drug and *not* putting it in the notes be inappropriate?"

"Inappropriate? Good Lord. It's malpractice. Maybe even criminal depending on the specifics."

Price's hopes were soaring. "A moment ago, Doctor, you said he wasn't justified in what he was doing even if his premise were valid. Does that mean his premise was invalid? Or is the concept of 'implicit memory' invalid?"

"That's two questions, Ms. Price. Let me answer them in the reverse order of how you asked. 'Implicit memory' is a valid concept. It refers to memory that is a function of or is 'implicit' in behaviors and activities but is a memory of which we are unaware. Is that clear?"

"No."

Nieves was silent for a moment. "All right. Are you familiar the term in sports, 'muscle memory'?"

"Yes," Price said as all three attorneys nodded in silence.

"A behavior is made up of a series of individual component actions but, once the overall behavior is learned, the individual actions that make it up no longer need to be specifically recalled. Okay?"

"Right. Throwing a ball, for example. You just go ahead and remember how to throw it. The individual actions that go into a throw are forgotten. On the conscious level, anyway."

"Exactly. They're there — obviously. You just don't know it. But Dr. Fredrich has distorted the concept to his own ends and turned it into a theory that the mind can recall not only events it has forgotten but can recall events of which it was not aware, consciously anyway, at the time those events occurred."

"How valid is that?"

"How valid is any theory? By definition, it's a theory. A postulation. A proposal. The true measure of a theory is acceptance."

"Okay. How accepted is it then?"

"It isn't. Almost no one buys memory as a purely physical activity independent of intellectual or even emotional considerations. Far more accepted is the idea that memory is almost a purely intellectual — and conscious — activity that exists only in the present."

"You're losing me again, doctor."

"Okay. Think of it as the difference between a videotape of something that occurred six months ago versus a narrative of the same occurrence that you sit down and write today. One shows the actual event. The other is a compilation of your perceptions as they exist today. The idea being that memory isn't a 'recall' of anything but that rather it's a contemporary recreation of events or cognitive items that were perceived at some time in the past. But," his voice added emphasis, "the essential thing is that the items had to have been perceived in the first place. At some level." He added even more emphasis. "At some perceptive or perceptible level. Otherwise they wouldn't be available for the re-creation."

"So, if I've somehow absorbed something in the intervening six months that didn't occur at the time but that I now relate to that event, it may form a part of my narrative even though it didn't occur?"

"Once again, very good," he confirmed. "You've stated the essential dichotomy of recovered memory versus false memory. It may be something you've actually experienced or, as with Dr. Fredrich, something that he consciously places into your perceptions to alter or even fabricate a memory."

"Why?"

"Why what?"

"Why does Fredrich do it?"

"To prove his theory. Based on discussions I've had with others in the field, it no longer even matters to him if the theory is valid. He is obsessed with proving to his peers that he's right and they're — we're — wrong. Reality be damned."

"Even if it harms the patient?"

"Even if it harms the patient."

"What about the oath, Doctor. 'First do no harm.' "

A touch of indignation was apparent in Nieve's tone when he spoke. "Oh, he's been disciplined, Ms. Price, I assure you. Several times. In fact, his license has been suspended in two states and revoked in a third."

"But I checked with the medical licensing board and there's nothing about that," Price said slowly. "Actually there's nothing at all," she added almost to herself.

"Well, yes. Such matters are confidential. In all three instances that I know of, Dr. Fredrich was allowed to surrender his license and cease to practice in that state. In return, his records were sealed."

"What did he do? What was he accused of?"

"Well, I have no more access than you do to the specifics, but from what I've heard, there have been several adverse medical consequences reported from his treatment. There are even rumors of at least one death."

"And your profession has no problem with letting him just move on and do it again?"

"The rationalization is that mistakes happen and good doctors would be inhibited along with the bad if disciplinary actions were made public. Lawyers make mistakes, too, you know."

"Yes, doctor, but, as the saying goes, our mistakes can generally get up and walk out of the office."

Nieves didn't answer right away. "Yes, I suppose," he said finally. "Look, I have no regard for Dr. Fredrich and, for what it's worth, would not object to seeing such willful and dangerous behavior dealt with more harshly."

"And we appreciate your assistance in this. You're our savior. A young lady's savior. You're in Chicago, right?"

"Yes."

"We'll have a round trip ticket, first class, waiting for you at — O'Hare or Midway. Which is closer? I know it's incredibly short notice but —"

"Ticket? What for?"

"There's a hearing the day after tomorrow, doctor, and, frankly, right now, your testimony is not only what we need but it's all we have. I —"

"Testimony? Oh, no. This is case analysis, only. I can't testify to any of this. I'd —"

"If it's cost —"

"Not at all. I never agreed to testify. And can't. I would be ostracized in my profession."

"Dr. Nieves, a young lady's health and stability — her safety is at stake. What about what you just said about —"

"I know what I just said, Ms. Price. But how much weight would it carry if I were portrayed as a charlatan and turncoat. No, no. I cannot. Please understand."

"I do understand. Sadly, I do." Price thought about severing the connection but held off. "Please reconsider, doctor. Please. As I said, you're all we have."

There was no response and it took the three people around the table a moment to realize that the connection was closed.

Things only got worse when, later that day, the audiotape that Kewen intended to offer as evidence was delivered. Price, Quinlan, Marks, and Valdez listened as Fredrich's voice — soft, smooth, professional — began the session.

> "I'm going to talk to you very softly, Janie, and I'd like you to focus in on the sound of my voice and what I'm saying and let your mind go where I direct it. Okay?"
>
> " 'Kay."
>
> "You remember when we spoke before, I asked you about your favorite places, don't you?"
>
> Janie nodded.
>
> "And you remember your most favorite place of all, that grove of Spanish oaks you told me about with all the moss hanging from them, the soft grass on the ground all around them, the tiny pond with the frogs."
>
> "An' the salama'ders. They were ev'rwher'."
>
> "Right. Let's go there."
>
> " 'Kay."

The tape continued as Fredrich led Janie to her "safe place." But soon the tone began to change as Janie was led back to her ordeal.

> "Where are you now, Janie?"
>
> "Nowher'. Can' see anythin'. Feels like a bi' open space. Hallway, mayb'."
>
> "But you can't see anything?"

"No. 'T's dark."

Silence for a moment.

"S' a light."
"What, Janie?"
"A light. An' — oh — oww! — oh —"

The three people listening all tensed.

"What is it, Janie? Is someone hurting you?"
"Mmmm."
"Is he doing anything else?"
"Ow!"
"Who is it, Janie?"

A silence, then, after a moment, they heard Janie whisper.

" 'Fessa Cann."
"John Cann? Your guardian?"
"Mmmm."
"He did all those horrible things to you?"
"Mmmm."
"Tell me again, Janie. Who did all these things to you?"

Again there was a pause and again Janie repeated the name.

" 'Fessa Cann."

28

Hotel Berghausen
Just outside Garmisch

The girl was young, extraordinarily pretty, with a figure that combined athleticism and voluptuousness. Stepping out of the shower, she toweled herself off in front of the full-length mirror opposite the bathroom door. When she was done, she stood for a moment, the towel dangling down her right side. Her head tilted from side-to-side as she looked at herself in the mirror with a clinical disinterest, examining her body as though it were something separate from the rest of her.

Turning slightly, she tossed the towel back into the bathroom and crossed to the dresser. She rummaged in the top drawer, then picked up two pair of thong panties, red in her right hand, white in her left. Dangling the lingerie in front of her on extended index fingers, she turned and raised her eyebrows at the man seated in the corner of the room.

"The white," the man decided.

The girl took the decision with indifference, dropped the red panties into the open drawer and stepped into the scanty white underwear. Then she crossed to the closet and pulled out a white mid-thigh length cocktail dress that she dropped over her head.

After smoothing it down, she extended one foot at a time into the closet and brought each out shod in an open sandal with two-inch heels.

The girl turned and faced the man and held out her palms. The man looked at her critically for a couple of seconds then made a circle with the forefinger of his right hand.

She turned slowly in response.

"The dress should be shorter," the man said in Serbo-Croatian. The girl didn't understand him and he repeated the statement in English. It was not either's first language, but they both understood it.

"But my ass is hanging out now," the girl began to protest softly but stopped abruptly as the man's eyebrows arched.

"And if I tell you to walk down the streets naked you will, won't you?"

The girl lowered her eyes.

"I didn't hear your answer, Lukina. You would, of course. Yes?"

"Yes," she said quietly nodding, remembering when she'd been forced to do exactly that.

"Yes, you would," the man said with finality, pleased with her compliance. He'd be reluctant to beat her, given her exquisiteness. Damaged goods bring less.

Riessersee Hotel
Garmisch

Cann had a late dinner and decided to have a drink before going up to his room. There were only two other people at one end of the bar. He seated himself at the other end of the bar where he could see the entire room and anyone who came in. He was now armed, and planned to keep it that way.

From where he sat, he could see a man in his thirties and a much younger, very attractive girl in a short white dress coming across the lobby toward the bar. Several yards from the entrance, the man grabbed the girl's arm, jerking her to a halt. He leaned down and spoke to her then pushed her forward.

Lukina walked into the lounge. She stopped in the doorway briefly and then crossed to the bar. Cann noticed she had an unsophisticated walk that didn't match her stunning appearance. She took a seat about halfway down the bar from Cann and gave him a quick look.

She ordered a drink and took a small sip. Staring for a moment into the mirror behind the bar, her eyes seemed to see nothing. Then she looked over at Cann and held his gaze for a second. She smiled and took another sip of wine, then fished in her purse for a pack of cigarettes. She took one out and made a show of searching for something. Then she turned to Cann and asked, "You have fire?"

Cann shook his head. Rather than seek elsewhere, though, Lukina put the cigarette back into the pack and put the pack back into her purse. Then she looked nervously toward the lobby and Cann saw the man out there frown and make a 'get on with it' motion of his head. Looking stiff and awkward, Lukina stood and came over to Cann.

"May I sit with you?" she asked with a glowing but nervous smile.

Cann extended a hand toward the seat next to him. He was not big on bar pick-ups but in this case he was struck, not only by Lukina's beauty, but by her youth. As he grew older, Cann had found his natural inclinations increasingly challenged by a growing paternalism. And he felt that now.

"You would like to buy me drink, yes?" Lukina asked, still smiling and positioning herself so that she was facing him full on.

"Sure," Cann said and signaled to the bartender. "The same?" he asked her as he pointed to the still half-full glass of wine she'd left only a few seats away. Cann saw a moment of fleeting panic as the girl realized her mistake. "I . . ." she was breathing in short breaths. Then she pasted the dazzling smile on her face yet again. But her eyes weren't smiling.

"You think I am pretty?"

"Very."

The smile relaxed slightly but the eyes seemed to get sadder. "Yes," she said and placed her hand on Cann's thigh, just above the knee. "You want to come with me?" Cann didn't know if the double meaning was intentional although the girl did raise her brows and curl her lips as she said it.

"That would be very nice," Cann said, "but I don't think so. Thank you." He patted the girl's hand and then gently lifted it from his leg.

Cann knew that at this point, the more polished ladies of the evening would either make some additional effort, or excuse themselves to seek greener pastures. But Lukina remained in her seat. As Cann watched, her eyes clouded and her lower lip trembled and she looked more and more like the frightened child she was. She put her hand alongside her face to block any view from the lobby. And let the tears flow.

Cann let her cry and said nothing.

After a moment, Lukina caught her breath and muttered, "I don't know how to do this." She looked at Cann. "I am sorry. I am —" Then she made a partial turn of her head toward the lobby but immediately brought her face back to Cann. When she did, he saw more fear.

"You don't know how to do what?" Cann asked.

"This," Lukina rolled her hand around. "To make you want me. To make you go with me. I —" she looked down. "I am — they bring people to room. I don't know how to —" she waved her hands to indicate the whole context and left it at that.

Cann glanced out to the lobby where the man was pacing with an occasional glare into the bar. That in itself rankled him. "And that man out there?" he asked.

"They call him Senka, I think," Lukina sniffled.

"You think?"

"I only meet him tonight. Branko sent him to —"

"Branko —"

"Branko Jost."

The last name was not lost on Cann.

"And Branko sent him to what?"

"To —" She started to look toward the lobby again but stopped herself. "To make you like me. If I fail, he will —"

Cann recalled the graphic images of the sex trade Nikolic had described. He leaned forward and lowered his face so that he could look up into Lukina's eyes.

"Talk to me," he said gently. When she didn't say anything, he asked her, "What's your name?"

"Lukina," she said softly.

"Talk to me, Lukina," he repeated. "Where are you from?"

Lukina looked up at him as though surprised he would ask. She'd not allowed herself to think of her home for what seemed like a very long time. After a moment, she answered. "Causeni. Is in Moldova. You know it?" she asked with a naïve hopefulness.

Cann shook his head. "No."

Lukina twisted her mouth and nodded, "No. Is far away." As was the look in her eyes. "Very far away." Her face crumbled again into tears and despair. "I miss it," she sobbed quietly. "My mother. I miss all of them. So much. I only wished to — And now I can't go home. They say someday. When I pay. But, I know that day will not come."

"Because you have no money? And they took your papers?"

Lukina looked at him with curiosity and uncertainty. Then she nodded. "But even without papers, I would try if I could. But they do not leave us alone." She moved her eyes toward the lobby. "Someone is always watching. And if we try to escape and are caught, they beat us. Some die." She nodded vigorously. "Is true. They have made us watch."

Cann lifted Lukina's chin with his forefinger. "Lukina, you don't know me. But I can help you. Do you think you can trust me?"

She looked deep into Cann's eyes and shook her head. "Trust?" She smiled sadly. "I cannot." Before Cann could say anything, Lukina

continued. "But how can it be worse than now?" For the first time
Cann saw life in her eyes. "So, I will hope. Perhaps I am foolish
but —" She shrugged. "I would rather be dead than do this."

Cann gave her hand a squeeze. "Okay. Tell me what you were
supposed to do exactly."

Lukina explained that she'd been ordered to get Cann to take her
outside where he would be seized by Senka and some other men.
That was all she knew.

Cann put the earpiece for his cell phone into his ear and hit the
"8," which he'd programmed to speed dial Nikolic. Pretending to be
talking to Lukina, he said, "Rade. It's John. Are you around?"

"That depends on where around is."

"I'm in the hotel lobby bar."

"I am not far. Why?"

Cann didn't answer directly. He scanned the people in the room.
"Do you still have people watching me?"

"Of course," Nikolic responded without hesitation. "Wait."
Through the earpiece, Cann heard a couple of beeps and then one
of the men seated at a table across the room gave him a look and a
short nod.

"Just the one?" Cann asked.

"No. There are two more outside. Why? What is going on?"

Cann gave him a quick rundown. Rade said he would direct the
men outside to determine who was waiting, where, how many. "I'll
also brief the man in the bar with you. Keep the line open so I don't
have to ring you back."

"Right. Thanks."

Lukina, who seemed to have caught on quickly, mimed responses
as if the conversation were with her. When Cann was done speaking
with Nikolic, he took Lukina's hand and said, "Now, we wait."

Several moments later, Cann heard Nikolic's voice through
the earpiece. "There were two men, John. We have them now. I am
reasonably certain there are no others. May I suggest you let things

go forward. Our friend in the lobby will be a bit surprised when he finds he is alone. We will be waiting outside."

"Got it." Cann nodded. He put his hand on Lukina's cheek and pulled her face close to his own. "Okay, Lukina, we need to act like you've been successful with me. Are you ready?"

She made a face. "I think so, but I am afraid."

Cann moved his hand from her cheek to her shoulder and squeezed "That's okay. But you can't act like you're afraid. Just take my arm and put your face into my shoulder like you're snuggling."

"What is snuggling?" she asked with a quizzical look on her face.

"Just put your head on my shoulder," Cann smiled. Lukina nodded. They stood and Lukina put her arm through Cann's, pressing closely against him. She put her face into his shoulder and they walked through the lobby, ignoring the man called Senka. Once outside, Cann maneuvered Lukina toward Nikolic's men. Senka followed and, by the time he began to sense that things were not as planned, he had two SAJ guns pointed at him. He glared venomously at Lukina. "You are dead, bitch," he spat. "And you will die in a way that —"

The words were cut off and replaced by a gurgling sound as Cann seized the man's windpipe with his fingers and twisted. Nikolic stepped up behind him and said, quite conversationally, "I'd rather you didn't do that, John, if you don't mind. We have some questions and, well, you know."

Cann loosened his grip. Slowly.

Nikolic turned to Lukina. "And you are the brave young lady who has assisted us?"

Lukina managed a tentative smile.

"Where are you from?"

"Moldova," she said.

"You will see it soon. I promise you. You are done with these men. But I have a request. We will help you in every way. But you could help us. Answer some questions. Help us learn how the operation works."

Lukina chewed her lip and said nothing.

"I promise you will go home. And until then, we will protect you."

She looked at Cann. "You promise this too?"

"I promise it, Lukina."

When Lukina spoke again, it was in a soft yet strong voice. "I want to go home," she said looking from Cann to Nikolic. "And, yes, I am done with these men. But first —" She crossed over to Senka and without a word swung her arm in a full, open-handed slap of such force that he stumbled back several steps. She watched Senka lick the blood off his lip, then turned back to Nikolic and Cann.

"If I stay," she said, "you help others too?"

"Yes, I think we can. Probably."

"Then I stay."

29

Schloss Grunberg
South of Munich

"Nikolic! Twice!" Erwin Jost rapped the ash end of his cigar on the brass ashtray and pointed the tip at Dubran Mribic who was seated across the desk from him. "We would have taken Cann if Nikolic had not interfered. Twice!" the old man repeated. "Why? What's Nikolic's connection to Cann?"

"Besides me, I don't know of one."

"Precisely," the old man shouted. "You. Nikolic would not be here if it wasn't for you."

Mribic said nothing.

"We knew Nikolic was on your trail. That's why we pulled you out. But you were supposed to come here and drop out of sight. Instead, you get yourself arrested in Garmisch. That was foolish."

Branko Jost was slouched in an armchair. "In fairness to Dubran, Father, you wouldn't have gotten your chance at this Matsen fellow if he hadn't."

"Pah!" the elder Jost scoffed. "We haven't got Matsen, have we?"

"Not yet," Branko shrugged, "but as long as Cann is around, we have a chance to use him as bait. And our KLA friends have their own special interest in Cann. We can use that."

"I hope so, Branko," Erwin Jost said. "We've stirred a wasp's nest here and I would hate to see it go for nothing." He looked at Mribic. "And you should hope so as well, Dubran," he said darkly. "You may be my son, but I have my limits."

Cann and Nikolic were learning that Lukina had been a very small part of a very large smuggling operation, but what she did know filled in a lot of blanks.

How had this all begun?

She had answered an ad for domestic help positions located throughout Western Europe and an interviewer had come to her home to talk to her and her parents.

Didn't she know about the dangers of such advertisements, Nikolic had asked her.

Yes. As did her parents. They had said "no" many times.

But this man was different. He had papers. And, while Lukina couldn't remember the details, she was able to produce a recognizable sketch of the logo they contained. A wreath, open at the top, encircling a pair of praying hands that were tented over a human figure.

"United Nations Commission on Refugees and Human Rights," Nikolic said tightly to Cann. The SAJ captain turned back to Lukina.

Were these the papers they used to travel from home to Brcko?

She didn't know. She traveled in a van with other girls and the man who had signed them up, but from Moldova to Brcko they had their own papers.

What was the trip like? Were they treated well?

From Moldova to Brcko, yes, it was good. Not luxury. But they were not mistreated.

When did they realize something was wrong?

As soon as they got to Brcko.

What followed was more awkward for Cann and Nikolic than it was for Lukina. For the most part, she told the story dispassionately as though it had happened to someone else.

They were taken inside a warehouse and immediately their papers were taken. Then they were told to take off their clothes. After some of the girls were beaten, they did as they were told. One of the girls was then made to have sex with two men. Very fast. Very rough.

Every girl was made to — The dissociation failed momentarily and Lukina looked down as she described the programmed humiliation. They were all made to perform every kind of sex act so that they would know there was nothing they could refuse.

One of the girls, the youngest, Lukina didn't know how old she was, but she looked young, was taken away by a man in a suit. In her mind, Lukina had named him the bird man.

Why?

Because he looked like a bird. He was tall. Spiky hair. He had a sharp, pointed nose and his eyes were dark and piercing. He kept bouncing his leg all the time while the girls were performing. And, all the while, his head went forward and back like a bird's does when it's walking or eating or watching.

She remembered something else about the bird man. He'd held a leather folder on his lap as he watched. At one point, he left the folder on the chair. Lukina saw it had the same logo as the one she'd drawn. The same as the one on the papers she'd been shown during the interview at home.

Nikolic gave Cann a hard look. "I think I know who this is," Nikolic said, his lip curled in contempt. He looked at Cann. "Gustav Bakken, assistant deputy high commissioner in the Tuzla office of the United Nations Commission on Refugees and Human Rights." He turned to a computer and brought up an image on the screen and showed Lukina. "Is this the man?"

Her eyes grew cold. She nodded.

Nikolic nodded in turn to Cann. "Bakken." He looked back to Lukina. "When did you see this man? Just that first day?"

The girl again blew air through pursed lips. "I see him often. Many times. That first day, he took young girl away. After that, next day, he came for me. I had to spend day and night with him. He is not nice man."

"You said many times," Cann asked. "You saw him after that?"

"He came many times. He brought others. Some times I see them arrive. In white cars and vans with that" — she pointed to the drawing of the UN logo — "picture on it. He brought many people — not always men — to parties, they called it. Many people, many different languages, I think. Different countries.

"Sometimes, we were dressed in nice clothes. Sometimes, no clothes. We would stand around. We could not drink or eat. We just wait until one of them takes us to another room. Sometimes more than one of them." She looked down again. "Sometimes they make us to do sex in front of everyone. But we cannot refuse.

"Other times," Lukina continued. "we were driven somewhere. I don't know where. We would have eyes covered. It was hour, maybe more. Two times, we drove perhaps two hours." She shook her head. "But it was same when we get to place. Always same."

"Tuzla, is my guess," Nikolic said. "About an hour away from Brcko. Sarajevo is another hour." He shook his head. "Entertainment for diplomatic receptions: visiting dignitaries." He sneered. "Dignitaries, indeed!"

"So, what's next?" Cann asked.

"We will put surveillance on Bakken. We have looked only in Brcko so far. Now we watch Tuzla and Sarajevo. Follow the leads, see how high this goes."

"Until you get to a certain point, then you get hit with diplomatic immunity. You know that."

Nikolic's look was ice cold. "Then we weigh alternatives."

Lukina interrupted them, her voice rising. "But what about now? What will you do? You help other girls, no?" She looked back and forth between the two men.

"We'll get this information to the authorities," Nikolic assured her.

"Pah! Authorities. Yes. Tell them. But is not enough. You must tell newspapers, television. If other girls don't know, they still go."

"We'll do that, too, Lukina," Cann answered, "but the newspapers may not even go with the story unless we can show them proof. If word gets out that we know about this, before we have proof — some proof at least — they'll destroy evidence. Hide the girls. Or worse."

"What can be proof? I am not proof?"

Both men nodded and Cann said, "You are. But if we had more. Documents. The papers themselves."

"Interpole," Lukina said.

"Yes, we work closely with them and —" Nikolic began.

"No," Lukina interrupted. "Not Interpol, police. I mean Interpole. Club. Documents are there."

Nikolic looked at Cann with raised eyebrows. "If we could get Lukina's papers — the fake ones. And the real ones."

Lukina shook her head rapidly. "No. Not *my* papers." She shook her head again, frustrated. "Yes, my papers. But other papers also. I hear others talk. Branko keeps all papers for all of girls in office in Club Interpole."

"Do you know where in his office the papers are?"

"In . . . ah . . . how you call in English?" She made a square in the air with her hands. "Where money is kept."

"A safe."

"Safe," Lukina repeated.

"How is it opened. Keys? Combination?"

"Is numbers. Turn thing in front."

This time Cann raised his eyebrows. "Think about it, Rade. If we can actually get the papers away from them, that'd be very persuasive proof. Even better, we clean them out and then blow the whistle with the local authorities. They go in. The girls get pulled out, right? Sent home?" He smiled at Lukina then looked back at Nikolic. "It won't stop the trade. But it'll hurt."

"And help other girls now," Lukina said tightly.

"For sure," Nikolic agreed. "A win would be nice. But it won't be so easy to do."

"Not easy, maybe. But you must have people who can handle something like this," Cann said.

"Of course, but we are not on our home territory. This is powerful organized crime we are dealing with. And the Interpole is open twenty-four hours a day. Often crowded. And always staffed. There's no time when the place is empty."

"You've got nobody inside?"

Nikolic shook his head.

Lukina was deep in thought. Then she looked up. "Oma is inside."

"Oma?"

"Yes," Lukina said, "she is old woman who looks after girls. Is good to girls. Cares about girls but —"

"But?"

"She also cares for Branko. I think she has been with Branko for long time. Like nanny? Or nurse. I have heard her speak with Branko and she speaks for girls. Tells him he must be nice to girls. Most times he doesn't get angry with her. Sometimes he listens. Most times he tells her she is wrong, that she is remembering wrong. Other times, he gets angry and tells her is not her concern. Then Oma forgets so that the next time is like first time."

"I don't understand," Cann said.

"Oma is not . . . how do you say . . . not right?" she said tapping a finger on her forehead. "Not crazy," she made a clutching gesture in front of her face. "She is —"

"Slow?" Nikolic suggested.

Lukina shook her head. "No, not slow. Oma is smart. She learns everyone's language," Lukina snapped her fingers, "and she translates for them with Branko. But she forgets. She will know something one time and later she will not know it. And then sometimes she will know it again." She shrugged. "One time after new girls come to

Brcko, I am bring to Interpole. I see Oma with girls. I know she cares for girls. I can see this. Feel it. One time, I ask Oma, 'Oma,' I say, 'how you can do this?' and she asks me, 'Do what? I help girls.' I tell her, 'But we don't want to be here. We want to go home.' And Oma looks at me and she is . . . what is word?" Lukina made a wide open-eyed expression and put her hands up in front of her.

"Surprised? Shocked?"

"Yes. Surprised. Like she doesn't know this. Doesn't know what I am telling her. So I tell her that I think I am going for job in West. Good job. Not this. I never want to do this. And I don't want to stay. And Oma she looks at me and she gets sad. And she says she didn't know this. 'What can I do?' she asks me. I say I need my papers so I can leave and she looks at me, still sad, and says, 'I will help.' But just then Branko comes in and he takes Oma with him.

"The next day, Oma is like, 'Hello, Lukina' — she remembers names always — 'how are you?' I ask her if she will help like she said and she doesn't know what I mean. So I start to tell her again and" Lukina stopped and shook her head as she recalled the image. "And Oma is surprised again. Is like we didn't talk the day before. And she is not . . . how you say . . . making pretend. I can tell. So I decide I must be ready when I talk to Oma so we can go right away and get papers and I try to go. Before she forgets. But before that happens, Branko comes to me and says I am not staying at Interpole. I am going to 'Park.' I don't know what this is but —" She put her head down but brought it up again defiantly, "— but it is to do what I must do in Brcko."

Cann waited a moment before he asked, "How can she help, this Oma? What can she do?"

"Oma knows numbers to safe. Where papers are."

"The combination? But you said she forgets."

"Not numbers. I tell you Oma is not . . ." once again she searched for the word, "is not — is *prost* in Romanian. What is *prost* in English?" No one knew. "But she is smart, I tell you this. With numbers especially. She remembers numbers. All numbers. She knows all girls' birthdays. Everyone's birthday. Telephone numbers. Is like magic she remembers every number. One day, girls and men at Interpole are playing game, asking Oma what is my birthday, his birthday, what is number on Branko's cars — he has many — and she knows all. Then man asks Oma what is combination to safe and she starts to say it and Branko, he says, 'No, no, Oma, you don't say that!' and he is laughing, but he hits man who asked and says to him he don't ask that again. So I know Oma knows numbers to safe."

"And you think Oma will help so long as something doesn't happen to interrupt the — thought process. Between the time she is asked and —"

"Yes, I believe this."

"Will she talk to me? Do it for me?" Cann asked.

Lukina shook her head. "I don't think Oma will do it for you. For a stranger," she said. "But she will do it for —" Her face drained of color as she realized what she was saying.

"Lukina, we can't let you go back there," Cann protested. "No one would expect that of you. We'll think of something else."

"What something else?" Lukina said her voice cracking. "Oma will only do it for someone she knows." She reached up and touched her lips with her fingertips. Her hands were shaking badly.

Cann and Nikolic looked at each other.

"Do you think you can, Lukina?" Cann asked.

"I must," she said firmly. "All the time, I am angry that no one does anything to help us. Now I can do something. If I don't —"

Cann spoke to Lukina. "Rade and I know a Dutch man — a good man — who is very brave. I owe him my life. He once said to me, 'Courage is not about *not* being afraid. Courage is about being afraid and doing it anyway.' I know you're afraid, Lukina. And I know you're very, very brave."

Lukina tried to smile but didn't quite succeed.

"Just don't forget promise," she said. "I am trusting you."

30

Safe House
Chatham County

Price and Furden sat in shadows at the kitchen table sipping coffee. It was approaching dusk but they hadn't turned on the lights. Janie was resting on the couch in the next room.

Just finding Janie and Sara had been no small feat. Belker's "no visitors" order remained in effect and even if it wasn't, Price knew Matsen wouldn't tell her Janie's whereabouts. For her own protection.

So she'd gotten on the phone to D.C. and threw some senior partner weight around to find out who this Ted was that Arthur had called earlier. Then she'd called Ted who'd professed complete and utter ignorance. But she'd finally persuaded him to call his associates and ask them — only if they existed, of course, and if they could somehow know such a thing — to contact someone named Sara who, of course, Ted had never heard of and have her call Katherine Price on the number that Price didn't need to give to Ted because Sara already knew it.

It was, she hoped, sufficiently circumspect to meet Ted's standards. Sara called within fifteen minutes.

"We've got nothing," Price told Sara. "Zero. Zip. Nada. In fact we've got worse than nothing. In addition to no expert, no witnesses, and no admissible evidence, we've got a judge who's been antagonistic toward us from the beginning. I certainly didn't help on that score."

"What if I testify?" Furden asked.

"I don't think it would be enough. Belker made it clear that the only thing that could offset Fredrich's testimony is another medical professional's, which we don't have, or Janie's testimony. And anyway, Belker also made it clear that he's going to have you taken into custody if you show up. My guess is that even if he did hear what you have to say, he'd discount you as an accused felon, a fugitive."

"Is there anything we can do?"

Price shrugged. "I'm trying to get an appointment with one of the justices on the Appellate Court. I'll ask that Belker be removed on the grounds of bias."

"Will it work?"

"Not likely." Price said matter-of-factly. "Judges just don't get removed. Almost never."

"So what's going to happen?"

"Unless we come up with something, Belker will enter an order turning Janie back over to Fredrich."

"I won't let that happen," Furden said, her voice tight.

"Neither will I, Sara."

"You'd defy a court order?"

Price nodded. "If it comes to that, yes, I will. But that still leaves Arthur in jail. Belker's not going to let him out unless he reveals where you and Janie are. And he won't do that."

The small voice behind them took them by surprise.

"Mis'er Ma'sen's in jail?" Janie was standing in the door. "Cuz a me?"

Price turned. "Not because of you, Janie. Because of me too. But he's okay. Don't worry."

Janie stepped unsteadily into the kitchen. "But he's in jail cuz he knows where I am, righ'?"

"Well, yes, but —"

"And you said the only thin' that the judge wan's to hear is a esper' or me."

Price nodded.

" 'Kay, then I'll tes'ify."

Sara stiffened. "No, Janie."

"I don't think that's a good idea, Janie," Price suggested.

"Why?" Janie asked. "Cuz I talk funny? Cuz I don' walk straigh'?"

Price was direct. "Partly. The judge will take your condition into account. Even Fredrich's records say he'd medicated you heavily."

"But I still 'member. I 'member everythin'."

"Janie, you can't —" Furden began to protest, but Price interrupted her.

"What do you mean you remember, Janie? What do you remember?"

"Ever'thin'. I knew wha' was happ'nin'."

"Even though you were drugged?"

Janie nodded. "The med'cin' just made me weak, you know, 'thargic. But I 'member."

"Did Fredrich get you to remember anything from before?"

"A li'l. A few secon's. I 'membered it hurt."

"If you testify, they might try to bring that up. Can you handle that?"

"Handle wha'?" Janie asked forcefully. "I don' 'member wha' happened b'fore 'cep' for a cupla seconds. Those other guys didn' need me to be co'scious for wha' they were doin'."

"You know what they did?"

"Well, yeah — people tol' me. But I don' 'member. I's like i' happen' to someone else. This time, Fredri' needed me co'scious so I could answer his questions. So I 'member. An' I wanna tes'ify."

Furden and Price were struck by Janie's strength.

"Lis'en," Janie said. She crossed unsteadily to the table, sat down between Price and Furden, and took the hand of each. "Ever since ever'thin' happ'n'd, ever'one's been takin' care a me, doin' everythin' for me. Now, fin'ly maybe I can do somethin'." She looked intently back and forth at Price and Furden. "For two years now, I been a victim. I don' wanna be jus' a victim an'more."

Not two hours earlier, Price couldn't have imagined letting Janie listen to the tape of her and Dr. Fredrich. Now she knew it was the right thing. It wasn't reality that had changed. It was perception.

> "I'm going to talk to you very softly, Janie, and I'd like you
> to focus in on the sound of my voice and what I'm saying and
> let your mind go where I direct it. Okay?"
> " 'Kay."

Janie nodded as she listened to the tape.

> "You remember when we spoke before, I asked you about
> your favorite places, don't you?
> "And you remember your most favorite place of all, that
> grove of Spanish oaks you told me about with all the moss
> hanging from them, the soft grass on the ground all around
> them, the tiny pond with the frogs."
> "An' the salama'ders. They were ev'rwher'."

Janie smiled.

> "Right. Let's go there."
> " 'Kay."
> "Where are you now, Janie?"
> "Nowher'. Can' see anythin'. Feels like a bi' open space.
> Hallway, mayb'."

Janie asked Price to stop the tape. "There's stuff missin' there. It di't happe' tha' fas'."

"Of what's missing, is it significant?

Janie thought for a bit then said, "No, I don't thin' so. Jus' gettin' down to the place." A wry expression formed on her face. "The safe place," she said sarcastically.

Price restarted the tape.

> *"But you can't see anything?"*
> *"No. 't's dark."*

Janie was listened intently. Then she saw Price and Furden watching her and she gave them a small smile. "I'm 'kay. Hones'." They went back to the tape.

> *"S' a light."*
> *"What, Janie?"*
> *"A light. An' — oh — oww! — oh —"*

This time when Price looked over at her, Janie had her lips pursed and she looked pained. Price stopped the tape.

"Still okay, Janie?"

"Yeah, 's 'kay. Tha's when I 'membered from b'fore. I thin' the drugs were wearin' off. I don' mean Fredri's drugs. I mean the drugs those guys gave me. It hurt — tha's all I 'member. An' it was jus' a second 'r two." She shrugged and then nodded to indicate she wanted to go on with the tape.

Price restarted the tape.

> *"What is it, Janie? Is someone hurting you?"*
> *"Mmmm."*
> *"Is he doing anything else?"*
> *"Ow!"*
> *"Who is it, Janie?"*
> *" 'Fessa Cann."*

"Wha'?" Janie's looked up, stunned.

"John Cann? Your guardian?"
"Mmmm."
"He did all those horrible things to you?"
"Mmmm."
"Tell me again, Janie. Who did all these things?"
" 'Fessa Cann."

"No way!" Janie said fiercely. "I didn' say tha'. I never said tha'."
"You're sure?"
" 'Course I'm sure," Janie said. "He kep' tryin' to ge' me to say tha' but I never did. I *know* I never did. It was the on'y way I could beat 'im."

"When I was at the observation window," Furden confirmed, "I heard Fredrich trying to get her to say it then too. And she wouldn't." She looked anguished. "That's when you were banging your head."

"I know," said Janie. "I 'member."

"Well, it's no surprise the tape's doctored," Price said. "If we could prove it, we'd have something."

"How can we prove it?" Furden asked.

"We'd need the original."

"The bastard probably destroyed it."

"I don' thin' so. He kept ever'thin'. He's a reser', 'member?"

"A what?" Price and Furden asked at once.

"A reser . . ." Janie let out an *'urrgh'* out of frustration and tried again. "A re . . . er . . . cher," she said slowly.

"Oh, a 'researcher,' " Furden realized. She looked at Price. "Of course. He not going to throw away any data." She looked at Janie. "Any idea where he keeps it?"

Janie nodded. "A' the en' of ev'ry session, he put ever'thin' in a draw' in a file cab'net tha' looks like a ol' radio."

"Locked?"

"Mmm-hmm."

"What kind of a lock. Do you know?"

"Com'ination. The tunin' dial."

"In his office?" she asked.

"Mmm-hmm," Janie nodded.

Price looked at Furden. "You know where his office is?"

"I've been in it. I even know the cabinet she's talking about."

"Sketch the layout for me," Price directed.

"Uh-uh," Furden said. "You don't know the place. I do. I can be in and out a lot faster."

"Faster isn't always better, Sara," Price said. "How do you plan to open the file cabinet?"

Furden had no answer. "I'm still going," she said with icy intensity.

"All right," Price said. "Give me an hour to get some things together. We'll both go."

The main parking lot at Whispering Marsh still had several cars in it despite the late hour. Price pulled into a far, unlit corner and turned off the engine. Reaching into the backseat for a small duffel, she asked Furden, "Where are we going?" Furden pointed through the windshield to a three-story building about two hundred yards away. They crossed to it without incident. Not surprisingly, the main entrance door was locked.

"Still got your key?" Price asked.

"Yes, but they change the locks whenever there's any kind of incident, so I don't know if mine will still work." She tried it. It didn't.

Price quickly stepped past Furden and pressed up close to the door so that her body shielded what she was doing with her hands. A few seconds later, she pulled the door open.

"Learn that in law school?" Furden asked.

"Different school," Price said without elaboration. They stepped inside. "Where's Fredrich's office?" Furden pointed toward the end of the hall. Once again, the lack of a key was not a problem and they were quickly inside.

At first, Price didn't see anything that looked like an old radio, but Furden crossed directly to a cabinet in an opposite corner. She pulled its doors open, revealing an old-fashioned floor model radio inside. Price went to it and examined the face of the radio closely. After noting where the tuning dial was set, she gingerly turned it, feeling more than hearing the telltale clicks. She then reached inside the knapsack and took out what looked like a large suction cup with wires coming out of its base. Price pressed the cup over the tuning dial and then plugged the free end of the wires running out of the base into a small box that had also been in the knapsack. She then plugged a set of earphones into a jack on the top of the small box and began to manipulate a sliding control switch.

"How does that work?" Furden whispered. Price shushed her without breaking her concentration. Truth be told, Price knew generally what the device was doing but had no real idea how exactly it did it. Something about magnets turning the tumblers and an acoustic monitor that sensed when they'd fallen into place. When they had, the device locked that gear in place and displayed the number on a digital readout on top of the box. The instrument did all the work. Price wrote down the numbers as they came up and listened for the significantly louder click that would indicate the door was open.

Furden couldn't hear it when the *thut* alerted Price that the device had done its job, but she knew as soon as Price removed the earphones and pulled the dish off the knob and pulled the front of the radio open. Inside were two drawers containing a number of accordion folders labeled by name, many of them containing tape cassettes. Price found one marked Reston. She reached again into the knapsack and this time pulled out what looked like — and was — a somewhat oversized tape recorder with a place for two cassettes instead of one. She also took out a number of blank cassettes and stacked them on the floor by her right knee, except for one that she put into the oversized recorder. Then she reached into the Reston file and removed a cassette and put it into the second receptacle of the recorder. Then she pushed a button and she and Furden both heard a crescendoing *whhhheeeppp* sound that lasted about six or seven seconds then ended abruptly. As soon as it did, Price popped out the two cassettes. She copied the date on the original onto the previously blank one, put the copy into the knapsack, and the original on the floor next to her left knee. Price repeated the process until all the tapes in Janie's folder had been duplicated on the high speed "duper," all the copies and blanks were back in the knapsack, and all the cassettes that had been in Janie's folder were stacked neatly by her left knee. Finally, she put the stack of original cassettes back into the Reston folder, pushed the drawer shut, and closed the front of the radio. The very last thing she did before standing was to carefully put the combination/tuning dial back into the exact position it had been in before she'd started.

The outer door of the Fuller building locked itself behind them as they left and they saw no one during the walk back to the car. As they got into the car, the security guard inside the admin building glanced up for a brief second, then went back to his book.

Back at the safe house, Price was setting up the tape player again. Furden was still parking the car.

"Kad'rin?" Janie said tentatively.

Price looked up.

"I been thinkin'. Tha' maybe Sara shouldn' listen."

"Why?"

"She's havin' a har' time. She's blamin' herse'f again." She pointed toward the tape player. "There's stuff on there —" Her voice trailed off.

"I don't know how we'd keep her from listening, Janie. Sara won't —"

At that moment, Furden came into the kitchen. "Are we set?"

Price looked at Janie who just nodded and looked down.

*   *   *

They listened to the tapes in chronological order. The first couple were brief, clinical, relatively uneventful. They came to the one of Furden's session with Fredrich. Janie's eyes grew wide when Furden mentioned the videotape of her ordeal.

"There's a vid'o tape?" She looked at Price and then back at Furden. "I didn' know tha'."

"Arthur told me John destroyed it," Price said. "That very night."

Janie tilted her head and looked at Price. "D'jou see it too?"

"No. I only know what Arthur told me. I thought that John was the only one who'd seen it." She looked at Furden. "How much of it did you see?"

"Just a couple of seconds." She looked at Janie then back at Price. "That's what made me —" She looked uncomfortably at Janie.

"Has anyone ever told you what happened to the men who did this to you, Janie?" Price asked.

"I figured it ou'," Janie said in a voice that chilled Price. "All John or Mis'er Ma'sen said was that they'd neve' hur' me again."

The statement hung in the air for a long moment, then Price put another tape into the player. They heard Fredrich's voice leading Janie to her safe place, and tensed when they realized they were listening to the original of the evidence tape they'd listened to earlier.

> "Where are you now, Janie?"
> "Nowher'. Can' see anythin'. Feels like a bi' open space. Hallway, mayb'."
> "But you can't see anything?"
> "No. 't's dark.
> " S' a light."
> "What, Janie?"
> "A light. An' — oh — oww! — oh —"
> "What is it, Janie? Is someone hurting you?"

> "Mmmm."
> "Is he doing anything else?"
> "Ow!"
> "Who is it, Janie?"
> "Don' know."

All three exchanged looks. That was *not* what they'd heard on the earlier tape.

> "Yes, Janie. You know."
> "No. Don'."
> "Look hard, Janie. You can see. You can see his face."
> "No. Can' see."
> "Tell me, Janie. Tell me who it is."
> "Don' know. Can' see."
> "It's Professor Cann, Janie."
> "No. 'S Not."
> "If you can't see, Janie, how do you know it's not?"

It was obvious from the silence on the tape that the question had thrown Janie. Finally she responded.

> "Don' know. Jus' know."
> "No, you don't know, Janie. And I do. And I'm telling you it's John Cann."
> "No."
> "Yes, Janie. It is. You know it is. Say it! Say it's Professor Cann.'"
> "No, 's not."
> Crack!!

All three of them stiffened at the sound.

"Did he just hit you?" Furden hissed, almost choking on the words.

Janie nodded.

Furden's face registered shock, grief, and hate. Her eyes were wide and unseeing. Price placed her hand over Furden's arm. It felt like a wound steel cable.

> *"You have to say it, Janie. We don't stop until you do."*
> *Silence, then "No."*
> Crack!!

Furden jumped up from her chair and spun around in a single movement. She crossed to the wall of the kitchen, placed her palms against the surface, and pressed her forehead against the wall. She didn't appear to be breathing, then suddenly gasped like a drowning person coming up for air. Janie got up slowly and crossed over to Furden. She put her hands on Sara's shoulders and said, " 'S 'kay, Sara. 'S 'kay."

Sara didn't look around at Janie. "No, Janie. It's not okay. It'll never be okay. I . . . How could I —" She was wracked by a gasping sob.

"You didn' know, Sara. 'S 'kay. Hones'. I'm 'kay." Janie put her arms around Sara from behind and hugged her.

A long moment later, Furden turned around and put her arms around Janie. Her breathing slowed and she seemed to regain some of her composure. But Price could see that Furden's eyes were burning and focused somewhere else.

Price had paused the tape. She waited then, after a while, asked, "Would you rather I listened to this alone?" Janie looked at Furden who shook her head. Janie nodded and Price pressed play.

> *"Come on, Janie, this is important."*

On the tape, Janie still didn't answer.

> *"Okay then, Janie, tell me this. Who visited you last?"*
> *"My paren's."*
> *"Before that?"*
> *" 'Fessa Cann."*
> *"John Cann? Your guardian?"*
> *"Mmmm."*
> *"And did he stay for a long time?"*
> *"Mmmm."*
> *"And did he bring you anything? Any presents?"*
> *"Mmmm."*
> *"And did he help you exercise? And take a walk with you?*
> *And have dinner with you before he left?"*
> *"Mmmm."*
> *"Tell me again, Janie. Who did all these things?"*
> *" 'Fessa Cann."*

"Ya' know," Janie said after they'd absorbed what they'd heard, "I kinda knew what he was doin' with those questions at the en' but I couldn' help answerin'."

"That's what sodium pentathol makes you do, Janie," Price explained. "It makes you compliant. It can't make you lie, but it does make you want to tell the truth."

"So, does this help Janie?" Furden asked stonily. She was sitting at the table wringing her hands in front of her as she spoke. "Will this keep the judge from giving her back to Fredrich?"

"Well, as it stands now, the tape's not admissible. Certainly not the way we got it and —"

"Wha'd make it 'missible?" Janie asked.

"Well, for one thing we'd have to show we got them legally. And they still would need to be authenticated."

"I can 'thenica'e 'em. I can tes'ify," Janie said earnestly.

"No," Furden repeated. She turned to Price. "If Janie shows up in that courtroom, she's in custody, right? I mean once she's there. She can't leave."

"Unless Judge Belker rules in her favor."

"And if he doesn't, Janie's surrendered to Fredrich?"

Price started to speak, stopped, and then, "Yes."

Furden put her hands on either side of her head and pushed her fingers into her hair, shaking her head from side to side.

"I's the on'y way, Sara," Janie said. "I can' spen' the res' of my life hidin'. And I don' wan' you bein' a fug'ive." She reached up and took Furden's hand. "I'm willin' to ta'e the chance, Sara."

But I'm not, Furden thought. *I'm not.*

31

The idea came to Price in the middle of the night. She telephoned Jonathan Priestly, attorney for Whispering Marsh, LLC, first thing in the morning and asked if she could meet with him immediately. Priestly was a courteous, courtly man and, in spite of the short notice, he'd cautiously agreed.

He greeted her in his office and they sat. "I have to say, Ms. Price —" he began.

"Katherine, please."

He smiled and nodded. "I have to say, Katherine, that I'm still not entirely certain we shouldn't have Ms. Kewen here, particularly if it concerns the issues related to Dr. Fredrich. Does it?"

"Well, under the circumstances, it's not unrelated, of course, but, as I said on the phone, there are issues exclusive to the relationship between Janie Reston and Whispering Marsh. Just as there are issues exclusive to the relationship between Whispering Marsh and Dr. Fredrich."

Priestly considered for a moment then said, "True enough. If it's the former, excluding Ms. Kewen might be appropriate. If it's the latter —" he tilted his head, letting the unfinished sentence hang. After a brief silence, he went on. "So, what's this about?"

Price lifted her briefcase onto her lap. "Have you heard the tape that Kewen provided yesterday? The one where Janie says John Cann abused her?"

"I have."

"Can I ask you what you think of it?"

He raised his shoulders almost imperceptibly. "With proper foundation it would be admissible evidence, I should think."

"That's your legal analysis. What about what it contains? Do you believe it? Personally? Do you know John Cann?"

Priestly didn't answer right away. "I've met him several times. And, frankly, I find it hard to believe. I've seen him with Ms. Reston and I never considered him to be a threat to her. And I never felt Ms. Reston saw him that way either."

"I'd like you to listen to that tape again."

"I remember it quite clearly, actually, so perhaps if you tell me what it is you —"

"Please."

Priestly looked at his watch then put his hand out palm up. "Go ahead."

Price quickly set up the tape player, and played the copy that Kewen had couriered over the previous afternoon. When they got near the part where Fredrich pressed for Janie to make an identification, Price paused the tape. "Please listen very closely." She hit "play" again and the tape went on to where Janie named John Cann as her assailant.

Price ejected the first casette and put a second one in. Priestly watched her with a questioning look on his face, but he said nothing. The two lawyers listened again as the same conversation took place. This time, Price didn't stop the tape and, this time, Priestly heard Janie deny knowing who hurt her and specifically deny that it was John Cann.

Priestly's expression went from quizzical to concerned and when he heard the "crack!" sound on the tape, it turned to shock, then anger.

"Did he just hit her?" he almost snarled.

Price nodded. "Janie confirms it."

"Janie con —?" He stopped himself and held up a hand. "Don't tell me. I don't want to know." He was silent for a moment, then said softly, "But she's safe." It was a question.

Price nodded.

"And according to this, she never said John Cann was her assailant."

"Right."

"Fredrich doctored the tape."

"Right. And the technology is readily available to conclusively establish which is the original and which one has been tampered with."

"Okay," he nodded. "So that second tape you just played is the original?"

"No, it's a copy."

"A copy. Where did you get it?"

Price hesitated. Then, "I copied it from the original under circumstances which prevent me from being able to authenticate it."

"Ahhh," Priestly raised his chin and his eyebrows. "But you're saying that what I just heard on this second tape is what actually happened?"

"Absolutely. And, as I said, Janie can confirm that's exactly what happened."

"She recalls it?"

"Yes."

"Even though she was medicated? Drugged?"

"Yes. She's explained it. And she's credible."

Priestly thought about it for a moment then asked, "Why didn't you take the original, then? If Janie can authenticate it with her testimony?"

"At the time, I didn't know what was on the tape. But mostly because I would be hard pressed to explain how I came by it."

Priestly nodded.

"The original needs to be obtained —" Price was trying very hard to phrase things so that Priestly wasn't burdened with awkward information "— in such a way that there's no question of its legitimacy or where it came from."

"Yes, I get it, Katherine." Priestly tapped his chin for a second or two then, again, looked into Price's eyes. "I assume the original tape is on the Whispering Marsh premises?"

"It's in Fredrich's safe in his office in the Fuller building."

"The Fuller building," he repeated. "Okay."

Price was treading lightly at this point. "Does that mean you'll help?"

Priestly nodded slowly. "The contract we have with Dr. Fredrich gives him significant control over the Alger Wing. But you say the tape's in Fuller." He looked at her over the top of his nose. "Please notice I'm not asking how you know that," he said with a wry smile. "But Fuller's completely under our control. Plus the contract also allows us to audit files and treatment records at our discretion so any proprietary or privacy objections should be moot."

"Are you concerned about liability for Whispering Marsh?" Price asked.

"For getting the records? The tapes? No. I think we're okay there." Priestly looked up at her. "For being held responsible, even partly responsible for Fredrich's actions? Sure," he said with raised eyebrows. "It's my job to worry about such things." He grew even more serious and leaned forward in his chair with his elbows on his knees and his hands clasped together. "But let me tell you something, Katherine. Whispering Marsh didn't become one of the outstanding

facilities in the world by failing its patients. Or shirking its responsi-
bilities. If there's to be liability, we'll take our lumps. But this —" he
jabbed his finger again at the tape player "— will not happen on my
watch."

Less than two hours later, a security guard rapped on the door to
Fredrich's office and got no response. He turned and looked at Dr.
Karlson, the medical director for Whispering Marsh, who in turn
looked at Jonathan Priestly, who nodded.

"You're sure about this, Jon?" Karlson asked. "I mean we usually
give advance notice of an audit. Perhaps we should wait until we can
have Dr. Fredrich present."

"The contract doesn't require notice. And you insisted on leaving
a message on his service. That's sufficient."

"That was only a half hour ago. It's not much time."

"We're talking patient abuse here, Peter. How much delay do you
want to explain to the families of his patients? Or the board?"

Karlson looked at him for only a second before he turned to the
guard and repeated the nod.

It took the locksmith two tries to get the safe open. All the files
and tapes were quickly transferred to storage boxes. "Let's get these
to the conference room in Admin," Priestly directed. "I want them
inventoried and reviewed immediately. With witnesses and certification. And we don't let them out of our sight for a second."

Fredrich pulled into his assigned slot in the Whispering Marsh parking lot, turned off the engine, and got out of the vehicle carrying his
briefcase. He just got to the start of the walk that led down to the
Fuller building when he saw the group of men trooping out carrying
several boxes. The presence of both Director Karlson and Jonathan
Priestly, combined with a polished instinct for self-preservation that
bordered on paranoia, made him veer off onto a side path until the

group had passed. When they turned the corner and disappeared in front of the admin building, he continued to his office. As he approached the end of the hall, he could see the door to his office was open and felt a surge of indignation. When he reached the open doorway and saw that the file cabinet was open and empty, he was angry.

His first impulse was to call Kewen but, as he mentally inventoried what was in the folders, his anger turned to resignation. It would be just like before. He knew. The frustration, the futility of trying to explain to people who would never, could never understand.

He gathered up the few items he would take with him and left the office. Avoiding the admin building, he got to the parking lot without incident and hurriedly got into his car. Then he felt the knife at the side of his throat.

"Do exactly as I say," Furden said quietly and coldly from the backseat, "or I'll slice your throat right now."

Fredrich didn't move but his eyes looked into the rearview mirror. "You can't be serious, Furden. This is kidnapping. Assault. It's —"

"Shut up and drive. Slow moves only."

Fredrich started the car, put it in gear, and drove out of the parking lot. Furden directed him to drive down the road, then to make several turns as they went farther and farther out into the country. After a while, she told him to turn right off a county highway and onto a state road and then stop.

"Slowly, very slowly, and keep your hands where I can see them, slide over into the passenger seat."

Furden kept the knife within inches of Fredrich's throat as he did as he was told.

"Now, put your hands, slowly, under your thighs and clasp them, then put your head down between your knees." Fredrich did so.

Furden slipped into the driver's seat, put the car back into gear, and sped away. The road in front of them was perfectly straight as far as the eye could see and was lined on both sides by huge swamp chestnut oak trees. As their speed increased, the trees began to blur.

"Can I sit up?" Fredrich said into his knees.

"Yeah," Furden said. "Keep your hands where they are and together."

Fredrich raised his head and inhaled sharply when he saw how fast they were going. "Mind if I put on my seat belt."

"Actually, I do."

They continued to accelerate.

"Are you trying to scare me?" Fredrich asked.

Furden shrugged. "Whatever."

Fredrich looked from Furden to the road to the trees more and more rapidly. "Okay, okay," he said shakily, "you've made your point. What do you want?"

Furden continued to look ahead and responded without emotion. "Punishment."

Then Furden tweaked the wheel and the car began to weave.

"I'm sorry," Fredrich said.

Furden didn't respond.

"I said I'm sorry," he whined. He started to reach out toward the steering wheel but pulled his hand back. "Look, I'll surrender my license. Everywhere. In writing." He looked from Furden to the trees, which appeared to be leaping in and out of the road. "What? What can I do?" he wailed. "What?"

"Nothing." Furden pulled hard on the wheel one last time. The car veered right and slammed straight into an eight-foot-diameter tree trunk.

They were both killed instantly.

32

Club Interpole
Schwabing District
Munich

It was dusk and the Club Interpole was beginning to fill with the just-leaving-work crowd stopping for drinks and diversion before heading home. A large, raised, rectangular stage dominated the center of the room. On it, two girls, one wearing just a G-string, one wearing nothing at all, danced languorously, mouthing the words to the soft rock song playing in the background.

All the bar stools around the perimeter of the stage were occupied by men who sat, elbows on the edge of the stage, heads raised, eyes glazed. The only time they moved was when they sipped their drinks or leaned forward to give the girls money, always trying for a brief touch of skin.

Cann stood a few feet inside the front entrance, casually attired in slacks and a hip-length leather jacket and driving cap. He peered under the brim of the cap and over his glasses as he gazed about the room. At the far end, beyond the stage, just as Lukina had described, he saw the door that led to the girls' dressing rooms/living quarters. Also as Lukina had described, the door was guarded by a very large individual in a black T-shirt, his arms folded across his chest in a way that exaggerated his already oversized biceps.

Cann scanned the mirrored rear wall of the room, checking the patrons on the far side of the stage reflected in it. Out of habit and experience, he also used the mirror to keep an eye on the room behind him.

On the wall to the right of the stage, Cann saw the small square in the otherwise solid wall through which Branko could monitor activities in the main room. To the right of it was a hallway and, from where he stood, Cann could see what should be the door to Branko's office. Past that, according to Lukina, there was a closet, and then a storeroom at the end of the left side. On the right were rest rooms — one *Damen* and one *Herren*. At the very end of the hallway was a door leading out into an alley. Somewhere on the other side of that door, Cann knew, a terrified Lukina sat in a car with Nikolic waiting for a signal.

A customer vacated a seat at the bar, and Cann crossed to it quickly. From where he now sat, he could see both the main room and the hallway. A waitress came over and took his order for a draft Augustiner, although Cann doubted that's what he'd really get. In less than a minute, she was back carrying eight ounces of a pale beverage that cost him eight euros. He added a two euro tip and got a small smile in return. Then he settled in to play the part of a customer.

He and Nikolic and Lukina had come up with a plan "A" and a plan "B." Both started out the same. Cann would go in, sit down, and observe. Plan "A" would be events driven in that he would wait to see if an opportunity presented itself. Plan "A" required enormous luck. For example, ideal situation: Oma was in the office alone, and Cann could get Lukina in through the back door and into the office and they would get into the safe, get the documents, be out in no time at all and get safely away.

It was not likely to go that way but Cann prayed it — or some-thing like it — would. For Lukina's sake. She was scared to death. And she was trusting him.

He waited. He watched. At one point, he saw a woman he assumed was Oma waddle into the doorway where the girls entered and exited. He willed her to come out and across the room, but she didn't.

He watched and waited some more.

Thirty euros later, it was clear they would have to go to plan "B."

Cann got up and went down the hall toward the men's room. As he got to the door marked *Herren* he stopped and looked back toward the main room. No one was looking his way. The customers were all looking at the girls and the girls weren't looking at anything.

Cann darted across and down the hall and turned the knob on the storeroom at the end. It was unlocked. He checked it quickly; it was indeed a storeroom and there was enough room for him and Lukina. He crossed back and went into the men's room. He checked under the stalls ensuring he was alone, then bit down twice on the wireless device clipped to his back teeth through which he could both speak and hear. Through the bones of his jaw, he heard two clicks signifying, "Ready."

"B." Cann uttered just the one syllable.

Nikolic gave two more clicks in acknowledgment. Cann did the same.

Cann busied himself with the normal business of a men's room visit until he heard another set of two clicks. Lukina was in place. Again, he acknowledged.

He made sure the hallway was still clear. Three steps and he was at the back door. It didn't appear to be alarmed but if it was, Lukina would dash back to Nikolic and Cann would act the part of a con-fused drunk. He held his breath, pressed the bar down, and pushed. No alarm sounded. None that he could hear anyway.

Cann opened the door wide enough for Lukina to slip inside. She was dressed in pants and a coat and her hair was tucked up under a workman's cap. No one would mistake her for a male up close, but they hoped it would be enough amid the planned diversion. Cann guided her into the storeroom and closed the door.

In the darkness, Cann could hear that Lukina's breathing bordered on hyperventilation. He took the sides of her face in his hands for a moment and then wrapped his arms around her shoulders. Lukina's arms went around Cann's waist and she held on tightly. Only when Cann felt the pressure reduce somewhat, did he pull back his head and speak in a whisper. "Stay here until I come for you. There'll be some loud noise in a minute, but don't panic. If you don't think you can go through with this, get back to Rade as quickly as you can. Okay?"

Cann felt Lukina's head bob up and down against his chest.

"Okay." Cann disengaged. He checked the hallway again and returned to his seat in the bar. He knew Nikolic had initiated Plan "B" when two men on opposite sides of the bar began to raise their voices, arguing over a dancer. Immediately, the bouncer guarding the backstage entrance focused his attention on the disturbance. Two other men on Cann's side of the bar shouted at the first two to shut up and the conflict widened. Voices grew louder, words grew angrier, and when a glass exploded against the rear wall, the bouncer left his post and charged around the stage.

Showtime.

Cann raced down the hall and got Lukina. Keeping himself between her and the growing brawl, they made their way to the backstage doorway where many of the girls had gathered to watch the fight. Cann signaled Lukina to lose the cap and jacket and let her hair cascade around her shoulders, the better to fit into the crowd.

While Lukina looked for Oma, Cann positioned himself on the edge of the group of girls, and acted as a goalie whenever a body fell or was thrown in that direction. He saw Lukina touch the old woman's arm to get her attention. Oma turned to Lukina and smiled, showing no surprise. Lukina leaned down to speak and Oma cupped a hand to her left ear and tilted her head. Cann saw Oma lose the smile and look up at Lukina with a more serious expression, then nod. The old woman and the young girl started to make their way around the battling crowd with Cann leading the way.

As they entered Branko's office, Lukina was explaining to Oma why she needed her documents. Oma was startled when Cann came into the room but said nothing and returned her concerned expression to Lukina. They were speaking Romanian so Cann couldn't follow but it was clear from her reaction and gestures that, just as Lukina had predicted, Oma was hearing what she was hearing for the first time.

As Cann kept an eye on the continuing melee through the window in the wall, Oma went to Branko's desk and scribbled the combination numbers on a scrap of paper. Lukina took the the paper over to Cann. "The numbers," she said. "To open. You do?"

Cann took the paper from Lukina and read the numbers as he crossed to the large freestanding safe in the corner. He bent down and started turning the dial. On the second try, there was an audible click and when he pressed down on the handle, the door pulled open. Cann had a good idea what he was looking for and, on the second shelf from the top, found several neat stacks of passports and other documents. He made a quick check to satisfy himself and cleared the shelf, stuffing the contents into the numerous pockets sewn into the inside of his leather coat.

Lukina suddenly pointed toward the window. "They come," she hissed. Cann looked, then made a pushing motion with his hands. "Go, go, go."

Lukina ran out into the hallway and darted to the left toward the exit door. Oma stood in the middle of the room with an uncertain look on her face. Cann hesitated. "*Komme mit?*" he asked. She shook her head. It was against Cann's instincts to just leave her there, but he had to make sure Lukina got away.

Two men appeared at the door blocking his exit. The first one charged low at Cann and got a front kick to the top of his head for his trouble. The second man pushed in close behind, staying upright. He stopped several feet from Cann and pulled a large wide-bladed knife from a sheath at his back. The action froze momentarily and then recommenced in slow motion as both men crouched and circled each other. Several times the other man slashed the blade out at Cann in a horizontal arc. Cann responded by going up on his toes and bending forward slightly while pulling his stomach in as far as it would go. Even so, the knife managed to cut his shirt on one of the passes.

Cann timed the next slash perfectly so that, as the knife swept left to right, Cann was able to grab the back of the attacker's wrist and forearm in his two hands. Holding the arm, Cann raised his leg and cracked the forearm over his knee. There was a loud snap of bone accompanied by a shriek of pain and the knife dropped to the floor. Cann slammed the heel of his palm into the assailant's forehead, dropping him.

Cann barreled out the door and crashed into two more men. One fell when they collided but the other grabbed Cann by the arm and spun him. Cann used the momentum to smash an elbow into the jaw of the one who had fallen and was getting up. This time he stayed down. Cann then snaked his right arm over and under the other man's arm and grabbed his throat. With his right foot behind his adversary's legs, he shoved backward and simultaneously swept the man's feet out from under him. The back of his head hit the floor hard and he, too, was out.

Cann raced to the exit door with two more men pounding down the hall after him. He got through it and slammed it shut behind him just as his pursuers crashed into it from the inside. He put his back to the door and leveraged his feet against a railing. Then he he clicked his back teeth on the wireless device and shouted to Nikolic.

"Are we set? Is Lukina with you?"

Nikolic's voice came back instantly. "I don't have her. I haven't seen her since she went in."

"*Shit!*" Lukina was still inside. Cann didn't hesitate for a second. He pulled his feet from the railing and threw himself to the side of the door. The men who'd been pushing from the inside came flying out and went sprawling over the railing and onto the concrete below. Cann dashed back inside.

He yanked open the storeroom door. Empty. He ran down the hall to the office and crashed his left shoulder into the frame to stop himself. Inside the office, Oma stood with a hand covering her mouth.

"Oma," Cann shouted at her in German, "*wo ist Lukina?*"

The old woman looked at him blankly.

Through the small window in the wall, Cann saw Lukina being dragged through the continuing brawl toward the back. He charged out of the office and without breaking stride, slammed into the man holding her, breaking his grip, and slamming him headllong into the wall. He slid to the floor and stayed down.

Cann grabbed Lukina's hand and looked for a way out. There was no escape through the mass of tangled and flying bodies at the front of the bar, so Cann pulled Lukina behind him and headed for the hallway again. As they turned into it, another Interpole guard stepped in front of them and pulled out a gun. Cann grabbed the weapon with a sweeping upward strike and smashed it back down onto the man's forehead. They dashed around him, reached the exit door, and got it open. Cann whipped Lukina around and shoved her ahead of him just as someone on the floor wrapped his arms around Cann's lower leg. Cann shook himself out of his coat and threw it at Lukina yelling "Go, go, go." Lukina grabbed the coat, hesitated for a second, then turned and ran.

"She's out!" Cann yelled to Nikolic through his mike as he brought his free leg up in an attempt to disentangle himself. He stopped when he felt the cold steel of a pistol press against the side of his head. In his earpiece, he heard Nikolic shout, "I see her." Another moment, then, "She's here. We've got her, John."

The man holding the gun on Cann said, "Enough."

Cann froze.

"Turn around, slowly," Branko Jost ordered.

As Cann did so, a fist crashed into the side of Cann's face crushing the transmitter between his teeth.

Outside, in the car, Nikolic heard nothing more.

33

Pretrial Conference
Judge Belker's Chambers
2:00 P.M.

Judge Belker entered the conference room, stopped abruptly, and stared.

On one side of the table sat Martha Kewen. Alone.

On the other side was Katherine Price, Beth Quinlan, and Richard Marks. And, next to Marks, was Jonathan Priestly.

Behind Price and the others, seated in chairs along the wall, Janie sat next to Helena Valdez. Belker correctly surmised who Janie was and felt smugly gratified. He didn't see anyone who might be Furden, though, and that didn't make him happy.

No one knew where Furden was. No one had seen her leave and she was nowhere to be found in the house. They'd waited until the very last minute before they left for the courthouse. Price had a suspicion Furden might be there when they arrived. She wasn't.

Then Belker realized there was no Petitioner here either.

"Where's your client, Ms. Kewen. Why isn't he here?"

Kewen shook her head. "I don't know, Your Honor. He was aware of the hearing and that his presence was required." She shrugged her shoulders. "I just don't know. Hopefully, he'll be here shortly."

"Hopefully, indeed. I realize that much of my attention and, frankly, my orders yesterday were directed to Respondent, but I'm quite certain I made it clear that the requirements of presenting evidence and witnesses at this pretrial applied to both parties."

"I know that, Your Honor, and I advised Dr. Fredrich of that. Hopefully —" she began to repeat herself and stopped.

Belker looked at Kewen for a moment longer, then turned and stared over Price's shoulder at the two people seated against the wall behind her. He raised his voice and shouted back into his chambers.

"Everett!"

The bailiff appeared in the opening.

"Introductions, Ms. Price," Belker said nodding toward the wall.

Price stared coldly at the judge, then said, "Directly behind me is Ms. Jane Reston, and you recall Ms. Valdez, our paralegal from yesterday."

Belker nodded and smirked and said, "Where is Ms. Furden, Ms. Price?"

"It was our intention that she be here, but — I don't know."

"She's a good' person, jud'," Janie began. "She —"

"Be still, young lady." Belker softened his tone but only slightly. "I'll listen to you shortly," he said. "For now, be quiet."

"Paul," Priestly interrupted. "If you're raising the issue of the warrant for Ms. Furden, it isn't necessary —"

"*Paul?*" Belker questioned. "We may have known each other for a long time, *Mr. Priestly*, but in my courtroom I'll have decorum. And I'll point out it's not your place, in my courtroom, to decide what issues will or will not be raised."

"Of course, Your Honor, I apologize. But I must tell you that the warrant for Ms. Furden's arrest is being quashed as we speak. We are dropping all charges against her. And in fact, in view of new evidence, Whispering Marsh may very well commend her."

Belker frowned at Priestly. "What the hell are you talking about, Jonathan? And why are you sitting there, by the way?"

Priestly pushed several sheets of paper toward the judge. Marks and Quinlan and Price passed them along. "That's Whispering Marsh's withdrawal as a copetitioner. We no longer are a party to the matters involved here and we hereby request to be allowed to appear on behalf of the respondents either as witness or friend of the court. But there is new evidence particularly germane to the issues here which —"

Belker swiveled his head to his right. "Have you been apprised of this new evidence, Ms. Kewen?"

"I have not, Your Honor. I have no idea —"

"You don't feel required to share it with counsel, Mr. Priestly?"

"That's what I'm doing right now, Your Honor."

"The Rules of Discovery are intended to prevent surprises from being sprung at trial, Counselor," Belker lectured.

"Of course, Judge. But this is a pretrial. And pursuant to your order," he said pointedly, "we're advising the court of evidence that will be presented. Evidence that not only contradicts the allegations of the petition, but places into issue the actions of Dr. Fredrich himself."

"Why wasn't it mentioned before?"

"We didn't have it before. It has only now come to our attention."

Kewen jumped in. "Where did it come from?"

"It was discovered in the course of a treatment audit that was done this morning."

"Treatment audit?" Kewen's voice rose. "What the hell does that mean?"

"Whispering Marsh has the authority and duty to monitor the treatment of patients within its care. In the course of reviewing certain files of Dr. Fredrich's, certain materials were discovered that are both in opposition to Dr. Fredrich's representations in this matter and also exculpatory with regard to the allegations he has made against others."

"Wait a minute, wait a minute," Kewen interrupted. She glared at Priestly. "Are you telling me that you seized and examined files of my client, knowing full well he is represented by counsel, without notifying me?"

"Dr. Fredrich was notified prior to the audit."

"You contacted my client directly knowing —?"

"I didn't. His employer did. And properly so as part of an internal process."

Kewen turned to Belker. "I object in the most strenuous terms to this, Your Honor. This clearly involves inappropriate contact and interference in the attorney-client relationship."

"Mr. Priestly?" Belker asked with eyebrows raised.

Priestly responded instantly. "I completely disagree. Dr. Fredrich is represented by counsel in this matter," he jabbed the tip of his finger into the table, "this one right now. The audit and the discovery of these new materials are part of an internal process involving Whispering Marsh and Dr. Fredrich. What Ms. Kewen is asserting is that, having been retained for *this* matter, she is somehow now entitled to be consulted if Dr. Fredrich's parking space is changed or some other term of employment is discussed. That is simply not so. If, and I stress if, Dr. Fredrich or Ms. Kewen feel there's an issue involving the audit, they may bring it. But it would be, and is, a separate, independent matter unrelated to this matter before the court."

"Except, Mr. Priestly," the judge interjected, "that this 'internal proceeding' as you put it, resulted in evidence you are now saying is relevant and material to these issues."

"Which we didn't know until after we saw it, did we? So giving Ms. Kewen prior notice was neither appropriate nor required." Priestly stared straight into Belker's eyes as he spoke. "We're here now. Mere hours later. Acting pursuant to your order. What would you have us do? Withhold exculpatory evidence from the court?"

Belker's mouth moved around as if he were trying to dislodge something stuck in a tooth. "Does this have anything to do with Dr. Fredrich not being here then?" he asked finally.

"How am I supposed to know?" Priestly asked.

"Watch it, Jonathan," Belker said, pointing a cautionary finger at him. He turned once again to his right. "Ms Kewen?"

"I'm at a loss here, Your Honor. I don't know where my client is. I still don't accept that this evidence was obtained properly. We don't even know what this evidence is so —"

Priestly jumped at the opening. "You have that tape that was discussed yesterday, Ms. Kewen? That you were going to put into evidence."

Kewen glanced at her briefcase, "Yes."

"Can we play it?" He said it to Kewen and then looked at the judge.

"You want me to listen to *her* evidence?"

"Hers first." He reached into his own briefcase. "Then mine." He tossed a cassette onto the table. "Dueling cassettes."

"Yours, Mr. Priestly? You just withdrew. You have no standing to be introducing evidence."

Price grabbed the tape off the table. "But I'm offering it, Your Honor. And I do have standing."

"Yes," Belker smirked. "But do you have foundation?"

"She does, Judge," Priestly said. "Me. And I assure you I can testify to a complete and proper chain of custody, certified from the time they came out of Fredrich's office to the moment I just placed it on the table."

"Your Honor!" Kewen cried in frustration.

Belker held up his palm. "I'm reserving judgment on this, but let's hear the tapes."

They listened first to Kewen's tape and then to Priestly's. Belker couldn't help looking at Janie as the recorded dialogue played out, especially on the second tape. Janie held his gaze throughout.

After the second tape finished, Belker looked at Priestly. "Why should I accept this as authentic and not the other?"

Price answered the question. "We have the chain of custody, Your Honor, and we are making arrangements to have it certified forensically as an original. Perhaps Ms. Kewen would submit her evidence as well for forensic examination and comparison?"

Kewen was trapped. "Of course," she said, having no choice.

Belker pondered for a long time before he spoke. When he did, his voice was cold, imperious. "I don't like any of this. I believe I have made it clear that I don't like hanky-panky. And I will not tolerate it in my court." He looked first at Priestly and when he didn't respond the judge turned his gaze grudgingly toward Price. "I have serious reservations about this tape and particularly the manner in which it was obtained. Frankly, I'm not inclined to admit it into evidence."

Price struggled to contain her anger. "Your Honor, this evidence is proper and admissible on any number of bases. But even more than that, for heaven's sake, listen to what's on it. You heard what this man was doing."

"And there are other tapes too, Judge Belker," Priestly offered. "Showing similar activity with other patients."

"Which would be irrelevant to this case, Jonathan. Bring them to the attention of the proper authorities if you feel that's warranted. But it's not admissible here."

"Plus he has a history of such acts as these in other jurisdictions," Price jumped in. "His license has been suspended —"

"Also irrelevant. And blatant hearsay."

"It's evidence of prior acts, and character —"

Belker waved his hands around the table in front of him. "Evidence? I don't see anything before me on that? You want me to make findings against Dr. Fredrich based on what's not here?"

"*Fredrich's* not here, for crying out loud! Why is that getting a pass?"

Priestly saw Belker inflate himself and tried to intercede. "Paul. Sorry. Judge Belker, let's back up a second here. Ms. Price is right. The essential point is that there is no longer a moving party. Whispering Marsh has withdrawn. And under your order of yesterday, an absent party or witness won't be allowed to testify. Without Dr. Fredrich —"

"Your Honor," Kewen interposed, "I should at least be allowed to find out *why* Dr. Fredrich isn't here."

"I might be inclined to grant a continuance under the circumstances," Belker offered. "I assume you would object, Counselor," he said sarcastically to Price.

"Oh, I don't know, your honor," Price said with undisguised sarcasm of her own, "I suppose if you give them the same continuance you were prepared to give us regarding Ms. Furden's absence —"

"I suspect you know where your witness is. Ms. Kewen doesn't. Big difference. In fact, I'm not sure I don't see your hand in that too, Price."

"In what?"

"Dr. Fredrich's disappearance."

"That's crazy."

"That's contempt."

Price came within a breath of repeating Arthur's riposte of the previous day but at the last minute managed to calm herself. "For the record, Your Honor," she said coldly, "I have no knowledge of either Ms. Furden's or Dr. Fredrich's whereabouts. Or why they are not here. In Dr. Fredrich's case, I would suggest it has something to do with liability of his own."

"Objection!" Kewen shouted predicatably.

"We're not at trial yet, Ms. Kewen. But I take your point." He drew himself up and glancing cynically at Price, intoned, "Hearing scheduled for two P.M. tomorrow is continued pending a report from counsel for petitioner on her client's absence —"

"You're giving them an indefinite continuance?" Price demanded.

"Indefinite."

"Oh, no you're not," she countered. "By statute Ms. Reston is entitled to a hearing within five days of the petition. Give us a date certain, Judge, within the statutory time frame."

Price had him and he knew it. Peering at Price through squinted eyes, he hissed. "Okay! You want a date certain? A hearing? You got it," he bluffed. "Today! Right now!"

"Fine by me!" Price called his bluff. She looked at Kewen. "Ready to proceed with your first witness, Counselor? You're the moving party."

"God damn it," Belker jumped out of his chair. "This pretrial is over. I will notify counsel of the hearing date at a future time. Pending further proceedings, I am issuing a bench warrant for Ms. Furden over and above the warrant already issued."

"And not for Fredrich?" Price accused. "Why am I not surprised?"

"Judge, I told you, the warrant for Ms. Furden is being quashed."

"I don't know that, do I, Jonathan? When I am notified, officially, I'll deal with it. In the meantime, mine isn't. As for Dr. Fredrich, fine, Ms. Price, one for him too. And as for Ms. Reston," he worked his jaw for a moment. "Everett, take Ms. Reston downstairs and hold her. In the absence of Dr. Fredrich and in view of my growing concerns over the actions of counsel here, I'm placing her in the custody of the Department of Social Services."

Price came out of her seat and put her face inches from Belker's. "Listen to me, you —"

"Kad'rin!" Janie shouted. She got to her feet and stumbled into Price. "I's 'kay. Don'. I . . . we nee' you. It won' he'p if you're locked up too."

Priestly also had a hand on Price's arm, but it was Janie who got through to her.

Belker drew himself back from Price and stood. "Ms. Reston is giving you good advice," he said straightening his robes. "You're the one who needs to listen." He turned to leave. "That's all. We're done here."

Price's glare followed him out the door.

"Oh no we're not, Judge," she said after him. "Oh no we're not."

34

Price stormed down the hallway, then suddenly whirled around to face Priestly. "Is this how you normally run your courts down here? Locking up innocents on a whim?"

Priestly understood Price's anger but still resented the question. "No, Katherine, this is not how we typically run our courts '*down here*,'" he said sharply. "But before you start teeing off on me or the courts '*down here*,' consider that you weren't exactly a model of moderation either."

"I know," Price said vehemently. "Why do you think I'm so pissed?" She took several deep breaths to compose herself. "I'm sorry, Jonathan." She looked anguished. "Arthur was bad enough. Now Janie. What are we looking at here?"

"Right now, Janie's being held for DSS pick-up. So if we're going to do something, we have to do it quickly. Once she's in DSS custody, there'll be hell to pay getting her out. They complain about overwork but try to take what they call a 'client' away from them and they fight tooth and nail. It's a numbers game. Funding."

"Where will they take her?"

"I don't know. Hell, they may not know. They've literally lost people in their system. Locked away and forgotten, farmed out to predators, abused by the people who are supposed to protect them." He was shaking his head as he spoke.

"Might the Appellate Court stay the transfer to DSS?"

"On what basis? As bad as Belker's rulings were, every one had *some* basis. I don't see a single valid appellate issue."

"What about federal court?" Marks suggested. "Habeas corpus?"

"Same thing. What's the justiciable issue? Belker has the authority to do what he did and the fact that his motivations stink doesn't change that. No, if we're going to get anything done quickly, it'll have to be right here. At this level."

"How?" Price, Quinlan, and Marks all said it at once.

"The chief judge of the Circuit Court is a reasonable man. He doesn't care for the way Belker runs his court. And he's a long-standing critic of DSS." He shrugged. "Maybe we can get him to take a second look at it."

"Overturn Belker?" Price was skeptical.

"Not overturn him. But he could reassign the case."

"How likely is that?"

"Not very," Priestley admitted.

"I don't have much time, I'm afraid," Loren Troy, chief judge of the Circuit Court, said at the outset. "Today is Ask the Judge Day. I have to be in the cafeteria in fifteen minutes. Twice a year, we give the staff the opportunity to grill the chief judge." He made a wry face. "Rank has its privilege," he said sarcastically. "But they're very popular. Everybody shows up. Then again, attendance is mandatory. Except for the judges." He shrugged. "So what have you got?"

Price and Priestly made their pitch quickly but thoroughly.

"You're asking me to remove a sitting judge from a case?" Troy asked. "Because you don't like his rulings?" He looked at Priestly. "I'm surprised at you, Jonathan."

"It's not because of his rulings, Your Honor," Price interjected.

"Judge Belker has exhibited a bias from the very beginning. If it were just directed at me, that's one thing. I can live with it. But his bias has placed a vulnerable young lady in jeopardy."

"What bias? The fact that he's made all these rulings against your side? That's not bias. This is Paul Belker we're talking about. He rules against everybody." He looked at Price. "And you allege he made discriminatory remarks to you. For Paul Belker, discriminatory treatment would mean he was being nice to you." He smiled but no one joined in. "There are other, more appropriate forums to take such a charge to anyway," he said more quietly.

"Your Honor, this isn't about me. I can take the rough and tumble of the system. But Janie Reston — please."

"I'm sympathetic with that issue, Ms. Price, I am. But this is just forum shopping. We don't second-guess each other. If you want to appeal, you're free to take any ruling or issue up."

"Loren, there's no time for an appeal," Priestly said. "We've already described what this girl has been through. And there is no basis, other than bias or ill will, to have her turned over to DSS."

"Bias or ill will?" Troy questioned. "Those are serious words."

"But what else is there? It isn't like there are no alternatives. She could be released to her parents —"

"Who are named as corespondents in the petition."

"Or guardians who would —"

"Who have been alleged to be the source of her injuries."

"The credibility of that allegation has been destroyed by the tapes. Which," Priestly held up a finger, "he refuses to consider. And there's no basis for that either. Loren, I hate to use the word but, even for those of us who know Paul, the depth of his hostility in this matter has been —" he'd started to say "irrational" but retreated from that word "— extreme. And look at the consequences here. Loren, you're one of DSS's biggest critics. Please. You can't let this happen."

Troy looked like he was giving it serious thought, then started shaking his head. "I am concerned about that. It sickens me. But I can't be seen as stepping in on another judge just because the lawyers protest. That would lead to chaos in the system. Everybody would be lined up outside my door every time they got a ruling they didn't like. On top of that, the system requires that judges be free from outside influence."

"Even when they're wrong?" Quinlan couldn't help chiming in.

Troy looked at her. "That's what the appeals system is for."

"But the potential for irreparable harm is huge," Quinlan pressed. "We've got all three requirements for injunctive relief. Irreparable harm, likelihood of prevailing, and no other adequate remedy at law."

"Even if I agree," Troy responded, "I can't issue an injunction. As chief judge, my authority is limited to reassigning him. And I won't do that."

"Your Honor, please," Price argued. "Balance the issues here. One judge's feelings against the safety and well-being of one who's —"

"But it's not just one judge. I have to look at the system as a whole. Imagine the reaction, not just of the lawyers but the other judges to my stepping in and taking over a case."

"Imagine the harm to Janie."

"I do." Troy shook his head. "But I can't do what you're asking. Not with what you've given me." He scanned the room as if looking for eavesdroppers. "Look, I don't like Paul Belker." He looked at all the faces in the room one by one. "Now, if anyone claims I said that, I'll call them a liar to their face. But I don't care for the way he conducts his courtroom. As smart as he is, I think he makes a lot of bad decisions precisely because of his ego and arrogance. But I cannot step in and take him off a case or substitute my judgment without a significant rationale that would allow me to justify it to both the bar and the bench. And the public, for that matter. What you've brought me is, frankly, run-of-the-mill attorney complaints. I need substance. More than substance. I need a hell of a reason to do what you're asking me to do. And a way to justify it. I don't have one." He looked at his watch. "I'm sorry. I have to go." He stood up and started to say something else then stopped and just repeated himself. "I'm sorry. I really am. Until the Bailey Act issue is resolved, I'm afraid Ms. Reston belongs to the State."

35

By the time they'd filed out of Judge Troy's office, Price was formulating a plan. As soon as the chief judge headed for the cafeteria, she grabbed Quinlan by the wrist and started pulling her toward the ladies' room. As she moved away, she pointed a finger at Marks. "Work on the habeas corpus option, Richard. It's worth a try." To Priestly, she gave an earnest, "Thanks for everything, Jonathan. Could you help with that?"

"Okay." He couldn't read the expression on her face. "What are you planning on doing?"

Price shouted over her shoulder as she pulled Quinlan down the hall. "Don't ask, Jonathan. You don't want to know."

Inside the ladies' room, Price spun Quinlan around until they were back to back. She looked at their reflection in the mirror. "Same height."

Quinlan nodded, but said nothing.

Price turned Quinlan again, this time so that they were both facing the mirror. Then she stepped behind her and reached out and pulled the younger associate's hair back into a chignon like her own. Up close, their hair was a slightly different texture and maybe a shade different. But pulled back tight, the variations disappeared. In the mirror, Quinlan watched Price examine the reflection and then make a face of approval.

"Want to be me?" Price asked.

Quinlan was embarrassed by the question but answered, "Well . . . yes. Someday I . . ."

"Not someday," Price said. "Today."

Quinlan was clearly confused at first, but then her expression began to take on a mischievous, conspiratorial look. "You mean like a plan?"

"Exactly like a plan."

"I'm in."

"Not so fast, Beth," Price cautioned. "There could be some risk. Professional risk in this instance. But risk. Think it through. No penalty for playing it safe, I promise."

"Are you kidding? I lay awake at night hoping ten percent of the stories I hear about Loring, Matsen, and Gould are true. If I wanted to play it safe, I could be reviewing contracts for the State Department of Transportation." Her grin just kept getting wider and wider. "What are we doing?"

"Are you up for a little *Mission Impossible*-type thing?"

"I suppose," Quinlan said slowly. "Though *Mission Impossible*'s a little before my time."

Price gave her a deadpan look.

"No offense," Quinlan shrugged.

"Okay," Price smiled. "Come on."

As they opened the door, Price asked, "Which, by the way?"

"Which what?"

"Which was before your time? The movie or the television show?"

Quinlan hesitated. "There was a television show?"

Price shook her head. "Sorry I asked," she mumbled as they entered the hallway.

· · ·

Price ran down the courthouse steps and flagged the first cab and told the driver to take them to the closest department store. Nothing fancy. They didn't need originals.

A few minutes later, Price ordered the cab driver to wait and dashed into the Kmart with a bemused but curious Quinlan right behind. They quickly picked out two identical orange dresses, not gaudy but bright enough to stand out in a crowd, two pairs of identical low-heel shoes, and one pair of white dress gloves.

Back in the courthouse ladies' room, they put on the dresses and shoes and Price redid Quinlan's hair. Then they posed side by side in front of the mirror to check the resemblance. Even up close, it was quite uncanny. "This just might work," Price mumbled.

"Okay, Beth, anything else you can think of to make us twins?"

"Just that thing you do with your hands when you're watching something but are bored."

Price twisted her head and squinted at Quinlan. "What thing?"

Quinlan adopted an exaggerated pose of nonchalance and put her left hand on her hip with her fingers pointing straight down at the floor. The she drew her right hand up to her face and placed her ring and little fingers along her chin and her middle and index fingers along her cheek. Then she turned her head to the right and sighed.

Price recognized herself. "Yikes," she said. "I do do that, don't I?" She was impressed and flattered. Quinlan smiled.

"Okay." Price gave them another once over in the mirror. "Put your coat on over the dress and cover your head. It's show time. Here's what we're going to do —"

The cafeteria tables were set up in two rows about twenty deep and they were all full. There was about thirty feet of open space between the last row and the entrance to the room where Chief Judge Troy stood in discussion with several other people waiting for the Ask the Judge session to begin. Price strode up to him. "Mind if I listen in?"

"By all means," Troy responded. He directed a staff member to find Price an empty seat, but she demurred. "No, I'll just stand in the back, if that's okay." She looked down at herself bringing attention to her outfit. "I spilled something on the dress I was wearing and had to change. This one's a bit snug, I'm afraid. I think I'll be more comfortable standing."

"Sure," Troy said. "Whatever you prefer, Ms. Price."

"Judge, we're ready to begin."

The mini-entourage marched to the front of the room.

Price backed up so that she was standing just inside the entrance. A conveyor belt for dirty dishes and trays ran along the wall to her right, then through an opening in the wall. Where the belt met the wall there was a narrow door that led out into the hallway. Out of the corner of her eye, Price saw it open slightly, then Quinlan appeared, bent over, almost on her hands and knees, as she slipped inside. Over the next few seconds, concealed by the conveyor belt, she sidled her way down to where she was only a couple of feet from Price. Then, wriggling out of the coat and scarf she had on, she watched Price splay the fingers of her right hand down by her side indicating to Quinlan that it was not yet time.

At the front of the room, Chief Judge Troy was trying to look appreciative of the rather tepid round of applause his introduction inspired. As the clapping tapered off, he looked down at the papers on the portable dais in front of him and then leaned down farther to retrieve a glass of water from the shelf underneath. At that instant, Price gave Quinlan a "come on" signal and took a single step back. Quinlan stood up directly in front of Price who performed exactly the opposite maneuver by dropping down to where Quinlan had just been. Now standing where Price had been, Quinlan looked around. Everyone seemed to be watching Judge Troy and, to all appearances, the switch had gone off without a hitch.

Price grabbed the coat and scarf and sidled along the wall behind the conveyor belt to the narrow door. Before opening it, she wriggled into the coat and scarf just in case she was seen. Opening the door a crack, she checked the hall and saw nothing. Out the narrow door, she darted across the hall to the door marked STAIRS and went into the stairwell.

Back in the cafeteria, Judge Troy shuffled the papers on the dais in an apparently futile search for something. After several seconds, he looked up and announced, "You'll have to forgive me, ladies and gentlemen, but I seem to have left some of my notes in my office. I'll just get them and be right back."

At the rear of the room, Quinlan who was about to adopt her Katherine Price pose stiffened. To get to his office, the judge had to go right past her and, while she and Katherine had created a good resemblance from a distance, there was no way that Troy would not see the ruse from up close.

As a low rumble of conversation started to grow, Quinlan raised her hand to get Troy's attention before he left the dais. The judge saw the wave and Quinlan began a turn. Obscuring her face with her arm as much as she could, she pointed a finger down the hall and followed it with an upraised palm. "I'll get it," her actions said.

"Why, thank you, Ms. Price," Troy said to her retreating back. Almost everyone in the room turned. "They're on the chair just inside the door. Thank you very much."

It only took Quinlan seconds to get the notes and return. In her brief absence, the judge had apparently fielded a question and everyone's attention was focused on him. Quinlan entered quietly and approached the rearmost table. Without saying a word, she tossed the papers between the shoulders of two people and walked quickly away. One of the women at the table commented on her rudeness, but another picked up the notes and passed them forward.

Judge Troy saw the action. "Thank you again, Ms. Price," he said with a smile.

Quinlan raised her hand in a dismissive gesture but kept her head down and turned away. Then, when everyone's attention was once again directed to the front, she put her left hand on her hip with her fingers pointing straight down at the floor, drew her right hand up to her face and placed her ring and little fingers along her chin and her middle and index fingers along her cheek. Then, with the slightest of smiles on her face, she turned her head to the right and sighed.

On the second floor landing, Price peered out of the stairwell door and saw another empty hallway. She quickly covered the distance to the conference room adjoining Judge Belker's chambers and, once inside, doffed the coat and scarf and pulled on the white dress gloves. Then she crossed to the door that led into the judge's chambers and gave the knob a gentle turn. It was unlocked.

Price had decided that the bigger the entrance, the greater the shock would be to the judge and so she stood coiled on the conference room side of the door generating an energy that would help her explode through the door with maximum effect. Three, two, one, Price gave herself a mental, "Heeeeeeeeere's Kathy" and burst into an empty room.

Her adrenaline ebbed briefly but immediately began to rise again when she heard the toilet flush in Belker's private john. Adapting and improvising, she hid beside a floor-to-ceiling bookcase so Belker wouldn't see her as he crossed back to his desk. Of course, if he was doing some research and needed a book —

But he wasn't and he didn't. He went straight to his chair and sat down and picked up the file he'd been working on. As he settled in, Price stepped up behind him and said matter-of-factly, "We need to talk, Judge."

Belker's entire body shuddered and he bounced a foot off his chair. He spun around with a gratifyingly disturbed expression on his face. "Jesus Christ, Counselor! Are you crazy? You almost gave me a heart attack!" His shock was quickly turning to outrage. "What the hell do you think you're doing in here? How the hell did you get in here?"

"I came in through the wall. You didn't see me, did you?"

"You came in through — What the hell are you talking about? Get out of here! I'll be the one who decides if we need to talk."

"Shut up," Price ordered.

Belker went silent, more out of shock than compliance, his head bobbing twice and his mouth moving, though nothing came out. He continued to watch open-mouthed as Price sauntered around the perimeter of the room turning each and every painting or photo on the wall just a little so that, when she was done, none hung exactly straight. She then came back behind his desk and leaned over him. Belker slid his chair back and Price reached under the well, pulled out his wastebasket, and flipped it upside down on the floor. "See how nothing spilled?" she said. "But when you try to straighten it up, everything will fall out."

By now, Belker was concerned. Very. And it showed.

"You were wrong, you know," Price lectured him with a wag of her index finger. "You should give some serious thought to what you did today. Especially about sending Janie to DSS. Will you do that?"

Belker just stared at her.

"That's all. That's what I came here to tell you." She stepped behind Belker who swiveled his head to the left and right trying to see what she was doing.

"No, no. No peeking. I'm going to go out the way I came in. Through the wall. And I don't want you to see me. It's a secret how I do it. Okay?" She put her hand on the side of Belker's head and pointed his face forward. Then, before he could react, she leaned over until her head was just to the side of Belker's, their cheeks almost touching.

"Ms. Price this is —"

"Shh," Price whispered in his ear almost seductively. "Think about what I said." As she spoke her left arm curled around the front of his neck slowly and gently in what might have been a caress. It wasn't. Price squeezed her forearm and upper arm into the carotid arteries on either side of Belker's throat resulting, after ten seconds of relatively mild pressure, in transient cerebral ischemia. Temporary loss of consciousness. Ten to twenty seconds of it after which there is no damage, no side effects, no aftereffects. And frequently no memory of the seconds just preceding unconsciousness.

Belker's head dipped forward and Price lowered his face gently onto the surface of the desk.

She quickly exited the office into the conference room, put on the coat and scarf, shoved the gloves into the pockets and reversed the entire journey back to the stairwell, down the stairs, across the hallway, and in through the narrow door of the cafeteria.

As she sidled over to Quinlan, Price half listened to a heated discussion about the clerical and administrative staff perception that their efforts were not fully appreciated. By Price's count it had taken her twenty to twenty-five seconds to make the return to the cafeteria, which meant that Belker should have awakened and was just about now getting his bearings. Of course, it could be shorter or longer depending on his powers of recovery, so she wasted no time getting over to Quinlan. Same process as before but in reverse and just as Quinlan got back to the narrow door at the end of the conveyor belt, everyone in the immediate vicinity of the cafeteria heard a bellow.

"Everett! Take that woman into custody. Right now!"

Price and everyone else in the cafeteria turned to see Belker charging down the hallway with an arm outstretched in front of him and his finger pointing at Price. Everett, Judge Belker's bailiff, who was seated toward the front of the room, also turned around at the sound of his name and looked quizzically, first at Belker, and then around the rear of the room, his gaze falling upon Price. While all this was going on, Quinlan slipped out the narrow door.

"You heard me, Everett, damn it! I want her in a cell now!" His eyes were blazing.

The bailiff got up slowly and started walking toward the rear of the room looking back as he did so, seeking guidance from Judge Troy. The chief judge quickly came around the assembled tables and reached Belker before Everett did.

"Paul, easy. What's the problem?"

Belker was practically hyperventilating. "I'm holding that woman in contempt. And that's just for starters. I'll be filing assault charges. Trespass. Obstruction of justice. Extortion."

"Easy, Paul, please. What are you talking about? What did she do?"

"She showed up in my office. Came out of nowhere. Snuck up on me."

"What do you mean, 'came out of nowhere'?"

"She said she came through the wall and —"

"Came through the wall." Troy repeated the statement in a monotone. "Paul, I doubt —"

"*I* didn't say she came through the wall," Belker shouted angrily. "*She* said she came through the wall."

"When was this?"

"Just now. A few minutes ago."

"What did she do?"

"She messed up all my pictures, she stood my trashcan upside down without spilling anything —"

"Messed up your pictures how?"

"She went around the room and tilted them. So that they were all crooked."

"Why?"

"How the hell should I know why. She wanted me to change my rulings —

"Why would making your pictures crooked make you change your rulings?"

"It wouldn't," Belker's voice broke as he shouted that answer too.

"That's what's so crazy. Then she came around behind me where I couldn't see her and said she was going back out through the wall and then . . ." Belker hesitated ". . . she leaned over and put her arms around me and —" Belker began to notice the expressions on the faces of the people watching him. "No, no," he waved his hand at them. "I know this sounds crazy, but that's what she wants it to sound like. None of what she did made any sense and that's why she did it. So that when I say it, it sounds like I'm crazy." He turned his glare on Price. "Well, it's not going to work, Ms. Price." He turned to the bailiff. "Take her downstairs, Everett. Now."

No one really liked Judge Belker and that included Everett. He again looked at Judge Troy for guidance.

"No, we're not going to do that, Everett."

Belker was outraged. "Why not?"

"Because Ms. Price has been here the entire time, Paul. She's never been out of my line of sight."

Price had stood motionless and said nothing throughout the tirade, shifting her gaze from Belker to Troy and every now and then frowning or raising an inquiring eyebrow.

"No, Loren, she has not been here the entire time, obviously." Belker said with exasperation. "Do you think I'm making this up? Do you think I'm crazy?"

"No, Paul, but she was right here. I could see her the whole time."

Behind Troy, Belker could see many of the attendees nodding their head in confirmation of Troy's statement, and a few offered words of commiseration and agreement.

"She was here, Judge, really."

"I saw her."

"Me too."

"Damn near hit me in the face with those papers."

The comments and the sea of concerned faces finally punctured Belker's confidence. He was by no means persuaded that he was wrong, but he did realize that no one believed him.

"Loren, listen, perhaps we can talk about this in your chambers. But —"

"Good idea, Paul. Why don't you go on down? I'll be right there."

"Fine." Belker gave Price a glare and started to say something but thought better of it.

Troy watched Belker go down the hall, and then turned to look at Price. For a moment he neither said nor did anything, then he crossed to her. "May I have a word with you?" He gestured for her to walk out into the hallway with him. When they were away from the crowd, he said, "I'm not going to claim that I know exactly what occurred here, Ms. Price, but I believe I could come up with a couple of very good guesses." He waited for Price to speak but when she said nothing, he continued.

"I take it this is the public justification I said I needed. Handed to me on a silver platter." He was nodding, but his attitude was not positive. "Let me tell you that I find it to have been a little too public. I may not like Judge Belker, but this was excessive. And it casts a shadow over the bench and the process. I don't like it."

There was nothing for Price to do or say. They both knew that. They stood looking at one another for a very long moment. Finally, Troy took a breath and spoke. "Judge Belker will very likely demand an inquiry into this. I won't encourage it but I want you to know, I will not impede it." He continued to stare into Price's eyes. "But what he did was wrong, particularly with regard to Ms. Reston. And I'm not going to do the very thing I've criticized him for, which is to let my feelings or ego or resentments alter my judgment." He paused again briefly before he said, "I will take this case back from Judge Belker and I will immediately call down and order your people released. I will, by the way," he held up a finger, "condition Mr. Matsen's release on a written apology to Judge Belker and the court for his 'we're even' remark."

Price nodded.

"I will also use this to see if I can't get Judge Belker to moderate his actions somewhat but what I won't do, Ms. Price, is allow this to hold him or the bench up to public ridicule. For that reason, Ms. Price, I strongly suggest that you go get your people and get out of my sight, out of my courthouse, and out of my jurisdiction."

36

Price took Judge Troy at his word and got everybody out of town. Pronto. She stayed to oversee the paperwork involved in freeing Janie and Matsen, but ordered Valdez, Marks, and particularly Beth Quinlan to leave immediately. There were no flights to Washington readily available so a car was hired; the driver was given directions to head north at maximum legal speed until they crossed the state line. Price also felt that the team could use some down time and had the D.C. staff reserve several rooms in a bed and breakfast outside Beaufort, South Carolina. They would all meet up there.

Janie's release was procedurally simple, since she was not yet technically "in custody." She was merely being "held." And the "hold" was dissolved with a stroke of the pen.

Matsen's release was a little more complicated. Judge Troy's order didn't purge him of contempt and conditioned his release, as the judge had said, on Matsen's written apology for the "we're even" comment. He was not released outright, but to the custody of Price who saw it as a way for Troy to keep her honest.

Queen Anne House Inn
Beaufort, S.C.

The Queen Anne House Inn was a sprawling southern mansion surrounded by lush lawns and gardens overlooking Beaufort Bay. Quinlan, Marks, and Valdez checked in, then gathered in a sitting room on the southeast corner and shared a bottle of wine. There was little conversation.

When Price, Matsen, and Janie arrived in the second hired car, there was an air of restrained celebration. For now, Janie was safe and she and Arthur were free. Sara's unexplained absence remained a great concern and, for Price, any sense of satisfaction was diminished by the knowledge that there might yet be repercussions. But for now, they could at least take a step back and breathe.

Price had briefed Matsen on the drive up. Matsen had said little, just listening, absorbing, except to express mild disapproval as Price told him how she and Beth had handled Belker.

Now, in the Queen Anne sitting room, Matsen drew Price aside. "About Sara and Fredrich," he said, "I don't like that they've both disappeared at the same time. I assume we're checking with the police? Hospitals?"

"Everyone's on it."

Matsen nodded. "Hopefully Sara's all right. But as for Fredrich, if he ever attempts to practice medicine again, we'll find him. And licensing issues will be the least of his concerns."

When a cell phone rang, they all scrambled to check their display. The call was for Price.

"Ms. Price. This is the office. Is Mr. Matsen with you?"

"Yes, he is. What is it?"

"Well, we received a streaming video file here. Attached to an e-mail. The IT people did — well it's — you should see it."

"Video file? Of what?" The somber voice on the other end of the line made Price worry.

"It's a scene like, you know, on the Internet. It looks like Mr. Cann." Price heard the voice on the other end pause and take a breath.

"IT made a digital file. Do you have a PC or a laptop available? They have it set up so you can access the network and open the file from there."

The others watched with concern as Price called Valdez over and asked her to bring her computer down as quickly as possible. Then she wrote down the access information and the name of the digital file. It was only a minute before Valdez was back and the computer was turned on and ready to go.

Price quickly accessed the Loring, Matsen network and followed the required paths to the appropriate folder. Then she typed in the file name IT had given it and hit enter. The others in the room had grouped themselves behind her and there was a collective gasp when the image came up on the screen.

In a scene that had sadly, terrifyingly, infuriatingly become all too familiar, a man sat on the floor in an orange suit, legs folded in front of him, his hands apparently bound at his back. The camera closed in on the cut and battered face of John Cann. The eyes were blackened, but they held firm on the lens as Cann stared icily into the camera.

Behind him stood five men, heads wrapped in checkered keffiyahs, faces partially covered. Four of the men — two on each end — held Kalishnikov rifles at an angle across their chests. The man in the center had a curved sword in his waistband and held a document in his hands. As the group in the Queen Anne siting room began to grasp what they were seeing, the man in the middle of the armed group began to read the document. He spoke in Arabic, but IT had superimposed a voice-over translation.

> In the name of Allah the Merciful and Compassionate, prayer and peace be upon the master of mankind, our master Muhammad, may Allah pray for him and give him peace.

By his grace and beneficence, the great Lord has given unto us and placed into our hands the infidel Cann to answer for his crimes against Allah and His people and the shedding of the blood of the shuhada Sami, Basheer, Abdullah, and Naji.

We do not mourn or weep for them. Rather we rejoice in the eternal reward that has been given to them by their martyrdom for they are in Paradise. Allah said, "Therefore let those fight in the way of Allah, who sell this world's life for the Hereafter; and whoever fights in the way of Allah, then be he slain or be he victorious, We shall grant him a mighty reward."

As Allah blesses those who die for Him, so He condemns the infidel who dares do violence against His chosen. The infidel who smites the faithful is as a jackal, a hyena with no honor, shame, religion, manhood, morality, or credibility and it cannot be that such as this will remain on this earth when his own eternal damnation awaits him.

The sentence of death is pronounced on the jackal Cann and shall be carried out in forty-eight hours when his head will be separated from his body like the animal he is. However, we show to the world the wisdom and beneficence of Islam and that we are just in our goals and just in our deeds. We summon and offer to the jackal Cann's great friend, the lawyer Matsen, to come and stand with him to present evidence why Cann should not be sent to his eternal punishment. Stand with your friend, lawyer Matsen. Come to where we have taken him and you may save the dog from slaughter. If you do not or you fail in your endeavors, on the appointed hour at the time that is right and proper, our shuhada will rejoice as the hyena is sent to his rightful place in Hell.

"Good God!" Matsen muttered. "This was all about getting their hands on John?" He was stunned and confused.

Price turned to him. "Who are those people they named, this Sammy and the others?"

Matsen looked to see where Janie was before answering. "The men who abused Janie," he said softly.

Price nodded. No further explanation was needed.

" 'Come to where we have taken him'?" Price shook her head. "How are we supposed to know where that is?"

"I think we have to assume Munich. Bavaria, anyway."

Price looked at Matsen. "I don't suppose I could suggest you shouldn't go?"

Matsen just looked at her.

"Arthur, it still could be you they want. That this," she flicked her hand toward the computer, "is a scheme to get you over there. That John's the bait for you."

"Well, it's good bait then."

Price knew she wasn't going to prevail. "Arthur, I'm not suggesting we don't move heaven and earth to find John and get him out of this, but," she hesitated only for a second before stating the chillingly obvious, "you know that there's no way they're going to let him go. Not after all this *shuhada* business. If you do this, all that will be different is they'll have both of you."

"Perhaps," Matsen agreed. "But there's no way I would consider *not* going. You know that."

Price didn't argue the point; just nodded and said, "Me too."

Matsen frowned. "No, Katherine. Stay here. Coordinate things, maintain an overview —"

"Cut the crap, Arthur. I'm going."

Matsen, too, knew argument was futile. "It would be unbearable for me if something happened to you too" he said.

"Funny," Price said, unsmiling. "I was thinking the same thing."

37

Forty-eight hours.

Price and Matsen headed immediately for the Hilton Head airport where they chartered a plane to Dulles International Airport. During the flight, they called ahead and were met by Loring, Matsen staff with fresh clothes, equipment — including satellite phones, and a number of other "necessities."

Price was used to traveling in style, but she soon discovered what it meant to travel under emergency conditions with Arthur Matsen. They received VIP treatment from Customs and Border Patrol and TSA at Dulles, and were on board in their first-class seats well before the other passengers.

They used the nine-hour flight from Dulles to Munich to go over everything from the beginning. Price knew the story of Djilic and Savka and Milica, and Matsen filled in as many blanks as he could. Then Price briefed Matsen in detail about what they'd learned of Erwin Jost from Nikolic. And finally, gently, apologetically, she told Matsen about Mribic's statement that Savka hadn't died in the fall.

Matsen accepted the information quietly. "It's always possible, I suppose," he said after a while. "Did he say —? Is she still alive?"

Price shook her head. "All I know is what John told me; that Mribic said Savka survived the fall and —" She hestitated.

"And what?"

"It turns out she was pregnant."

Matsen looked out the window for a long time before he asked, "Did she have the child?"

"He didn't say."

Matsen nodded but said nothing.

"I'm sorry, Arthur. We meant well, John and I. Not telling you. John wasn't at all sure that Mribic was even telling the truth."

Matsen was silent for a while longer, staring once again out the window, seeing nothing. Then with a deep breath, he brought himself back to the present.

"Let's concentrate on getting John back in one piece." They winced at his choice of words. "Tell me more about this Rade person."

"Radovan Nikolic. John said he was SAJ."

Matsen raised an eyebrow. "SAJ?" He reached under his seat for his carry-on and, after clearing its use with the flight attendant, took out a satellite phone and punched in some numbers. That call led to more calls. Then Matsen spoke to someone in what Price assumed was Serbo-Croatian. He clicked off and turned to her.

"There is a Radovan Nikolic with the SAJ. Highly regarded and not just by his own people. And apparently he's in Bavaria. So that's where we start. He'll be meeting our plane."

Nikolic viewed the video of Cann on a laptop in a quiet secure corner of the VIP lounge at the Franz-Josef Strauss International Airport some forty-two kilometers northeast of Munich. When it was done, he looked up shaking his head. "This *shuhada* business the speaker is talking of, what is this?"

Matsen gave Nikolic the entire story of Janie and Cann and the terrorists named Sami, Basheer, Abdullah, and Naji.

"Good," Nikolic said nodding. "It does not surprise me that John did this. And this girl, Janie? She survived?"

Matsen and Price both nodded

"She is well?"

"Making progress," Matsen said with a tilt of his head. "Or was."

They'd received the news of Furden's death just before landing. They'd also learned that Janie was heartbroken and confused, convinced she was a jinx. Their hearts went out to her. So did Nikolic's. "I wish her well," he said.

After a moment, bringing them back to the matter at hand, he flipped a thumb toward the laptop. "The one reading on the video may be speaking in Arabic, but I can tell you that at least two of the other men are not Arabs. They are KLA — Kosovo Liberation Army." He looked pointedly at Price and Matsen. "You know what this is?" They nodded and Nikolic continued. "They tried to take John before."

Matsen frowned.

"The morning Mribic escaped, some men tried to grab John off the street. They were KLA."

"I knew it," Price said with intensity. "I knew something had happened,"

"As you know, the KLA are part of the global terror network. So there is this connection to this *shuhada* business. But there is another connection for KLA as well." Nikolic gave Price and Matsen a run-down on Jost and his associations with the KLA as hired guns, enforcers, couriers. The sex trade.

Matsen was appalled. "I would never have agreed to represent Mribic if I'd known all of this." He shook his head. "My God."

"Yes," Nikolic said, "John told me the same thing. I believe that."

"So you think John's kidnapping is related to Jost's criminal activities?" Price asked. "It's not about revenge for the *shuhada*?"

Nikolic raised his shoulders and looked at Matsen. "Artur, let me ask. When you first heard from these people, did they ask specifically for John to come?"

"No." Matsen shook his head. "They just said 'you.' 'We want *you* to defend Mribic.' I assumed they meant the firm."

Price jumped in. "But even the last time I talked to him, John felt it was about getting you here, Arthur. Especially after the message about . . ." She hesitated, looking at Matsen. "About Savka surviving the fall. And being pregnant."

"What is this?" Nikolic asked.

Matsen let Price explain. When she was done, Nikolic looked at Matsen. "Do you think this Savka is alive?"

Matsen shook his head slowly. "No. I want to think it but I've lived a long time. Most people don't make it this far. For that reason alone, it's unlikely. And I don't see how they could have survived that fall." He paused, then looked at Price. "Maybe that's cowardly of me, Katherine. If I thought they'd lived, it would be hard to accept that I didn't go back."

"But you did."

"But I didn't find them. Maybe I didn't look hard enough." He took a breath and let it out slowly. "And let me tell you," he said to Nikolic, "it would be exactly like Djilic to use Savka and Milica — even after all these years — to get at me. He bragged that he never forgot."

Nikolic was shaking his head. "John told me you identified Pred-rag Djilic as the same man on the tape that I know as Erwin Jost. I believe now, they are one and the same. How else would he know about this Savka? And the significance to you?"

"Then what about John being taken?" Price wondered.

"I don't know. It was perhaps a matter of opportunity. At some point, these KLA realized who John was." He pointed at the computer. "The terrorist network is global. These organizations communicate with each other all the time. And they work together. You can be sure there has been a price on John's head for some time now. The U.S. is not the only one that offers rewards. Perhaps, for the KLA, John was a . . . what is the word in English . . . *nagrada?*"

"Bonus," Matsen said.

"A bonus, yes. An extra prize.

"And once they felt I wasn't coming," Matsen continued, "they were free to go after John."

"And still use him to get you too," Price added.

"Yes. They tried twice to get him and failed. It's ironic that the third time we went to them." He described their trip to the Club Interpole and, as best he could, how Cann had been taken.

"He went back for Lukina," Matsen observed.

Nikolic nodded. "He and I both swore on our honor that we would get her out no matter what." He looked earnestly at Price and Matsen. "Otherwise I promise you I would have gone in after him." The others nodded.

"Do we have any idea where they took him?"

"More than an idea." Nikolic answered. "One of our men was close enough to hear Branko Jost say 'take him to my father.'"

"Branko Jost?" Matsen asked.

"Branko Jost runs the Club Interpole. Has his office there. He is heir apparent to Erwin Jost."

"So where's the father?"

"Almost certainly Schloss Grunberg. About thirty kilometers southeast of Munich. The elder Jost rarely leaves it. We already had loose surveillance on it and our man saw them arrive. He didn't see John specifically but he did photograph one of Branko's men from the Interpole as he got out to open the gate."

"And you think John's still there?"

"We've not seen anyone leave since then."

"What are we up against, Rade?" Matsen's voice had changed. There was a whole different affect to it. Businesslike. Cold. "How strong is it? Schloss Grunberg."

"It's a fortress," Nikolic answered. "Schloss means castle. That's what it is. It would take an army."

"How much of an army?" Matsen asked.

Nikolic gave a bitter laugh. "More than what I have. I have perhaps six men total with me."

"That's not what I asked. I asked what it would take." Matsen pushed a pad and pencil over to Nikolic who realized Matsen's question wasn't hypothetical. "Write it down. Whatever we need. I've already made calls. If I've missed something, I'll ask for that too."

And with Matsen doing the asking, Nikolic realized, they'd get it.

"And, Rade, I will defer to you on specific tactics and personnel — with one exception." There was ice in that last phrase. "We're not going to do a full frontal assault with John in there. Not in the first instance. What I want is a three-level plan. Set up an assault force around the castle. Be prepared if it becomes necessary. Overwhelming force so that, if we have to go in that way, it's over as quickly as possible. But let that be the third level, the last resort. Before that, second level, I want to try to get people in there covertly. There's a team in Augsburg already on the way here that specializes in that. Do we have information on security? Personnel? Electronics? Devices?"

"Some but —"

"Okay, the team from Augsburg will be bringing its own equipment. Acoustic, thermal, laser. What you already know will give them a start. If we can mange to get them inside, put them in place before anything has to happen or better yet locate John and get him out without a fight."

Nikolic was thinking, nodding, and writing all at the same time.

Price waited for Matsen to continue and when he didn't she asked warily, "And the first level?"

"That would be me."

"No, Arthur."

"Yes, Katherine."

"Arthur, you can't —"

"Stop," Matsen snapped. He rarely raised his voice and that alone had an impact. "I wouldn't like to think you're about to lecture me on the inadequacies of age or the vastly superior suitably of Rade and his men for the task at hand. With regard to the latter, I agree with you. With regard to the former, this is not the posturing of a foolish old man. The fact is my presence is required. Without it, John will be beheaded. If you think I could be dissuaded from doing anything in my power to prevent that, you shame me."

Price was taken aback. "I don't think that, Arthur," she said, sounding both chastised and resentful, "but I won't apologize for being concerned. At least I can go in with you."

"No, you can't."

"I can be your assistant. A stenographer. If it's a trial, they'd have to accept that."

"They don't have to accept anything. This is their show. They're making the rules."

"Being a woman could help. If they're Muslim —"

"They are thugs," Nikolic interjected. "Understand that Jost is a man who has children raped just to make a point. He will have no respect for you."

"But —"

"Discussion over, Katherine. I will not have it."

"Now who's —?"

"I am. And I'm pulling rank." He softened his tone slightly. "Katherine, I need you out here, working with Rade. And I'm not being patronizing." He turned to the SAJ captain. "Don't underestimate her, Rade. She's a professional. I mean that. Katherine is the best of the best. She wouldn't be with me otherwise."

Nikolic gave Price a long appraising look and Price held his gaze. They exchanged nods.

"Okay. The clock is running," Matsen continued. "It's clear Djilic wants me. The KLA already have John. They believe that gives them all the cards. So let's take control of events as much as we can."

"It's likely they don't think we know where John is. That means they expect to be the ones initiating contact. When and where they choose. If there's a time they'll be complacent, it's now. So let's use that." He turned to Nikolic. "I want you to sneak me out of here, Rade. Once we're clear of the airport, I'll dress up in my best court-room suit and show up unannounced on Djilic's doorstep."

Price shook her head in frustration.

"You've got people in place. Watch for any reaction when I arrive. If we're right and they don't know we know, they probably don't have optimal security in place. When I do show up, they'll almost certainly scramble to maximize their defenses. And you'll be watching."

"I like that. Sieze the initiative," Nikolic said.

Price could admire the tactic, but still hated that it was Arthur doing it. "Are you going to be wired?" she asked.

"No. They'd find it and that would just alert them that there was someone listening. The Augsburg team will be bringing several laser eavesdropping devices. The kind you point at a window and they pick up the vibrations and relay them back to a receiver that trans-lates them back into words."

"But we don't know where in the castle you'll be."

"That's why they're bringing several of the lasers." Matsen pointed at Nikolic's pad. "You'll have sufficient people to cover the castle. Spread the devices around; try different windows. With luck, some-one will pick me up."

"And what?"

"Hopefully, someone will say something helpful or —"

"Hopefully — With luck —" Price mimicked angrily. "And if they don't?"

"The best we might be able to hope for is to keep John alive long enough for the Augsburg team to get inside."

"You realize he could already be dead," Nikolic said, clinically analytical.

Matsen nodded.

"Or once you're in," Price protested, "what's to keep them from killing John immediately? And you?"

"I don't know, Katherine. I don't claim to have all the answers. But I do feel this is the best way for John." He paused for just a second. "And it's how I want to do it."

Price saw something in his face. "My God, Arthur! You *want* to go in there!"

"Yes, Katherine, I do." His look was chilling. "I left a lot on that mountain," he said distantly. "If there's anything left of it, Djilic has it. I want it back."

38

Cann sat on the dirt floor in a corner of the small, unlit room. He was turned slightly, his hands bound behind him by handcuffs. They'd been on him, too tight, for well over twenty-four hours and the pain in his shoulders and wrists had gone from searing to throbbing to numbness. His chest and torso remained stiff and uncomfortable from the repeated blows with batons and rifle butts. Taking a deep breath was out of the question.

The pain from the injuries to his face had also deadened. One eye was nearly closed, the other cut along the upper eye socket. His lips were swollen and cracked and his nose was flattened, probably broken, which was good since it kept him from having to endure the smell of his own waste.

His captors hadn't allowed him any breaks and had made it clear they wouldn't. So there had been no reason to go through the discomfort of holding it in. It was demeaning. To soil oneself. It was meant to be. That was why Cann had made very sure to glare defiantly at the KLA men as he let go. So they would know it was not done out of terror or fear. That it was directed at them. It was a small thing in the overall scheme, but it was all he had. And he'd had the perverse satisfaction of knowing they'd gotten the message when he'd received an angry beating. It also had the side benefit of making it pretty unpleasant to be in the same room with him, so he found himself alone more often than not.

He cocked his head to the left when he thought he heard sound coming from the other side of the door. For a moment, there was nothing, then he heard the scrape of the deadbolt. *Showtime again.*

A vertical slit of light between the edge of the door and the frame widened and brought an ugly dawn into Cann's tiny world. The new brightness temporarily blinded him before a single silhouette started to form in the doorway. He heard before he saw, "Phew, John! No wonder they're leaving you alone. Phew!" Mribic repeated waving his hand in front of his face. "I think I'll stay out here, if you don't mind. Phew!" He stepped back slightly and leaned his face away from the opening.

Cann pulled his legs up under him in preparation for a lurch and a lunge that never materialized. His brain gave the command but the muscles of his legs, numbed by immobility, failed.

Mribic sensed the threat and pulled his right hand in from outside the door frame and displayed the semiautomatic pistol he was holding. "Don't, John. Please. I didn't come here to add to your discomfort." He was keeping himself a step or two outside the cell but could still see the entire room. "I'll tell you I don't like this. It's unnecessarily — well, you know." He flipped his hand dismissively.

"No, I don't know. Tell me." Cann's words were slurred through swollen and broken lips and had that nasal twang that comes from being unable to breath through the nose.

Mirbic nodded. "These people don't like you. I think you know that. And you know why. It's no consolation, but it wasn't about you to begin with, John. Originally this was about getting Matsen over here. These people were just the hired help. Bad karma for you. Or kismet, I suppose."

"That's what I don't get," Cann interjected. "You spent the war killing Muslims and these people are Muslims. All that stuff you said about Serbians and differences and history?" He shrugged his shoulders. "What was that about?"

"I meant every word. But I was killing Bosnians, not Muslims in general."

"And these people," Cann tossed his chin up, "they're Kosovars. You're okay with that?"

"I have no use for them, but this is business. As I said, they were the hired help, the muscle for the plan."

"Which was?"

"It started when I got myself arrested in Garmisch. I can tell you my father wasn't pleased. I think he thought about leaving me there. But then, he got this idea —"

Cann was shaking his head in a questioning manner. "Your father?" He squinted at Mribic.

"Erwin Jost." Mribic enjoyed the look on Cann's face. "As I said, he wasn't happy with me getting myself arrested, but he owns enough of the authorities in Bavaria. As you saw." He shrugged. "Apparently he has some history with Matsen —"

Cann laughed out loud, stunning Mribic into silence. "You don't know what that history was?" he asked, wincing from the pain the laughter caused him.

"Something that goes back to World War II." Mribic shrugged.

"Tell me something. All those things you said about the atrocities against the Serbs and your hatred and what you said about retribution. You meant that?"

"Of course," Mribic said indignantly. "Why wouldn't I? It's all true."

"And you don't know who your father really is?"

"What's that supposed to mean?" Mribic seemed more offended than angry.

"Erwin Jost had no history with Arthur," Cann told Mribic. "Erwin Jost didn't even exist during World War II."

"So what? Lots of refugees assumed new identities. Whatever

happened between Matsen and my father made them deadly enemies. And my father has carried the hatred with him for years. So
when I was arrested, my father decided to use that videotape to —"

"On the tape, your father was one of the prisoners?"

"Well, he was to begin with. He was caught up in a sweep during
one of his trips back to Bosnia. We had to get him out of there."

"So at the end of the tape you were helping him escape."

"Exactly. And my father sent Matsen the tape. The idea being that,
when he saw Erwin Jost on the tape and learned he was still alive, we
could get him over here."

"Except Arthur didn't see Erwin Jost on the tape."

"Yes, you said that. But whatever name Matsen knew him by, he
recognized him, right?"

"Yes. As Predrag Djilic."

There was silence as the words penetrated.

"Predr —" Mirbic scowled. Out of reflex, his face darkened at the
name. "What are you?" He suddenly pointed the pistol directly at
Cann's face. After a moment, he slowly lowered the gun and took
some breaths. "No. No. Nicely done, John. Though, I don't know
what you thought you'd gain by that." He had a crooked smile on his
face. "Predrag Djilic?" he scoffed. "That's too much. That's like saying
he was really Hitler or the bogey man." He shook his head some
more. "But Djilic? No. That's too over the top. I don't think so."

Cann spoke evenly. "Arthur was in Yugoslavia with the OSS in
World War II. Djilic was with Miljkovic. Hell, you know the history
better than I do. Arthur's the one who took Djilic's — your father's
— eye. And your father made two people Arthur loved jump off a
cliff. That Savka you told me about? That's why it's personal."

Mribic stared coldly at Cann. "I don't believe you. But you can
believe this. The KLA want you. They have you. My father — Erwin
Jost," he said sharply, "wants Matsen. Whatever his reasons. And he'll
get him." He grinned at Cann's expression.

"We sent that videotape of you and the so-called terrorists to

Matsen. We told him he could save you if he came. And you know he will." He chuckled without a hint of humor. "Maybe we'll let you see him before you die. And you will die. Just as they said on the tape. And so will he." He stepped back and slammed the door shut.

As Cann heard the bolt slide home, he began again to struggle with the cuffs.

Further surveillance and the array of state-of-the-art laser, thermal, sonic, and infrared surveillance devices brought by the team from Augsburg fed a wealth of information into the construction trailer serving as the command center set up about three-quarters of a mile away from Schloss Grunberg. All the data gathered was transmitted in real time to technicians in the trailer who entered it into computers that generated a three-dimensional holographic image of the castle structure and the people inside.

So Nikolic, Matsen, Price, and the others assembled in the trailer knew the castle had three levels and every indication was that the top floor was empty. There were about a half dozen people on the second floor, some appearing to be sleeping or at least stationary and others more mobile. Best conclusion was they were looking at living quarters. Based on that, the plan would incorporate a way to seal off the second floor from the first to interdict reinforcements from above.

On the ground level, an entry foyer and then an enormous great hall ran down the middle of the castle from front to back. To either side were hallways running off in either direction; off the hallways, rooms of various sizes and indeterminate purpose. The surveillance indicated the presence of another half dozen men on the first floor. And to the right of the great hall at the rear of the castle was Erwin Jost's study where acoustic surveillance picked up conversations confirming that Cann was indeed a prisoner inside.

But the surveillance had been unable to identify any person inside specifically as Cann; nothing visual, no thermal image, nothing that might be interpreted as someone bound or restricted.

Based on that, it seemed likely he was being held underground and even though they had both ground penetrating radar and light/laser enhanced imaging available, the distances to the target surface were too great for it to penetrate. Even with everything they had learned, if they had to go below the surface, they'd be going in blind.

Matsen looked at his watch yet again and stood. "Time, ladies and gentlemen. We need to move."

Level three of Matsen's plan, a main assault force to be held in reserve unless absolutely necessary, was in place around the perimeter of the castle at a distance of a quarter mile from the outer surrounding wall. The plan was that the assault force would move up to the perimeter of the castle once the stealth team — generically a Special Missions Unit (SMU) — began its surreptitious entry. It had already been decided that the SMU, designator Sierra 1, would go in first, before Matsen's arrival generated the expected increase in security.

A brief debate arose when Price announced her intention to accompany the stealth team. Even before Matsen could respond, Fohler, the SMU team leader, politely said, "No, ma'am, with all respect you will not."

"But you don't even know what I —" Price began, her frustration growing by the second.

"Ma'am, it doesn't matter. What matters is that we eat, drink, play, sleep, train, and work together." He tapped the earpiece he was wearing. "We don't even need these things most of the time. We know what each other is thinking, we know what every one of us is going to do before we do it. There's no place for you."

"Because I'm a woman?"

"No, ma'am," Fohler responded evenly. "You could be Joan of Arc, but if you haven't trained with us, you're not going in with us."

"And you think you could stop me?" Price said defiantly.

He nodded and patted the holster strapped to his thigh. "I do, ma'am. And I will. With regret. But I will."

Price knew he wasn't bluffing. She also knew he was right. She'd been there. In similar situations. And she knew she would be saying — and doing — exactly the same thing in his position.

There was nothing more for her to say. She'd tried suggesting, asking, persuading, demanding, arguing. She turned and headed for the door.

"Katherine," Matsen reached a hand out as she passed. "Where are you going?"

"Not far, Arthur," she said evenly. "Not far."

39

Price crouched with her back to the wall several yards from the gated main entrance to the castle grounds. Surveillance had indicated that the security measures did not extend outside the castle compound and the outermost line of electronic defense consisted of sensors along the top of the wall. She also knew that the stealth team was about to disable those sensors as they began their infiltration. She watched the handheld meter closely for the change in reading.

When the numbers on the LED suddenly went from 13.8 to 0, she stood and swung the briefcase she was holding onto the top of the eight-foot wall. Then, most unladylike, she hiked the skirt of her smart business suit up around her waist and raised her arms above her head. She crouched slightly and leaped up to grasp the edge of the top of the wall, then quickly pulled herself up to the top. She spent only a second or two there before she dropped the briefcase to the ground on the inside and followed immediately after it. Once down, she resumed a squatting position and waited. She knew that there were several more stages of security that the stealth team would have to deal with sequentially, but those did not concern her. This was as far as she was going. For now.

• • •

Sierra 1 cleared the wall in seconds and immediately restored current to the sensors. In the absence of enhanced security, it was unlikely the brief disruption would cause alarm. They made their way, slowly and methodically, avoiding the known hazards and sensors, across an expanse of open ground, through a wooded area, and then across a second cleared area up to the walls of the house without detection or incident. Once there, the plan was to gain entry into the cold, unlit, and apparently empty west wing of the castle and wait for further intelligence.

Every member of the team was trained in all the "arts" of their profession but Davis had a particular aptitude for electronics and so, by default, he set to examining the small outer door at the west end for triggering or detection devices. He found a simple magnetic-field arrangement, which he neutralized by simply inserting an additional magnetized metal sheet between the two contacts that adhered to the fixed plate even when the door was opened. Once done, the team slipped inside and took up positions just off the great hall.

The town car pulled up to the main gate of Schloss Grunberg. The driver opened his window and pressed the call button on the intercom. There was a chirp as the connection was made and a voice said simply, "Yes?" The driver pulled forward so Matsen could speak into the microphone.

"Arthur Matsen to see Predrag Djilic."

"Who?"

"You heard me. Ask the man you call Jost what I mean."

There was silence then the voice came back. "Which Jost, sir?"

"Are you there, Djilic?" Matsen challenged into the speaker. "Speak up if you are."

"I am just the guard, sir," the voice came back.

"Then go ask your boss if he's still too much of a coward to face me."

"I don't think I want to do that, sir."

Matsen paused for a second then, "M-a-t-s-e-n. Arthur. Tell him."

The receiver on the desk in the study buzzed and Erwin Jost reached out and pressed a button putting the call on speaker. "There's an Arthur Matsen at the front gate, Herr Jost. He says he is here to see a Herr Jilich, I think he said? What do you want me to do?"

Jost flipped his head at his son who was already out of his chair and moving to a side table where he picked up a phone that rang automatically on the second floor. In the meantime, the elder Jost instructed the guard to put the call through.

"Matsen," Jost/Djilic said calmly.

"Djilic."

"If you prefer." A pause. "Welcome to my home."

"Let's get on with this, Djilic. Have your people open the gate."

"So brusque, Matsen," Djilic clucked. "Of course, we will open the gate. But not for your vehicle. Please exit the automobile and walk if you please."

"I'm over eighty, Djilic. It's a bit of a long walk."

"Yes. I'm sending a cart for you. But you will leave your car and driver behind. Send them away. Understood?"

"Perfectly."

On the other side of the wall, Price waited. She'd considered and rejected the idea of walking up to the town car when it came through the gate. Arthur would still be in control of the situation at that point and could still call it off. Instead, her plan was to wait until the car had passed and then simply walk up the driveway behind it, like she'd been left behind. She knew there was a very real danger of being shot since security would be heightened, but a woman in a business suit carrying a briefcase and making no attempt to hide herself?

L'audace, Price, toujours l'audace, she smiled to herself.

But the car didn't come through. She heard it pull away and, a moment later, the gate opened a couple of feet. She saw Arthur walk into the grounds and continue up the drive. A moment later, a large surrey-topped, multipassenger golf cart appeared with two large men seated on the front bench seat. It pulled up to Matsen and one of the men got out to help Matsen into the backseat. The driver made a quick three-point turn and was about to drive back up to the castle when they heard a woman's voice called out.

"Mr. Matsen, you'll need these papers."

Both guards drew their weapons and pointed them back down the driveway at Price who was walking confidently up to them. She held up the briefcase and beamed a smile. One guard was already keying his handset. The other returned the smile uncertainly. Matsen glared.

"He has a woman with him," the guard reported.

"Put him on," Jost/Djilic ordered.

The guard handed the phone to Masten.

"You said you were alone," Djilic growled.

"No, I didn't. You didn't ask. But no matter, she just brought me some papers. She can go now." It was Price's turn to glare.

"Give the guard the phone."

Matsen complied, never taking his eyes off Price.

"Bring the woman too," Djilic ordered the guard who waggled his weapon from Price to the cart.

She climbed into the back seat beside Matsen.

"I will never forgive you for this," he said harshly.

"Yes, you will, Arthur." She placed her hand on his knee. "At least I dearly hope you will. But I could never forgive myself for *not* doing it. So let's just get this done."

They were led into the castle through a small paneled door to the right of an enormous wooden one attached on both sides to the castle wall by huge cast-iron hinges. Once inside, they found themselves in a small room that looked more like airport security than part of someone's home. In addition to the two men who'd brought them from the gate, there were two more men in the room accompanied by two large German shepherds who watched the proceedings with intelligent yet neutral gazes, not particularly concerned with what they were seeing unless they were told to be.

First Matsen, then Price were required to walk through a metal and explosives detector, then each was scanned by a handheld wand. Lastly, each was subjected to a thorough physical hand search that left no surface untouched or unprobed. Price stoically tuned out the indignities noting that at least the man searching her did so professionally.

When that was done, they were led to another door at the rear of the room that opened into the great hall. As they exited, Price looked down at one of the German shepherds with a smile and received an almost imperceptible wag of the tail in return.

The four of them clacked down the marble-floored hall to a door near the rear of the building. One of the guards rapped on the closed door. In reply they heard the single word, "*Komme!*"

Matsen recognized the voice at once.

Inside, Predrag Djilic sat relaxed behind his desk, his right elbow resting on the arm of the chair and his right hand holding a large cigar up by his face. He watched without expression as Matsen and Price were marched into the study and stood before his desk.

Matsen's and Djilic's eyes met and held. Neither of them wavered or spoke. After several moments, Djilic slowly slid his gaze over to Price and insolently surveyed her from head to toe and back up again. In return, Price examined Djilic, especially his eyes. The prosthetic was first rate, but she did see that one eye was too clear to be real and didn't move when the other did.

Djilic noted her examination of him and deduced its purpose. "I see you're aware of our —" he flipped the cigar so the bite end was pointing at Matsen "— history. Some of it anyway. Perhaps you're more than a secretary?" He spoke to the guards in German. "She has been searched?" They nodded. "Thoroughly?" They nodded again. He looked back at Price but directed his question to the guards. "And how did she take it?"

"She did not react at all, Herr Jost," one of them said.

Djilic nodded with pursed lips. "More than a secretary, I think. Yes." He gave her an unpleasant grin and turned to Matesn. "Still hiding behind women I see," he sneered. When Matsen didn't respond, Djilic continued. "I caught up with Popovic, you know," he announced with icy satisfaction. "She was tough but, in the end, she died. Hard." He stared again at Matsen for a long time relishing the moment. "I told you I never forget."

Matsen vividly recalled the woman Chetnik officer who'd helped him and Savka and Milica and promised himself he would mourn her later.

But for now, he sat down in the chair behind him. Price did the same.

"I didn't tell you to sit," Djilic snapped. Matsen didn't respond and he and Price remained seated.

"I want to see John," he said.

Djilic huffed a laugh. "You do, do you?" He leaned his face forward just a bit and peered intently. "You do realize you have no say whatsoever about what happens from here on out, don't you?" Matsen said nothing and Djilic nodded again. "That's right," he reminded himself, "you were always insufferably arrogant." The smile grew more unpleasant. "Well, we shall see. We shall see."

"And the trial?"

This time Djilic guffawed. "Please Matsen, don't. You were a lot of things, but stupid was never one of them." He laughed some more. "Very well, you want a trial, we'll have one." He rapped a knuckle on the desk. "Guilty! There, that was easy," he smirked. "And I promise you'll see your friend." His face darkened. "You'll see him die." He rapped his cigar hard on the ashtray on his desk, his eyes boring into Matsen's.

"Still a man without honor I see." Matsen stared back.

"Honor?" Djilic opened his arms in an expansive gesture. "I am honored. Everywhere. By everyone." He looked at the guards in the room and switched again to German. "You honor me, not true? Yes?" he said to them.

"*Ja*, Herr Jost," they both said emphatically.

"They fear you," Matsen retorted. "That's not honor."

"Ah, but it will do," Djilic said with genuine satisfaction.

"And Savka?"

"Savka?" Djilic acted perplexed. Then he feigned recognition. "Oh, yes, Savka." He chuckled. "What about her?"

Matsen knew he was being played with but wanted — needed closure. "Did she survive the fall?"

Djilic prolonged the moment. "You know, Matsen, I must be getting old." He tipped his head and lifted a shoulder. "Of course, I *am* old. Obviously. But I must be mellowing. I had planned to play that one out a bit, but things have gone so well and there are so many better things to move on to so I will tell you. Of course she didn't survive the fall. It was, what, sixty, seventy meters down, perhaps more, almost straight down onto trees and rocks. You'd have to be a fool to even entertain the possibility. But then —" He exaggerated the grin on his face and flipped his hand dismissively declining to state the obvious.

Matsen wasn't surprised. But he'd hoped.

"But listen," he continued to grin, "you know the jokes, 'There's good news and bad news'? Well, that was the bad news. Savka, I mean. She died right there, Matsen. Count on it." Then he leaned back and puffed imperiously on his cigar. "Want to know why I know? How I know for sure?"

Matsen knew he didn't.

"I dug her up."

The words ripped into Matsen's gut, and his head burned. Price sat stunned by the evil of the man across from her. His next words sickened her.

"And I pissed on her."

Matsen lurched out of his chair with surprising speed and got to Djilic before the guard could stop him. As the man reached for Matsen from behind, Price leapt at him and grabbed his right wrist with her right hand and placed her left hand on the back of the man's elbow. Then she rolled herself against his back and using the man's own body as a fulcrum, pulled back hard. The arm snapped with a loud crack. The second guard reached for Price, but she stopped him with a front kick to the groin. Matsen and Djilic were face to face, hands on each other's shoulders wrestling weakly, but equally, for an advantage.

Price stepped forward and rammed the heel of her hand into the second man's forehead. She turned back toward the first guard and froze when she saw a man holding a semiautomatic pistol pointed at the back of Matsen's head.

"Enough!" Branko Jost shouted. He signaled with his left hand for several men armed with machine pistols to come in and restore order. Matsen, oblivious to the development, had managed to get a hand on the front of Djilic's neck and was gratifyingly, satisfyingly squeezing as hard as he could.

Branko reached around him and cracked the barrel of his pistol across Matsen's knuckles shattering several of the fragile bones as well as his grip. His men then dragged Matsen back to his chair and this time, restrained him with rope. They also shoved Price into a far corner and bound her to a chair. Armed men were posted above and behind each of them. Branko shoved the man with the broken arm out of the room and shot a contemptuous look at the second man who sat on the floor nursing his wounds and his pride.

Djilic fell back into his chair and was rubbing his throat and staring hard at Matsen. His first attempt to speak came out as a rasp and he cleared his throat and tried again. "Enjoy that, Matsen. Now it's my turn." His face was an evil sneer that was probably meant to be a grin. He was silent for a very long time before he finally spoke.

"So let's see. Where was I? Oh, yes. Your precious Savka. I went back not long after and learned that she'd been buried by nearby villagers." He leaned forward over the desk and overarticulated his words to drive them deeper. "And I dug her up." He was spitting the words out. "And pissed on her. Right in her face. All over that pretty blond hair." He gave a low laugh and searched Matsen's face for the pain he wanted to inflict. "And when I left, I left her unburied." He smirked. "I assume the villagers reburied her eventually, but I made my point."

Matsen didn't want to react but he couldn't help closing his eyes in pain and fury.

Djilic wasn't done.

He relit his cigar and took several puffs before he spoke again.

"But," he postured, leaning back and opening his arms, "remember I said there was good news and bad news? It's true that Savka did not survive the fall." He mock pouted. "That's the bad news. The good news is —" He let a dramatic pause hang in the air.

"Milica did."

Once again he peered at Matsen's face looking for a reaction, but Matsen managed to keep the churning and twisting inside. All Djilic saw was a cynical disbelieving look.

"No, it's true," Djilic said in an earnest protesting tone. "As she fell backward, Savka clutched Milica to her chest and when she landed on her back, she cushioned the fall enough so that little Milica lived. Isn't that wonderful news?" he said with an insincere, mocking imitation of excitement. "Of course, there were injuries. To her spine. Head injuries. But she survived. She really did. A local family took her in. Good people. They raised her. As their own. Want to know their name?"

Matsen said nothing.

"Mribic. Their name was Mribic."

In the corner, Price looked at Matsen and even from behind she could sense the shock of the revelation.

"Intriguing, isn't it?" Djilic gloated. "And it gets better. I went back. Not right away, of course. Too many people were looking for me. But I became Erwin Jost and," he waved off the subject, "I suspect you know the rest.

"Anyway, it was about five years before I went back again. That would make Milica, what, twelve, I think." He paused for effect. "And that's when I first had her, Matsen. At twelve." His grin was pure evil. "She was quite lovely. Beautiful. A little defective, perhaps, her injuries and all, but that was easily overlooked. Considering.

"And I kept going back. Many times. And I raped her every time. And every time I raped her, I did it roughly. I hurt her and I frightened her. And each time I thought, *This one's for you, Artur*. So — think about this — it's because of you. It's on your hands." He sat back with a vicious sneer on his face and puffed on his cigar. "I told you I never forget."

"Her people should have killed you."

Djilic dismissed the notion with a wave of his hand. "No one defied me. I'd have killed them if they even thought of it. But it never got to that. I don't think they ever knew. I don't think Milica ever told them. It took a long time for me to realize that she didn't remember it. Which made it even better." He leaned forward and his smile became even more diabolical. "Every time I came back and took her — every time I raped her, she didn't remember the time before. Every time was the first time. It was delicious."

Dubran Mribic stood on the second floor balcony smoking a cigarette, a desperate debate raging inside.

Impossible, he repeated to himself. It could not be that his father was Predrag Djilic. He would know. He would feel it. It could not be that the blood of Predrag Djilic was coursing through his veins.

Could it?

No. Cann was lying. He had to be. He looked like he was telling the truth but — And how could he know anything about it anyway?

Thousands had searched for Djilic or evidence of his fate over the years since the war. And found nothing. Cann wasn't there.

But Matsen was there, the other side of the debate nagged. And no question there was something between Matsen and his father.

And there was the matter of the eye.

Pah! That could be anything. A lucky guess. A plan. Cooked up to —

To what? As far as he knew his father had started all of this.

But the name Savka. It was not a common name, for sure, but not so rare either.

And the story.

The chase.

The fall.

The man named Artur.

He'd always thought it a fable. Or a dream.

He tossed away his cigarette, the spray of sparks getting the attention of the unseen surveillance. Then he turned and went back inside and down the hall to another room. He rapped softly.

Inside it, Oma said, "*Komme.*"

Mribic came in and saw her seated by a window. She smiled at him. He crossed over to her and placed his hand on her cheek. "I need to ask you about something, Mama."

40

Cann wriggled and stretched in an effort to get some feeling into his limbs and upper torso. Stabbing pins and needles heralded success and when they subsided, he had at least some use of them. Leaning forward, he pulled his cuffed hands down to his rump but couldn't get them past his buttocks and down to his thighs. He sat back on his hands and took deep breaths stretching his chest cavity, elongating his body as much as he could and putting as much pressure on the connectors in his shoulders to give him the extra flexibility he needed to accomplish the goal. It was difficult and painful. But it worked.

Once that hurdle was overcome, Cann slid his hands down the backs of his legs and over his feet. He sat for a moment with them clasped in front of his as if in prayer until the burning stopped. Then he steeled himself for the next step.

Inside handcuffs, near the teeth that mesh to keep them closed, is a spring that can be manipulated and sprung with a metal probe, which Cann didn't have. But he'd heard that a sharp blow accompanied by an immediate pull could cause the teeth, or a tooth, to jump out of the grooves and, if timed precisely, a pull could loosen, even open, the cuffs.

He got to his feet for extra leverage, took a deep breath and, bending his wrists so that his hand were angled left, he swung his clasped hands to his right as hard as he could striking the outer edge of the cuff on the rough surface of the wall. Metal stunned bone and his knuckles scraped the wall but the cuffs remained secure. The pain was like an electric shock and made him want to doubt the theory. But it was all he had.

He swung again.

Clang! Pull.

Nothing.

Clang! Pull.

He sensed more than heard or felt a click, but he'd not pulled quickly enough. The cuffs stayed locked.

His hands were bloodied and if some bones in his wrist weren't broken they were so badly bruised the pain was the same. Excruciating.

But quitting was not an option. He swung again and hit the wall.

Clang! Pull.

The right cuff sprang open.

Cann gingerly removed his right hand from it and waited for the pain to subside.

Predrag Djilic continued his venomous narrative. Matsen kept his gaze on the wall behind and to the left of Djilic, denying him eye contact. Back in the corner, Price continued to clench and unclench her fists while at the same time straining at her bonds in an attempt to expand the ropes binding her wrists. She kept watch on the man guarding her but he was focused on what Djilic was saying.

"Then, when she was about sixteen, she got pregnant." Despite himself, Matsen's teeth clenched and he shook his head slowly. Djilic pursed his lips and shrugged. "I didn't care really, not one way or the other. I mean, a half-breed Serb bastard. Why would I?

"Anyway, as you've figured out by now, Dubran was the half-breed Serb bastard." He chuckled to himself. "And I had no intention of being particularly involved with either of them. But I was aware of them from a distance and Dubran turned out well, considering. Big. Strong. Very intelligent. And mean. Very mean. But, then, he had my blood, didn't he?

"So I brought them here. I wanted Dubran under my wing. I didn't care about Milica, but Branko took to her. And she to him. And then to the girls. And it worked out well." He took a long draw on the cigar and blew the smoke out and up. "Till now." He shook his head. "A shame, I suppose. For her. For you."

"Mama," Dubran Mribic began, "when I was a child, sometimes you would be sad and would cry and I would ask what was wrong and you would tell me a story of you and your *mamice*, my *baba*, and how you were chased by bad men and fell. Do you remember?"

"I cannot remember that I told you the story, Dubran. You know I cannot. But I remember the story. The bad men. The chase. The fall."

"When you told it to me, Mama, I thought it was a tale. Or a dream, perhaps. But it was real?"

Oma looked at Mribic, but her gaze was distant. "It was very long ago. Sometimes I wonder if it was a dream, but I think, yes, it was real."

"In the story, you told me of your *mamice* and you. You were in a town, you said. Do you remember what the place was?"

"No," Milica said quietly. "It was far away because we walked a long way. The tall man —"

"Yes, the tall man. You said his name before, Mama. What was it, do you remember?"

"Oh, yes," she smiled. "Artur was his name. He was very tall. Very handsome." She smiled some more. "I said to Mama he was pretty, but she told me men were handsome, not pretty. I remember that. He carried me."

"And the bad men, do you know who the bad men were?"

The smile faded. "There were so many bad men, Dubran. And they were very bad to your *baba* Savka." She looked inquiringly at him, protectively. "I did not tell you about . . . what they did, did I?"

"No, Mama, you didn't tell me that." He patted her hand. Nor was there any need to tell him now.

"This Artur, Mama, the tall man. Do you remember his last name?"

Oma's eyes squinted and moved around as if they were looking inward, trying to read something. After several moments, she shook her head. "No, I . . . I called him Artur. I don't think I knew it. I don't know."

"What about the name Predrag Djilic? Do you know that name, Mama?"

Again, Milica's eyes showed the search going on behind them. Finally, "Perhaps." she struggled some more and then shook her head again. "I don't know. I was very young." She shrugged. "But why do you ask me this, Dubran? Something is wrong, yes?"

"No, Mama." He sought to reassure her. "Why do you say that?"

"I feel something. In this house. There is something — something terrible will happen, I think. It frightens me." She looked at him. "Do you feel it, Dubran?"

Mribic nodded slowly. "Yes, Mama, I feel it too."

Djilic pointed his cigar at Matsen again. "This is so much better than I planned." He leaned his head back and took a long pull on the cigar, then slowly blew the smoke up toward the ceiling. "My intention was to get you here. And kill you. In my own way. In my own time. By my own hand. That will still happen, Matsen. Count on it.

"But before you die, I will take so much more from you than I could have thought possible." Djilic spoke slowly, evenly. "This Cann is important to you, I know. He will die too, Matsen. Because you sent him. His blood, his death is on your hands. Like Savka and Milica." He paused.

"Cann will die first." He said with a bob of his head. "I should like to drag this out, frankly. But our friends are impatient. They want their pound of flesh." He smirked at his own joke. "And you will watch him die. And know it is because of you."

Djilc glanced at Price. "Then we have this lovely creature here." He looked back at Matsen. "Once again, only because of you. I'm not sure what her role is, but I can see you care for each other. That's good." He leaned forward. "Because she will die next. But not until my men are through with her. And you will watch that, too, Matsen. And all the while, remember. It's all because of you.

"Then, I will let you see Milica. After all these years. It's amazing how the circle has closed." He took another puff, savoring the moment more than the cigar. "She looks different from the last time you saw her, of course. But it is little Milica. You will see that. And then," Djilic tapped the cigar on the ashtray again, "you will get to watch Milica die. Again. For a second time. For you, she died when they jumped off that cliff. Because of you. And now she will die a second time and, again, it's because of you."

Matsen was looking down, his shoulders heaving. Djilic leaned his head forward and down to examine Matsen's face. "Oh, come on Matsen," he mocked, "you're not breaking already, are you? Don't quit. Not so soon."

Matsen breathed in and looked up at Djilic. "It's not quit, Djilic," he said in a near whisper, "it's rage. That a coward like you has lived so long. Take off these ropes. Face me."

Djilic laughed. "And have us two antiques roll around on the floor making fools of ourselves? No, I don't think so."

Matsen looked around the room then back to Djilic. "Choose the weapons then. You must have a set of dueling pistols — something."

"Broadswords, perhaps!" Djilic proposed mockingly. "We can

have a contest. The winner will be the first of us who can even lift the bloody thing." He chuckled. "A duel. It's an intriguing idea, Matsen, I must say." He looked like he might be considering the idea. "But no."

"Because you're a coward."

"No," Djilc answered. "I'm a lot of things, but we both know coward isn't one of them. The fact is that I am not going to duel with you because I don't have to. I am where I am because I'm the better man. And you're where you are because you're not. And they," he tossed a look in Price's direction but it included the others, "are where they are because of you. It's that simple."

He turned to his son. "It's time, Branko. Our friends below have kept their end of the bargain. Now we shall keep ours. Go tell them I have what I want and they're free to do what they want with Cann. But he doesn't die till I get there." He locked his eyes on Matsen's. "Till *we* get there. And bring Oma down too."

Branko nodded and turned to leave.

"Don't you love her, Branko?" Price called across the room. "How can you?"

"He is his father's son," Djilic said proudly.

Branko looked coldly at Price, said nothing and left.

"What about Mribic, then? She's his mother, for God's sake."

"Yes, well, Dubran will have to choose, won't he."

41

"Control to Sierra One. Tango Two is moving to Papa One."

The communications tech in the command trailer relayed the information received from the surveillance team behind the castle to the stealth team, designator Sierra 1, which was hunkered down in the west wing.

From the start, Cann had been designated Primary 1: P1 or Papa 1. Matsen was P2 and Price, when she turned up unexpectedly with Matsen inside the castle, was given P3. At the top of the target food chain, Erwin Jost/Predrag Djilic and Branko Jost were T1 and T2 not only because of their status in the hierarchy of bad guys but also because their ready visibility had yielded more identifiers — voice and visual — early on in the surveillance. The remaining bad guys, the ones they knew of, were T3–T15. Among them, though the surveillance didn't know it, was Dubran Mribic.

Surveillance also had one unknown female subject, U designator, who had remained in one of the second floor east wing rooms from the beginning of the surveillance to the present. Oma.

• • •

The Sierra team acted on the report that Branko Jost was heading for

Cann. They had a flat digital camera under the door to monitor the great hall itself and, even as control advised that he was coming, they saw Branko march down the hall toward them, turn left and go down the hallway into the east wing.

All else seemed quiet in the hall so they withdrew the camera and slowly opened the door. One by one they silently crossed to the east wing hallway. As with all their disciplines, every one of them was highly trained and skilled in stalking and pursuit, but some were better than others. In this respect, Mattera had an almost preternatural ability to remain out of sight and sound. He took the lead, the rest strung out behind him.

In addition to remaining undetected, Mattera's capacity for total silence allowed him to hear what was going on around him and, in this case, ahead of him. He followed Branko down the hallway by the sounds he made, calculating distance by time and volume, and spaced himself accordingly. His own confidence was matched by his peers confidence in him.

The hallway ended in a "T" and Mattera could tell by sound that Branko had gone to the left. Still, he held up a hand as he reached the end of the hall and, as one, the team came to a stop behind him. He listened at the corner and interpreted from what he heard that Branko went several yards further, then stopped. Then, metal rasping, opened a door, then the sounds faded.

Mattera rolled himself around the corner and rapidly advanced to where Branko had exited the hall. He did a quick examination of the ancient wooden door. No keypad, no obvious wires or plates. Instead of a knob or handle, the door had gate latch-type hardware. Mattera knew there could be a low current running from latch to plate, which would activate when the flow was broken. But he also knew that Branko had not taken any time at the door and so — sometimes you have to take the chance. No one breathed as he opened the door. Silence. He went in.

They were at the top of a narrow-walled circular stairway. An ancient design for defensive purposes; it forced attackers into a single file with little room to wield a weapon. Of course, that was before the time of firearms. Especially automatic firearms. Especially suppressed automatic firearms. Who knows where the ricochets would go in such a confined environment? Presumably forward and down. But then, that works in reverse too. Mattera and the others could picture someone at the bottom of the stairs firing up into what was essentially a spiral funnel. It would be virtually impossible *not* to hit anything and everything in it. But not going down was not an option.

Mattera reached the bottom of the spiral staircase and slowly moved his head around to where his eyes could see what awaited them. The staircase ended in the middle of a narrow corridor that ran left and right away from it. To the right the corridor ran into another "T" and to the left it ended at yet another huge oak door with cast-iron hinges.

Just as Mattera was about to raise an arm to signal the team to follow him into the corridor, he heard voices off to the right. As the sounds quickly grew louder, he signaled the team to retreat up the staircase to where they wouldn't be seen. Fohler moved ahead of Mattera and found a spot where the geometry of the outer circular wall met the curve of the inner circular wall so that there was a slit through which he could see, barely, into the corridor at the base of the staircase. He positioned himself so that the top of his head pressed into the low ceiling, and one eye and one eye only, was out beyond the surface to where it could see through the slit.

He recognized Tango 2, Branko, as he marched past followed by one — two — three — four men, all wearing keffiyahs, all armed. At this point, designators didn't matter. They were the bad guys. The men of Sierra then heard metal rasping followed quickly by shouting and muted thudding sounds, the kind made when someone is being beaten.

Whether they were born with it or whether it evolved over time, men like these had a compulsion to rescue. While theirs was a world fraught with complexities, it eventually came down to a question of right and wrong, good and evil, "us" versus "them." And since Tango 2 and the others were "thems," it stood to reason that whomever was being beaten was an "us." And they ached within themselves to do something about it right then. But there were too many unknowns at that particular moment and through intelligence, training, and common sense, the men of Sierra knew that rescues were only rescues if they succeeded. The odds were that the "us" in question right now, almost certainly Papa 1, was not being killed at the moment. A single shot would have done that. So Sierra held back and waited for the "thems" to pass on their way back, dragging — yes, it was Papa 1. As they passed, Fohler saw Cann's right hand, hanging limply at his side, a bloody mess.

A fighter, Fohler thought.

One of ours.

Price and Matsen were led out of the study by the remaining guards, followed closely by Erwin Jost/Predrag Djilic himself. They turned left and marched down the center hall taking the same path Branko had just taken moments ago.

From their observation point behind the castle, the surveillance communicated the group's exit to Nikolic in the command trailer and he relayed it to the Sierra team. The Sierra team, below ground and encased within what was probably eight to twelve feet of stone, heard nothing.

In his exuberance, Djilic was talking nonstop and loudly and it was the sound of his voice that alerted Duggan at the rear of the Sierra team still lined up in the spiral staircase. With a tap and a hand signal he communicated the imminent problem to the man in front of him and the message flashed down the line. At the lead, Fohler checked the hallway. He didn't know what was around the corner to the right but it was a good bet there was an empty room to the left. He led the team out of the stairwell and to the cell formerly occupied by Cann. It had been small for Cann and the eight men of Sierra team almost didn't fit. They had to struggle and cram to even get the door shut. Once they were closed up inside, the stifling odor hit them but no one spoke. They all understood.

Price took Matsen's arm as they descended. At the bottom of the stairs, the group went right and right again at the end of the hall. As they made that turn, Branko was coming back that way and his father stopped him.

"They are all in there?" he asked.

"Cann and the Kosovars. I am going for Oma now."

Djilic frowned. "Well, hurry. I'm anxious to get started."

Branko nodded and moved off. As he reached the bottom of the circular stairwell, he glanced at the room where Cann had been held and saw that the door was closed but not bolted. More out of instinct and habit than anything else, he went to the door and slammed the bolt home.

Branko ran up the stairs to the second floor and went quickly to the room where Oma was being kept. He rapped softly on the door.

"Oma, it's Branko."

"*Komme*," came the reply.

He opened the door and stepped in. Mribic stood and faced him. The two men looked at each other. Then Branko spoke.

"I'm glad you're here, Dubran. I thought I would have to go look for you."

Mribic nodded but said nothing.

Branko took a moment to smile at Oma. "How are you, Oma?" he said.

"I am well," she smiled back. Still, Branko noticed the concerned look on her face and the way she looked from Dubran to him and back.

He turned back to Mribic and flipped his head toward the door. Mribic crossed the room and joined him in the doorway. Branko took a step back out into the hallway and Mribic followed. Oma watched from the other side of the room.

"You have to get her out of here. Now," Branko said firmly.

"Why?"

Branko looked off to the side and didn't answer immediately. Then he brought his gaze back and looked directly into Mribic's eyes. "Father is going to kill Cann and Matsen and the woman." Mribic nodded. "And Oma."

"Why?" Mribic asked again, but this time with much greater intensity.

Branko shook his head. "It goes way back. Something to do with Matsen during the war. It wasn't a pretty story, Dubran. I didn't know it before. And I still don't fully understand, but I do know our father. He is serious. Get her out of here. I'll tell him she was gone when I came up."

Mribic felt his body chill.

"Branko, does the name Predrag Djilic mean anything to you?"

Born and raised in Germany by Erwin Jost, it didn't. He shrugged his shoulders and shook his head. Then he stopped. "Although —"

"What?"

"Matsen called Father something like that when he was at the gate. I think that was what he said."

"And what did Father say?"

Branko thought about it. " 'If you prefer,' I think he said."

Mribic nodded. He took a deep breath. Then he reached out and grabbed Branko by the shoulder and squeezed. "Thank you. This will be difficult for you, you know that."

Branko nodded and looked warmly at the woman he knew as Oma. "She is the only mama I have ever known." He looked back at Mribic. "Perhaps I am not my father's son after all," he shrugged. "Perhaps that is not such a bad thing."

Mribic gave Branko's shoulder another squeeze and then turned to his mother. "Come, Mama, we must go now."

Oma rose and with her rocking gait crossed the room. She stopped in front of Branko and wrapped her arms around his waist and looked up into his face. "I don't understand all of this, Branko. But I thank you. You are a good boy."

Branko laughed. "Not everyone would agree with that, Oma. Sometimes a not-so-good memory is a good thing, I think." He kissed the top of her head.

"Now go."

42

— and the Exalted One said, "Do not consider those who died for the cause of Allah as dead, rather as alive, at their Lord sustained." Verily, Allah's words are true. But he who strikes the hand of the true jihadi, strikes at the heart of Islam and will feel the wrath of Allah —

Price and Matsen recognized the room from the videotape. And, just as in the tape, Cann sat on the floor in the middle of the room, arms tied behind him, the handcuffs replaced by leather bindings. He looked up when they came in and, despite the gravity of the situation, felt embarrassment to be seen this way. Price and Matsen saw no shame for Cann. What they felt was rage.

Also just as in the tape, five men with their faces masked by checkered cloth stood against the rear wall behind Cann. The one in the center was reading from a clipboard he held in his left hand. As before, the other four held rifles while the speaker had a short sword stuck in his waistband. Every now and then, the man who was speaking hitched his waist band and fondled the haft of the sword.

Price looked around the room, which she estimated to be twenty feet by twenty feet. One guard stood with her just to the left of the door through which they'd entered. To the right of the door, another guard was posted next to Matsen. Two more flanked Djilc. Nine — ten counting Djilic — against three.

In the command trailer, Nikolic stood stiffly in front of the bank of monitors processing what he'd heard from the study. If he'd needed confirmation that Jost was Djilic, he had it. And much more.

"Units report," he commanded into his mouthpiece. The various elements of the assault force announced their readiness. Nikolic thought for a few more seconds, then. "All units," he called for their attention. "We have lost contact with Sierra 1 and P1, 2, and 3. Subjects are believed — repeat, are *believed* — to be below ground under the east wing of the structure. Security on the surface remains in place. All units will move forward on my command, but you will exercise maximum stealth unless and until there is contact. Then you will implement 'chaos.' Acknowledge."

All did.

"Charlie 3 will move forward to disable the wall sensors again." It had been turned back on after the initial penetration so as not to arouse suspicions. Now, they would have to take their chances.

"Understood."

"Go."

Nikolic waited and watched the monitor as the designated unit moved up to the wall. When the readout told him the electrical current had been interrupted, he said, "All units. Go."

In a room on the second floor of the castle, the guard assigned to monitor the electronic security saw the flashing light that indicated an electrical circuit had been broken. He identified the specific circuit that was down and keyed his mike. "All personnel, be aware of a circuit interruption on the outer wall security. Possible breach. Report any visual confirmation."

Mribic knew that most of the castle personnel were outside or otherwise occupied with the higher alert level but he was still exceedingly cautious as he led his mother down the hallway. From the second floor landing, he examined the central staircase and beyond for any activity on the first floor. Seeing none, he reached his hand back for his mother's and led her down the stairs. Given Milica's short legs and awkward gait, it was slow going. They reached the first floor and crossed the great hall and slipped into the west wing through the same door that Sierra 1 had used earlier. Once inside, Mribic relaxed slightly as they headed in darkness for the far end of the building and the garage where the castle vehicles were kept.

> — for without a doubt, fighting the infidel is a duty of all who are able and divine laws have agreed about fighting them back so they leave humiliated and diminished, God willing. The basis of this call to the struggle is what God meant when he said, "To those against whom war is made, permission is given to fight, because they are wronged and verily, Allah is Most Powerful and will certainly aid those who aid His cause for He is Full of Strength, Exalted in Might, able to enforce His Will —

Though he'd been raised a Muslim and was still one in name at least, Predrag Djilic was neither inspired nor moved by the words he was hearing. In fact, he was tempted to call a halt to this performance except he knew it was being staged and taped for those who had commissioned Cann's death. Djilic shook his head. *Will this idiot never shut up? Let's get on with this.*

•   •   •

Inside Cann's former cell, Sierra 1 had heard the bolts slam home but maintained silence in case anyone remained outside. After a few minutes, Duggan and Woodowski, the two team members last in and thus pressed against the door, set to work to see what they were up against. It was clear that aside from the bolted door, the biggest hurdle they faced was the lack of room to move, a factor they had to take into account in choosing the means they used to effect an escape.

Normally, their first choice would have been the modified detonation cord they carried with them for such purposes, but in such close quarters they had to take into account the effect the intense heat would have on those closest to it. And then there were the fumes. They were as concerned with alerting someone outside the cell to their presence as they were with any possible ill effects to themselves. So, initially, they'd rejected that option.

The low-tech alternative was to use their knives to dig and cut through the old wood of the door and the two set to doing just that. As expected, they were seriously hampered by the tight quarters. Even more of a problem, the wood was old but, rather than being weaker because of it, it was close to petrified in places and would require far more time than the team had.

Back to Plan A.

Mribic and Milica made their way down the corridor that ran the length of the west wing and ended at a door that led into the garage area. Mribic tested the handle and found it unlocked. He slowly pressed down and pushed the door open just a crack. He waited, then stepped inside, listening intently. He heard nothing. His eyes, already adjusted to the darkness, saw nothing. He reached back and again took Milica's hand and pulled her into the garage. He took a final look past Milica to check the corridor. It was clear.

He closed the door and crossed to a gray metal box on the wall where he turned the key disabling the alarm wired into the outer doors and frame. As he started to move deeper into the garage toward the vehicles, still holding his mother's hand, he felt Milica stop suddenly and pull back on his hand. He froze and then looked back at her. She nodded toward the front of the garage. The doors each had four panes of glass and, through one of them, he saw about a third of the head of someone standing outside with his back to the doors. Mribic crouched down and had his mother do the same. He signaled her to stay where she was. Then he moved slowly and silently to the corner at the front of the garage. He squatted down with his back to the wall then slowly raised himself to where he could see outside. From that angle, he could see that the man wore a black jumpsuit, was talking into a mouthpiece, and carried a suppressed HK MP5K submachine gun. Mribic was momentarily thrown. He'd been concerned with avoiding detection from within — unaware of the force massed outside the compound.

So who the hell is this? he asked himself. But the most logical conclusion was obvious. Matsen hadn't come alone after all. Far from it.

Suddenly, the man outside slid down and out of view. A moment later, the tip of a pry bar probed under the garage door not six feet from where Mribic was crouched. He reached back and removed the 10mm Glock from the back of his waistband and waited in the dark corner. The tip of the bar tilted downward and pressed into the concrete as the man outside raised the other end. The garage door offered little resistance and rose about two feet. The man outside waited, listening for an alarm or other response. When none came, he lay flat on the ground facedown and quickly slid himself under the open door and into the garage. When he raised his head, he came face to face with the muzzle of Mribic's Glock 20.

The guard monitoring security had seen the light on his panel go out when Mribic shut off the garage alarm and, as before, had passed the information over the channel to all personnel and units. Making his

way back to the staircase, Branko heard the transmission and considered for a moment and then keyed his own mike. "All personnel,"
he ordered, "draw back from the outer perimeter and reposition at
designated stations close in. Repeat. Withdraw from current grounds
positions to designated positions for primary castle security immediately."

The Sierra team finished affixing the det cord to the door around the
lock area and then compressed themselves as far back as they could
against the rear wall — which wasn't very far. There was at most a
foot between the door and Duggan and Woodowski who had wriggled themselves around so that their backs faced out. The standard
main ingredient of det cord, PETN, was highly explosive but for this
usage was mixed with a suppressant so that, rather than explode, it
would burn. Rapidly and intensely. The other team members struggled out of their shirts and jackets and passed them forward so that
they could be draped over the heads and backs of the two men who
would bear the brunt of the heat. They hoped it would be enough
and feared it wouldn't.

Mribic kept the Glock 20 pointed at the intruder and peered into
his face. "I know you," he frowned. "You are —" He peered more
intently. "You are with Nikolic, yes. What are you doing here?"

The man was silent.

Without hesitation, Mribic lashed the pistol into the man's head
stunning him momentarily — long enough to seize the submachine
gun and turn it on its former owner. When the man could focus
again, this time on the suppressed muzzle of the MP5K 'room
broom,' Mribic asked, "Is Nikolic here?"

Again the man said nothing.

"Give me your radio," Mribic ordered.

The man didn't move.

"Don't be foolish," Mribic warned him. "You can do it and live or

I will shoot you and take it anyway. I only want to communicate with your captain." The man considered the incontrovertible logic and started to move. Mribic flicked the weapon up. "Slowly, very slowly. Put it on the floor and push it away from you." The man did so.

Mribic took the headset and held it to his ear and mouth with his left hand. He pressed the small button on the earpiece. "Nikolic?"

There was silence before Nikolic responded cautiously. "Who is this?"

"Mribic."

More silence, then, "I see. Have you killed my man?"

"No, Captain Nikolic, he is not dead. A bit damaged. But I want to give him back to you."

"That's not like you, Mribic. You must want something. And you know I don't deal with —"

"Shut up, Captain. I'm not asking for a deal." Mribic looked over at his mother crouching in the shadows. "I'm asking for a favor."

> And God said, "If a man kills a Believer intentionally, his recompense is Hell, to abide therein forever. And the wrath and the curse of Allah are upon him, and a dreadful penalty is prepared for him." Thus does God protect the people of Islam everywhere, and through his servants he will he stop the harm of the infidels for He is mightier and stronger and will prevail.
>
> Prayers be upon his prophet Muhammad and his companions, and we thank God the Lord of the two worlds.

The man finished reading, then slowly placed the clipboard on the floor by his feet. He stood erect and drew the sword from his belt. As one, the five men moved forward chanting, *"Allahu Akbar, Allahu Akbar, Allahu Akbar —"*

43

"A favor." Nikolic repeated the single word. "How can you —?" He shook his head as if to clear it, then finally asked the obvious. "What favor?"

"I want you to get my mother out of here."

Nikolic stiffened. He didn't expect *that*. "Your mother," he said.

"Oma she is called. My father —"

"Yes, Mribic, I know. I heard it all."

"Heard what?"

"Your father told the whole story to Matsen in the office. About your mother and her mother and Predrag Djilic."

"So my father really is Predrag Djilic." It was a statement, not a question.

"Yes."

After a pause, Mribic asked, "Will you do it?"

"Get your mother out?"

"Yes."

Regardless of his feelings toward Mribic, Nikolic knew it was the right thing to do. "Yes," he said. "We'll do it."

"Thank you."

"I'm not doing it for you, Mribic," Nikolic felt compelled to say. "You should come with her. Turn yourself in."

"No, I don't think so, Captain Nikolic. I know what your mission is in my regard so —"

After a pause, Nikolic said, "Give the headset back to my man Zamonja then. You also have his weapon?"

"Yes."

"You will return it to him?"

Mribic thought about it for a second but, "No," he said slowly, "I won't do that."

"How is he to protect your mother if he is unarmed."

"He came in quietly. I want him to go out that way. I don't want a firefight."

"And you are concerned he will shoot you also."

"That too," Mribic acknowledged, "but I'll also cover them from here. I assume you know there is security out there."

"We do."

Mribic handed over the radio and gestured to the man that he should talk to Nikolic. Then he turned to his mother and took her hands in his. "This man will take you to safety, *Mamice*. Go with him."

"I would stay with you, Dubran," she replied squeezing his hands.

"I know, Mama, but this is best. Please. I will try to be with you later. But for now, please go with this man." He stood and leaned down and kissed her on the cheek. *"Ti si mi tako draga, Mama."*

Milica's eyes clouded at the sentiment of love. *"Znam sine, i ti meni,"* she told him in return. "You are dear to me also, my son."

Unseen in the small of her back, Price's right wrist was raw and bloodied to the extent it looked like she was wearing a "web of thorns" tattoo. But her right hand was free.

She willed Cann to look at her and, when he did, her eyes communicated a clear message: *On my move.*

Cann nodded almost imperceptibly.

Still chanting, the five KLA men stood directly behind Cann. The man in the center tilted his head backward and extended his arms straight out from his shoulders. The blade of the short sword he held in his right hand momentarily caught the reflection of the single bulb hanging in the center of the room. The assassin's lips moved silently for several seconds. Then, slowly, deliberately, he bent at the waist and leaned over Cann, his left hand reaching out for Cann's hair and his right hand beginning to extend the blade out and down toward Cann's throat.

Cann focused completely on Price's face and waited. As the man who would behead him bent at a forty-five degree angle, Cann saw the flash of imminent violence in Price's eyes and the movement of her hand out from behind her. Only a fraction of a second later he made his move. He rolled onto his back, hands still bound behind him, knees pulled into his chest as tightly as possible. He compacted himself under the man bent over him and pushed up and off his shoulders, blasting his legs straight up into the man's chin. The sword flew out of the man's hand and Cann heard the crack of snapping vertebrae as the man fell with his head at an unnatural angle.

Cann's explosive movement distracted Price's guard just long enough for her to pull her left hand out from behind her, cock her arm and slam her left elbow into the man's forehead. Then she threw her left arm over the man's right forearm taking control of the machine pistol that dangled from his shoulder. In a fluid motion, she swung the pistol toward the center of the room and — blessedly, for-tuitously, it was on automatic — pulled the trigger as she swept the muzzle down the line of KLA terrorists killing the two on the left outright, missing the prone center man who was already dead, and severely wounding one of the two men on the right. The last of the five terrorists had time to drop to his knee as he struggled to bring his assault rifle to bear on Price.

From the right of the door, one of Djilic's escorts fired at Price but she, too, had dropped to one knee and the bullet flew over her head.

She fired in that direction and the shooter fell. The two guards still with Djilic and Matsen shoved them out the door. Price whipped her attention back to the remaining KLA man. There was no need. Cann, still with his hands tied behind him, and on his back and still with his center of gravity up around his shoulders, swung his right leg in a horizontal arc as the man pointed his weapon at Price. The toe of Cann's boot caught the point of the man's chin, dazing him. He froze, suspended, and was an easy target as Price put a three-round burst into his face.

Price turned back to the man who had been guarding her. He put his hands up in front of him in a gesture of supplication. Price didn't pull the trigger. Keeping the gun pointed on him, she backed over to where the sword had landed and kicked it over to Cann who used it to cut himself free, then used it to check the condition of the five terrorists. Four were already dead, and it was clear that without immediate medical help, the fifth soon would be. Cann turned his back on him, put the sword into his belt, and picked up one of the AK-47s along with several magazines from the other downed KLA. He glanced at the frightened guard seated on the floor pleading with his eyes, then looked at Price. Without a word, he used his former bonds to secure the grateful but still fearful man. They left him face down on the floor.

"They've got Arthur," Price said.

"I know," Cann responded. He looked at Price for a moment and she returned the gaze with equal and reciprocal warmth. Finally, Cann said, simply, "Thanks." He looked down at himself. "I'd hug you but —" He extended his arms to encompass the entire situation including his own less than sanitary condition.

Price nodded. "I'll take a rain check."

Cann put a hand up and softly pressed his palm against Price's cheek. Price tilted her head into it. They held each others eyes for a moment then suddenly came back to reality.

"Arthur," Price said.

"Arthur," Cann agreed.

They turned and moved to the doorway.

Djilic had been first out of the room propelled by a guard pressing hard on the small of his back. Another guard pushed Matsen out after them and a third followed close behind, clutching his bleeding right side.

Led by Djilic, the group turned right and continued straight, passing the hallway on the left that led to the cell where Sierra was trying to escape. The way grew increasingly darker as they went on. When they reached the end, they could only go left. After about twenty more yards, they came to another old wooden door with rusted cast-iron hardware. Djilic stepped aside to let the guard behind him do the heavy work of getting it open. After several seconds, the door groaned and swung out to reveal another flight of stairs, straight up, not circular. Djilic motioned for the second guard to get Matsen through the door and up the stairs and then looked back down the corridor for the third guard who had been struggling to keep up. The man was slumped against the wall two-thirds of the way back. Djilic barked an order and the guard beside him ran over, grabbed the man by the collar, dragged him to the door, and propped him beside it. It wouldn't stop any pursuers, Djilic knew, but it might delay them. He shot another quick look down the corridor and, seeing nothing, went into the stairway followed by the guard who pulled the door closed behind them.

Inside the cramped confines of Sierra's mini-prison, the det cord was burning intensely. Duggan and Woodowski pressed harder into the rest of the men trying to put as much distance between their backs and the heat as possible. But they could still feel it even through the several layers of cloth that covered them. The smell of burning fabric began to fill the room and combined with the smoke to make it difficult to breathe. The men could only hope that the door would give out before they did.

Branko noticed a burning smell as he wound his way down the circular staircase. He peered cautiously around the wall and into the hallway toward the old wooden door. The burning odor was clearly coming from that direction and he could see the beginnings of smoke or vapor appearing on the outside of the door. As he watched, a bright red square began to appear on the outer surface of the door around the locking plate. *Someone was inside and was burning their way out.* He started toward the door, then stopped. He didn't know *what* was on the other side. It was only common sense to get reinforcements. Thinking his father and the other guards were just around the corner, he turned and ran for the "T" at the end of the hall.

Inside the cell, the heat and the smoke were unbearable and not just for Duggan and Woodowski. In desperation, Fohler who was pressed up against them facing outward raised a leg and inserted it between the two seared men, cocked it, and slammed his heel into the locking plate on the door. The burning det cord had by then etched a perimeter around the plate so that the blow cleanly dislodged the mechanism and the part of the door surrounding it. The cord flared briefly then quickly burned itself out on the floor. The men inside fell out into the hallway, for a moment operational security taking second place to the need for cooler air. The sounds of the escape got Branko's attention and he looked back over his shoulder to see the men stumbling out into the corridor. He reached for his weapon but, seeing the numbers, again decided that discretion would be the better part of valor.

Branko started to round the corner just as Cann put his head around the edge of the dungeon doorway. Both men saw each other at exactly the same time. Cann raised his weapon as Branko pulled back into the corridor where the Sierra team was recovering. At that moment, Fohler looked up and, before Branko could react, the team leader raised his weapon and fired two short bursts, one into Jost's head and the second into his torso. Several of the rounds passed through Branko's body and struck the back wall.

"What the hell —?" Cann muttered as he pulled his head back into the room. He exchanged a questioning look with Price who had heard the shots. He brought his face around the edge of the doorway and saw Branko's body slide down the wall.

"What the hell —?" he repeated, still struggling to place these events in context. But he'd recognized Branko and, on the principle that "the enemy of my enemy is my friend," called out, "Who's there. This is Cann." Fohler, who had advanced to the corner, answered, "That's P One to us, Mr. Cann. Can we verify?" He hand signaled and the other men who could move joined him. Fohler went down on one knee and carefully edged his weapon around the corner. Another Sierra team member did the same above him and two more did the same from the far wall of the corridor.

Price quickly gave Cann a rundown on the tactical plan and who the men outside were *supposed* to be. Then she took a turn at peering cautiously down the hall. "It's Price, Fohler," she called out. "You still planning on shooting me?" she asked as a means of identification.

"Consider it withdrawn, Ms. Price. If it's you."

They incrementally exposed their faces until the mutual tension subsided. Price led Cann out of the room and down the wall where they were joined by the remaining Sierra team members. Duggan and Woodowski could barely move and the team had left Taylor, the best at the medical stuff, with them.

"Nice to see you again, Ms. Price," Fohler smiled. "And to meet you, Mr. Cann. Now let's get out of here." He turned toward the circular stairwell.

"Whoa, we still don't have Arthur," Cann interrupted.

"Sometimes you take what you can get. I've got two men badly burned over there."

"So go," Cann said abruptly with Price nodding her concurrence beside him, "we're not leaving without Arthur."

Fohler quickly made his decision. "Chetrie, you and Taylor get Woody and Dug out of here. Get back to ground level and reestablish communications with Control. Apprise them of the situation — that we have P1and P3— and are going for P2. Go." Chetrie ran back up the corridor and he and Taylor began to gingerly lift the others.

"Mattera, Sepp, Davis, you're with me," Fohler ordered. He looked at Cann and Price then down at a series of round dark spots on the ground leading off into the darkness. "Somebody's hit. And leaving a trail. Mattera's the best. He'll take point and we'll see where this leads. Ready?"

He didn't wait for an answer and the six moved off into the darkness.

44

Inside the garage, Mribic had placed himself under one of the vehicles where he was mostly concealed in shadow. He could see under the garage door and watched as the shadowy figures of Zamonja and Oma crouched low as they moved away from the castle. They had to cross three hundred meters to reach the outer wall of the grounds and there were places where the cover was sparse.

Suddenly, beyond the two figures and off to the left, Mribic sensed movement. Two other figures were moving toward the castle, not twenty meters away from Zamonja and Oma. Mribic looked back over at his mother and saw that she and Zamonja were bent over and moving very slowly, clearly aware of these others nearby. The MP5K he held didn't have a night scope but Mribic sighted its muzzle as best he could on the moving images and held his breath as the inward bound pair passed his mother and her escort.

Before Mribic could breathe a sigh of relief, a shot rang out and Mribic saw one of the men in his gunsights fall. The second man immediately dropped to the ground and began firing in the general direction of the first shot. Fire was returned from that direction and it was answered by more fire from behind the original pair. Mribic couldn't tell who was who or who had started it. But whatever the source, whoever the combatants were, the fact was that, in an instant, a full firefight had erupted between castle security and the assault force.

With Oma and Zamonja caught in the crossfire.

When they reached the top of the stairway, one of the guards gave Matsen a shove into the windowless room adjacent to the study. Matsen stumbled and grabbed the back of a chair, wincing at the pain in his broken fingers. Djilic entered the room a moment later and, without looking at Matsen, crossed quickly to an intercom in the wall as the second guard took a position in the doorway at the top of the stairs.

Djilic pressed the call button and attempted to contact security without success. Unaware of the Sierra penetration and the assault force, his immediate priority was additional security for himself. Once he had that, he would seek out and destroy Price and Cann. Then he could deal with Matsen at his leisure.

At that moment, the shooting outside spread like a fuse around the grounds and the sounds of the conflict penetrated the walls of the castle. Djilic's first reaction was surprise, then confusion, then suddenly, realization. For the first time, his sense of absolute control was shaken.

The sounds of the shooting didn't penetrate below ground though.

Matterra reached the corner and positioned himself with only his ear out beyond the edge of the wall and listened. He heard no sound and slowly rolled his head until a line of sight was established. He jerked his head back when he saw the body propped against the wall. After another few seconds passed without sound, he looked again. He saw no movement and moved the muzzle of his weapon around the corner and activated the laser sight onto the seated figure. No reaction. He prepared to move out into the corridor, knowing if the guy was playing possum, he would be exposed and caught in a narrow shooting gallery. Fohler came up to cover him and Mattera went low and around the corner. He approached the seated figure cautiously until he was close enough to see that the man was dead. Still, the body was there for a reason and Matterra called for Davis to come up and check for booby traps. When they were sure there were none, the others joined them. They unceremoniously shoved the man's body out of the way, and formed up to address whatever was behind the door.

From inside the garage, Mribic had seen Zamonja throw Milica to the ground and fall on top of her when the first shots rang out. From his position of concealment, he watched with concern as Zamonja attempted to get Oma to the nearest cover, a large fountain about thirty yards ahead of them. To do it, they had to raise themselves slightly. But it was enough to backlight them against the muzzle flashes of the opposing sides.

Mribic's gut tightened and his muscles contracted involuntarily when he saw several figures on the left targeting his mother and Zamonja. Without hesitation, Mribic sent three-round bursts from the MP5K at every muzzle flash he could see on the left. He began to receive return fire from that quarter. The assault force on the right also saw the flashes coming from Mribic and unleashed a fusillade into the garage. Despite his cover, Mribic was hit several times up and down his right side. He knew the wounds were serious and he felt his consciousness begin to slip away. As blackness took him under, he saw Zamonja spin around and enlarge his own body to cover Oma and he was grateful. But even in the darkness, Mribic saw the puffs of impact on Zamona's body, which convulsed each time it was struck until it could no longer support its own weight. Behind and under him, Milica struggled to get up on all fours. Less than a second after Zamonja succumbed, Mribic watched helplessly as his mother's back arched suddenly and her head snapped violently to the side as she, too, fell.

Then, all was still.

The guard at the top of the stairway heard the door below creak when Cann and the others started to pull it open. He fired down in the direction of the sound as Djilic crossed the room and cracked open the door to the study. He checked to make sure it was empty and motioned to the other guard to bring Matsen, then crossed to his desk and armed himself with two handguns. He kept one in his hand and stuck the other into his waistband.

Once in the study, he could hear the magnitude of the assault more clearly. He considered putting a bullet into Matsen then and there, but couldn't let go of his dream of prolonged revenge. But evasion was a prerequisite to realization of that dream. He gestured to the guard to follow him and bring Matsen along. The three men left the study, crossed the great hall, and went into the west wing corridor that led to the garage.

The surveillance behind the castle detected the movement in the study and relayed the information to Nikolic. The intelligence available to Nikolic was enhanced further when Chetrie's voice crackled into Nikolic's headset advising that he, Taylor, Woodowski, and Duggan were at the top of the circular stairwell just outside the center hall and that P1 was free and was accompanying P3 and Fohler and the rest of the Sierra team in a search for P2.

At the bottom of the stairway, still in the bowels of the castle, Cann and Fohler crouched on their haunches on either side of the open door. The shots from the guard above had ricocheted dangerously in the corridor, but no one had been hit. At a nod from Fohler, the two men raised their weapons and pointed them into and up the stairway and fired. They stopped firing and waited a beat but didn't pull their weapons back. Then, in a purely timed maneuver, they fired again, one low and one high just as the guard moved into the stairway to return their initial fire. They knew the exercise had worked to perfection when they heard the clatter of the guard's gun bouncing down the stone steps. That was confirmed a moment later when the body slid to the bottom of the stairs.

After a quick but careful check to make sure the man was dead, Fohler charged up the stairway followed by Cann, then Price, then the others. At the top, they cautiously checked the room, then moved inside.

The first thing Fohler did was reestablish contact with Nikolic and get his bearings. Nikolic immediately advised him that they were mere steps behind Djilic and Matsen and another, armed man. And that the three had only just left the adjacent study and were, at that moment, crossing the great hall toward the west wing of the castle.

Notwithstanding the intelligence, Fohler, Cann, Price, and the others entered the study with caution. Once they confirmed that it was secure, they quickly crossed to the door. Still in the lead, Fohler peered out into the great hall. At the far end, near the front of the castle, he saw one man only, apparently the last in line, as he was about to exit the great hall into the west wing corridor. In an instant, Fohler raised his weapon and dropped the man where he stood. An unseen hand tried to push the door shut but it banged against the outstretched foot of the now dead guard. As they dashed down the great hall, the team watched as the offending appendage was roughly shoved out of the way and the door thudded shut followed by the clang of a bolt slamming home.

Djilic kept Matsen at bay with the gun in one hand while pushing the door shut and bolting it with the other. Then he turned back and pointed the gun straight at Matsen's face. "Perhaps it's time, Matsen,"

Djilic said with chagrin. "I'd rather hoped for a more elablorate, more enjoyable conclusion but —" He shrugged. "One makes do."

Matsen stood stoically, chin high, saying nothing.

Djilic looked at him for a moment then said, "I don't suppose you'd beg for your life, would you? Give me that much?" he said with a smirk.

"I'll see you in hell first."

Djilic pursed his lips, tilted his head to the side and lifted a shoulder. "If we're to meet again, I suppose that's as good a place as any." He glanced at the door again as the sounds from the other side grew louder and the smell of something burning started to seep into the hallway. "If it's any consolation, you won't get there much before I do, it seems."

"My regret is not being the one to send you there." Matsen said calmly.

Djilic smirked, then fired past Matsen's ear into the wood of the door. The sound carried through to the other side, and Cann and Price exchanged looks of increased fear and concern. Inside the hallway, Matsen refused to react to the shot. Defiance was all he had.

"No reaction?" Djilic said with irritation. "Come on, Matsen, show me something. Don't just stand there."

Matsen continued to stare.

"I know," Djilic said, brightening. "Do you still want that duel!" He reached into his belt and took out the second handgun. With his left hand, he ejected the magazine and let it drop to the floor. Then he jacked the slide back ejecting the round that was in the chamber. It clattered to the floor and rolled toward Matsen. Djilic put the empty gun on the floor as well and kicked it over to Matsen who looked at it but made no attempt to pick it up.

"Come on, Matsen, go ahead. Look —" Djilic removed the magazine from the gun he was holding, and cleared the round from its chamber. When he was done, he held the single round in his left hand

and the gun itself in his right. "Go ahead, Matsen. We'll count to three and then load and fire. Fair?"

Matsen held up his swollen right hand with its broken deformed fingers. "With these? You *are* a coward."

Djilic was unaffected by the insult. "It's better than no chance at all, isn't it?"

Matsen knew he was certain to lose the "duel." The spring that holds and returns the slide on a semiautomatic handgun is tensioned at about sixteen pounds of pressure. Pulling it back with an uninjured hand isn't easy. With his damaged hand, Matsen doubted he would be able to pull it back at all. Still, there was always the possibility — or Djilic could miss his shot.

Whatever happened, Matsen would not give Djilic what he wanted most. He would not panic or show fear. He didn't want to die but he wasn't afraid of it. He'd lived a good long life. Perhaps Djilic was right. Perhaps it *was* time.

Calmy, without looking at Djilic, Matsen bent over and picked up the loose round with his left hand and put it between his teeth. Then he picked up the gun, also with his left hand, and cradled it against his chest, holding it in place with the wreckage of his right. Then he looked straight at Djilic, and waited.

The hint of a smile appeared of Djilic's face and he gave the slightest of nods.

"Good, then. Ready?" He arched a brow. "Okay, one-two-three."

Matsen pressed the gun to his chest with his right wrist and tried to pull back the slide with his left hand. But the spring resisted and, with his injuries, it proved impossible. Matsen tried again, holding the weapon even tighter with his right wrist, but it suddenly flipped out of his grasp and clattered across the floor.

Not that it mattered. With two good hands, Djilic had already pulled back the slide, inserted the single round, and let the slide slam forward chambering the round. He had his weapon once again pointed into Matsen's face even before Matsen had dropped the gun.

"Go ahead, Matsen," Djilic said smirking, "Pick it up. I'll give you another chance."

Matsen looked directly into Djilic's eyes and shook his head slowly.

"As you said, Djilic, it's time. Just do it."

The shot reverberated throughout the hallway and out into the great hall just as Cann and Price got the door open and thrust their own weapons into the space beyond.

They saw Matsen with his back to them, just standing there, not moving.

In front of Matsen, they saw Djilic, standing, not moving.

Not seeing.

Not living.

The exit wound in the top center of his forehead made him a dead man standing.

After a long moment, Djilic began to totter and then, slowly, he fell forward smashing face first into the floor.

Behind him, lying on the floor with his Glock 20 in front of him and pointing up, a long double smear of blood extending back down the hallway where he'd dragged himself from the garage, Dubran Mribic slowly lowered his own face into the floor and allowed himself to die.

45

"But Janie's okay?"

Cann sat in an orange jumpsuit borrowed from one of Nikolic's men, having taken a quick shower before joining Price and Matsen on the veranda. After the warm reunion, Matsen had moved off some distance and was standing by the balustrade staring out over the grounds in silence. Price was bringing Cann up to date.

"Not completely. Sara's death has hit her particularly hard. Such a waste."

"It is," he agreed. He and Sara had never grown close but he still mourned the loss. Especially for Janie.

"Janie's not back at Whispering Marsh, is she?"

Price shook her head. "She's going to stay with her folks for the indefinite future. Whispering Marsh is providing twenty-four-hour on-call care so she can do that."

"Sounds like the least they can do after what happened."

"They did step up to the plate once they found out what was happening, John."

He nodded. "I suppose." He looked at Price. "You should have told me."

344

"Like you told me about the attempts on your life? Like we told Arthur about Savka right away?" She put her hand over his. "We felt it was the right thing to do at the time. We meant well."

Cann curled his fingers around Price's. "I know." He took a deep breath and squeezed her hand. "I know," he repeated.

Behind them, Nikolic cleared his throat. When they looked at him, he came over.

"I wanted to let you know we've received word that the team we sent to pick up Bakken missed him. It seems the UN has already transferred him and he is gone. East Timor, I am advised."

"What do you think will happen?" Price asked.

"We'll issue a warrant, but you can be sure the UN will assert diplomatic immunity on his behalf. And," he went on, "it is almost certain that the East Timorese authorities, who need the UN assistance, abuses and all, more than they need Serbian gratitude, will honor it."

"Are you going to leave it there?"

Nikolic shook his head slowly. "No. We'll get him. One way or the other."

"If we can help —" Price offered accompanied by a nod from Cann.

"Thank you. I'll keep that it mind," Nikolic answered. Then he brightened. "On a happier note, I received word that Lukina has arrived home safely and is happily with her family again. It may not be easy for her at times but —"

"She'll make it," Cann said. "She's incredibly strong."

"I wish I'd met her," Price said.

Cann nodded. "You'd like her. She's quite a girl." He looked at Price. "Too."

Behind them, they heard a soft rustle.

They turned and saw Milica standing in the open doorway leaning on two canes. Her head was swathed in bandages that showed red stains leeching through.

"Her injuries aren't too serious," Nikolic told them. "We wanted to take her to hospital anyway, but she wouldn't hear of it."

Milica looked past Price and at Cann and he saw a flicker of recognition, but she didn't linger on him. Her gaze continued without stopping to Arthur. She stared at his back for a moment then began to make her way across the veranda. Matsen didn't appear aware of her presence.

"Artur?"

The voice was too small and timid to startle Matsen, but it did take him out of his reverie. He turned and looked down into Milica's eyes, which stared up at him.

Arthur's mouth wrinkled in a crooked smile and his eyes filled with tears. He reached out and took Milica's shoulders in his hands and slowly, gently pulled her to him. Milica let go of the canes and put her arms around Matsen's waist. The canes clattered to the ground. Cann started to get up and go over. Price gently held him back.

Arthur and Milica continued to hold one another without saying a word. At the table, Price had her hand over her mouth and she was crying. Cann blinked back his own tears.

Many, many moments later, Arthur and Milica hesitantly began to release their embrace. Finally separating, Arthur gently turned Milica so that her back was to the balustrade. He helped her into a half leaning-half sitting position on the railing before sitting himself, facing her.

"I remember you, Artur," Milica said softly looking up at him. "I have always remembered you."

"And I've always remembered you, Milica," he responded. "Not a day has gone by that . . ." his voice broke and he stopped. Milica took his hand in hers and she comforted him. "It's all right, Artur, it's all right."

They sat in silence for a moment longer.

"I . . . how do I say . . . adopted you, you know," Milica said in a slightly lighter tone. "When I needed someone — something to — I always thought of the tall handsome man my *mamice* loved, and I decided that you would be my father. I mean, I knew you weren't but — Do you mind?"

Matsen slowly shook his head. "I wish I had been."

She smiled up at him.

"Did you ever marry, Artur?"

Matsen nodded and reached into his pocket and pulled out his wallet. He took out a small photo and showed it to Milica.

"That's Margaret. She's been gone for some time now."

"She's very pretty."

"Yes."

"She . . . may I say . . . it is a long time and I was very young but I think, perhaps, she looks like my *mamice*. A little. Yes?"

Matsen nodded slowly. "Yes," he said again. "Margaret was a wonderful women and I loved her for herself." He looked again into Milica's eyes. "But, yes, she looked like your *mamice*."

This time, it was Milica's turn to nod. "It was good, Artur. It was a good thing you did. You gave her the chance to love. That was important."

Matsen smiled sadly. "You're comforting me?"

"It's what I do best, I think. I am happiest when I have someone to take care of." She stopped and her face became sorrowful and fearful at the same time. "I have lost my sons, Artur," she said haltingly. "And my girls, they tell me. I don't — I am lost myself, I think."

Matsen slid closer and enveloped Milica's head in his arms and held her close.

"What will you do?" he finally said. "What would you like to do?"

"I don't know." She looked at him. "I have never . . . I don't know," she repeated.

"Would you like to come to America?"

Milica didn't say no. She looked past Matsen and off into the distance.

"America," she said mostly to herself. "It is like a dream." She smiled up at him again. "But my whole life is like a dream to me. The parts I remember." She looked at Matsen drawing him into the moment. "What will I do? I need — something. I need —"

Matsen gently interrupted her.

"There's a young lady in America I'd like you to meet."